THE
NEVER
WITCH

PRAISE FOR THE NEVER WITCH

McLean's writing has never been more stylish and powerful—this book raises the bar on craft.

—Ottawa Review of Books

Original, unique, clever, deftly crafted, and a simply riveting and fun read from start to finish.

—Midwest Book Review

The Never Witch *is perfect for readers who like their fantasy grounded in emotion and their magic served with a side of grit.*

—Literary Titan

This author clearly has a talent for creating magical universes beyond our ken.

—Elinor Florence, national bestselling
author of *Finding Flora*

Action-packed, thrilling, and entertaining, author JP McLean's **"The Never Witch"** *is a must-read occult suspense and urban fantasy.*

—Anthony Avina, Book Blogger and Reviewer

PRAISE FOR JP MCLEAN

A cleverly plotted, supernatural thriller that'll keep you hooked to the very last word.

—The Wishing Shelf Book Awards

Featuring a fearless, badass heroine and plot twists that will leave readers breathless, J.P. McLean's **Blood Mark** *is a gritty, sexy, fast-paced thrill ride from start to finish.*

—E.E. Holmes, award-winning and bestselling
author of The Gateway series

An exciting blend of action, mystery, suspense, and thrills with a supernatural kick that will leave you wanting more!

—Ann Charles, USA Today bestselling
author of The Deadwood Mystery series

A profoundly intelligent story of a captivating young woman whose victories and struggles with a unique gift will grab your every emotion.

—Jennifer Manuel, Ethel Wilson Fiction Prize Winner
for *The Heaviness of Things that Float*

A captivating nail-biter that will leave readers thirsting for more! . . . This gripping tale should be on every bookshelf this year!

—InD'Tale Magazine

Titles by JP McLean

The Thorne Witch Novels

The Never Witch
Hexborn

The Dark Dreams Novels

Blood Mark
Ghost Mark
Scorch Mark

The Gift Legacy

Secret Sky
Hidden Enemy
Burning Lies
Lethal Waters
Deadly Deception
Wings of Prey

The Gift Legacy Companion

Lover Betrayed (Secret Sky Redux)

Novellas

Crimson Frost (A Supernatural Noel)

THE NEVER WITCH

JP McLean

The Never Witch
The Thorne Witch Novels ~ Book 1

First Canadian Edition August 2025

WindStorm Press, Vancouver, Canada
Copyright © 2025 by JP McLean

ISBN 978-1-988125-72-5 Paperback
ISBN 978-1-988125-73-2 EPUB
ISBN 978-1-988125-74-9 PDF
ISBN 978-1-988125-75-6 Audiobook

Book Cover Design by ebooklaunch.com
Author Photo by Crystal Clear Photography
Editing by Donna Tunney and Amanda Bidnall
Excerpt from Hexborn copyright © 2026 by JP McLean
Cataloguing in Publication information available from Library and Archives Canada.

A Note on Spelling

This novel is written in Canadian English, which means you'll find honour with a "u," dialled with two "lls," and centre with an "re." Rest assured—they're not typos, it's just Canadian English. So grab yourself a double-double and enjoy *The Never Witch*.

Cast of Characters

A complete list of *The Never Witch* characters can be found at the back of the book.

To the booksellers who hand-sell my books, and
the readers who share their love of my stories,
—this novel is for you.

ONE

Had she been a witch in anything but name, Adeline Thorne would have taken the tingling sensation between her shoulder blades as a warning that someone was watching her. For the second time in as many days.

But she wasn't a witch. Maybe it was a sixth sense, something plenty of humans had.

She rolled her shoulders and stole a glance through the solarium's glass wall, first left, then right. But no one lurked in the garden. She chalked up her feeling to an annoying habit and reminded herself to stay in her own lane. *Right.* Not a witch, not even a human with a sixth sense.

She was a reluctant graphic designer, a better-than-average portrait painter, a big sister, auntie, daughter, and ex-wife, and that was enough. Besides which, it was a beautiful spring day with perfect light. She turned back to the canvas, where Mrs. Doppler's portrait awaited the final brush strokes that would capture her unique essence.

The roll and slam of a van's door in her driveway brought her head around. *Damn.* She'd forgotten she'd agreed to look after her sister's kids for a few hours. She swirled her angle brush in the murky water of the jelly jar. There'd be no more painting today. Tomorrow, she'd tackle Mrs. Doppler's eyes again. They weren't quite right, and the heart of any portrait rested in the eyes.

Adeline's tranquil morning scattered with the thud of her front door. Jack blurred past the living room, sneakers squeaking on hardwood as he thundered toward the back of the house. A clunk, an abrupt stop, a whispered apology, and the sneaker squeak resumed with vigour. She knew she should have moved the fern further into the alcove.

"Hi, Auntie A. Sorry about Fernie. Charlie home?" Her nephew didn't wait for an answer before he threw open the kitchen door and raced to the back stairs. At almost thirteen, his shoes were the size of Mini Coopers.

Adeline's sister called after him. "Jack Booth, where are your manners?" Jack's tall, gangly form had already disappeared down the stairs.

Ever since Charlie had moved into her rental suite, Adeline had dropped down to second billing.

Olive chased after her brother as fast as her four-year-old legs could carry her. "Wait for me!" Her mass of blonde curls bounced with each step.

"Hands on the rail, Olive," Sarah said, her voice a warning as she closed the front door behind her. "You here, Addie?"

Adeline poked her head out the solarium door. "In here."

Sarah Booth should have looked frazzled. She appeared anything but, striding in as if she'd just stepped out of a younger Cameron Diaz's Instagram feed. Artfully mussed blonde hair framed her impossibly fresh face. Her yoga getup clung to her slim frame like haute couture. Adeline felt like Sarah's inferior prototype: older, darker, and flawed. She stood and removed her smock, draping it over the back of the bar stool.

"I hope Charlie doesn't mind company." Sarah stopped in front of Mrs. Doppler's likeness. "It's coming along," she said. "What's the deadline?"

"Next month. Mr. Doppler wants to present it to her on their thirtieth wedding anniversary. It'll be ready. Has to be. Can't disappoint my first five-figure client."

"You won't. He's going to love it. It's beautiful. She's beautiful. Must have married right out of the womb." She leaned in close, studying the brush strokes. "I don't know how you do it. Swipes of purple and orange, and yet when you stand back, the colours just . . . work."

"You need help with those?" Adeline asked, gesturing to the heavy tote over her sister's shoulder and the shopping bag in her hand.

"I'll just put them in the kitchen," Sarah said, walking into the adjoining room. "Thanks for taking the kids on such short notice. Joe was called away." Sarah's husband was an architect with no role in the Stonewater coven or interest in the governing council. "I won't get another salon appointment before the summer solstice."

Adeline cocked her head. "It's only April." She followed her to the kitchen.

Sarah dropped the bags on the counter. "It seems Natalie's been 'discovered.' She cut some influencer's hair, and suddenly everyone on the west coast in need of a stylist is beating a path to her door."

"You could fix that," Adeline said, twirling an air wand.

Sarah turned, her expression morphing from surprise to amusement. "Is Adeline Thorne suggesting I use magic?"

Adeline grinned. "That was my monthly allotted effort." Her sister, wisely, didn't push the subject, but she did laugh, which smoothed over the magical fissure in the room.

"I'd never *fix it*. I wouldn't do that to the poor girl," she said, pulling apples and bananas from her tote. "Natalie's worked hard. I don't begrudge her the success." She dropped her hand in the tote a few more times, removing half a dozen sandwiches wrapped in wax paper. "Although I could arrange for a cancellation in a pinch, I suppose." Her next dip produced a six-pack of pudding cups. From the canvas bag, she liberated a Halloween night–sized box of assorted potato chips.

"Sarah," Adeline said, staring in disbelief at the crowded counter. "I have food. You don't need to bring all this for a few hours."

Sarah dropped her hands to the counter. "Oh. It is quite a lot, isn't it?" She offered Adeline a wince of apology. "I don't want to be a burden."

"You never are. I adore Jack and Olive and love having them all to myself for a while. Well, myself and Charlie."

"They love you too, and Charlie is a gem for putting up with them," Sarah said, folding the canvas bag. "Still, Jack eats as much as three linebackers these days. Can't believe how fast he's outgrowing his clothes." Sarah grabbed the six-pack of pudding and the stack of sandwiches and set them in the fridge. She straightened and tugged the hem of her form-fitting jacket. "Well, I should get going." With a subtle turn of her wrist, she unfurled her fingers, and a steaming cup appeared in her hand. "A little treat for you. Mocha cappuccino. Extra whip." She raised her other hand to put a cork in Adeline's protest. "I know. Don't think of it as magic. Think of it as aversion therapy." She leaned in and kissed her sister's cheek. "I love you. And thank you. Again."

Adeline accepted the gift with a roll of her eyes and took a tentative sip. "Perfect. If you lose your day job, you're a shoo-in at Starbucks."

Sarah's laughter trailed behind her as she started down the hall. "I won't be more than two hours, but if something comes up, Joe will be home soon. I can ask him to pick up—" She stopped mid-stride, stumbled, and reached a steadying hand for the staircase balusters.

Adeline rushed to her side. "What's wrong?"

Sarah grimaced, taking short, sharp breaths. "Don't . . . know." She held her stomach like she'd been sucker-punched. Adeline wrapped a protective arm around her sister's waist and guided her to the sofa in the living room. Sarah bent over and Adeline rubbed slow circles on her back until her breathing evened out.

"Feeling better?" Adeline said.

Sarah nodded and straightened. "Yes. It's passed."

"Do I need to take you to Emerg?"

"No. It was the grid. Feels like . . . something hit it. Hard." The grid was the warp and weft of power that fuelled the magic of witchkind. Adeline stiffened. Damaging the grid was like taking an axe to the tree of life.

"What was it?"

"Who, I think. Someone's targeting the grid, and it's not the first time. Probably a warlock. A powerful one." The phone in Sarah's pocket buzzed. She pulled it out. "I've been summoned. Shit."

᛫)) ᛫) ● (᛫ (᛫ (᛫

Luke Churchwell stormed into his office, tie in hand, pulling at the top button of his shirt. He tossed his suit jacket onto the sofa and rounded his desk, staring blankly out the floor-to-ceiling windows that overlooked downtown Vancouver.

He spun at the soft ding of the intercom on the desk. *Not wasting any time, are they?* He punched the flashing button.

It was Connie. She'd self-titled herself his PA and had an office one floor down. "Boss? Kai Oxen and his escorts are here. You expecting them?"

"Yeah." As if she didn't know. He rubbed his forehead. "Park them in the conference room. I'll be right there."

Luke strode into his private bathroom and planted his hands on either side of the sink. Just three years into a twenty-five-year sentence and he didn't think he was going to make it out intact. Or alive. Nicholas Tanner, the pompous son of a bitch he'd tried to overthrow, had outplayed him, out-magicked him, and now owned his hide.

He splashed cold water on his face, headed back to his office, and retrieved the silver cuff from his suit jacket. Then he composed himself, tucked the cuff into his pocket, and headed to the conference room.

Kai Oxen lounged in one of the plush chairs that surrounded a massive raw-edge slab of cedar. He scrolled through his phone, giving off a not-a-care-in-the-world vibe—unlike his escorts, dressed in black body armour. They stood at attention, one by the door, the other behind Kai.

"Hello, Kai," Luke said, greeting his childhood friend.

Kai dropped his phone in his pocket and leaned back in the chair. "Luke. You're looking good. Lord Tanner treating you well?"

Luke deflected the underlying sarcasm that only a comrade-in-arms would hear. "Your sentence has come down, as you may have guessed," he said, nodding at the guard behind Kai. A guard behind each of them, Luke observed.

"I figured as much, though the guards are overkill," Kai said, straightening in his chair. "How big's the fine this time?"

Luke rubbed the back of his neck. He hated what this was going to do to Kai. "No fine," Luke said. "Not this time."

"What's going on? Tanner's usually begging for cash."

Luke cringed. Tanner was no doubt listening in, and he'd have a visceral reaction to Kai's disrespect.

Kai narrowed his eyes with a tilt of his head. "Surely not corporal?"

"No. The high court's not inclined to be lenient with a third conviction."

"Lenient? Their version of corporal isn't anything I'd call lenient. So what punishment does a minor siphoning infraction get a lowly warlock these days? A magical block?" Kai said, raising a calculating eyebrow, as if he were already working out a way around it. "For how long?"

"Not a block." Luke drew in a long breath. "Forfeiture."

Kai jerked to his feet, sending his chair rolling backwards. "For siphoning? For Christ's sake. We all do it. The high court's punishing me for the equivalent of masturbating? I barely touched her."

Luke didn't doubt it. Kai siphoned magic like an Olympic-level pickpocket. That, and his low regard for the no-siphoning laws, resulted in him possessing a breadth of magic few warlocks could match.

"The 'her' in question is one of the king's inner circle. How did you think this was going to play out?"

"She didn't even fucking notice!"

"Not until she tried to form ice. And couldn't." Luke hated the position Kai had put him in.

"This isn't right! A minor third offence? The correction is a magical block, a time out. Not an express train to the fucking end of the line."

"It's forfeiture, and Lord Tanner has charged me with carrying out your sentence."

Kai nodded, hollowing his cheeks. "And you're going to be a good soldier? That's a little below your station, isn't it?"

"I believe that is the point. He finds these types of reminders . . . amusing." Luke pulled the cuff from his pocket. Kai's eyes flashed surprise. Luke soft-lobbed the cuff, and Kai caught it deftly with his right hand.

Kai glanced at the cuff with disdain. "Is this really necessary? It's not like I can escape with these two clowns glued to my ass."

Said clowns didn't bat an eyelash. *Clown* wouldn't even register on their list of insults. The King's nulls were trained assassins immune to all magic but his. It was a lifetime commitment they escaped only upon their own death or the death of the king. The sight of them struck terror in most warlocks.

"Right wrist. Put it on."

"What the hell happened to you? We used to be friends."

"Put it on. It'll take me a few days to find a suitable host. The high court's not going to any further expense to find you when I do." The cuff would track him, but its similarity to ankle monitors ended there. If he tried to magic it off, or remove it in any way, it would detonate. The loss of his hand would be the least of the damage. He wouldn't be able to access higher magic; rune magic required two hands.

"Unnecessarily harsh, wouldn't you say?" Kai flared his nostrils at Luke and then turned the cuff in his hands, carefully examining the runes engraved on the inside.

"Not my choice." Luke looked to the floor. He had no leeway to offer Kai. Not this time. And if Kai didn't comply, the nulls would put the cuff on for him.

"This your work?" Kai asked, referring to the runes.

Luke shook his head, keeping his regret from leaking through. "No."

Kai nodded absently. "You sure it's going to work the way it supposed to and not blow off my hand prematurely?"

"It'll release the moment you've completed serving your sentence."

"You mean after I've forfeited the magic I've worked my entire life to create?"

He'd lose most of his magic, but not all of it. Only death could take the seed magic that warlocks were born with. "I warned you, goddamnit. Was I not clear?" Luke hated that his friends paid the price for his own infraction. Guilt hollowed him out every time. But if he showed his former ally any kindness, the price would only get steeper. "You knew the law. You got caught. This is the ruling."

"Fuck you," Kai said. He slipped the cuff over his hand, and the metal immediately shrank to a snug fit.

A lump formed in Luke's throat at the sight of Kai in a cuff. They were both prisoners now.

"You feel like a big man?" Kai said. "A real asset to your lord and master. Traitor."

The words would have eviscerated him if he wasn't already impenetrably numb. "Lord Tanner wants to be present. I'll call you when we're ready. You'll have sixty minutes to get to the court. Don't be late."

TWO

Adeline followed through with her promise to call Joe. Sarah's husband, also a witch, would have felt the hit on the grid as well, and after Sarah materialized inside the council's chamber, its wards would prevent her from contacting him.

But Joe was with a client, and Adeline got dumped into voice mail. It was a relief. Joe wasn't a big fan of Adeline's. She left what she hoped wasn't an end-of-days message. After she disconnected, she noticed the family's van was still parked in her driveway. Either Joe or, hopefully, Sarah would collect it before the night was out. Maybe there'd be some answers by then.

She'd never understood what had driven her sister to seek a position on the governing council. The GC was a nest of vipers at the best of times, and a crisis in the coven would only fuel their never-ending power games. Sarah wasn't like them. She was diligent, scholarly.

That she hadn't mentioned the earlier attacks on the grid was in keeping with Thorne family tradition. She didn't blame her. Isolating Adeline from witches and magic had begun as a kindness, but Adeline had weaponized it. Her isolation became a trip wire, and lord help anyone who breached it.

It made sense that Sarah suspected the warlocks. Warlocks didn't draw their magic from the grid but went directly to the source, draining any nearby living organism. Those living things, all living things, fed the grid. Kill the grid, kill the witches.

Hearing an excited shout from the basement brought a smile to her lips. The only time she heard laughter was when the kids were over. It was a lovely change from the normal hush of the house. She snagged the box of potato chips and headed down the stairs.

"Come in," Charlie called at her knock. The house was built on a sloping grade, allowing for a walkout basement suite. His private entrance was near the base of her back stairs.

"I brought snacks," Adeline said, dropping the box on the kitchen counter. The roar of racing cars and canned cheering came from the next room. Charlie and Jack teetered on the edge of the sofa, hunched over hand controls, faces scrunched in concentration.

"We being too loud?" Charlie asked, darting a glance away from the big flatscreen. Dew still sparkled on the back lawn outside the patio doors.

"No," she said, dismissing his concern with a swipe of her hand. Olive had made herself at home in Charlie's overstuffed recliner, though Adeline suspected Charlie had settled her there himself. A well-worn teddy bear sat on one side of her and a china doll on the other. Olive's feet were straight out in front of her as she studiously read to her captive toy audience from a picture book in her lap.

Adeline smiled to herself, ever grateful for her good fortune in finding a tenant like Charlie Tucker. He was the first and last guest she'd ever had in her newly renovated bed-and-breakfast suite. A spry senior and war vet, he'd never married and preferred the flexibility of renting versus owning. He had no desire to amass possessions, he'd explained, and their arrangement suited him. He'd arrived with one duffle bag and nothing else. It had been almost two years now, and she still brought him breakfast every weekday. He'd drifted into her family without a ripple and taken up the vacant grandfather berth at the family wharf.

"Send them up when you need a break." She started for the door then turned back. "Join us for lunch. Sarah dropped off enough sandwiches to feed your old battalion."

"Oh, I doubt that," Charlie said, without breaking his concentration. "I'll bring them up at noon."

Back upstairs, Adeline nudged the fern a little closer into the nook under the stairs. A small octagonal window let in enough light to keep Fernie happy. The architectural feature was just one of many that had drawn Adeline to the house. A wide front porch across the full width of the house was another. Even in bad weather, she found solace there, wrapped in a blanket on the porch swing, her legs tucked up and a book in her hands.

Later that morning, Joe returned her call. He was pleasant. Offered to collect the kids, but she held him off. They weren't a bother, and they were having fun, she assured him. She liked the life they breathed into the house.

After lunch, Adeline and Jack sat on the living room floor, working on a crossword puzzle she'd laid out on the coffee table. Olive slept soundly on the sofa with the teddy bear tucked under her arm.

"Auntie A," Jack said. He kept his attention on a puzzle piece he tapped against the table. "My first unbinding is at summer solstice." Traditionally, a newborn witch's magic was bound for their own protection. Too many accidental fires, floods, and tornados had prompted the precaution. Children were brought into the magical fold at twelve years of age, and if they proved trustworthy keepers of that knowledge, their magic would be gradually unbound. "I've been practising. A lot."

Adeline's anxiety ramped up, unbidden. "Your mom told me. She's so proud of you." Adeline shut out unwanted memories of her own unbinding experience and prayed Jack would be spared that humiliation.

"I want you to come." He darted a tentative glance at Adeline, and it nearly broke her heart in two.

"Jack," Adeline started, and then stalled, searching for the words to disappoint him graciously. "I wouldn't be welcome. I'm sorry."

He didn't say anything for the longest time. Eventually, his shoulders slumped. "You aren't a jinx."

"Probably best not to test that," Adeline said, covering the sting with a wink. She hadn't known Jack was aware of her reputation. "And I'll be at your party, which is the best part anyway."

As the afternoon sun began to fade, and with no word from her sister, Adeline made dinner. Jack had asked for mac and cheese, which got an enthusiastic nod of approval from Olive on the condition she be allowed to put *Ketsup* on it.

Jack had two helpings and was eyeing a third when a screech of tires close by sent a jolt of adrenalin through Adeline. She set her napkin on the table and rose.

"What was that?" Jack asked.

"I don't know. Stay here," she said, and walked to the living room window. Outside in the street, a car was stopped in the middle of the road. A dark hump lay crumpled on the asphalt in front of the vehicle, illuminated in the beam of its lights.

"The car's hit something," Jack said, bringing her around. She hadn't noticed he'd followed her.

"I'll see if they need help. Keep an eye on your sister? I'll be back in a minute." *Please don't let it be the neighbour's dog*, she thought, her heart sinking.

Adeline grabbed her phone and raced out the front door. She slowed as she approached the vehicle. The man behind the wheel appeared to be unconscious. Had the driver suffered a stroke? A heart attack? She crouched near the crumpled figure on the road. Oh no. Not a dog. A man, groaning and barely conscious. She pulled out her phone and dialled 911. Where were her neighbours? Had no one else heard the accident?

"Help's coming," she said to the stranger. "Hang in there." At least he was breathing. Maybe he'd just banged his head. Adeline felt wholly unprepared. At thirty-four years of age, her Girl Guide first aid training was but a distant memory, as was high school CPR. The operator kept her on the line.

The stranger opened his eyes, his mouth forming words she couldn't hear. She leaned in, trying to catch what he was saying. If these were his final words, she was the only one who'd hear them. He lifted a shaky hand and reached out to her. All she had to offer was comfort, so she put the 911 operator on speaker, set the phone on the road, and took his hand in both of hers.

He strained forward, but Adeline was unable to decipher what he was trying to say. She stroked his hand, assuring him that help was close. His other arm came around, his fingers working, though erratic, which she took as a good sign. "It's going to be all right," she said, praying the cliché wasn't a lie.

His grasp on her hand tightened, his strength surprising her. And then he wrapped his other hand around her wrist and met her gaze. Fear smothered her surprise. His gaze was steady, his grip a vise.

He sat up and brushed his lips by the shell of her ear. "Tell Luke that Kai has served his sentence."

And then her body exploded in pain.

S arah left Stonewater coven's sanctuary on foot, needing fresh air and forward motion to clear her head of the politics and grid trauma she'd been steeped in for the last six hours. Early-blooming honeysuckle bushes by the front doors scented the cool night air. She filled her lungs and then started down the steps of the sprawling mansion. It had been built in the Tudor Revival style in 1912. The building's ground floor was a stone-walled fortress, with the glaring exception of a glass sunroom that protruded around the back. White stucco and great wooden beams painted green adorned the upper floors.

When they were children, she and Addie had spent many happy hours in the sanctuary. It's where she learned her love of ballet, and where Addie learned to love painting.

As she walked, she spoke with Joe on the phone. "There was a tear this time. In the southwest. Lady Brighton is involved. She sent her spellcaster to help repair it. Our own spellcaster joined him, but poor Odette, she was as wrung out as I've ever seen her when she returned. It'll be a few days before she or the grid are functioning properly."

"Lady Brighton? The high priestess? Damaras must be overjoyed to have her attention."

She would be, Sarah knew. As its priestess, Damaras ruled over the Stonewater coven, but the high priestess ruled over all the covens. No witch was more powerful than Lady Brighton and few were invited into her confidence. Damaras had been working on an invitation for years.

"Has the coven any idea who did it?" Joe asked.

"No. They're assuming warlocks, of course. Lady Brighton's sentinels are searching for residual magic. Damaras's war mages have sent out their spies. They're hoping to find surveillance footage somewhere. Lady Brighton sent word to the warlock king."

"Have they talked yet?"

"King Lochlan was outraged, or so he'd have us believe. He says he still stands firmly behind the peace accord. He's making inquiries. Assigned Lord Tanner as his envoy. I'll fill in the rest of the details when I get home. I left the van at Adeline's and have to figure out what to tell her. I'm going to walk for a bit, then pick up the kids."

"Take your time. Adeline has already fed them. And be careful."

"Always am. Love you," she said, and hung up.

She continued along the gravel footpath through the sanctuary's grounds. The gardens teemed with the very life that fed the grid. Only witches were able to see the faint glow that surrounded every living thing. The oldest among them, usually trees, had the strongest hues, like a coating of baby powder. The glow was more apparent in the dark. She'd spent many evenings in her witch's garden, watching the tiny specks of life break away from trees and spiders and drift up to become a part of the living grid. Brushing her hand across the tops of tall grass sent the specks scattering like sparks from a bonfire before they rose in a twisting vortex.

The war between witches and warlocks had ended before she'd been born. All her life, she believed the grid was immutable. And now it was threatened. It unsettled her.

Sarah wished Adeline hadn't witnessed her reaction to the grid's hit. If she hadn't crumpled against the staircase, she wouldn't have to explain why. She was in the damned-if-she-did-or-didn't place. Magic and witches were salt in Adeline's wounds, but if Sarah told her nothing, it would make her as bad as the coven, which had shut her sister out.

The imminence of Jack coming into his magic was what had finally cracked the wall Adeline put up between herself and witchcraft. Adeline's love for Jack had done that, which moved Sarah to tears if she allowed herself to dwell on it.

Sarah understood Adeline's need to protect herself. Before Adeline's final unbinding, her sister knew the craft inside and out. She could recite spells and perform their requisite hand motions at first-degree levels. She had an encyclopedic knowledge of potions. There was even talk she might skip the initiate level and be placed in the first-degree ranks.

But despite her studious preparation, each of Adeline's four unbinding ceremonies had failed to release her magic. No one was able to say for certain why. It could have been a bad binding when she was a newborn. Or she may have been that unluckiest of witches who simply didn't inherit the power that should have been their birthright. In the end, the why of it didn't matter. Adeline's simmering resentment had erupted, and her backlash had left scars. She'd been banned from the coven and unfriended by her peers. And that was before she married a warlock.

So Sarah respected Adeline's wishes. She pried at the crack Adeline had opened, but didn't push her. Sadly, though her sister didn't have magical abilities, she was still a witch, and subject to the peace accord and the coven's rulings.

She sent Adeline a text that she was on her way, found a quiet spot from which to dematerialize, and spurred herself to Adeline's kitchen.

·))) ● (((·

Luke watched the light fade from the sky, his hair still wet from the shower. He'd worked out his frustration at the gym in the atrium, and the ache in his muscles felt good. Not much distracted him these days, not even the Crown Royal in the glass he held by his thigh.

He stiffened as a whisper of rune magic swirled past his ear like an airlock releasing. Kai Oxen's name spoken in a hiss.

Kai's cuff had been deactivated.

Luke's day had just gone from bad to shitshow. He reached for his phone and dialled Kai. The call went to voice mail.

Tanner's runecaster didn't make mistakes, which could only mean that Kai had found a way around the sentence. Tanner would be apoplectic.

His phone rang, as he knew it would. Tanner.

"Please tell me how Kai Oxen's sentence was served without me being apprised and present?"

"I'm as surprised as you are. He must have circumvented the cuff."

"Impossible! Find him. I want that cuff. And I want a report within the hour." The line went dead. Moments later, the shields of Luke's prison wavered and fell. His magic released.

Which was the only good thing that would come out of that night.

THREE

Sarah rematerialized in Adeline's kitchen. "Addie? Jack?" she called, seeing the dinner dishes on the table.

Jack's voice rang out. "Mom?"

"What's going on?" Sarah said, walking into the living room. Jack and Olive stood in front of the window, looking out to the street.

"An accident," Jack said. "Auntie A told us to stay here."

Sarah rushed to the window. Adeline was crouched in the road with her back to them.

"Watch your sister. I'll be right back."

A siren wailed in the distance. Sarah took off at a dead run toward the accident but quickly slowed when she caught the metallic scent of ozone in the air. Warlock magic was in play. She called to Adeline to get out of there, but neither her voice nor her magic could pierce the illusion the warlock had cast. And then it was too late. Sarah shielded her eyes from a blinding flash of red that lit up the warlock who held Adeline in his thrall. Adeline let out an agonizing shriek, struggled, and cried out again before finally falling away from him. Abruptly the illusion shattered. Gone were the car, the unconscious man behind the wheel, the accident scene, and the warlock.

"Addie!" Sarah ran to her side. Sirens approached and abruptly cut off. She and Adeline were spotlit in the vehicle's headlights. Sarah quickly encased the vehicles, and their sirens and lights, inside a veil to hide them. Anyone watching would see the vehicles carry on. Car doors slammed and footfalls drew near. "Addie?" Sarah said, touching her arm. Adeline hissed.

"What happened here?" a police officer said.

A paramedic moved in, crouched down, and opened a medical bag.

"I . . . don't know. I found her here. Her arm—"

"Please stand back and give the paramedic room to work," the officer said. Another paramedic hustled in with a gurney.

"Are you the one talking to the 911 operator?" the officer asked.

"No," Sarah said. She stuffed a hand in her pocket.

The officer scanned the pavement nearby then spoke to the paramedics. They'd found Adeline's phone and handed it to him.

The officer returned to Sarah. "Can you identify the woman?"

"No. I was just walking by."

The officer told her not to leave the scene. She retreated, feeling helpless. Now that outsiders were involved, she'd have to let the situation play out. The paramedics loaded Adeline on their gurney.

The moment the ambulance left, Sarah got to work erasing all traces of her presence from the police officer's memory. She retrieved Adeline's phone from him, sent him on his way, and called Joe. After her husband arrived, she let the veil collapse.

Human medical professionals would be able to treat Adeline's physical injury, but only a witch healer would be able to identify and treat whatever magical damage the warlock had unleashed.

Sarah called the coven's priestess. "A warlock attacked Adeline. I need help."

·)·)·)·●·(·(·(·

Luke dressed and dematerialized, following the cuff's fading residual magic. He re-formed on a quiet residential street in Dunbar and kept to the shadows. Something wasn't quite right. The sweet scent of cloves hung in the air. Witch magic. A lot of it.

If the cuff was still there, he could no longer sense it. He took to the air and flew over the homes in the vicinity of the witch magic. An ambulance wailed a few blocks over. Nearby, a minivan idled in a driveway. And then, in a wash of power, the van vanished. Interesting. Hovering over the house adjacent to the driveway, he pulled a coin from his pocket, inscribed a rune onto it, and dropped it. The coin bounced off an invisible barrier and fell to the road. Warded. But a witch ward wasn't the magic he felt infusing the night air.

It couldn't be a coincidence that Kai's cuff vanished in the vicinity of a warded house. What had Kai gotten himself mixed up in?

A gust of wind dissipated the last of the witch magic, and Luke took form opposite the warded house. The lights were out inside. Further along the street, he noticed a flash of white on the asphalt. It was a paper square of wrapping from medical gauze. He knelt and picked it up. It wasn't damp, so it hadn't been on the ground for long. He scented burned flesh. What had happened here?

Luke stood. He scribbled a finding rune on the wrapping and tossed it into the air. The paper floated, circling, and landed at his feet. Which meant the cuff was no longer nearby. He scrubbed his face. Tanner would go nuclear if he thought a witch had possession of the cuff. Anyone but a witch. Rune magic was a tightly guarded secret. A death sentence awaited the warlock who revealed it. Tanner would certainly blame Luke if he could. Was that Kai's goal—to infuriate Tanner and get Luke killed? Two birds, one cuff?

Not a bad strategy. He supposed death was one way out of his sentence, though it wasn't his first choice. He walked into the shadows and dematerialized.

He took form outside Tanner's gatehouse. The runes buried around the estate prevented warlocks from dropping onto the grounds unannounced. A guard called ahead and escorted him to the front door. The first guard left only after another guard took possession of Luke, like he was infirm and might wander off.

"He's expecting you," Luke's escort said, taking him to Tanner's study. The guard knocked once and entered. Luke followed.

Tanner stood before a stately bow window. He cut an imposing figure, with his thick neck and broad shoulders. One hand rested in the pocket of his slacks, rustling coins. His shirt was silk, and custom made. "You have something to report?"

"I followed the cuff's residual to a neighbourhood in Dunbar. Lost its trail there. Couldn't locate it."

"And Kai Oxen?"

"Gone. I did, however, catch the scent of burned flesh. No body, though it might have been moved."

"A human?" Tanner turned his back to Luke. "The cuff wouldn't have released on forfeiture to a human."

This is the point at which a younger, stupider version of himself would have questioned that assumption.

"Did you check the runes before they were activated?" Tanner asked.

"No. I wouldn't presume to know better than Liam Nunez." He wasn't foolish enough to diss Tanner's pet runecaster.

Tanner swivelled back around, his eyes narrowed. "You were charged with carrying out the sentence . . . in my presence."

"Yes. I apologize that you weren't advised. You should have been." A little grovelling went a long way with Tanner. "Perhaps your runecaster can shed some light on the anomaly."

"*Perhaps* if you had found the cuff, he could have done so. Not only have you failed to carry out the sentence as I ordered, you've now lost the cuff."

Luke glued his gaze to his feet. There were two explanations for the cuff's premature deactivation, and neither involved Luke. Either Liam had screwed up, or Kai had outfoxed him. Surely Tanner knew this.

"You have forty-eight hours to find that cuff and return it to me. If not, Kai Oxen will be found and executed." Tanner, once again, turned his back to him. "You are dismissed."

· ☽ ☽ ● ☾ ☾ ·

Confusion accompanied Adeline's awakening. She lay in a hospital bed, her right arm bandaged from shoulder to wrist. An IV line snaked from a translucent bag above her shoulder into a needle taped to the back of her other hand.

Sarah sat beside her bed. "You're awake," she said, putting her phone aside and standing. "How are you feeling?"

"Like someone took a blow torch to my arm," Adeline said, clearing her throat. "What the hell happened?"

"What do you remember?"

Adeline struggled against the sheets to sit up.

"Let me," Sarah said, finding the bed's remote. The head of the bed started to chug up.

"There was a car accident. We heard it from the kitchen." Adeline lurched upright. "Oh no! Jack? Olive?"

"They're fine," Sarah said. "Joe took them home." She rolled the tray table close to the bed.

Adeline lay back and closed her eyes, exhaling with relief.

"What else do you remember?"

Careful of the IV line, Adeline reached for the water glass on the overbed table and took a sip from the bendy straw. "Tires screeched outside, as if a driver had nailed the brakes. There was a car in the road. It looked like it had hit something. I worried it might have been a dog, so I sent Jack away from the window to watch over Olive—you can't unsee that kind of carnage.

"But when I got out there, the driver was unconscious, and what he'd hit was a man. I called 911. Tried to comfort him. But he was stronger than he looked. His grip sent an inferno up my arm." She lifted her bandaged arm with a wince. "And now I'm here in fluorescent city. What did I miss?"

"There was no accident. It was an illusion. As effective as veil magic. You were attacked."

Confusion flooded Adeline's thoughts. "By whom? Why?"

"The man on the ground was a warlock. I felt his magic, but I couldn't break through it."

Adeline tensed. "What did he do to me?"

"Other than the burns? I don't know. I can't read any magic coming off you."

Adeline shook her head with a derisive laugh. "Good to know some things don't change."

"All kidding aside," Sarah said, "I'm worried he targeted you. Had you seen him before?"

"No. I didn't recognize him."

"He could have glamoured his looks. Is there anyone new in your life? Someone trying to befriend you? A clerk at the grocery store who's asking too many questions? A new date?"

Adeline shook her head. "No one." Especially not a new date. She still hadn't recovered from her last dip into that cesspool.

"I saw him briefly," Sarah said, avoiding eye contact. She handed Adeline the bed's remote, smoothed the sheet, straightened the bendy straw in her water cup.

Adeline noted the stalling tactics. "What is it?"

Sarah looked up. Straightened her shoulders. "Damaras has agreed to a regression. They might be able to get an ID on the warlock from my memory."

"Dumbass? Why would the princess help me? And why would you agree to that?"

"It's Priestess Damaras," Sarah said, barely restraining an eye roll. "She's our coven's leader, whether we agree with the results of the election or not. And she turns into toads those who dare call her *princess* or *dumbass*."

"We all called her Princess Dumbass."

"When we were twelve. And she's helping because I asked her to. Please don't be angry. Someone attacked you. We need to know who . . . and why."

"We?" Adeline said.

"Warlocks are attacking the grid. And now a warlock has attacked a witch. The peace accord is at stake. So, yes, answers would be prudent."

Adeline nodded, considering her sister's words. "He wouldn't have known I'm a witch. You said so yourself. I have no witch tells. None."

"Maybe he knew you were witch adjacent. Attacking you would get our attention."

"Witch adjacent?" Adeline said, cocking an eyebrow.

Sarah suppressed a smile. "Kind of liked that one myself."

"Does she know I saw him?"

"Damaras?" Sarah shook her head. "Saying her name wouldn't kill you. And no. I wasn't sure how much you'd remember."

"Don't tell her. I'd sooner swim in sewage than let Damaras root around in my head."

"You have second-degree burns on your arm. When the drugs wear off, you may think differently."

"My memory where Damaras is concerned is painfully clear. She has no more interest in my well-being than she does a paperclip's."

"Damaras needs me. She wouldn't act against me."

"Damaras's loyalties blow in the wind."

Sarah raised her hands in surrender. "All right. Let's see how my regression plays out. We might ID the warlock and that'll be the end of it."

Adeline pressed her lips together and reached for her sister's hand. "I'm sorry. Damaras's name brings out the worst in me. Especially after what she did to Mom."

Sarah offered her an understanding smile.

"How are the kids?" Adeline asked. "How much did they see?"

"They're okay. Joe explained to Jack what happened. Olive was inconsolable. Thank heavens she's just four and her mind is malleable. He adjusted her memories. She's fine now. Charlie thinks you burned your arm on the stove."

"Joe must be miffed with me." He'd been with Sarah long enough to have witnessed some of her more colourful acts of rebellion. This was yet one more black mark against her.

"He's not."

"Liar."

Adeline remembered something else. Before the pain, the warlock had spoken to her.

"Do the names Luke or Kai mean anything to you?" Adeline asked.

"No," she said, with a slow shake of her head. "Who are they?"

Adeline looked away. Sarah would want to run the names up the coven's flagpole. But Adeline didn't trust the coven. They hoovered up information but weren't so good about sharing what they learned with outsiders, and Adeline was an outsider.

"If I tell you, you have to promise it stays between us. You tell no one in the coven." If there was any leverage to be gained from the warlocks' names and message, Adeline wanted it for herself. She could bargain with that information.

"The coven can help find them."

"No one. Promise me. Swear on our father's grave."

"Addie, be reasonable."

"Swear it. On our father's grave."

Sarah hesitated, as if she were running through counter-arguments. Ultimately, she came up empty. "I swear it. On Dad's grave."

Adeline searched her sister's face but found only resignation. "The warlock told me to tell Luke that Kai had served his sentence."

FOUR

Sarah pocketed the nurse's home-visit schedule and thanked the burn unit's staff. Insurance requirements dictated Adeline be wheeled out of the building and released into Sarah's care. The opioids in Adeline's system rendered her impaired and hence unable to drive. But they didn't stop her from grinding away on the coven in general and Damaras Deschene in particular during the drive back to Dunbar. It seemed the crack in Adeline's wall only allowed family in.

Sarah carried Adeline's plastic bag of patient belongings and helped her up the front steps. The door had barely closed behind them when the doorbell rang.

"I'll get it," Sarah said. "You sit."

Sarah groaned when she looked through the front door's diamond pane of glass. "Come in," she said, holding the door open. She'd expected Damaras to show up, but not this soon.

Damaras, an attractive woman in her sixties, swept in. She was the same age as Sarah's mother, but whereas the lines on her mother's face were born from laughter, Damaras's lines had been etched on a marble tableau that rarely cracked a genuine smile. Sarah led her into the living room, praying Adeline kept her cool.

"Adeline," Damaras said.

"Princess Dumbass."

Sarah sucked in an audible breath.

"Schoolyard taunts are a little juvenile, wouldn't you say?"

Adeline, thankfully, didn't respond.

"I heard what happened," Damaras said. "I'm incensed. We all are."

"I was attacked by a warlock, and now you're incensed? Why weren't you incensed when the abuse was coming from witches?"

"Adeline!" Sarah said. Angering the priestess wouldn't help the situation.

Damaras raised her hand to Sarah. "It's okay." She turned back to Adeline. "It's been fifteen years. How long are you going to carry the victim torch?"

"You don't think I have a right to be angry?"

"I do understand. Anyone who'd been in your position would have been . . . upset. To be denied your power? With such promise?"

"Oh, you think *that's* why?" Adeline pressed her lips together, bobbing her head.

Sarah opened her mouth, desperate to cut off her sister before she dove into a well-trod rant. "Perhaps—"

"Not even close, but let's start there," Adeline said, ignoring Sarah's cue. "Sure, the failed unbindings were humiliating, but what you allowed the coven to do to me was degrading."

"You threatened witches. That cannot be tolerated."

"You had me banished for threatening witches who were using me for magical practice."

Banishment wasn't like being tossed from a movie theatre without a refund. Witches were forbidden from associating with banished members. Only blood relatives of the banished were excepted.

"Again, fifteen years. Let it go."

"Well, it's only been six years since you refused to open an investigation into my father's untimely death. You know, the death that happened in the middle of an election you were losing? And that you subsequently won."

Damaras rubbed her forehead. "I'm sorry you're still having difficulty accepting that your father died of a heart attack, but an investigation wouldn't have changed the coroner's findings."

"He was murdered. Are you also sorry that just four years ago you contrived to replace my mother with another archivist?"

"Your mother retired."

"My mother had the nerve to question you."

"Your mother never recovered from your father's passing. What happened to your father was tragic. We all mourned him."

Adeline took a breath, sat back.

Sarah chewed her lip, praying her sister chilled out.

"I'll rescind the ban," Damaras said, mistaking Adeline's posture for acquiescence.

"The ban? Too little, too late, I'm afraid," Adeline said. "Now, if you were to open an investigation . . . Otherwise, I've grown comfortable being on the outside. I've accepted that I'm not a witch. I don't want back in."

"You may not have powers, Adeline, but you are a witch."

"That's convenient. Now that you want something from me, I'm a witch? What is it you want, Damaras? And don't try to peddle that it's my best interests motivating you."

"Fine. You want to spend your days steeped in anger? Your choice. Just know it's not healthy. And you're dragging your sister along for the ride."

Sarah hid her distress behind her hand. Provoking Adeline was like shooting at a full propane tank.

"Yada yada, Damaras. What do you want?"

"Did you see the warlock who attacked you?"

"No."

"Do you have any sense of what he was after?"

"No."

Damaras nodded in a way that questioned the veracity of Adeline's denials. "Some of us believe your attacker might have been a siphon."

Adeline drew her brows together. "That doesn't make sense. Siphons go after witches with power to steal. I have nothing to siphon."

"Not all warlocks are strong enough to detect a witch's powers. But this house is warded. He might have sensed that. Assumed you were a witch."

"Apparently, I am a witch," Adeline said, deadpan.

"A barren witch," Damaras clarified, using the formal term for what she was.

Sarah held her breath.

"Which brings us full circle. Why would a warlock mistake me for a witch with anything worth siphoning?"

"She has a point," Sarah said, wading in to the discussion. "Speaking as a binder, I can tell you there's no reading from her of any of the elemental threads: earth's green, water's aqua, air's white, or fire's orange. And no witch's blue aura. She reads as human."

"Our assumption is based on Adeline's burns," Damaras said. "The archivist is aware of siphon attacks on witches prior to the accord. Some suffered similar burns."

"Well then," Adeline said. "I guess the good news is the warlock didn't get the magic he assumed was his for the taking."

"No," Damaras said. "But we don't know what he might have left behind in you either. Warlocks are vengeful, and he didn't get what he wanted."

Sarah hadn't considered that possibility, and, given Adeline's sudden stillness, she hadn't either.

"But . . . our magics are incompatible. If he'd left magic in her, it would have killed her," Sarah said. It's why unions between witches and warlocks never produced offspring.

"And Sarah doesn't read anything in me," Adeline said.

"Yet," Damaras said. "And, given your history, there's a good chance nothing will materialize. Still, I'd rather be certain."

"Nice," Adeline said. "Do you enjoy rubbing that in?"

"Not at all. But I thought you'd prefer I be forthright with you. I've brought Marcus. He's outside. If you'll allow him, he'll see what he can do to speed the healing of your burn."

"You should have led with that, Damaras," Adeline said.

Although Adeline's emotions were hidden, Sarah knew her cynical side would see the healer's pain relief as the bribe that it was.

"I'm offering now."

Addie stared at Damaras for an uncomfortable moment, before nodding once. "Thank you, Damaras," Adeline said.

Sarah considered how painful Adeline's burn must have been for her to accept the offer, let alone express gratitude to the woman.

"You will, of course, keep us apprised of any changes in your . . . health?"

Adeline replied with a smile.

The mistake Damaras had made was not specifying the price of the bribe beforehand.

Luke's only lead on the cuff was in the warded two-storey clapboard house in Dunbar. Someone in that house had to have seen Kai or knew what had happened, and the clock was ticking.

His research had coughed up the homeowner's identity: Adeline Thorne. She'd made a name for herself as a competitive black belt and, more recently, an artist. Her website pointed him to the Bolt Gallery on Granville Street, where he'd met Suzanna Bolt the previous evening. She'd been about to lock up, but his fine clothes and charm bought him a private showing of Adeline's work. Suzanna had been very helpful.

In the chilly early morning hours, he parked in the street near the butter-yellow house with white trim. It was still dark outside. The car was a nuisance, but he might be in the neighbourhood for a while. Best to be comfortable.

Given the wards, he had to assume Adeline was a witch. The knowledge gave him a leg up. He left the car and approached the house cautiously. Using magic near a ward could set it off. At the foot of the stairs, he felt a kiss of power. A warning. The ward let him mount the few steps and approach the front door. He reached out, and his hand hit the ward's invisible barrier. The sensation was familiar. It was calibrated to repel magical beings and bad intentions. The rubbery texture had a little give to it, like an inflatable exercise ball. He could knock on her door or ring her doorbell, but he couldn't muscle through the ward. His magic might be able to break it, but that would only announce his intentions.

He descended the steps and followed the membrane around the exterior of the house, down the sloping driveway. A side door on the lower level had a mail slot with the name *C. Tucker* on it. A tenant? Another witch, likely. He continued along to the back of the house, where a stairway leading to the second floor jutted proud of the wards. Beyond the second-floor landing, a solarium poked out, providing cover to a patio beneath. The ground-level windows revealed a darkened kitchen and living room.

Turning, he found a small, detached garage that wasn't warded. Sage and rosemary grew in the small garden, but there was no sign of wolfsbane, belladonna, or mugwort. The home's membrane continued all the way around the house. He wouldn't be getting in, not without some help.

Luke returned to the car, reclined his seat, and settled in. He slept until the sun came up. The neighbourhood slowly awakened. Lights popped on inside homes. Cars pulled out of driveways. Dogs tugged sleepy humans from lawn to lawn.

He kept out of sight, watching Adeline's dormer windows for signs of life. But it was the side door opening that got him out of the car. He timed his arrival so the older gentleman who'd exited Adeline's downstairs suite would see him looking up at the house while studying Suzanna Bolt's business card that had a scrawl of handwriting on the back.

"Excuse me," Luke said. "I can't quite make out this writing. Is this Adeline Thorne's home?" The man—Tucker, he assumed—wore a houndstooth cap and leather bomber jacket.

"What have you got there?" the man asked, approaching with a steady gait. He may have been elderly, but he was fit. Luke handed him the card. The man flipped it over. Naturally. "The gallery shouldn't be giving out her home address."

"So this *is* her house?" He gently probed the man's mind. Not a witch, or at least he had no barriers.

"Who's asking?" the man said, taking in Luke's bespoke suit, his Prada oxfords.

"The name's Churchwell." Luke produced a business card. "I'm on a tight schedule. Do you know if she's home?"

"Did you try the doorbell?"

"There was no answer."

"I'm not surprised. It's 7:00 a.m. She's likely sleeping. Come back in a few hours." He turned to leave.

"I've got a flight to catch. Would you be so kind as to give her my card? Ask her to call me?"

"Sure," the man said. "You have a nice day."

If Adeline's tenant noticed the rune on the card, he didn't react. It was a single-use compulsion rune. Handy as hell. He always kept a few on him. Luke returned to his car and watched until the man got to the next street, far away from the ward. After Luke activated the rune, he waited until the man turned around and started back before he pulled away from the curb.

FIVE

Adeline sat on the edge of her bed. A part of her wished she'd had the strength to turn Marcus away yesterday, but the pain of the burn was like nothing she'd experienced before. His healing ended the excruciating agony. She'd find a way to live with her hypocrisy.

Marcus was truly at the top of his game, Adeline thought, examining the burn. He'd knitted together the nerves and mended her skin beautifully. The burn had been reduced to nothing worse than the result of a sunny midsummer day at the beach. There wouldn't even be a scar. She'd have to make sure Sarah was present when the burn care nurse came by to change her dressing. Not that she wanted Sarah to have to alter anyone's mind, but there'd be no explaining the rapid healing to someone with human sensibilities.

Her thoughts tumbled again into that dark hollow of wondering. Had the warlock left something behind inside her, something incompatible? Was she a ticking time bomb?

She needed a binder, and the irony of it wasn't lost on her. In her teens, Adeline railed against binders. The one who'd bound her magic as an infant. The one who'd performed her unbindings. Blaming a person had heft to it. Blaming some nebulous hereditary lottery was as unsatisfactory as punching shadows.

Over the years, she'd mellowed, even if she didn't understand Sarah's drive to make binding her specialty. Now, only a binder could save her life. They were trained to see the threads of magic, even the red threads of warlock magic. Sarah would be able to see if her attacker's magic was manifesting inside her.

How Adeline felt about allowing Sarah to bind her was a muddy creek she'd cross when, or if, it happened.

She'd have to apologize to her sister. As good as it had felt to let off some steam blasting Damaras, it had the potential to blow back on Sarah. For some incomprehensible reason, Sarah had accepted a role on the GC. How she stomached working under Damaras, Adeline didn't know, but Adeline knew the role was important to her.

She checked the time again. She'd slept late. Probably because of the healing. She wouldn't get any work done on Mrs. Doppler before she made Charlie's breakfast. She headed to the kitchen and put on a pot of coffee.

When they'd started this bed-and-breakfast routine, Charlie had four meals on rotation, and they all included bacon, home fries, and bread. The only variable was whether the egg would be fried, scrambled, poached for a Benny, or soaked into French toast. She would include a fruit cup from time to time, which sent his eyeballs rolling, and the occasional bowl of oatmeal snuck onto his tray, but she still hadn't broken him of his cholesterol habit. Today's breakfast was a scrambled egg.

As Adeline prepared the meal by rote, she glanced into the solarium. One more day and, thanks to Marcus, Mrs. Doppler's portrait would be done. It was Adeline's best work by far. She'd had the luxury of time to do it justice. It was an interesting observation that the higher the commission, the longer the deadline. The inverse was also true. She'd done enough five-hundred-dollar dog portraits in fourteen-day windows to know.

She set the bacon cooking and started the washing machine. The shirt she'd worn last night was ruined, but her cargo pants were probably salvageable. She topped the load with Charlie's sheets and a towel.

Back in the kitchen, she turned the bacon and dropped the potatoes in the rendered fat. She wiped Charlie's breakfast tray and dressed it with a plate, napkin and cutlery.

She turned at a knock on the back door.

"Charlie?" she said, opening it. "Are you early, or am I late?"

"I'm early, but I come bearing gifts," he said, handing her a business card. He sniffed the air. "Ahh, nothing like the smell of a good double-smoked rasher."

Yeah, he wouldn't be giving up his bacon anytime soon.

"What's this?" she asked. *Churchwell* was the name on the card. Gold lettering on a black background. A phone number appeared below the name, but nothing else and nothing on the back.

Charlie nodded at the card in her hand. "I found that well-to-do fella out front this morning on my way out for my walk. He'd rung the door-bell, but you hadn't answered."

"I was probably in the shower. Well-to-do?"

"Fancy threads. Drove a Jag. Had 'tude, as Jack would say."

Adeline laughed. "It's an odd name, isn't it? First or last, do you know?"

"No. Introduced himself as Churchwell. Maybe he fancies himself a celebrity, like Bono or Prince."

"What'd he want?"

"Asked me to have you call him. Seemed urgent."

"Okay. Thanks." Adeline tucked the card in her jeans pocket. "You want to wait a few minutes? Your breakfast is almost ready."

"Sure," he said. "Mind if I help myself to coffee?"

"Please do. Cups are out." She cracked his egg and whisked it in a bowl.

"How's the arm?" Charlie asked, pouring the coffee.

"Much better. It wasn't as bad as the doctors originally thought."

"Glad to hear it." Charlie topped up Adeline's mug. "That man, Churchwell?" Charlie said. "He got your address from the gallery on Granville that sells your paintings. You ought to have a talk with them. Safer to meet clients at the gallery than here."

Adeline frowned. "I'm surprised Suzanna would do that." In fact, Suzanna was the one who'd suggested that very arrangement.

When his breakfast was ready, Charlie refilled his coffee and left with his breakfast tray and a reminder for Adeline to call Churchwell. He kept mum about the glass of orange juice she'd snuck onto his tray.

When she'd finished cleaning up, she pulled Churchwell's card from her pocket and dialled his number.

After the introductions, he suggested they meet to talk about her work.

"How about next week?" she said.

"I'll be out of the country. In fact, my flight leaves in a few hours. Could we meet this morning?"

"I can't today. I'm sorry." She was determined to get Mrs. Doppler finished before the light faded.

"It won't take long. Let me buy you a coffee. I think you'll find it worth your while."

Oh damn. If Suzanna had sent him, it was probably a commission, and a good one. Her dream of ditching graphic design, which sucked the life out of her, and making a steady income from her art, felt like a real possibility. She agreed to meet him and raced upstairs to change.

On the way out the door, she remembered to transfer the laundry from the washer to the dryer. While doing so, a silver bracelet dropped to the floor. She picked it up. Oddly, the outside of it was unadorned, but the inside was intricately etched. *Must be Charlie's.* She set it on the laundry room windowsill and left for her meeting.

·))))●((((·

L uke had chosen the coffee shop not for its coffee, but for the privacy of the booths it offered. He was seated facing the door when Adeline arrived with a portfolio in her arms. She was dressed simply in a lightweight trench coat over dress slacks. He stood and waved her over.

"Mr. Churchwell. Pleased to meet you. I'm Adeline Thorne."

"I recognized you from your photo," he said, shaking her hand. "At the Bolt Gallery. Please, join me." She was in her thirties, dark hair, which she wore in a long braid over one shoulder. Attractive, for a witch.

She slid into the booth, and the overwhelming clove scent of witch magic followed her. His eyes watered. A server, unaffected by the aroma, came by before Adeline was settled and took their order.

"Thanks for coming on such short notice." He asked her about her work, and while she gave him her history, he probed her mind, slipping inside like she had no mind guards in place at all. He took the surprise in stride and flitted through her thoughts, treading lightly so as not to alert her.

He didn't gather any more information than what she was talking about. He saw images of art classes, museum tours, and her early work. A nude male model she'd taken to her bed. She thought about the portfolio and wished she'd had time to sort through it before their meeting.

"What exactly are you interested in having me paint for you?" she asked.

"I would be pleased if you'd agree to a portrait."

"Yours?" Her thoughts flipped to a sketchbook and his likeness from a slideshow of angles.

She pulled at her coat's cuff, her mind tumbling around the irritation of the itchy fabric. As she tugged the sleeve, he got the image of another man, his hands hovering over her arm. An injury, painful. The man was a witch; he was healing a burn. Perhaps the burned flesh Luke had scented in front of her house?

"Give me a moment," she said, and slid out of the booth. She removed her coat, and, as she did so, he got another strong waft of magic. The turtleneck she wore was sleeveless. When she was once again seated, she rubbed her right forearm in a soothing motion. The scent of cloves was coming from her arm. The witch magic that had healed her burn. He got a flash of a car in the road, a body.

And then a clear picture of Kai's face, his hands encircling her wrist.

He sucked in a breath. The bastard had dumped his magic into a witch? How was that possible? And why couldn't he sense Kai's magic in her? That amount of magic should have been leaking out of her pores. And if Adeline knew that she harboured a warlock's magic, he'd eat his Armani.

Adeline rubbed her temple. Luke pulled back, studying her. She didn't read or conduct herself like any witch he'd ever met. At best, she was untrained and inexperienced. She had no defence against Kai's magic, that was for certain. Was she even a witch?

Then he remembered who he was dealing with. Kai was diabolically clever, and for the most part unscrupulous. If it served his purposes, he wouldn't hesitate to plant those images in her head. Burn her for the optics of it. He'd been cornered, desperate.

Still, Tanner's runecaster had a reputation for excellence. Any cuff Liam Nunez made wouldn't be so easily fooled. Now, more than ever, he wanted to get his hands on that cuff.

"You brought some work to show me?" Luke said, distracting her.

"Yes." She cleared space on the table and unzipped the portfolio. Shy pride flitted across her features.

"These are stunning," he said. Her expression turned hopeful. While he took his time studying the pieces she'd selected, her mind drifted to the gentleman Luke had talked to this morning. Tucker. She cared about him.

And then she pictured Kai's cuff. Yes! She had it. It was in her hand,

and she'd set it on a windowsill. She was wishing she'd put it by the back door so she wouldn't forget to put it on the old man's breakfast tray come morning.

Well, now, that was something he could help her with. She pictured the tray in her hands going down the outside stairs.

Perfect. Once the cuff was outside her wards, it was his for the taking.

SIX

Sarah danced from foot to foot, and not in a graceful ballet movement. She stared out Adeline's living room window, worrying her lip and cranking her head left and right to watch both ends of the street, as if she were at a tennis match. But there were no players. Adeline was late. Really late. She stretched her fingers, knit them together, ran them through her hair. When Addie's Jeep finally pulled into the driveway, Sarah raced to the front door.

"Where have you been?" Sarah said, confronting Adeline the moment she closed the door.

"Why are you so worked up?"

"Did you forget the burn care nurse is coming today?"

"Oh, damn! I did. When is she due?"

Sarah stood on her toes and peered out the front door's window. "That's her now, pulling into the driveway behind your Jeep. Let's hope she didn't see you. Go to the sofa, lie down. I'll have to work fast, and . . . I'm sorry, I know you hate me releasing magic, but you've left me no choice."

Adeline apologized again and nodded her assent. Sarah would have bathed in her sister's momentary acceptance, but there was no time. She spoke in whispers, raising her hand like a conductor. The air around Adeline rippled and wavered. When it settled out, Adeline's burned arm was once again encased in white gauze. She wore hospital scrubs, was propped up with a pillow, and a blanket covered her lap. The end table was laden with tissues, pill bottles, and half-full water glasses.

The doorbell rang. "Try to look the part, would you?" Sarah said, heading to answer the door. She smiled. It felt good to be in the big-sister role for a change.

The nurse was easy to manipulate. She was overworked and worried she wouldn't have time to dress the wounds of everyone she needed to treat today. Sarah created the illusion that Adeline's wound was healing much better than expected. She planted the idea that the follow-up appointments they'd scheduled wouldn't be necessary. There were far more serious cases requiring the nurse's attention. She closed off with a suggestion that the nurse direct them to their GP if they needed further wound care.

"Thank you so much," Sarah said, escorting the nurse to the front door. She watched until the nurse made it safely out of the driveway.

"Thanks," Adeline said, sitting up when Sarah came back to the living room. "You mind returning my clothes?"

"Do you want me to ..." She swirled her finger in the air. Adeline was either feeling charitable or guilty, and nodded. She closed her eyes. Sarah drew on the grid and returned Adeline and the living room to the condition they'd been in when she'd arrived.

Adeline opened her eyes, checked her clothes, and started for the solarium.

"Where were you earlier?" Sarah said, following her. She stopped to admire the tower of blooming orchids Adeline had inherited from their father. He'd built the tower by repurposing an old lampstand. Arms with disc-like hands rotated around the lampstand at intervals from the floor. He'd be pleased to see how well his orchids were doing.

"Met with a potential client," Adeline said, her face lighting up. "I may have another commission. A portrait."

Adeline told her about Churchwell having gone to the Bolt Gallery and that he'd been taken with her work. "I'll check with Suzanna, but I think the guy will go as high as twelve, possibly even fifteen grand."

Sarah whistled. "More than Mrs. Doppler?"

Adeline nodded, her smile infectious. She set down her portfolio.

"Congratulations."

Adeline asked her to stay for lunch, but she couldn't. She'd already rescheduled her appointment with Natalie and didn't dare skip it.

"I thought Natalie had been discovered. That interlopers had her fully booked," Adeline said, insinuation in her tone.

"What can I say? A spot opened up."

Adeline simply smiled, and Sarah positively wallowed in the change that had come over her big sister. All her life, she'd hoped one day to be able to share the magical world with Adeline. She knew it would be difficult for Adeline, but her hope had never left. For the first time since they were kids, she let herself feel that hope again.

Sarah spotted her purse in the kitchen and went to collect it. She called over her shoulder. "What's your thinking about what the warlock told you, the names he mentioned?"

"I've given it some thought," Adeline said. "The way I see it, the message the warlock wanted me to deliver is his problem, not mine. I'm more concerned with what he was up to. What he may have done to me, other than the burn."

"I agree," Sarah said, returning to Adeline. "Besides, Damaras is already working on the warlock's ID. She had Simon do my regression this morning. He was able to produce a likeness." Sarah had been surprised by how much detail Simon was able to retrieve.

"Weren't you worried what else he might find in there?" Adeline said, pointing to Sarah's head.

"No. The regression was very specific. I knew the approximate time when I'd seen the warlock's face. Simon just ran the clock back to the twenty-minute window I gave him. I could feel where he was searching. I would have blocked him if he wandered too far."

"You can do that?"

Sarah nodded. "I probably couldn't stop Damaras, but no one else gets in my head unless I let them." It was a prideful boast, but Sarah wanted Adeline to be proud of her accomplishments as a witch, not just as a mother.

"I'm sorry about yesterday. It was careless of me to go off on Damaras the way I did. I may not understand why you want to work with her, but I hope I didn't cause problems for you."

"I'm working for Stonewater coven's priestess. It won't always be Damaras, but I do appreciate that she's given me a chance to make a difference. I can help you, too. Let me."

"You're sure you can keep this away from the coven? Because if there's an advantage to be gained as a result of this information, I want to be the one who gets it. Not Damaras."

"I've already promised."

"You're right. You did. Okay. From what the warlock said, whoever this Kai was, he was serving a sentence. So he'd committed a crime and been caught. It would help to know which warlock sentences result in burns like this," she said, rubbing her arm. "If he's left something behind in me, it'll be mentioned in the sentence."

"I have access to the archives," Sarah said. "I'll start there."

"Great. I'll dig out my old notebooks. I may have written something useful during the lectures on warlocks. I've got some of dad's old books too."

"I thought you burned your witchcraft books." Sarah retrieved her car keys from her purse.

"I tried. Mom took them away from me. I'm pretty sure they're in a box in the back closet."

Sarah laughed. "Sounds like Mom. Speaking of which, you going to tell her?"

"No. I don't want her to cut her cruise short. She's been looking forward to it for ages, and you know she'd fly back here in a heartbeat if she thought one of us was in trouble." She'd left on New Year's Eve for a year-long, around-the-world cruise on a small luxury liner.

"You're right. She would." Sarah slung her purse over her shoulder. "I'll head to the archives after my appointment. You sure you're okay?"

"Just tired. Have a bit of a headache."

Sarah nibbled her lip. "Something you'd attribute to the attack?"

"No. Marcus's magic is a little overwhelming. That's pretty much all I feel right now."

"Makes sense. Still, be careful in the coming days. A warlock attacked you. You can't take that lightly."

"Don't worry. I'm not. Can you sense any change?"

Sarah sent out her binder feelers, but Adeline still registered as non-magical. "No threads, no blue aura. You're good."

"No magic. What a surprise. Can you please report that to Princess Dumbass and get her off my back?"

So much for hoping Adeline might be coming around. "I will, but she's not going to drop it. I know her. She'll try to weaponize your attack to use it against the warlocks. You'd better prepare yourself. She's not done with you."

Luke had less than eight hours to retrieve Kai's cuff and deliver it to Tanner. If he failed, he had no doubt Tanner would follow through on his threat.

He materialized with the sun's first rays in Adeline's back garden. The ground floor was lit up. Inside, Adeline's tenant, Tucker, appeared in a sleeveless undershirt. Standing at the kitchen window, he downed pills with a glass of water then moved out of view. A television came on. Luke bided his time. He was patient when he had to be.

At precisely seven o'clock, Tucker left the house wearing the same cap and jacket as before. Luke probed his mind. He was thinking of flowers and wondering if Leung's grocers would have any out this early.

Luke kept still in the shadows beside the garage. The lights on the top floor directly above the solarium came on. A figure moved behind gauzy curtains. Adeline. He was sure of it. When the upstairs lights went off, the main floor's lights came on. Adeline moved about in the kitchen then walked into the solarium and disappeared. Sunlight glared off the solarium's glass, turning it into a mirror. Thirty minutes passed before she reappeared in the kitchen.

Tucker returned. Flowers peeked out the top of a paper grocery bag. He hummed a tune as he fitted his key into the lock and ducked inside.

Anytime now, Adeline would start down the stairs with her tenant's breakfast. He considered that not only did Adeline have a tenant who was most definitely human, but that she served him breakfast. On a tray. Every morning. Witches didn't usually live in such close proximity to humans. And even young witches coming out of their barbaric bindings had better mind protection than she possessed. Like most warlocks, Luke considered the witches' practice of binding their infants' magic abhorrent, effectively stunting their magical development. Perhaps Adeline's magic had been similarly restricted. Regardless, something didn't add up, and once again he found himself wondering if she was a witch or simply a witch's pet.

When Adeline shouldered the back door open and turned around, Luke snapped to attention. He held off until she reached the second landing, the farthest point from the house and its wards. She held the tray aside as she monitored her feet on the steps. Luke drew a rune in the air that called the cuff to his hand. At the same time, the replacement cuff, a cheap knockoff, appeared in its place on the tray. Adeline stopped and swivelled her head toward the garage. Had she sensed movement? Magic? Whatever it was, she dismissed it with a shake of her head and continued down.

"Charlie, your breakfast is here," she called, and Luke disappeared.

He re-formed near Tanner's gatehouse, the cuff heavy in his hand. He examined the runes but found no anomalies, no mistakes—not even an errant scratch that might explain the cuff's premature release. Kai Oxen's name was correct. His third conviction for siphoning was noted. The sentence of forfeiture was clear, as was the note that the sentence had to be carried out in the presence of a higher authority.

All standard rune work. It could have been more specific about which higher authority, but Luke knew the wording's built-in flexibility allowed Tanner to appoint a stand-in should he change his mind about attending.

There was nothing in the script specifically barring forfeiture to a witch. It simply went without saying that a warlock would never do such a thing. Shouldn't even be able to. Their magics were incompatible. Kai's magic would kill a witch. Spilling your magic into an inhospitable host was not forfeiture. It was the equivalent of flushing it, which Kai would never do. He was far too proud of his magic to flush it, and Luke didn't believe Kai would risk losing his hand.

So, if Adeline Thorne was a witch, she was no normal witch.

"Where did you find it?" Tanner said, when Luke's escort delivered him to the study.

"A human had it." Luke felt Tanner trying to probe his mind. Tanner would never be able to get inside his head, but that didn't stop him from trying.

"Has Kai tried to contact you?"

"No. I'm the last person he'd contact." *Other than you.*

Tanner ran his fingertips over the runes. "I'm sure you inspected these. Did you notice anything amiss?"

"No." Luke's thoughts turned to Adeline. Kai was a dead man if Tanner learned what Luke suspected.

"Nonetheless, I'll have it checked." He slipped the cuff into his pocket. "I want to know if Kai contacts you. And I want to know who that devious bastard forfeited his magic to."

SEVEN

Adeline woke feeling unrested. The headache she'd developed the day before had stayed with her into the evening and ultimately sent her to bed early. The dull ache was still with her, burrowed into the base of her skull. A headache that lasted two days? She struggled against the fear that it was connected to the warlock's attack.

She shuffled into the shower, hoping the spray of warm water would help. It didn't, and she was late again. She needed to get Charlie's breakfast started.

While she waited for the coffee to brew, she bent to the vase of fresh flowers Charlie had given her yesterday. They smelled like spring. He'd been so sweet, concerned about her burn, even though she'd assured him she was on the mend.

Today's breakfast was egg Benny. She dragged out the cast iron pan, the pot for the poached egg, and another for the hollandaise, then pulled the ingredients she needed from the fridge.

She downed an Advil with her first sip of coffee, and while the bacon rendered, she wandered through the solarium and into the dining room. Her witchling notebooks were strewn about the table. Reading through them had dug up old ghosts. Anger and humiliation at first, but as she worked her way through the notebooks, she rediscovered the wonder she'd lost. The curiosity. She'd been diligent with her notes. Thorough. The spells came back to her, the potions. She questioned anew how magic, something that had felt so natural to her, could have failed her.

She returned to the kitchen. The Advil hadn't kicked in yet. She tried to ignore the nagging ache as she turned the bacon and added the potatoes. She dribbled vinegar into the poaching water and dressed the tray as she waited for the water to come back up to a simmer. She'd come to love the game she played with Charlie, sneaking fruit and veggies onto his tray.

Today, she decided it would be a fresh tomato. She pulled the ripest one from the vine in her fruit bowl and set it on a cutting board.

After she assembled his breakfast and placed it on the tray, she turned to get the hollandaise. But the glass bowl atop the pot of heated water was empty. She hung her head. His breakfast would get cold in the time it took her to make it. She was off her game. *Damn it.* She'd made this same breakfast dozens of times. She could have sworn she'd whisked the damn sauce. She could picture it clearly in her mind.

She rushed across the kitchen, dropped a chunk of butter in a measuring cup, and set it in the microwave. Back at the stove, she cracked an egg, separated it, and reached to drop the yolk in the glass bowl. She stopped herself at the last moment . . . and blinked. Then blinked again. A pale yellow sauce covered the bottom of the bowl. She dipped her finger in and tasted it. Hollandaise. *What the hell?* More residual from Marcus's magic? Or something else?

She was halfway out the door when she noticed the tomato she'd sliced and set on Charlie's tray. It had turned black.

Sarah had phoned ahead, so Addie was expecting her. It was late afternoon, and Joe had the kids. She used her key to open Adeline's front door. "Addie?" she called out. "You here?"

"Dining room," Adeline said.

Sarah approached the table stacked with books. "I'm glad you called. Are these your old notebooks?"

"Yeah. Some of Dad's textbooks too."

"Have you discovered anything yet?"

"Other than I was obsessed with taking copious notes? Not much. But I'd forgotten how pervasive were the teachings that warlocks are a corrupt and untrustworthy lot. One bad apple spoils the bushel? Not that I needed that reminder." Adeline rubbed the back of her neck.

"Well, I learned something." Sarah pulled a sheet from her purse and handed it over. "That's a list of infractions the warlock high court professes to enforce."

Adeline studied the list.

"Siphoning is on there," Sarah said.

Her sister nodded. "This is a good start. Did anyone question what you were doing in the archives?"

"No. But Simon was there. He asked how you were doing."

"He didn't try to read you?"

Sarah shot Adeline a look of exasperation. "Simon's a good guy. He wouldn't do that. But he did volunteer that Damaras tasked him with searching for similar attacks. He was still there when I left." Though Sarah didn't dare voice it, she thought it was a smart move on Damaras's part.

Sarah pulled over one of Adeline's notebooks. "What's this?" she said, pointing to marks in the margin.

Adeline glanced over. "Just me last night. Doodling."

Sarah flipped a page and found more. Worry knotted in her stomach. "These aren't doodles, Addie. They're runes." And not just any runes. Complex runes.

Adeline jerked her head up. "Runes? You sure?"

"They teach these in third degree. Warlocks use them, but we don't know how."

Adeline pushed her chair back and stood. Sarah followed her into the kitchen. Adeline popped the lid on a bottle of Advil and swallowed one, washing it down with a glass of tap water. When she turned from the sink, her forehead was furrowed with worry.

"What is it?" Sarah asked.

"Nothing. Nothing important."

"Bullshit." She stepped closer. "Addie, you're shaking. What the hell is it?"

"Can you see threads in me? Magical markers of any kind?"

Sarah stepped back and drew on her binder magic. "No. Nothing. What's happened?"

Adeline crossed her arms over her chest and told her about the incident with the hollandaise sauce. She was petrified it might be a sign of warlock magic.

"If you were using warlock magic, I should be able to see red threads coming off you, and I don't," Sarah said, more relieved than she let on.

The news didn't erase the tension from her sister's posture.

"I know you don't want to hear this," Sarah said, "but maybe you should tell Damaras."

·)·)·)●(·(·(·

deline's reaction was visceral. She'd chum up to Damaras the moment she finished gouging out her own eyes. "If I tell Damaras, she'll want to put me under her control," Adeline said. "And I won't learn what's been done to me unless it suits Damaras to tell me. I'll become her pawn."

"You've already done all you can with your notes and Dad's books," Sarah said. "Damaras will keep you safe, and I'm not going to stop looking for answers."

"I have a life, Sarah. Charlie, my painting. And I have you. You can warn me if magical markers appear."

"I can bind you, but if word leaks out, I can't protect you."

"I know. But the house's wards can. I'm not ready to hand myself over to Damaras."

"You can't stay in the house around the clock. You'll go stir-crazy."

"Maybe whatever it is will pass."

"Maybe," Sarah said, with no conviction. "You'll tell me if anything else happens?"

"I promise." And though it killed her, she asked her sister not to bring Jack and Olive around. "Just in case."

After Sarah left, Adeline packed up her old notebooks and her father's textbooks and returned them to the back closet. Though the light was fading, she donned her painting smock and filled the jelly jar with fresh water. She was counting on Mr. Doppler's approval, which she wouldn't get if his gift wasn't ready in time. A recommendation in his circles would boost her reputation and bring in quality clients. How she would love to be able to choose what to paint and have the time to do it properly.

Her thoughts turned to Churchwell. She'd already considered which angle she'd paint. His right side would be the best if he wanted to hide the small scar under his left cheekbone. Not that the scar took away from his good looks. She'd never painted eyes so dark that she had difficulty picking out the pupil. The intensity of his gaze when he turned it on her had felt almost physical. She would use indigo highlights to bring out the black in his hair. He'd probably want to get it cut before he sat for her. Hopefully, he'd wear a suit. A costume or setting piece didn't feel right for him, and he wore his suit like a second skin.

Back at the easel, she studied Mrs. Doppler's photos again, and then the sketch she'd drawn as a reference. She squeezed small dollops of blue, white, and black on her palette, and then added a drop of *sienna*. Mrs. Doppler's eyes were a shade of blue that bordered on grey. And though the pose Mr. Doppler had settled on for his wife was formal, there was a hint of playfulness in her photos that she wanted to capture. The curve of her lip held some of it, but the rest would be in her eyes.

As she started with the blue, mixing in white, she wondered where Churchwell had flown to. He hadn't mentioned it. He hadn't even mentioned what he did for a living. Lawyer, possibly. Broker. A professional of some kind. He'd worn aftershave that smelled of cedar. She pictured him in a skyscraper, gazing out a window over the twinkling lights of a city, perhaps with a drink in his hand.

He should have called by now. How long could it take to check his calendar for dates to sit for her? She'd worked from a series of photos for Mrs. Doppler's portrait, which couldn't be avoided, given the painting would be a surprise. But she preferred to work with the subject in person.

Adeline's phone rang. *Damn.* Some days it seemed like the universe was conspiring against her ever finishing the portrait. She set down her brush and went to the kitchen to retrieve her phone.

It was Churchwell. Their conversation was brief and disappointing. He was unable to sit for her. His trip had been extended indefinitely. But he approved of her pose and angle suggestions. She rhymed off the photos she would need to do his likeness justice, and he said he'd get them to her in the next week or two.

"Out of curiosity," Adeline said, "where are you?"

"Stuck in an office tower with a view of a beautiful city I'll never get to explore."

"You don't get any time off?"

"Not even for good behaviour."

Before he disconnected, she could have sworn she heard ice cubes in a glass on his end.

Heading back to the dining room, her gaze landed on the flowers Charlie had brought her yesterday. The colourful flower heads, now a dull brown, drooped on blackened stalks. She took a step back. *Oh no.* Her heart rate picked up. *No no no.* She crept over to the fruit bowl, staring straight ahead, then sucked in a breath before looking down. The bananas and remaining tomatoes were black. She backed away and dropped into a kitchen chair.

The image she'd had of Churchwell was exactly as he had described. Had she somehow triggered his phone call?

No matter how hard she tried to find another explanation, her thoughts boomeranged back to what she could no longer deny. The warlock had done something to her, had planted a seed of some kind. And it was growing. She loosened the cuff on her right sleeve and examined her arm. Though still itchy from the healing, it looked perfectly normal. She almost expected to see the thing he'd left in her, a thing that could be removed.

She knew she should call Sarah, but her sister would want to involve Damaras. As she refastened the buttons on her shirtsleeve, dread and uncertainty overwhelmed her. Adeline's dislike of the Stonewater priestess went bone deep. Damaras drooled for the additional power the high priestess bestowed on her covens' priests and priestesses. Damaras was out for herself. She'd always been more interested in power and politics than what was best for the coven.

Adeline couldn't get past Damaras's greed for power. Not that she'd ever put much effort into trying.

The front doorbell rang. *Bloody hell!* She needed time and privacy for a breakdown, not company.

She sucked in a breath and marched to the front door to get rid of whomever it was.

But sadly, the *whomever* was Damaras, and she wasn't easy to get rid of. She was also capable of breaking the house's wards, so, albeit reluctantly, Adeline invited her and her elderly companion inside.

Damaras's presence normally fired up enough rage in Adeline to overcome her fear of the woman's power, but not today. Adeline's nerves were jangled.

"This is Beatrice," Damaras said, introducing her companion. "She's the principal binder from Seattle's Moonmere coven." The kindly-looking woman stood a head shorter than Damaras and clutched her purse in front of her as if it were a kettlebell—a cannonball with a handle.

"No disrespect, Beatrice," Adeline said, turning to address Damaras, "but Sarah's binding skills are second to none. And she's already told you her take."

"Given the gravity of the situation, I thought a second opinion was prudent. Shall we sit?"

"Does Sarah know you're seeking a second opinion?"

Damaras seated herself and invited Beatrice to do the same. Adeline resigned herself. The priestess and grandma wouldn't be going anywhere until they got what they'd come for.

"Has anything changed since my last visit?" Damaras asked.

Adeline took a seat and addressed Beatrice. "Sarah is my sister. I mean no offence."

The woman smiled. "I'm aware. And you're quite right. Your sister's skills are well-known. Damaras is also right. A warlock attack cannot be taken lightly."

Adeline absently rubbed her right forearm. She didn't disagree. But she didn't want Damaras involved. She sent up a prayer that whatever had just blackened the fruit hadn't left a thread behind. "All right. Let's get this over with."

"Beatrice, if you wouldn't mind?" Damaras said.

Beatrice stood in front of Adeline. "This won't take but a moment, dear," she said, and flooded her with binder magic. When she finished, she addressed Damaras. "I find no threads of any kind."

Adeline couldn't fathom why, but Damaras looked unhappy about that pronouncement even as she thanked her. Adeline, however, sighed in relief.

Damaras's attention swung back to her. "Have there been any changes in your health or otherwise since my last visit?"

"I got a new client. Another portrait."

Damaras pressed her lips into a tight line. She inhaled. "Magically. Speaking."

Adeline crossed her arms. "No. Nothing's changed."

"You're certain? Because I smell warlock magic."

EIGHT

Sarah's attention drifted to Adeline, as it had with worrying regularity since the previous day, when she'd learned about her episode with the hollandaise sauce. The blackened tomatoes were especially concerning.

"Ow! Mommy! That hurts," Olive cried.

Sarah glanced down at the brush in her hand. "Sorry, munchkin." She pressed a kiss to her daughter's head. "Let's get you to school."

After she dropped Olive at kindergarten, she drove to her sister's house. There'd be no rest for her until she'd read Addie's threads. She found her on the front porch swing with a mug in her hands.

"Coffee's on. Can I get you a cup?" Adeline said.

"Mind if I check your threads first?" Sarah didn't wait for a reply before she sent out her binder magic. That Addie didn't call her on the presumption meant she was worried as well. "You're good." Sarah pressed a hand to her chest, and her shoulders relaxed.

But the news didn't seem to relieve Adeline, who stared off into the distance.

"Has something else happened?"

Addie nodded then told her about her phone call with Churchwell and the demise of Charlie's flowers.

"And you waited until now to tell me," Sarah said.

"There's more," Adeline said. "We should go inside."

Adeline took a seat at the kitchen table and beckoned to her sister. "You may want to sit," she said, her face unreadable.

Sarah sat and chewed at her lips while Addie unwound the events involving her unexpected company and Damaras's parting remarks.

"It's a good bloody thing there were no red threads," Sarah said.

"Given what happened to Mom, Damaras is the last person I want questioning my loyalty."

"Can you smell it?" Adeline asked.

Sarah sniffed the air. "Not now. What'd you do with the blackened fruit? The flowers?"

"They're in the trash. Outside."

"It could be that's what she scented. There may have been an odour in the air, I suppose, after the incident."

"Maybe I should get in touch with Warrick," Adeline said. "See if he can shed some light on what's happening to me."

Warrick Flynn was Adeline's ex. A warlock. Every witch family's worst nightmare, and the bane of every wannabe grandparent. "He comes from old money," Sarah remarked. "His family's old school, traditional. They won't suffer a witch wielding warlock magic. You can't trust them with this information."

Adeline leaned forward, rearranging the salt and pepper shakers around the napkin holder. "I don't want this, whatever it is," she said. "It's taken me years to accept that I'm a barren witch. I've built a new life. One without magical complications. Outside the coven's political games."

Sarah reached over and took her sister's hand. "I know. And I'm so proud of you. That you've accomplished all of this," she said, gesturing around her, "with no magic? I couldn't have done it." She hated hearing the words *barren witch* come out of Addie's mouth. It was a term whispered among witches for fear saying it aloud would tempt fate.

"Painting is more than a hobby. It's who I am. Charlie is like family. This house is my dream home. I can't give them up, Sarah. If we tell Damaras, I'll lose it all."

"Why do you say that?"

"A witch with access to warlock magic? She'll want me where she can control me. Under her roof." Adeline's features hardened. She pulled her hand away and stood, skittering her chair across the floor. "I've got to get back to Mrs. Doppler before I lose another day."

Sarah looked up at her, pleading. "You can't ignore what's happening to you." Adeline's nostrils flared and a storm rolled in behind her eyes. It's what her sister looked like when she felt cornered. Sarah shifted in her seat. She hadn't meant to do that.

"I just need to finish her eyes," Adeline said, flexing her fingers. "If I wasn't interrupted every goddamned time I tried to work on her, it'd be done by now!"

Sarah stood and took a step back. "Adeline?"

"Two blue orbs. Her eyes are all that's left!"

"Adeline!" Sarah said. "Stop. Whatever you're doing. Stop!"

The acrid smell of smoke brought Adeline around.

Sarah dashed behind her and sprinted toward the solarium, tossing an extinguishing spell ahead of her. She whispered another spell to disengage the fire alarm and clear the smoke. Adeline stumbled in behind her.

A quick glance around the room revealed the source of the fire. They followed the last tendrils of smoke to the canvas sitting on the easel. Adeline approached it with her hands clasped on the top of her head. "What have I done?"

"We can fix this," Sarah said, approaching Adeline like she was a land mine.

All that remained of Mrs. Doppler's eyes were two holes burned through the canvas.

·)·)·)·●·(·(·(·

"What's happening to me?" Adeline wrapped her arms around her torso. Her gaze drifted to the tower of orchids. Her features fell. "Nooo."

Sarah left her side to inspect the plants. Adeline didn't have the stomach for it.

"It's not so bad," Sarah said with a pained face, poking at the blackened plants. "The roots look okay. They'll come back."

"Not if I can't stop whatever it is I'm doing." Adeline started for the kitchen, wanting to get away from the destruction she'd caused, but the kitchen wasn't far enough. She walked to the front porch and sat on the top step. Sarah sat beside her.

"What did you see in there? In the kitchen, earlier?" Adeline asked.

"Your aura was a tangle of red threads."

"Warlock."

"So it would seem."

"And now?"

"Nothing. The threads are gone."

"Warlocks draw their power from living matter. That's what's happening. With the hollandaise, Churchwell's call. The painting. Each time, something died."

"As distressing as that is, I'm more worried about what damage the warlock magic is doing inside you," Sarah said. "You may not have magical abilities, but you're still a witch. Born of a witch. It's in your DNA." Sarah worried her lip. "I wish I knew what the tangled threads mean. Why they disappear. Is it normal?"

"You mean for a warlock?" Adeline said.

"You're not a warlock," she said, with a brisk shake of her head. "But we need to find out what's going on inside you, and quickly."

"How?"

"You know how. Stop fighting it. Damaras is powerful and connected. She can find the answers we need."

"It would kill me to ask for her help."

"It might kill you not to. Our magics aren't compatible. That warlock has just given you the equivalent of the wrong blood type."

Adeline dropped her head into her hands. "Is it too early for a drink?"

"So you'll do it? You'll call her?"

Adeline would have considered the alternatives, but there were none. She straightened. "We have to take care of some things first."

Adeline's pride took a hit, allowing her sister to repair the holes in the canvas and the smoke damage. She'd had more magic released around her these past forty-eight hours than she'd experienced in the ten years prior. But there was no getting around it. Not if she wanted to deliver the portrait on time. Still, she refused to allow Sarah's magic near her paint or brushes. Adeline was determined to finish Mrs. Doppler's eyes herself—and without magic.

Two hours later, when Adeline stepped away from the portrait, it was finished.

"Beautiful," Sarah said, leaning against the archway to the kitchen.

"Thanks. It's just how I imagined it." Adeline gathered her palette and brushes and walked past Sarah into the kitchen. "It'll be dry tomorrow. Then I can crate it and get it to Suzanna."

"I can do that for you. The Bolt Gallery, right?" Sarah said. "Unless you're trying to put off calling Damaras for another day."

Adeline set her things on the counter and tore a paper towel off the roll. "No. I know I need help. I want this out of me before I cause damage I can't live with." She wiped the paint off the palette and dropped the paper towel in the garbage. "I'll call her. I just have to find a way to keep control of my life here, in this house."

"Negotiate with her."

"With what? My forgiveness?" Adeline laughed at herself. "Yeah. Right. She's got the power to force my hand."

"And you have the power of a warlock inside you. That's proof that the warlocks have broken the accord. She's a politician looking for any advantage. Use that."

Adeline's spirits lifted. She looked sideways at Sarah. "You're pretty clever for a baby sister."

"Baby? I prefer *younger* sister. And FYI? I'll always be . . . younger."

Damaras arrived on Adeline's porch within minutes of their phone call.

"I've invited Silas Vance to join us," Damaras said, settling on the sofa. "He's our senior war mage."

Adeline had almost made it to the chair across from her. She stopped and turned. "Please stop inviting witches to my home without asking me." Damaras really did bring out the worst in her.

"Silas understands warlock magic better than anyone. But if you'd rather play around until you kill something precious, I'll tell him to stay home."

"You could have mentioned him when we were talking on the phone."

The doorbell rang. "I'll get it," Sarah said, scooting out of the living room like her sneakers were on fire.

Moments later, she ushered Silas in. The dark-skinned man with close-cropped hair stood a pinch taller than Sarah. He dipped his head in greeting to Damaras.

Damaras stood. "Thank you for coming on such short notice." She turned to Adeline. "Silas sent his junior mages here the night of your attack. After Sarah called for help."

Silas shook Adeline's hand. "I'm sorry we weren't able to trace the warlock," Silas said. "They're slippery bastards."

"Marcus was able to heal her burns," Damaras said. "But we fear the warlock may have inflicted something magical on her." She retook her seat, smoothing the tails of her oversized linen shirt as she sat.

Silas circled Adeline, all the while mumbling a spell under his breath. "I don't sense any warlock magic. Sarah? Does your binder's magic sense anything?"

Sarah had also taken a seat. "Not now. But earlier, she was covered in a tangle of red threads."

Silas's eyes widened in alarm. "How can that be? She's a witch, is she not?"

"I have no powers. Never have," Adeline said, intervening before Damaras could draw satisfaction from telling him.

"Describe for Silas the events you hinted at when we spoke earlier," Damaras said.

Adeline paused. She glanced at Sarah, knowing the telling might put a dent in her reputation. Sarah nodded. Adeline took a deep breath then explained the incidents surrounding the hollandaise, her new client, and the canvas.

During the recounting, Damaras's body slowly stiffened. And when the telling was done, Damaras glared at her sister. "You disappoint me, Sarah."

"I apologize," Sarah said. "We suspected it was the healing magic that caused the anomalies. Marcus expended more than Adeline's ever been exposed to. I've been checking regularly. There were no markers until today. We called right away."

"You called when you needed help. I'm glad I followed my instincts and had Beatrice examine her."

"Beatrice wasn't able to sense any more than Sarah," Adeline said. "Don't make me regret calling you."

"You're dancing awfully close to a line you don't want to cross, Adeline," Damaras said.

"I'd like to have you come by the training centre at the sanctuary," Silas said. "If you're agreeable? I'd like to provoke this magic out of you. See it for myself."

"She'll move in tonight," Damaras said. "I'll make arrangements."

The thread holding Adeline's temper frayed. "I will not be moving in. Aren't you forgetting something? I'm banished."

Damaras's head swivelled back to Adeline, a thin smile on her lips. "I am a woman of my word. I rescinded your banishment after our last meeting."

"That doesn't change anything. I can't move in, Damaras. I have commitments here."

"Then break them. This is important."

"So are my commitments—"

"I'm sure we can work around your commitments," Silas said, sidetracking the heating argument.

Damaras finally broke eye contact. She turned to Silas. "Are you certain?"

"Yes." He addressed Adeline. "Can you be at the sanctuary at ten tomorrow morning?"

"I can. And Sarah will be coming with me."

·))) ● (((·

Luke convinced Tanner to extend his reprieve long enough for him to search Kai's usual haunts. Luke was working from the assumption that Kai had forfeited all but his seed magic, and he couldn't use that to hide. Of course, another warlock could be hiding him, and Kai had a wide circle of friends, but Luke made the effort because even the illusion of doing so kept him in Tanner's good graces.

Kai was probably already restoring his powers. First with a donation of magic to awaken his seed magic, likely from one of the warlock women he flirted with. Another siphon, to be sure. A siphon could replenish whatever they'd donated soon enough. After that initial injection of power, Kai would begin siphoning again.

As Luke strolled through his old friend's favourite bars and clubs, he sent out feelers, listening for chatter. A warlock who'd circumvented a runecaster's cuff would cause a stir. He heard nothing. Perhaps he'd underestimated Kai's ability to be discreet.

All too soon, he was forced back to his well-appointed prison. He hadn't found Kai, and if anyone knew where he'd disappeared to, they weren't sharing.

Luke lay in bed, thinking about Adeline. Tomorrow he'd find a way to keep tabs on her. If Kai had somehow deposited his magic inside her, he'd be back for it.

NINE

Sarah sat outside Damaras's office, feeling like an errant student awaiting the principal's scolding. As she shifted position once again on the hard wooden chair, she wondered if keeping her uncomfortable was precisely the intent.

The priestess had called Sarah in for a 10:00 a.m. meeting, precisely the same time Adeline was set to meet with Silas. Since she couldn't be in two places at once, Sarah had arrived early, hoping to see Damaras and be done with her before Adeline showed up in—she checked the time—twenty minutes. But getting in didn't look promising. Her assistant said Damaras was tied up with someone else. Whoever it was, they were being very quiet. Or maybe they were using a spell, because Sarah couldn't hear voices beyond the closed door.

She remembered the day Damaras had appointed her to the GC. She'd worked so hard to earn her place on the council—a place that gave her the opportunity to shape binder policy and decisions that affected them all. She tried not to think about how easily Damaras could un-appoint her.

Fifteen uncomfortable minutes later, the door opened, and Silas exited, his features softened by a contented smile. Her intuition flared. That smile was out of place. He jerked his head in her direction and his smile faded. "Sarah. You're early."

"Yes, well, Damaras asked me to meet her here at ten o'clock, so I'll be late joining you and Adeline."

"Of course. I'll see you later, then," he said, and turned to leave.

"Wait! Silas." Sarah jumped to her feet and then hesitated. She didn't know Silas well, but his reputation was brutal. "Don't hurt her. Adeline."

"I won't. She'll be fine. Perhaps a little uncomfortable, but nothing she can't handle."

After he left, and with just four minutes to spare, Damaras invited her into her office.

"I must apologize," Damaras said, her cheeks flushed, "for putting you in an untenable position. Please, have a seat." She motioned to a sofa and took a seat opposite. A low table sat between them.

"Untenable? What do you mean?" Sarah said, not comprehending.

"We all know Adeline's opinion of Stonewater coven, and her animosity toward me. It was unfair of me to put you between us."

"You didn't."

"We both know what my expectations of you were. I don't blame you for not telling me right away. She's your sister. Family."

"I brought you in as soon as I could." Sarah stood and walked to the fireplace. "She didn't ask for this. She needs our support."

"And she'll have it. But this is bigger than you and Adeline. The GC is meeting this morning to discuss our options in response to the attack. I want you there."

Sarah spun to face her. "This morning? I can't. Adeline is expecting me to join her and Silas."

"I know. That's why I asked Beatrice to attend in your place in the training centre with Silas."

"Are you trying to provoke Adeline?"

"That isn't my intent. This coven is my priority. Our meeting with the warlock lord is already set. We must be prepared to present our case and extract the steepest price we can for the crime."

Sarah felt torn. The opportunity to be a part of the team possibly reshaping the peace accord was beyond her expectations. But she wouldn't abandon Adeline. Not when she was so vulnerable.

"I'm sorry. Adeline put her trust in me. I won't break it."

"I understand. Truly, I do. Go to her. If you can make her understand the bigger picture, then I'll see you in the council chamber in ten minutes. If not, please send Beatrice to the chamber to attend in your place. A principal binder's vision is critical to our discussions."

Sarah left Damaras's office with a tightness in her throat. She swallowed. Damaras had made the choice clear. Family or coven. Sarah's loyalty was being tested. She resented the hell out of Damaras for the blatant coercion. Apparently, Adeline wasn't the only one harbouring old grudges.

Sarah collected herself before she pushed open the doors to the training centre. It was quarter past ten, Beatrice was on her feet, her face flushed, and Adeline had Silas pinned to the mat.

·))) ● ((C ·

"I may not have magic, but I'm not defenseless," Adeline said.

"Point taken," Silas said, his voice strained. "I yield."

Adeline removed the pressure of her knee from his lower back and stood. Silas rolled over and stared up at her. "Black belt? Third degree?"

"Fourth," Adeline said. She'd been training in martial arts since her first failed unbinding. Her father thought it would be good for her to learn to direct her anger. He'd been right. It had just taken a longer, rougher road than he'd imagined, ending with a spectacular wreck of a marriage to a warlock. She offered Silas her hand and helped him up.

"Adeline. May I have a word?" Sarah said, having witnessed their exchange from the doorway.

Adeline excused herself and walked across the floor to join Sarah. "Silas said you were in a meeting with Damaras."

"Yeah. She's called a council meeting to form a response to the attack on you."

"Today?"

"As we speak."

"Let me guess. She wants you in the meeting. A meeting she arranged for the exact same time I'm facing off with Uncle Silas and Grandma Bea."

"Looks like."

Adeline shook her head. "What is she so afraid of?"

"The meeting with the warlock lord has been scheduled. She wants to ensure we're prepared."

"What she wants is for you not to be here with me."

"No. Damaras left it up to me."

Adeline checked over her shoulder to see what Sarah was looking at. Silas was examining the enormous jade tree he'd wheeled into the room shortly after she'd arrived.

"What's that all about?" Sarah asked.

"The plant is sacrificial. It's my battery, though I have no idea how to find the on switch."

"How's it going so far?" Sarah asked.

"Good, if me not displaying a stitch of warlock magic is the goal here. Silas says he's not unleashing his magic until he's exhausted his physical options. Says he doesn't want to pollute his findings."

"Makes sense, I suppose," Sarah said. "What'd I walk in on?"

"Silas thought a physical attack might bring out my inner warlock." Adeline tried to put up a modest front, but she'd loved the surprise in Silas's expression when she'd knocked his feet out from under him. It'd been a while since she'd had a real workout, and the slow burn in her muscles felt good.

"You're enjoying this," Sarah said, her expression amused.

"A little. But it won't last. Not when he pulls out his magic."

"He knows that. He won't harm you."

Adeline wasn't entirely convinced. "The sanctuary hasn't changed a bit. Neither have the vipers in it."

"Do you need me here? Because I'll stay if you do," Sarah said.

"Go to your meeting. But don't leave the sanctuary without me. I'm driving you home. We can talk more then."

Sarah pulled her into a hug. "Try not to hurt our war mage, okay?"

Sarah walked through the council chamber's wards and took her seat. Damaras sat at one end of an oval table, surrounded by her hand-picked councillors. The two war mages who reported to Silas were present, along with the highest-ranking elementals, one each for earth, water, fire, and wind. The principal spellcaster was there, as was the principal potioner. Simon wasn't a regular member, but he was there and acknowledged Sarah with a nod. Marcus was in his place across from her, as was Carolyne, the archivist—a position her mother had held for many years before Damaras intervened.

Damaras cut through the idle chit-chat. "Now that we're all present, let's get to work."

She laid out the series of events, calling on Sarah to fill in some blanks, until those around the table had been brought up to date.

"The warlocks have broken the accord," Damaras said.

Daniel, the senior of the two attending mages, shook his head. "I disagree. A solitary attack on a barren witch? It's an affront, a minor transgression at best."

"She could have been killed," Sarah said, keeping her anger in check. If she jumped all over the mage's classist reference, they'd dismiss her for being overly sensitive because she was family. "Perhaps a reframing of the event would clarify the severity of the situation. A warlock perpetuated an unprovoked attack on a member of our coven who had no means of protecting herself."

"I'm sorry, Sarah, but I have to agree with Daniel," Kylie, the other war mage said. "Even reframed, this is not an elevated crime. Yes, it's reprehensible, but both sides of this accord have had rogue players before."

"That's true," Carolyne said. "As the archivist, I can confirm the precedent has been set. There's been no loss of life, and the physical injury has already healed. The warlocks will press for a lesser charge."

"Setting aside the severity of the crime, what proof do we have?" Odette said. Sarah had respect for the coven's spellcaster. The spiky-blue-haired witch's incantations were as imaginative as they were effective.

"Silas is with her right now, trying to tease out the extent of the damage," Damaras said. "Moonmere coven's binder, Beatrice, is with them. She'll report what she sees."

"The red tangle of threads Sarah observed could have been a temporary phenomenon," Casey, the fire elemental, said. "But even if a binder can identify them, warlocks can't see threads. They aren't going to take our word for it."

"Unless she can demonstrate warlock magic," Damaras said. The room fell silent. Incredulous councillors glanced about the table, searching for solidarity.

"That's impossible," Carolyne said. "I would have read of other cases in the coven's history."

"Adeline harbours a warlock's magic," Sarah said. "I've seen it myself."

Kylie huffed. "Errant blips that even you chalked up to residual healing magic. What are your thoughts, Marcus?"

Marcus was young for a principal healer, but his skills were unquestioned. "It took a lot of magic to heal her burns. There was bound to be residual. Probably for a few days, at least. Residual healing magic has been known to produce hallucinations, narcolepsy in humans, elevated levels of elemental magic in witches."

"Adeline was probably hallucinating, then," Daniel said. "You didn't see the magic for yourself, right?"

"Not the first two times," Sarah said. "But I was there when she burned holes through a canvas. I saw the red threads spring out of her and, seconds later, smelled smoke. The canvas was in the adjoining room. There's no other explanation for it."

Marcus pinched his chin. "A witch with warlock magic? It shouldn't be possible, but if she's severed from her witch magic, I suppose it's conceivable."

Daniel shifted forward, his elbows on the table. "Let's think this through. If we have a witch in our coven capable of wielding warlock magic, she could infiltrate their ranks, learn their weaknesses. Unlock their rune magic. She could be a strategic asset."

"This is Adeline we're talking about," Damaras said. "It will be no surprise to Sarah when I say that Adeline won't spy for us."

"She doesn't want the magic," Sarah said. "She wants it removed."

"Why?" Daniel said. "She's got a unique opportunity here."

Sarah tilted her head in disbelief. "I suppose the fact that warlock magic is incompatible and might kill her probably helped her come to that decision. She may be magically barren, but she still has witch DNA."

"A warlock is the only one who could remove her magic," Kylie said. Witches could neither siphon nor give away their magic. "And I would advise against asking for that. Siphoning is illegal and they'd see it as doing us a favour. It would be a waste of an opportunity to gain a more . . . impactful remedy."

Sarah stood, the heat of her anger flushing her cheeks.

"Let's take this down a notch," Damaras said. She reached to her forehead and swiped at a sheen of sweat. The stress of the meeting seemed to be affecting everyone in some way. The other witches around the table did their own stress dances, stretching necks from side to side, cracking jaws, rolling shoulders.

"Our meeting with the warlock lord isn't until tomorrow night. We'll break for lunch, and when we return this afternoon, I want your suggestions on which charge, and which remedy, would most benefit our coven."

Sarah was uncomfortably aware that Adeline's wishes weren't on the table. They weren't even a consideration.

"Does anyone else feel that?" Marcus said, his forehead furrowed.

Sarah felt it, but she couldn't put her finger on what it was.

A muffled boom from inside the building sent them scrambling.

TEN

deline waited until the door closed behind Sarah before returning to Silas. A short time later, Silas brought his magic to the party. Adeline sensed relief from Beatrice, who retreated to her corner, carrying her kettlebell of a purse, which never left her hands.

"Aren't you the expert on warlock magic?" Adeline said, rubbing the quad that Silas had kicked in their last hand-to-hand.

"Yes, and raw magic would have told me a lot more about your power than a contrived set-up. But our physical contest isn't causing the level of stress we need, so here we are."

Adeline watched as Silas marked a square about the size of an overstuffed armchair on the floor. He then walked around that space, chanting a spell. When he stood back, with a flourish of hand movements, a windowless closet appeared.

"Let's see how your warlock feels about environmental stress, shall we?" He swept his arm, and a door in the closet opened. "Make yourself at home."

Adeline peeked inside. "There's nothing in there. Barely room to sit down."

"You won't be sitting down. I'll invoke elemental magic. Unleash whatever power surfaces in response. The training centre is warded to contain any damage you might cause."

"You have a ward for you and Bea as well?"

"Don't worry about us. Go on. Get in," he said, with a shooing motion.

"Do I have a safe word or some way of getting out of there?"

"No."

Adeline took a step back.

"The healer can be here immediately."

"That's not very comforting."

"It's not meant to be. Stop wasting our time and get in."

Adeline stayed put. Sarah might have believed that Silas wouldn't hurt her, but he was under Damaras's orders.

"Killing you would defeat our purpose," he said, exasperation tingeing his words. "I thought you were as keen as we were to learn what the warlock left inside you."

"I am, but this," she said, waving at the box, "feels extreme."

He crossed his arms. "Do you have a better plan?"

She didn't. She had no plan. "If I do this, can you remove whatever you find inside me, or neutralize it?"

"I don't know. This situation is unprecedented. But until we know what we're dealing with, we have no target to remove or neutralize."

"So you can—if you learn what to target," she said, hopeful.

"You wouldn't like my methods. I'd need to consult with the other principals to come up with a non-lethal solution."

"Non-lethal would definitely be my preference." Adeline stepped toward the box. "Guess there's no getting around this." Adeline ducked under the short doorframe and stood in the centre of Silas's box. With her arms extended, her fingertips touched the walls. The door closed, and the room darkened. She closed her eyes and centred herself, relying on her martial arts training to draw her focus away from the overwhelming sense of being trapped in an enclosed space.

It started with a warm breeze, almost welcome, until the wind turned vicious, whipping around her body, pulling at her clothes, turning her braid into a weapon that slashed across her eyes. The wind slammed her into the sides of the box, lifted her off her feet, and bashed her head into the closet's ceiling. She tucked in her head and squeezed her eyes closed: small protection in the face of the onslaught. The wind pressed her back against a wall, compressing her chest until she could hardly breathe. When the wind finally died down, Adeline stumbled before righting herself. Her face felt like it had been sandblasted, and the body slams would leave bruises. She knew Silas wouldn't be easy on her, but he'd pushed it to the limit. She'd be hurting tomorrow. Just her luck that her warlock didn't mind the wind element.

Her reprieve lasted a minute, maybe two, before the next sensation hit. Water soaked her sneakers and rose up her ankles. If she were a witch, she could call on wind to drive the water out. The water climbed higher, swallowing her knees, creeping up her thighs. Witches could spellcast the water away or dematerialize. But how would a warlock deal with this scenario? *Wait.* Warlocks could also dematerialize. Was that her ticket out of here? The water rose to her hips. She struggled to imagine transforming her body into molecules that could be willed anywhere. She'd never made it that far in her witch training. Visualization failed, as did a concentrated effort to will herself outside the box that was quickly becoming an aquarium.

The water was up to her armpits. Buoyancy took her weight off her feet. If there'd been a current, she'd have been swept away. She was a strong swimmer, but she couldn't get fully horizontal. The best she could do was bob . . . until she was submerged. Her mind swam with visions of witches tied to planks being lowered beneath the water's surface, drowning. She shrieked.

Silas's disembodied voice floated into the box. "Fight it with the warlock's magic."

His voice halted her downward spiral. *Stop reacting and think, Adeline. Okay.* The box was just a tank. She had to kick out the glass, maybe blast the lid off.

The water reached her chin. Her toes were losing their hold on the floor. Floating now, she formed a ball and, with her feet on a wall, bulleted her back at the opposite wall. It had no effect. She couldn't develop enough momentum. She inhaled a breath, forced herself to the bottom, then sprang up, fists overhead, and punched the ceiling. Pain flared. She was pretty sure she'd broken something in her hand.

"I could use a little help here, Warlock," she mumbled, treading water. Surely Silas wouldn't let her drown. With her head now pressed against the top of the box, she closed her eyes and envisioned water the way she liked it. On a beach. Could it be that Silas's magic was just an illusion? She pictured herself in a lounge chair, seagulls overhead, and the sun a brilliant ball in the sky. The scent of sunscreen overwhelmed her senses. Silas's water disappeared, but her relief was tempered with anger. She should have known it was an illusion. The wind had probably been an illusion as well.

She was better prepared when Silas pulled his next trick out of his hat. Beneath her feet, the box turned to mud, suctioning her feet to the floor. The humidity and rot of a jungle invaded her sinuses. Soon something crept across the top of her foot and began twining up her leg. It wasn't a snake. Witches couldn't conjure living beings. A vine, maybe? Something tickled the shell of her ear. Something else brushed her shoulder. Silas was summoning earth's elementals.

Adeline kept herself centred, dismissing the sensations for what they were. Magic. Not real. Not consequential. To prove it to herself, she pressed her hand to the tickling sensation now on her neck.

Damn it! Not an illusion. Whatever it was stung her. She swore as she hurled it away. It swung back and stung her again, on the cheek. "Over the line, Silas!" She banged on the door. She'd had enough, and warlock magic sure as shit wasn't coming to her rescue. "Let me out of here!"

Silas ignored her plea. The vine on her leg made its presence known again, continuing its upward push. It was now around her thigh. She couldn't see it—the darkness in the box was absolute—but it rasped against her clothing as it grew.

If the stinging plants were real, this was too. She had to untwine it before Silas could turn it into something nasty. Gauging where the top of it was, she reached down, ready to pluck it off. But the moment her fingers touched it, thorns sprouted along its length. The vine thickened. Sharp points pierced her pants, pressing painful pinpricks into her skin. The pressure increased, thorns multiplied, stabbed, and dug deeper. Shallow breaths did nothing to ease her agony, and pulling on the wretched thing made it worse. With gritted teeth, she punched her fists straight out, left and right.

The box lit up with a red glow and shook violently. She fought to balance herself on the shifting floor as air swirled and then settled. The scent of jungle decay dissipated, and Adeline was once again standing on solid ground inside Silas's box of torture.

The warlock had finally shown up.

What had Silas seen from outside the box when she'd lit it up? Had Beatrice sensed warlock threads in whatever magic Adeline had expelled? Whatever it was, she wasn't controlling it, and she couldn't call it.

She shook out her hands and rubbed her cheek, where a lump was forming from whatever had stung her. Other lumps had formed on her legs where thorns had dug in. The hand she'd punched the ceiling with earlier hurt like Hades.

The final element was fire. Her throat constricted. She remembered with aching clarity how painful the burn to her arm was. In a futile attempt to put an end to the trial, she banged on the cube's door. Once again, Silas ignored her plea.

She sucked in a breath, trying her best to grasp onto the foundations of her training. Centre, breathe, reason. A whoosh of fire lit up the tiny closet with bright orange and yellow. Intense heat drew perspiration from her pores. She breathed out through her mouth. "It's not real," she repeated, vanquishing the images of witches on pyres that invaded her mind. Flames licked up the sides of the box. She fought back, envisioning arctic ice, the impossible blue of icebergs. The flames retreated and then re-formed—stronger, unrelenting, burning through her resolve.

The illusion shattered with her scream.

Sarah rushed to get outside the council chamber's wards so she could dematerialize to the training centre. Damaras, Marcus, and the two war mages did the same. The doors to the centre were intact, but the scene inside resembled the aftermath of a pipe bomb explosion.

Adeline stood amid the wreckage, gazing about with a blank look on her face. Silas and Beatrice were both slumped against a wall.

"Marcus, see to Silas," Damaras said. She personally attended Bea and issued instructions to get another healer.

Sarah hurried to Adeline. "What happened?"

Adeline looked from Silas to Beatrice. "Are they okay?"

"Are you hurt?" Sarah said, sweeping her gaze up and down Adeline's body. The floor was scorched, and blast marks radiated from the spot where they stood.

Sarah was alarmed by Adeline's confusion. Her forehead creased as she took in the damage, as if seeing it for the first time. "This is … Did I … How?"

"There are some chairs in the hall. Let's wait there."

Sarah tugged Adeline's hand. Addie followed for a few steps and then stopped. Sarah turned. Adeline was staring at three concrete planters embedded in the wall. Sarah remembered the jade tree that Silas had brought in to power her sister's warlock magic. If those planters were three of the same, all that remained of the trees were ragged stumps.

In the hallway, Sarah conjured a cup of tea, which Adeline took without complaint, but she just stared at it. A witch Sarah recognized as a healer trainee appeared, and rushed inside the training centre.

Sarah reached for Adeline's cheek. "What happened here?" It was swollen and red.

"I don't know. Something from earth's elemental magic."

"Stinging nettle, perhaps." Anger swept over her. Silas had hurt her intentionally, and it wasn't just the stinging nettle. Her pants were covered in small tears and blood.

A short time later, Daniel appeared in the hallway and sought them out. "Marcus sent me. Silas is conscious and talking. He's fine. Beatrice has a fractured shoulder. The other healer is working on her. She'll be up and about before the end of the day."

"Thank the stars," Sarah said.

"Damaras has postponed our follow-up meeting for a few hours. She doesn't want either of you to leave the sanctuary until she's had a chance to debrief her," Daniel said, nodding toward Adeline.

She looked to her sister, who didn't protest. "Okay. We'll be in the sunroom."

Sarah led the way. Adeline followed, still acting a little spaced out. The sunroom had been Sarah and Adeline's favourite room when they were kids visiting their mother at the sanctuary. With its glass roof and three glass walls, the room was as close as it was possible to get to the outdoors, but always warm and safe from rain. They were alone. They settled into matching wicker chairs and assumed identical poses, curling their legs underneath them.

Outside, bird feeders hanging from the post of an arbour swayed under the onslaught of birds vying for a treat. Crocuses and daffodils poked up through the white blossoms of sweet woodruff ground cover.

"What happened at your meeting?" Adeline asked.

"There seems to be a consensus that the warlock committed a crime. But to what level the offence rises is still being debated."

"You mean he may not have broken the accord?"

"You didn't die."

"Yet," Adeline said. She turned her attention back to the window.

"What happened in the training centre?" Sarah asked.

Adeline told her about the drills Silas had put her through. "My warlock made an appearance. He doesn't like fire."

"Silas went too far. But at least we'll have a better idea of what we're dealing with now," Sarah said. "How are your legs?"

Adeline looked down to her slacks and then held out her hand, where another series of red welts had swelled. "Not as bad as a fractured shoulder. I feel terrible having done that to Beatrice."

"It's not your fault. She and Silas both know that."

They retreated into silence, alone with their thoughts, gazing out at the birds in the garden.

Eventually, Sarah dispelled the quiet. "When the GC reconvenes, they'll be making decisions about which remedies to propose. Do you still want me to put forward your wish to be rid of the warlock magic?"

"I did before, but now I don't know. The power I experienced as the box blew apart was incredible. Even though the magic felt wrong, it took my breath away. If I could learn to control that power without hurting anyone?" She gazed unseeing into the distance. "My thoughts are all over the place. Having magic after all these years would be a seismic change in my life. I need time to think."

It was early afternoon when Damaras made an appearance. "How are you feeling?" she said, addressing Adeline.

"I'm fine. How are Silas and Beatrice?"

"She's not fine," Sarah said. "She's got a broken hand, two stings that I can see, and dozens of cuts on her legs. She needs a healer. Marcus, or one of the others if he's not able."

Damaras produced a phone and typed out a text. "To answer your question, Silas is healed. He was able to direct the repair of the training centre. Beatrice is coming along. She'll need to rest before she's one hundred percent."

"What did she see?" Adeline asked.

"Warlock threads. Much like what Sarah described. She also saw the red aura that signals a warlock wielding magic."

"Did she detect any witch markers?" Sarah asked.

"None."

"Well, that much is good," Sarah said.

"I'm reconvening the GC. Adeline, would you please stay here awhile longer? We may need to ask you some questions."

"I'll do you one better. I'll attend. After all, it's me you'll be talking about, isn't it?"

Eleven

Adeline knew she was pushing Damaras, but, damn it, her life hung in the balance.

Damaras looked taken aback. She paused. "All right. I'll adjust the chamber's wards. Join us when Marcus is finished with the healing."

Marcus arrived within minutes of Damaras leaving and swiftly crossed the room. "We have to stop meeting like this," he said, crouching in front of Adeline with a twinkle in his eye. "Sarah," he said, acknowledging her sister.

Marcus would have been just coming into his magic when Adeline left the coven. If she were into younger men with sweet smiles and soft curls, she'd have been swooning.

"You're not too tired from healing the others?" She remembered how much her healing had taken out of him.

"That was hours ago, and I had help. But thanks. What do you have for me?" He was already examining the swelling on her face. She held out the hand that sported matching stings.

"Leave it to Silas to find a way to turn earth's elemental magic into a weapon." He addressed the sting on her hand first, and soon the warmth of his healing magic soothed away the pain. When he was done, there was nothing left of the angry red swelling. He repeated the process on her cheek.

Sarah magically removed her pant leg, and, one by one, Marcus healed the puncture wounds. "I suppose we should feel lucky he didn't treat the thorns with poison," Marcus said in a tone that didn't hide his disgust. Accidents were one thing, but she suspected healers didn't condone intentional injury. The pain dissipated, and Sarah reattached her pant leg, magically repairing the tears.

Adeline sat and offered Marcus her other hand.

He made a pained expression. "How'd this happen?" he asked, hovering his hand over hers. "Broken third metacarpal. Punching injury. You take a swing at him?"

Adeline shook her head. "I should have."

Marcus's face contorted. "Think happy thoughts." He crabbed his fingers.

She cried out.

"Sorry," Marcus said. "There's no easy way to fix that quickly without the pain."

His features smoothed, and the heat of healing once again enveloped her. The pain eased. She wiggled her fingers.

"Better?" he asked.

"Thank you."

"You're most welcome. I'm attending the GC as well. Shall we walk together?"

Adeline had never been inside the council chamber. It was a cross between a conference room and a cigar bar. At one end, a large oval table dominated the space. Built-in cabinets surrounded it, filled with books, curios, and artifacts. Comfortable seating and casual tables sat at the other end of the room, surrounded by leaded windows. She almost expected to see Winston Churchill lounging with a cigar in one of the armchairs.

"You'll sit beside me," Sarah said, heading to two empty chairs on the far side of the table. Marcus took the last empty chair across from them. Adeline counted fifteen people seated. She knew four of them, five if she counted her sister. She was surprised to see Beatrice, but knew Silas would be there. The others she either didn't know or hadn't laid eyes on in more than a decade.

Damaras welcomed Adeline and introduced her around the table. Each of them acknowledged her with a nod, most without any genuine warmth.

"Silas, please report your findings," Damaras said.

"Through a series of escalating stimuli, I was able to provoke warlock magic from Adeline. The physical attacks and wind element didn't affect her. It was the water element that brought out the first signs of warlock magic. Beatrice noted red threads and monitored the draining of the first sacrificial jade specimen. We brought in two more jades and continued with earth's elemental. That's when Beatrice reported her first sighting of the red aura typical of a warlock using magic. That same magic caused the enclosure to shake until my elemental magic released. At that point, the two additional jade specimens we'd brought in were sagging, but not depleted. The fire element is what finally revealed the extent of her magic. You all saw the results in the training centre."

"The ramifications went farther than the damage to the training centre," Daniel said. "Around this table, in the moments before the explosion, Marcus asked a question: had anyone else felt what he had? I did. It was a drain on my power. Who else experienced that?"

Hands crept up around the table. Daniel nodded. "I thought so. She was draining us."

"It wasn't intentional," Adeline said, sensing accusation in the faces around the room.

"I would have to agree," Silas said. "She has no control over it. Which puts us all at risk."

"Beatrice, do you have anything to add?" Damaras said.

"A rumination, if you'd indulge me." Damaras nodded her consent. "The red threading I observed coming from Adeline, the aura and life-snuffing magic, I've seen it all many times before. The only difference I can detect between Adeline and a warlock is a tangling of the red threads. Which has me thinking. If I were a warlock and wanted to gain admission to this chamber, I might be tempted to set up the scenario we're dealing with now. How do we know this woman is who she says she is, and not a warlock in body glamour?"

Whispers rose around the table. Glamouring wasn't illegal for warlocks or witches, but full body glamour was highly discouraged because it was almost always misused. Worried looks were exchanged.

"Oh, for heaven's sake," Sarah said. "She's my sister. She may have been attacked by a warlock, but she certainly isn't one. I'd know."

"No disrespect, Sarah, but would you?" Beatrice said. "Warlocks can be very convincing. And your sister was married to one, as I recall. She'd be sympathetic." At this point, Grandma Bea's purse made an appearance, floating up from below and dropping with a thud to the table. "How about we be certain?" The purse peeled away, revealing a coal-black stone.

"A warlock stone?" Marcus said. "I didn't think there were any of those left."

"The warlocks destroyed most of them, but a few survive," Beatrice said.

Something about the stone made Adeline uneasy, as if the warlock in her knew what it was. "Would someone please tell me—what's a warlock stone?"

"It neutralizes warlock magic," Beatrice said. "When it's ground to a powder and spelled at a warlock, it neutralizes their power immediately. Enough of it will kill them or at least maim their magic, often permanently." Beatrice puffed out her chest. She looked at Adeline. "Warlocks convulse if they touch the stone with bare hands." She tilted her head, pleased with herself.

The old bat had been carrying that heavy stone from the moment she'd crossed Adeline's threshold. She was frightened of her. So much so that she'd been prepared to annihilate her all along. And Damaras didn't look one bit surprised at what Beatrice kept in her purse.

Beatrice waved her hand, her magic pushing the stone in front of Adeline.

Adeline hesitated. Having warlock magic didn't make her a warlock. Did it? If she touched it and convulsed, how long before Grandma ground off a chunk of the rock and killed her with it?

She glanced at Sarah. "You're not a warlock," Sarah said. "Go ahead." Her confidence encouraged her.

Adeline raised her hand above the stone. But she didn't touch it of her own volition. Beatrice used her magic to press Adeline's hand to the stone. Adeline watched in stunned disbelief.

Sarah jumped to her feet, swung her arm out, and spelled the stone across the room. "How dare you?" The stone scudded to a stop near an armchair.

"That's enough!" Damaras's voice commanded silence in the room.

Beatrice looked horrified, not for what she'd done to Adeline, but for the warlock stone, which she called back to her. It disappeared below the table.

All eyes switched to Adeline. "Terribly sorry to disappoint."

"My apologies, Adeline." Damaras swung her attention back to the group. "Let's get back on track, shall we? What compensation are we aiming for to address the warlock attack on Adeline?"

The principal spellcaster lifted her palms. "We still can't prove it. It's our word against theirs."

"We have Adeline on video in the training centre." Damaras crossed her arms, a smug smile on her lips.

Adeline should have figured as much, but it would have been nice to have been informed that she was being filmed.

"We have two paths of redress." Daniel held up a finger. "Seek retribution against the individual warlock." He unfurled a second finger. "Or aim higher."

Carolyn referred to her tablet. "Against an individual warlock, we might pull down a sizeable fine or force a permanent magical wipe."

"No. I think we've got some leverage here." Kylie had her arms crossed and tapped a finger against her cheek. "She could still die if her DNA reacts to the warlock magic. A death escalates the level of retribution to those remedies specified in the accord. We could get any crime against witches elevated to accord-level status."

The cold casualness of Kylie's words chilled Adeline.

Odette nodded, thoughtful. "An attack against the grid would be a good choice."

Adeline looked around the table, and it was an effort not to shake her head. These witches didn't care about her. Not her burns or the horror of being attacked. Not the stings or thorn pricks, the torture of Silas's box, or Beatrice's abuse of power. Her fear of what the warlock's magic might do to her didn't faze them. Not even her possible death tickled their concern.

She was a tool. Expendable. A means for witches to tilt the balance of power.

Maybe it was time for her to consider if she was better off with the warlocks on the other side of the accord.

Luke was summoned the following afternoon. He arrived at Lord Tanner's manor house to find him dressed in his regalia, an elaborate sash draped from shoulder to hip and decorated with the warlock king's and the lord's sigils.

"Any word from your friend?" Tanner asked.

"No."

One of Tanner's lieutenants knocked and entered. He too was dressed formally. "Your troops are in place."

"What's going on?" Luke asked.

"The witches just dropped a boon in our hands," Tanner said. "I think we know who Kai forfeited to. And because you're the one who knows his tricks best, you'll accompany us."

Within the hour, Tanner, the lieutenant, and Luke, wearing his black runecaster's cape, stood in a clearing opposite the priestess of the local coven and two of her war mages. The warlocks' magics were evenly matched by the witches. Each party would, of course, have backup in place nearby, but the intent was not to release magic. Accord meetings were set up to address the most serious breaches, whose remedies were already set out in the accord.

Introductions were not made. Their attire identified their roles.

Wearing a striking blue cape, the priestess laid out her complaint. Her war mages wore black fatigues. The priestess identified the location of the warlock's attack as being within Lord Tanner's territory. She then demonstrated their proof on a screen that she conjured between them. Luke's heart thudded at the sight of Adeline, clearly releasing a massive blast of warlock magic. It wasn't subtle, wasn't aimed, and wasn't contained in any fashion. Any doubt of what Kai had done evaporated.

"The resolution we demand is an addition to the enforceable infractions of the accord."

"What addition did you have in mind?" Lord Tanner asked.

"We want the sanctity of the grid elevated so that any attack on the grid becomes an accord-level breach."

"Has the witch died?"

"Not yet."

"Then your aim is high, Priestess. The infraction has not resulted in a death. We'll agree to take possession of the witch, remove the magic, and return her to you unharmed. I'll even agree to a financial penalty to compensate you for your time."

"Your warlock has delivered a death sentence. My aim is dead on."

"Not without a corpse for us to examine," the lord said.

Without a body, Kai's infraction couldn't be elevated to accord level. The warlocks would suffer a financial penalty at most. And Tanner would happily siphon Kai's magic out of the witch himself, adding to his already considerable powers.

"Her death is inevitable. Your warlock knew what he was doing when he attacked a witch."

"As I said, we'll remove the magic. We can do it right now, if you wish. If not, you will have to assume responsibility for her death."

The priestess's smile broadened. "And just how do you propose removing the magic?"

Luke sensed the trap moments before Tanner paused.

"The only way possible, of course," Tanner said.

"Siphoning? You're suggesting compounding the initial infraction with an additional breach?"

"To save her life." Tanner's tone suggested she was testing his patience.

"Ah, so you agree. Her life is in jeopardy. And the only way out of the mess your warlock has gotten you into is to break the accord. Again."

"Even two lower-level infractions do not meet the criteria for an accord-level remedy," Tanner said.

Damaras was not deterred. "Let's review, shall we? We've agreed your warlock's attack left incompatible magic in one of our witches—a death sentence. We all agree that siphoning is illegal, so you can't remove the magic. That makes her inevitable death your responsibility. Proof of an accord-level breach. When she dies, the remedy we demand is raising the sanctity of the grid to the highest-level infractions of the accord."

"You're willing to let one of your coven die rather than remove the magic that will kill her?"

The priestess tilted her head. "A sacrifice for the greater good."

Luke knew witches had a righteous streak in them, but letting someone die unnecessarily was cold.

"I doubt your coven would agree with you, and they will eventually learn what you've done," Tanner said. "May I suggest you allow the siphoning to save the witch's life? We'll double the financial compensation, punish the warlock responsible, and agree to work with you to repair the grid if it's damaged again."

The coven's war mage spoke. "Warlocks can't repair the grid without killing the very source of it."

"We can now. You agree to my terms, and I'll let you in on a secret I think you'll find worth your while. But not until after I've retrieved the magic. Deal?"

The priestess's eyes widened a fraction. Tanner had hooked her. "Give us a moment," she said, and her threesome disappeared.

Luke was certain the priestess would serve up Adeline—and he couldn't let Adeline recognize him. If she did, Luke wouldn't be able to hide that he knew Kai had dumped his magic into her. Tanner would realize he'd lied.

Luke took an imperceptible step back from Tanner and his lieutenant. After a moment, he did it again. He tugged the hood of the cape forward, hung his head, and used his magic to transform his features. He rounded his square jaw, set his eyes farther apart, flattened his nose.

The priestess returned, ahead of the two war mages. "You have a deal," she said. "The witch is unco-operative. I'm assuming you can handle her?"

When the war mages caught up, they had Adeline between them. With her features hardened and her jaw clenched, she looked anything but happy to be there. She studied each of them in turn through narrowed eyes. When her gaze fell on Luke, he didn't sense a whiff of recognition from her.

"I've explained to Adeline that you wish to touch her for the purpose of identifying the warlock responsible for the attack. She has agreed."

"Come to me," Tanner said, rolling with the narrative as he extended his hand.

When Adeline faltered, the priestess reassured her and then pressed her forward.

"I'm here to help," Tanner said. When she was in range, he stepped forward and rested his left hand on her shoulder. She immediately collapsed. He caught her and laid her carefully on the grass.

Tanner glanced between his lieutenant and the priestess, ensuring his second in command was monitoring her. With Adeline on the lawn between the two factions, Tanner lifted her closest hand. He rubbed it between his own and closed his eyes. A red glow extended down his arm and into her hand. His face, at first serene, slowly contorted. His brow furrowed.

Tanner released Adeline's hand and laid it carefully on her stomach. He reached across for her other hand and repeated the process. This time when his eyes closed, he pinched his face in concentration. Again, the red hue of his magic slid down his arm and into her hand.

His eyes were closed, so he didn't see Adeline open hers. "What are you doing?" she asked, her voice unnaturally calm.

Tanner blinked his eyes open, startled, but his magic didn't falter. The hue continued flowing down his arm. He dipped his head and reached for her shoulder to put her under again, but Adeline shirked away. Luke saw her mind flood with images of Kai gripping her hand and then the pain blasting through her.

Tanner was caught off guard by the speed of her movement. She nailed him in the ear with a knee and followed up with the heel of her hand to the underside of his nose. A sickening crunch and a gush of blood confirmed a broken nose. The lord fell to his side, and Adeline was on her feet. Flames erupted from her hands, setting fire to whatever they touched.

The lord's troops spilled out from the surrounding forest, encircling the gathering. Witches rose above them, their hands ready to spell.

"Get away from me. All of you," Adeline said, retreating from the warlocks as well as her own coven.

The lieutenant helped Tanner to his feet and pulled him away from her.

An elderly witch, short in stature, appeared above and behind Adeline and sent a swirling cloud of powder over her. Sensing deadly warlock stone, Tanner, the lieutenant, and Luke dematerialized. The action caused Luke to lose his hold on the magic transforming his features. They rematerialized a safe distance away, flanked by the lord's troops.

As the powder settled over Adeline, it snuffed out the flames from her hands. She stumbled and fell to her knees. Another witch, younger and blonde, materialized and called the wind to blow the poisonous dust off her.

The witches congregated near Adeline, and Luke had the sense they were containing her. Across the clearing, the priestess and her war mages started toward them.

"What happened?" she demanded.

"Whoever did this was clever enough to lock his magic inside her. I can't siphon it out. It would appear the only one who can is the one who deposited it."

"I want a name," the priestess said.

"Yes, so do we." Tanner touched his nose with a wince. Information was leverage in Tanner's court and had a price. He wouldn't give it to the witch without extracting a fee. "Did she see the warlock who did that to her?"

"No," the priestess said.

Luke knew differently, so they were both playing games.

"Our deal is off," the priestess said. "Your warlock inflicted a death sentence. You can't remove his magic to save her life, so you must accept our terms."

"I don't think so," Tanner's lieutenant said. "The witch should be dead, should she not? Incompatible magic and all? That witch isn't even sick. Why?"

"She's resilient," the priestess said, "but she's not immune. Eventually, your warlock's magic will kill her."

"So you say, but perhaps you've found a way around the incompatibility problem?" Tanner said.

"Sounds to me like you're trying to skirt your obligations as concerns the accord," the priestess said.

"Or maybe you're the one deflecting," Tanner said. "You've made her immune to warlock magic so that she's not in mortal danger, and you think you can fool us to gain an advantage through the accord."

"May I offer an observation?" Luke said to Tanner. Tanner nodded. "That witch wasn't co-operative from the start. She was already suspicious, and now she knows her priestess lied to her. When she backed away from us, she was backing away from them as well. She distrusts them. She doesn't distrust us, except for you carrying out whatever the priestess arranged. I think we can win her over. We have the means to hold her until the warlock who is responsible for the attack shows up to reclaim his magic. Which he will assuredly do."

"No. She's ours," the priestess said. "We will hold her."

"With warlock stone? That'll kill her faster than the incompatible magic," Tanner said. "Warlock magic is the only thing that can contain her safely."

The priestess stepped away to confer with her colleagues. When they returned, the war mage spoke. "We want the warlock who did this to be punished. We want double the usual financial compensation. We want protection of the grid elevated to accord-level status. And, finally, we want the secret you think is so worth our while. In exchange, we'll give you the witch."

"We'll agree to punishing the warlock, and the usual financial compensation, but not the secret and not the grid's status change," Tanner said. "You can keep the witch. If she dies, we're prepared to renegotiate."

The priestess tilted her head. A slow smile crept onto her face. "I can feel your greed, Tanner. You're vibrating with it. You want her magic. You agree to our conditions, and I'll sweeten the pot. I'll give you the key to earning her co-operation."

TWELVE

Adeline woke with a massive hangover. She tried to corral her thoughts, but they scattered like frightened birds. What had she had to drink last night? Her head suggested she'd consumed the entire liquor cabinet, and then some.

She swung her feet off the bed and sat upright. Her head swam. No matter how hard she concentrated, she couldn't remember a thing from the previous evening. She glanced over at the clock. *Damn!* She'd missed making Charlie's breakfast. She lurched out of bed, angry with herself. Maybe he'd forgive her if she made him a bacon-heavy brunch instead.

In the bathroom, she splashed water on her face and brushed her teeth. She picked up her phone, which she hadn't charged, and tapped it to life. Saturday. It was Saturday. She exhaled with relief. Charlie took care of his own breakfast on the weekends.

She was tempted to drop back into bed, but thought caffeine might help ease her headache. Tea, not coffee. She dragged on some sweats.

Down in the kitchen, she swallowed an Advil and put the kettle on. While it heated, she checked the liquor cabinet and frowned. Not empty. Not even a dent. She checked the trash. No empty cans or bottles. Nothing. She perched on the closest kitchen chair.

This was no hangover. Someone had messed with her head. With a mug in hand, she grabbed a pen and paper, snagged a throw from the sofa, and settled on the porch swing. The cool morning air revived her somewhat. She jotted down everything she could remember. The last thing she recalled clearly was burning holes in Mrs. Doppler's canvas. Sarah had been there; she'd repaired the canvas. The painting wasn't on the easel, so Adeline must have finished it. She hoped she'd finished it.

Wait. How had she burned holes in a canvas? There was a vague connection between the damage to the canvas and a burn on her arm. Her right arm. She examined it but found no evidence. She tapped her pencil, took a sip of tea. What day had that been?

She remembered going to the sanctuary's training centre. Flashes came to her: being thrown against a wall, a vine's thorns piercing her legs, wind turning her braid into a weapon. The healer, Marcus, rushing past her. A kettlebell. There'd been an explosion. Blast marks radiating out from where she stood. Whether the images were memories or dreams, she couldn't quite sort out. She saw no bruises on her body or evidence of puncture wounds.

Flipping the pages, she reviewed her notes. They were nonsensical, scattered. The musings of a broken mind. She returned to the house. There had to be clues as to what had happened. The dishwasher was empty, cupboards tidy. Nothing unusual in the fridge. She wandered into the solarium but found everything in its place. Upstairs in her bedroom, she came across her first clue. When she changed for bed, she always draped her clothes on the chair in the corner. There were no clothes on the chair.

The doorbell rang. Reluctantly, she traipsed down the stairs. Through the diamond pane of glass, she saw Damaras, the last witch in the world she wanted to see.

The doorbell rang again. "I know you're in there, Adeline. Open up."

Adeline let out a sigh of frustration. The witch would break her wards if she didn't comply. That much she remembered. She opened the door. "What do you want, Dumbass?"

"I'll ignore that in light of what's happened," she said, letting herself in. She pulled the door out of Adeline's grip and closed it. "Keep this closed."

Adeline grew alarmed. "What's happened?"

Damaras made no attempt to move past the hallway. "What do you remember about the attacks?"

Adeline narrowed her eyes. "Attacks?"

Damaras pressed her lips into a tight line. "I'm afraid so. What do you remember?"

A snippet of a memory drifted by. Adeline grabbed it. A man with a tight grip on her wrist. Glowing red light. "My arm. It was burned."

"Yes. By a warlock. Do you remember what he looked like?"

Adeline rubbed her temples. Had she seen his face? "I don't know.

My memories of the past few days feel scrambled. Did you say attacks—plural?"

"The warlock who attacked you is attacking others in the coven, too. Your sister. Marcus. And you again, it would seem. He's trying to cover his tracks by messing with your memories. The warlock lord has offered us refuge, in compliance with the accord."

"Where's Sarah?" Adeline asked, her throat tight.

"She's joining your mother on her cruise. Joe and the kids are with her. They'll be safe there. I've arranged for one of Lord Tanner's warlocks to protect you—"

"A warlock? To protect me?" The idea was laughable. She parked her hands on her hips. "The warlocks just attacked us, and now they're going to protect us. What have you been smoking?"

Damaras inhaled impatiently. "One warlock attacked us. One rogue warlock. It could as easily have been a witch attacking them, and I thank the stars it isn't. Lord Tanner wants him found and stopped as much as we do."

Adeline doubted that. "Thanks for the warning, but I'll take care of myself. A warlock won't get past my wards."

"He really has scrambled your brain. Think, Adeline. The warlock has already gotten to you. Twice."

The throbbing in Adeline's head picked up its pace. Damaras had a point. Adeline wasn't thinking straight. She rubbed her eyes.

"Refuge is the accord's remedy for unprovoked mass attacks," Damaras said, "and the warlock lord has taken responsibility. As he should. He's offered up a runecaster for your protection. No warlocks have more power than their precious runecasters."

In a coven, the equivalent was a spellcaster. Power-wise, they were on the same level as war mages and second only to the priestess.

"Why would the warlock come back now? Seems like he's achieved his goal."

"Have you forgotten that you harbour his magic? You are the living proof of his crime. He will kill you if he can. We can't let a lone miscreant, witch or warlock, threaten our peace accord."

The holes she'd burned in the canvas. That was his magic. The attack was real. Adeline breathed through the pain in her head. "And you trust them?"

"If we don't trust in the accord, we slide back into war. No one wants that."

Adeline paused. Her head pain subsided. She was too confused to argue, and not at all sure she was right.

Damaras took out her phone, swiped at the screen, and typed something. "The warlock who's agreed to protect you has also agreed to accommodate your commitments to your tenant, so long as it doesn't compromise your or your tenant's safety."

This was not the Damaras Adeline knew. She narrowed her eyes. "Why are you doing this?"

Damaras jerked her head back. "Safeguarding the coven? Everything I do is to protect our witches. Do you really think so little of me?"

Adeline wanted to say yes, but she wasn't that cruel, and Damaras did appear to be genuinely distressed. She softened her stance. "How can I help?"

"The warlock will be here shortly. Please co-operate with him. The passcode is *penny*. If he doesn't say it, don't let him in. I have to run. The elementals are exposed. I must coordinate their refuge with Lord Tanner."

After she left, Adeline teetered on the edge of the sofa. The sense of urgency Damaras projected bled into Adeline, clouding her thoughts. Nothing about this situation made any sense. Warlocks protecting witches? It had to be sub-zero in Hell.

And why hadn't Sarah called? Just as she reached for her phone, the doorbell rang. She stared in the door's direction for a moment. Instinct born from years of warnings about warlocks made her hesitate. She dialled Sarah.

"I've got a warlock on my front porch," Adeline said, instead of hello.

"Damaras arranged it?"

"She did. She just left. Are you okay?"

"My head hurts like hell, but yeah. I'm at the airport. An airport. We've been travelling so long I have no idea anymore what country I'm in or what day it is."

"So it's true?" The doorbell rang a second time.

"I don't know what's fact or fiction right now," Sarah said. "I'm not thinking straight. Didn't even feel the warlock's attack until it was too late. Getting the kids to safety feels like a good precaution. Keep your phone close?"

"I will. Stay safe. I'll let you know what's happening as soon as I figure it out."

Adeline rose and walked to the front door. A hood set the warlock's face in shadow. "What can I do for you?" Adeline said through the closed door.

"Looks like your bad penny is back," the warlock said.

She'd heard that voice before. She turned the deadbolt and opened the door.

· ⟩ ⟩ ● ⟨ ⟨ ⟨ ·

Luke lowered his hood. Adeline stood in the doorway, but she hadn't yet invited him through her wards.

"Churchwell." His name came out like a curse. "You're a warlock?"

The question was rhetorical. "So it would appear. And you're a witch?"

"Not really."

Luke quirked an eyebrow. "Well, that explains a few things. Are you going to invite me in, or shall we have this conversation on your porch?"

"I'm not inviting you in. You've already deceived me once. Why should I believe you now?"

"Deceived you? Because I didn't reveal what I am? Do you introduce yourself as not really a witch?"

She studied him, wary. "Did you know I was a witch?"

"No. You don't behave like a witch, you have a human tenant, and there's no witch's garden. Why would I think you were a witch? I simply liked your work. Is that so difficult to believe?"

Indignation swept over her demeanour. "When were you in my backyard?" she said, lifting her chin.

"The day I came looking for you. Thought you may have been in the garden when you didn't answer your doorbell. Your tenant took my card."

She crossed her arms. "What happened to your out-of-town trip? You told me it had been extended indefinitely."

"I work at Lord Tanner's behest. He thought I'd be more valuable here." More precisely, his value would be getting close enough to Adeline to find the key to the lock Kai had put on his magic.

Her stance seemed to soften. "You know Damaras?"

"The priestess? We've met. Lord Tanner struck an agreement with her." And he'd tasked Luke with carrying it out. "I'm to offer you shelter and escort you to and from here while you attend to your tenant. A completely unnecessary risk, in my opinion, but I wasn't consulted."

"I'd prefer you stay here," she said. "You can have the guest room upstairs."

"No. The warlock who attacked you knows this house. You're not safe here." And Luke wouldn't be able to monitor her closely enough.

Adeline flipped her dark hair behind her shoulder. "If you think he's coming back here, you can pick him off when he shows up."

Luke pinched the bridge of his nose. "A, he's motivated. He won't be easy to pick off. B, you'd be putting your tenant at risk. And C, he has a much better chance of getting to you here than he does where I live."

Adeline started a counter-argument, but his patience had grown thin. She couldn't stay here. He raised his hand to stop her. "You don't need to invite me in. I'll wait in the car. If you're not there in twenty minutes, I'll advise Lord Tanner that you refused my shelter." He turned and jogged down the steps.

In the car, he looked back at the house. Adeline had closed the front door. He hoped he hadn't overplayed his hand. She was stubborn, but he didn't think she was stupid.

Kai had humiliated Tanner. Not only had he foiled Tanner's cuff, but he'd stooped to new depths, dumping his magic into a witch. When Kai came back for it—and he would—Tanner wanted the witch under his control. She was bait.

If Luke drove off without her, Tanner would take it personally. Another failure. Another excuse to punish him by punishing those he cared about. He drummed his thumbs on the steering wheel. He checked the time. Ten minutes left. He put the ignition in accessory mode and the sultry notes of Billie Holiday dropped his anxiety level a notch.

He hadn't lied to Adeline, but he also hadn't told her the entire truth. He would. In time. Because, given the power he'd seen her demonstrate, he'd prefer to be on her good side if her memories were restored.

When he spotted her coming down the driveway from the back of the house, he tried not to sag with relief. He started the engine. She had a large tote over her shoulder, which she held tight to her chest after she settled into the passenger seat.

"You want me to put that in the trunk?" he asked.

"I'm good," she said. "So, where's your place?"

"Downtown."

She made no small talk, just stared out the window. When they got within sight of the building, he pointed it out to her.

"An office? Your home is in an office tower?"

"It's a safe house. You'll be comfortable." And as protected as they could make her from Kai.

He ran through some of what he framed as the suite's safety features during the elevator ride to the penthouse. "The unit is shielded. That's the warlock equivalent of your wards. You can't dematerialize in or out of the suite. There are cameras in every room apart from the bathroom and dressing room." A guard had removed those two hours ago. A modicum of privacy for their *guest*.

She turned to him. "There's a camera in my bedroom?"

"Yes. Three guards are on site at all times. One stationed at the hall door; the others roam."

"That's intense. What is it you do that requires that level of security?"

It was what he'd done, not what he did. "I can't say."

The elevator door opened. "After you," he said, sweeping his hand ahead of him. The guard at the door watched them make their way toward him. "That door is the only way in or out of the suite. The guard will want to search your bag."

Alarm swept across her face. Ah, no wonder she was keeping a tight grip on it. "Weapons can be used against you. It's best not to rely on them."

The guard rummaged through her bag and removed a collapsible bo staff and a baton. Adeline was clearly furious about it. "I want those back when I leave."

"Of course," Luke said.

The guard opened the door and watched them cross the vestibule. An alarm blared. The guard approached Adeline with his hand extended. She rolled her eyes, bent to lift her pant leg, and removed the hunting knife she'd strapped to her lower leg.

"Do you have any other weapons?" the guard asked.

"You running out of alarms?" she asked.

"Don't test him," Luke said. "He's not above a cavity search."

She widened her eyes. "No, I don't have any other weapons."

After the guard retreated, Luke toured her around the suite. "You can use this room while you're here," he said, showing her a bedroom suite that was a mirror to his own. He pointed out the bathroom and the dressing room. "You'll have privacy in those two rooms only. A cleaning crew comes in weekly to restock. If there's something you need, let them know."

She set her bag on the bed and looked around the room, spotting the cameras—one mounted in the ceiling by the window, the other near the door.

"They're for your safety," Luke said. He didn't tell her the cameras were also wired for sound. "Windows and doors are monitored."

Back in the hallway, he pointed out his bedroom. The door was closed. The bedroom hall separated those rooms from the rest of the suite. Beyond the hall was a living room area, and farther along was the kitchen.

"Nice view," she said, walking up to the wall of glass that overlooked Coal Harbour, a scenic neighbourhood on the waterfront. She wandered into the kitchen, taking in the six-burner gas stove, the side-by-side full-sized freezer and fridge, and the custom cabinetry. "A gourmet kitchen?" she said, sweeping her hand along the granite counter. "You cook?"

"No. Meals are brought in." Or not, depending on how testy Tanner was feeling. Adeline's presence would fix that. At least for a while.

She quirked her head. "You don't just conjure your meals?"

"Warlocks don't conjure." If he wasn't under Tanner's control, he could have served up a banquet, but his magic had been leashed. "There's an espresso machine, and the fridge is stocked. Feel free to help yourself."

"I can make breakfast, if you'd like. I've gotten pretty good at it if you take Charlie's word for it."

"Charlie's your tenant?" he said, feigning ignorance. She nodded. "I'm curious," Luke said. "Just how did you end up with a human tenant?"

"Lucky, I guess. I renovated the basement to make a bed-and-breakfast for a little extra income. Charlie moved in and never left. He's one of the family now."

Luke nodded, not understanding why a witch would need a tenant, let alone a human one, for extra income. He set the thought aside and continued the tour.

Behind the kitchen, closer to the hall through which they'd arrived, were two other rooms. A large meeting room and his office. He didn't point out the rooms behind locked doors. She wouldn't have access to those.

"There's also a gym and a pool in the atrium. A guard will accompany you if you wish to use them."

"Are there other suites like this in the tower? You know, where people live, not just work."

"The tower isn't approved for residential use." It was a minor problem Tanner had easily skirted.

"May I ask why you live here and not in a condo or a house?"

"The tenants here scatter to their homes at night. I enjoy the quiet. Can I make you a coffee?" he said, steering the topic in another direction.

They returned to the living room, and Luke set about making her a latte. While it brewed, he studied her. Her brow was pulled down low. She rubbed it like she was soothing a migraine.

"Why do you describe yourself as not really a witch?" he asked, handing her the latte. He'd startled her.

"Damaras didn't tell you?"

He shook his head.

She looked taken aback, but didn't explain why. "I have no powers. Well, no witch powers," she said with an awkward smile, correcting herself.

Seemed Damaras was keeping a lot of secrets. This perhaps explained how Adeline was able to hold Kai's magic without it killing her. "That must be difficult."

Adeline stared at him with an odd look on her face, like she was looking at an enigma. "It is difficult. Was, anyway. I've learned to accept it. Are there warlocks like me? Not really warlocks?"

He smiled, pleased she felt comfortable enough to joke with him. It would make getting close to her easier. "Not that I'm aware of. How did that happen? If you don't mind me asking."

"No one knows for certain. It's rare, for sure. Lucky me. It may be that I just didn't inherit the power I should have. Or it could have been that my newborn binding wasn't done properly."

"Witch bindings are barbaric," he said, spitting out the words. Binding magic was more detrimental than clipping a bird's wings. A bird would eventually regrow the feathers. A witch lost those formative years of magic and would never get them back.

"Oh?" Adeline swiftly shifted to the edge of her seat. "I'd rather be bound than cuffed. A binding won't accidentally blow your hand off. A binding doesn't cause irreparable damage. Bindings prevent horrific disasters, like setting your parents ablaze, or fuelling an indoor tornado. It's a safety precaution. A cuff is a life-altering sentence. *Amputation* is barbaric."

THIRTEEN

Adeline stalked to the bank of windows. She calmed herself with deep breaths.

"I'm sorry," Churchwell said. "I shouldn't have said that."

What the hell had she gotten herself into? She was standing in a warlock's lair, which she'd entered voluntarily. His guards were on patrol, and cameras were everywhere. Her mother and sister would have disowned her. She could thank Damaras for putting her in this position.

"We're going to be two sides of a clamshell for the next few days. Please accept my apology. I happen to agree with you about the cuffs. Can we put our difference of opinion behind us?" Churchwell said.

She turned from the window, retook her seat, and picked up her latte. "If I'm honest, after what happened to me, I'm not terribly fond of bindings either."

As it appeared she was stuck here with the warlock, she should at least try to fill in the blanks in her head. "What do you know about the warlock attack on the coven?"

"Only what Damaras has told us. Lord Tanner is taking her at her word."

"What has she told you?"

With a flick of his hand, the soft drum brush of a jazz tune floated into the room on invisible speakers.

"A warlock attacked you. He left warlock magic inside you. It's indisputable—we watched a digital recording of you using it. The priestess tells us the warlock returned and attacked others, wiping their memories of the evidence of his attack on you."

"My sister has gaps in her memory. So do I. I'm told our healer does as well."

"I'm sorry. I know there's no love lost on warlocks in the witch community, but we're not normally like that."

She nodded, knowing at least one other who was decent and kind. Her ex, Warrick. "Why would a warlock poison me with his magic?"

"Poison?"

"He must have known our magics were incompatible. That it would kill me." Just like it killed any chance witch and warlock couples could procreate.

"Perhaps. Is there a reason why he'd want you dead?"

"Not prior to the attack. I didn't know who he was. But Damaras says I'm proof of his crime now. So I guess that's motivation."

Churchwell leaned forward, his forearms on his thighs. "The history between our kinds has been long, and fraught with war, at least until the accord. But even now, a warlock would no sooner give his magic to a witch than a witch would give his book of spells to a warlock. It's unnatural."

"And yet . . . here I am," Adeline said. "A witch with a tank full of warlock."

"Yes. It's a puzzle. What do you remember about the attacks?"

"The first one? He cast an illusion of having been hit by a car. I tried to help him. Called 911. His magic burned my arm." She absently rubbed the shirtsleeve on her right forearm. She'd pieced together the original attack but still wasn't confident her memories were true or complete.

"You saw him?"

"I don't know." In her mind, she watched him reach out to her, saw a blurry face, but the harder she tried to focus, the more her head hurt.

"And the second attack?"

"That one's foggier." She'd experienced blips of warlock magic, inadvertently killing produce. "The coven's war mage tried to, I don't know, tease the warlock magic out of me?"

"That would be the evidence we saw. A blast?"

Adeline had a vague memory of being annoyed that Silas hadn't told her about the cameras in the training facility. "I think so."

"That was a risky game your war mage played. Uncontrolled magic is dangerous."

Silas. More memories rushed back. Her besting Silas on the mats in his training centre. His magic box of torture. She'd blown it apart. She smiled, remembering.

"What is it?" the warlock said, questioning her smile, straightening.

"Nothing." His expression said he didn't believe her. She could live with that. She might be irritated with the priestess and her war mage, but she wasn't ready to trust this warlock. She shifted in her seat and finished the last of her latte. There had been someone else in the training centre. A grandmotherly figure with a purse. An outsider. But Adeline couldn't place her.

"Are some memories coming back?" Churchwell said, interrupting her thoughts. He'd sat back and had an arm draped over the back of the sofa. A playboy pose. Was he aware of it?

"Snippets. Nothing that makes sense." Not yet. She needed time to stitch it together. "Tell me about you. How'd you end up working for the warlock lord?"

"That's a long story." Churchwell gazed down the length of his out-stretched arm, and then up to the camera, as if he were addressing someone on the other end of it. "We've known of each other for a long time, but stood in opposition on most issues in the territory. Eventually, we came to an . . . understanding. I've been here ever since."

An inexplicable shiver ran through Adeline. Churchwell had chosen his words a little too carefully.

"And your family? Where are they?"

"Here and there. They move around."

A non-answer. She stretched her head from side to side, trying to ease the headache.

"Damaras never did say. How do you want to deal with the warlock magic you've been saddled with?"

And now a deflection. Interesting. And a good question. Adeline had a sense of déjà vu. She'd considered this question before. "I don't know. The surge of warlock power felt pretty good, as I recall. But it kills things too. Witches don't do that. It goes against our grain."

"You don't have to kill things. Not anymore. You may find it hard to believe, given your low opinion of our kind, but we've evolved."

Adeline smiled. "Was that a sense of humour, Churchwell?"

"I wouldn't go that far." He stood and removed his suit jacket, the fine cut of which she'd been admiring. It would have been an excellent choice for his portrait. She caught a hint of cedar. He unbuttoned the sleeve of a perfectly fitted shirt and rolled it up. When he extended his arm for her inspection, she moved in, curious about the clear, gel-like patches the size of silver dollars on his skin.

She gazed up at him, a question in her face.

"Power cells. Not the infinite source of power witches can draw from the grid, but a decent substitute."

"Where do they come from?" Adeline asked.

"Runecasters make them. Vetted warlocks can buy them for the right price."

"Vetted?"

"The cells are powerful. Tanner doesn't want them in the wrong hands."

"And you're a runecaster. That must be lucrative. Is that your business with the warlock lord? Selling these cells?"

"No. But I can teach you how to use them."

She recalled a conversation with Sarah. A choice. Learn how to use the warlock magic. Or get rid of it. As if the magic understood the threat, it surged inside her. She lifted her arm and felt a tingle of power at her fingertips. Tiny bursts of white lightning. Her lips parted.

Sarah, Joe, and the children passed through the tender port in Naples and shuffled onto a water taxi that would take them to her mother's cruise ship anchored offshore. The last-minute travel arrangements had been hard on all of them. Red-eye flights and layovers left them tired and edgy. They all needed to sleep for a week just to recover and acclimatize.

Sarah transferred to the ship and took Jack's hand. He plodded along beside her, asleep on his feet. Olive's pink knapsack and a tote were draped over her shoulder. Joe had Olive in his arms and his own collection of bags and knapsacks.

Scanning the deck, Sarah soon spotted her mother, Morgan Thorne, waving to them. Her mother's white hair fell in soft waves to her collar and curled around her face. In capris and deck shoes with a cotton sweater tied around her shoulders, she looked at home with the cruise ship set. She'd been a beauty all her life, and that hadn't changed when she'd turned sixty last year.

"I'm so glad you came," her mom said, draping an arm around Sarah's shoulder and giving it a squeeze. She reached down and tousled Jack's hair.

"Mom," Joe said, leaning in to kiss her cheek.

"Hello, Joe. Good to see you." She turned to Olive. "Pumpkin." Olive reached out her arms. "Let me take her," she said to Joe. "You've got your hands full." Olive happily went to her grandmother. "I believe the guest suite I booked for you is ready."

The cruise director approached them and introduced himself. He led them to the check-in desk and ran through the safety briefing.

"A porter will follow shortly with your luggage," he said, and showed them to their suite. A bottle of champagne chilled in a bucket on the side bar.

It was too early, local time, to put the kids to bed, but they didn't fight it. The tiny room had a bunk bed, and Jack was delighted to get the top berth.

"We'll pay for this later," Joe said, but neither he nor Sarah had the energy to keep them awake a moment longer.

By the time Sarah and Joe returned to their sitting room, their bags had arrived.

"I had the porter open the champagne. I hope you don't mind," her mom said.

"Bless your heart," Joe said, and he filled their flutes.

Sarah's mom pulled her into a hug. Her mother had been Stonewater coven's principal archivist, but she was also a healer. She pushed the hair from Sarah's forehead and held a hand on either side of her temples.

"Your instincts were right. Someone's folded your memories. They're compressed, which tells me someone wanted you to forget something."

"There's more to it. I didn't want to tell you until I was able to do it in person. And Adeline will kill me if you cut your cruise short because of it."

She told her mother about the attack on Adeline, the warlock magic that had been spilling out of her ever since, and the explosion in the training centre.

"You checked Adeline yourself? It wasn't another binder?"

"No. I read her. So far, Adeline seems to be okay. The warlock's magic is making itself known, but there are no witch tells in Adeline's threads. Not a hint of blue in her aura."

Her mother pursed her lips, jutted her chin. She was displeased, but what mother wouldn't be if their child's life was threatened? And there were few bigger threats to a witch than incompatible magics.

"I'm not the only one whose memories are scrambled. The coven thinks the warlock who attacked Adeline is wiping the memories of those of us who knew about it. They think he's trying to cover his tracks."

"He's clearly not covering his tracks very well given that you remember every detail."

Sarah rubbed circles on her temples, trying to ease the pressure. "Not every detail. I don't know why I know this, but I'm positive I saw his face. Yet it's blurry now."

"When you say the coven thinks this warlock is responsible, I assume you mean Damaras Deschene."

Her mother and Adeline shared a low opinion of Damaras that Sarah had long tired of navigating. It wasn't as if Sarah put the priestess on a pedestal. She'd agreed to work with her for the better good of witchkind. It was the only way she could contribute at a policy-shifting level. "Well, yes, but the war mage as well."

"Of course. How is Silas?"

"Smug but competent. He didn't hold back when he was testing Adeline. Went too far, in my opinion."

"Adeline can hold her own," her mother said, with a note of pride.

"She knocked him out cold with that explosion." A conspiratorial smile curled Sarah's lips.

"Good. I've no doubt his pride will recover."

Sarah's mother set down her empty flute and rose to leave, probably because neither Sarah nor Joe were doing a good job hiding their yawns.

"I won't attempt to recover your memories until you've rested properly. I'll call Damaras when I get back to my suite. Given that she sent you here, I'm sure she'll be expecting my call."

The next morning, Sarah's family arose long before the Italian dawn. They wandered up to the top deck in the dark and found snacks available in an alcove off the dining room. On a ship that catered to adults, there were no water slides, arcades, or other children's play areas. She and Joe entertained them until the dining room opened and then joined her mother for a proper breakfast. Her mother had secured two small tables close together. Joe and the kids settled at one, and she joined her mother at the other.

"How's your headache, sunshine?" Sarah's mother asked.

"Better. Not gone. The sleep helped," Sarah said. A stunning diamond tennis bracelet sparkled on her mother's wrist.

"That's new," Sarah said, admiring the sleek line of princess-cut diamonds.

A shy smile crossed her mother's lips. "It was a gift from a friend."

"A *friend*?" Sarah said, thinking it was a *he*, and more than a friend. She waited for her mom to expand on the mystery man, but she didn't. "It's beautiful," she said, and then, taking her mother's cue, switched gears. "How'd your conversation with Damaras go?"

"She didn't return my call. And I haven't been able to reach Adeline. Have you spoken to her?"

"Not since she called me." She pulled out her phone and swiped through the incoming calls. "Yesterday. What time is it there?"

"Too early to call yet," Joe said. "We're nine hours ahead."

Over breakfast, her mother insisted on hearing again the details surrounding Adeline's attack.

Sarah and her mother kept their voices low. When Sarah finished, her mother ruminated out loud, sorting through details she found pertinent. "Damaras had proof Adeline was attacked by a warlock. Proof my daughter was in mortal danger. And as a result, the GC agreed to demand an accord-level breach remedy?" She shook her head, anger tinting her features. "The woman's first concern should have been for Adeline's life. The only remedy she should have been negotiating was for one of the warlocks to siphon the magic out of her."

"Adeline didn't want that." Sarah's headache ramped up, pounding in her temples. "She did at first, back at her house. She wanted the magic removed. Seeing Dad's blackened orchids nearly killed her. But after she experienced the warlock's magic in the training centre, she questioned her decision. Said she was willing to learn how to wield the magic if she could do it without harming the living things around her."

A stack of pancakes was set in front of Olive. Sarah left her seat to cut them for her.

When she returned, her mother continued in a quiet voice, "Your sister's life is worth more than any magic, more than any accord remedy."

"Mom. She's okay. If she has any witch magic in her, it's well and truly buried. And I'm not the only binder who read her. The binder from Seattle's Moonmere coven saw her and agrees with my assessment."

"Beatrice?" her mother asked. Sarah nodded. "She and Damaras are old friends from boarding school. Her loyalties are with Damaras."

"Then trust me. Adeline's witch magic is as dead as it's ever been." Sarah had been keeping one eye on the children and now turned to her husband. "Joe, the syrup," she said, drawing his attention to the bottle Jack had upended in free flow over his waffles.

"I believe you, sunshine. But the risk of incompatible magic is too great. The warlock's magic is an infection."

"Adeline's situation is unique. Maybe for her it's not incompatible. After all, mixed magic isn't a problem for warlocks." They could siphon magic from witches and warlocks alike.

"She's not a warlock. And that's not a chance I'm willing to take. We must convince her to let it be siphoned out of her before it reacts with her DNA and kills her."

Sarah rubbed her face. "I already know how she'll respond to that suggestion. *Fine for us to say*, and all that."

"Yes. It won't be easy. Sadly, now that she's had a taste of it, she'll resist letting it go. I'm not looking forward to that conversation. You remember how rebellious she was when her unbindings failed. Her anger at the world? This will be worse. I know she says she's accepted her condition, but she never truly has. I'm not sure I could if it were me."

"She's been doing really well," Sarah said. "Ever since Jack came of age last year, I've seen a change in her. She's loosening up on her no-magic stance. Not long ago, I conjured a latte for her. Not only did she accept it, but she made a little joke."

"My. That is progress."

"She also snagged a second portrait commission. Almost twice the fee of the first one. She's starting to earn a name for herself." Sarah smiled at Joe, who was doing a masterful job of distracting the kids.

"Neither money nor renown stand a chance against power like you described. It will be intoxicating, especially for someone who's never tasted magic before." Her mother summoned a passing waiter to bring them another urn of coffee. "Where were you when Damaras suggested you visit me?"

Sarah had to think. "At the sanctuary."

"And where was Adeline?" her mother asked.

"I . . . don't know. I assumed she was at the sanctuary too. What are you thinking?"

"Warlocks can't get into the sanctuary. So when did the warlock attack you?"

"Good point. Why didn't I think of that?"

Her mother patted the back of her hand. "Confusion is natural when your memories have been manipulated."

"I remember we both accompanied Damaras and the war mages to the clearing. To meet with Lord Tanner. It must have happened there."

"I see." The waiter returned with the urn and topped up their cups.

When the waiter left, her mother continued, "A rogue warlock attacks you, Adeline, and possibly others, folding your memories during a meeting with three of the most powerful witches in the coven in attendance, not to mention Lord Tanner and his minions?

"And now Adeline is under their protection, we can't reach her, and you and I are half a world away. Something doesn't add up."

FOURTEEN

Adeline hadn't thought to bring workout gear, so she was stuck wearing the clothes Churchwell supplied. Looking in the bathroom mirror at her bare midriff, the short shorts, and the sports bra with laces over her breasts, she had to wonder if the last woman who'd worn the clothes had been more comfortable on a pole than on a mat. The style didn't match the impression she had of Churchwell. If he showed up in some kind of Magic Mike stripper outfit, she'd have to look for a new dance partner.

She had doubled up on the pain pills, and they'd finally beaten down her headache. Adeline pulled a loose T-shirt over the skimpy outfit, rebraided her hair, and met Churchwell in the living room. He'd already cleared away the furniture. Much to her relief, he'd dressed in a loose long-sleeved T-shirt over workout pants.

His visual inspection of her suggested he didn't approve of the T-shirt addition to the ensemble he'd provided. She ignored him. She was a fourth-degree black belt. She wasn't about to slide into some sexist role he'd created for her with his clothing choices.

He called her to him and asked her to extend her arms. Nearby was a silver tray with six gel packs. They looked like miniature breast implants. "Your power will drain the closest life source. That's why we place them on our arms," he said. He inspected her arms, top and underside, and had her push up her sleeves. "You're right-handed?"

She nodded. He had her spread her fingers, and examined her hands carefully. "What are you looking for?" Adeline said.

"The best place to locate the cells." He had her hold out her right arm, palm up, then picked up the silver tray. One by one, he plucked the gel packs from the tray and laid them against her skin in a line between her wrist and elbow. "This one," he said, referring to the cell he'd positioned near the crook of her arm, "is set so you can feel it without looking at it. When that one's gone, your magic will start draining anything with a life force in the vicinity."

"They won't fall off?"

"No," he said, setting down the tray. "And don't remove them if you don't have to. They can't be reused."

She folded her arm, feeling the bulge of the gel pack at her elbow.

"The magic we'll call on today creates something from nothing. It's rudimentary. One of the foundational skills every warlock learns. Let's start with something small."

He held out his hand, closed his fist, and when he reopened it, he revealed a pair of dice. The magic was familiar. Conjuring. She'd learned the theory as a teenager, back when the possibility she might wield magic still remained.

He guided her through the process, explaining that after she had a clear image in her mind, she only had to desire it, and the magic would send power flowing from her body through her arm to her hand, creating what her mind imagined.

"It'll be easier at first if you close your eyes to avoid visual distractions."

She followed his instructions, visualizing the dice in her mind before extending her arm. She expected a tingle in her fingertips, like she'd experienced earlier. When no sensation came forth, she doubled down, picturing dice in her mind's eye, willing them to come to her. A feathering of warmth fluttered under her ribs. She inhaled. By some instinct, she knew that warmth was her magic.

She kept her eyes closed tightly and called to it again. The flutter returned. *There you are*, she mused, feeling the magic stirring, warming her body. It was an odd sensation—not the physical aspect of it, but beneath that. The magic had a personality, if that was the right word. Shy and cautious, as if it were testing her as much as she was testing it.

Welcome, she said, feeling that a greeting was appropriate. On the inside, she grinned in wonder. On the outside, she schooled her face in concentration. Warmth travelled leisurely across her shoulder, down her arm, and into her hand. But she couldn't feel dice in her fist. She concentrated harder, picturing the dice clearly in her mind, wanting them, calling to the magic to deliver them.

But again, nothing landed in her hand. "I don't feel any dice," she said, disappointed.

"Keep your eyes closed," Churchwell said. "Open your hand to release the magic."

She took his words on faith, reimagined the dice, then opened her hand. When she did, a flutter of magic raced down her palm. A loud crash jolted her eyes open. On the floor in front of her was a wooden board game. She recognized it immediately. Coloured marbles scattered in every direction, along with four sets of dice. Their family had played the board game, called Fragitation, all the time when they were kids.

"I guess we should be grateful you weren't imagining a craps table," Churchwell said, amused.

"Now I know why you cleared the room."

"I didn't think anyone could mess up dice. Not even an almost witch."

She smiled in response, enjoying his humour and the unexpected relief and gratitude at finding the magic inside of her, and directing it, at least somewhat. It all made sense now. Visualization was the key to warlock magic. And it rang true with her. She'd visualized the hollandaise. She'd visualized Churchwell calling her. She'd even visualized her frustration with not being able to finish Mrs. Doppler's eyes.

She checked the gel packs. The first one had flattened somewhat but wasn't gone. "How many of these would it take to conjure that craps table?"

"Conjuring is witch vocabulary. Warlocks call it compelling."

Ah yes. She nodded, remembering where she'd heard that before. Her ex. Contentment flooded her just thinking about him. Warrick was everything a woman wanted and didn't want in a man. Devastatingly handsome, creative in the bedroom, talented with a guitar. And with enough pent-up anger to burn down the world. She'd met him at the Sturgis Motorcycle Rally in South Dakota one August. Married him that September. He was hot, tatted, and most definitely not conforming to his father's wishes. Marrying a witch was his one-finger send-off to his old man.

"Okay, how much power to *compel* a craps table?" Warrick would absolutely approve of Adeline compelling a craps table.

"It depends on how much innate power you have, how skilled you are. In your case, it would likely deplete your remaining power cells and most of mine. I'd prefer we not test that, all right?"

"Can warlocks compel living beings, like a cat, or a person?"

"No. Let's move on."

He was a little quick with the no, but maybe he thought it an inane question. Witches couldn't conjure living beings either.

He then walked her through compelling different coloured dice and other small objects. Each time, the magic came when she called to it, and each time she thanked it. She was careful to be specific when she created the images in her mind. They moved on to larger items: a hair dryer, a toaster, a baseball mitt. Next up were combination items, like ice cream in a bowl, flowers in a vase. And then she smashed a teapot. Scalding tea splashed across the floor. She'd been aiming for a cup of tea, not the whole pot.

"You're tired," he said, clearing the mess with a flurry of finger movements and a swipe of his hand. "Let's call it a day."

Mentally tired, perhaps, but her physical energy was pent-up. "What is that you're doing with your fingers?" Her guess was he'd been forming runes.

"We're working on your magic, not mine."

So that was a yes on the runes. A small bulge remained in the power cell at the crook of her arm. "Can we try one more thing?"

"What?"

"It's not big or breakable," she said, and, hearing no objection, she closed her eyes in concentration. When she finally unfurled her hand, it held proper workout gear. A twin to his own, but in her size. "Did you say there's a gym in here?"

She rode down the elevator with a guard she didn't recognize, and he dropped her off inside the gym. "You don't need to wait," she said, seeing him take up residence beside the door. "I'll call you when I'm done."

He didn't answer. *Fine.* She turned her back to him and chose an elliptical machine in front of a glass wall overlooking a pool. She would pack her bathing suit next time she was home. Or maybe she'd conjure—compel—one.

Using her newfound magic felt good. Too good. On the verge of addictive. She wanted more. For someone who'd banished magic in her home, wouldn't even talk about it for fear the buried resentment would resurface, she'd certainly done a one-eighty in record time. She was acing hypocrisy.

But she didn't know the magic would feel like this, like a living being inside her. It was asleep right now, but it would wake if she needed it. She also knew it had more secrets to share, more power than it had yet allowed her to tap into. Having the magic removed was no longer under consideration. It would be tantamount to killing it. She wouldn't do that. Not when she could learn to wield it without sacrificing anything. The incompatible magic complication hadn't materialized, and she prayed it never would.

Near the thirty-minute mark, dripping in sweat, she spotted Churchwell on the pool deck below. He dropped his robe, giving her an eyeful of lean, toned muscle. The heavy silver necklace he wore emitted an unnatural glow. He dove in and surfaced into a front crawl. At the end wall, he did an underwater turn, kicked off, and launched effortlessly back into a crawl. She got off the elliptical and approached the glass. He had markings on his upper arms that continued across his shoulders and back. He was pushing too much water for her to see if he had marks on his chest.

A guard stood inside the pool deck door. One-on-one security for both of them? It was either massive overkill, or the threat was more serious than she knew.

·))) ● (((·

Luke suspected Kai had marked Adeline with a locking rune. Luke had to find it. He'd been certain the rune would be on Adeline's burned arm or fingers. But it wasn't. Nor was it on her legs, which he'd examined each time he'd encouraged her to close her eyes to create images in her mind.

There was a slim chance he might see it if she put on a bikini, but, failing that, he'd have to research a new runecast to do the job. Getting her naked to find it wasn't on his agenda. No matter how attractive she was, she was still a witch.

"You're back," Luke said, entering the suite. Adeline sat on the sofa with her phone in her hand, her hair wet. Coconut and honey scented the air.

"I saw you in the pool. Do you always have it to yourself?"

"Usually. Don't know why." He tightened the belt on his robe. "The water temperature's ideal for a workout. You're welcome to use it."

She didn't commit to donning a bathing suit, but he sensed she was thinking about it.

"Do you have Wi-Fi here? I can't get a signal."

"I'll get you the password." He walked to the kitchen and searched through one of the drawers. "Here," he said, handing her a piece of paper. He didn't tell her that her online activity would be monitored.

"Do you mind me asking about your markings?" she said, taking the paper he offered.

He shrugged, noncommittal. He rarely noticed them anymore.

"Are they runes?"

He paused. "What do you know about runes?" he asked.

"Nothing. It's just . . . I doodled marks that looked like them. After the attack. My sister told me the doodles were runes."

Interesting. "They're for protection. From . . . unwanted magic."

"Do all warlocks have them?"

"Very few." The price was prohibitive, and runecasters hid their proprietary designs within a larger piece so the rune configurations couldn't be identified or pirated.

"Would you mind . . . showing me?"

He took a step back.

"I'm sorry," she said. "Was that inappropriate?"

"Not at all. I've just never had anyone ask to see them." He didn't suppose it would hurt to settle her curiosity. *It's not like she would be able to pick out the runes.*

He lowered the robe to his elbows and turned around. Her clothing rustled as she rose.

"It's quite beautiful," she said. "Intricate." He felt her warm breath on his back.

Her hand brushed his shoulder. He twitched.

"Would these work on witches? You know, to prevent what happened to me?"

"I wouldn't know," he said, pulling up his robe. "Runes aren't something we share with outsiders."

Tanner's call came swiftly. "I thought you understood. No runes."

Tanner had been very specific. He'd intentionally exposed Adeline to the power cells, hoping she'd leak the information to the coven. It served his purpose: the news would unnerve them. But Luke wasn't to expose anything else that would give the witches more than they already knew about warlock magic. Runes topped that list.

He'd just hung up when his intercom buzzed. "Yes," he said, answering.

"It's Connie."

His *PA*. He pinched his brow.

"Two guards are on their way up for a collection."

"Thank you." He hung up, unlocked the vault, and prepared their package.

The following morning, he texted Tanner that he and Adeline would soon be leaving for her house. Moments later, his magic was released. He would have sagged with relief, but he wouldn't give Tanner the satisfaction. He felt the suite's shields fall. His necklace heated, an unnecessary warning.

"I'll need to stop for groceries," she said, as she buckled up. "My head's still a jumble. I have no idea what's in my fridge."

"A stop isn't necessary. I'll compel what you need at your place."

"Thanks, but Charlie is particular about his bacon."

Luke carried the groceries and waited while Adeline fit her key into the lock. He sent out feelers for warlock magic in the vicinity. Nothing came back to him.

"Please, come in," Adeline said.

He climbed the stairs and, even though she'd invited him in, detected resistance as he passed through the ward. It was stronger than he'd anticipated.

She hummed while she worked in the kitchen, unpacking the groceries, pulling out pans and utensils. He left her and wandered into the solarium, flipping through the stacks of canvases that leaned against the walls. There were squares and rectangles in a variety of sizes. Some appeared to be finished, others looked partially complete. They all had her signature style.

On the wall above one of the stacks hung a collection of framed photos. An elderly couple. Parents or grandparents, he presumed. Adeline as a child, a head taller than the other girl in the photo. Must be her sister. A laughing family of four. Her sister's family, he realized, recognizing the woman with blonde hair from the night in the clearing. More photos of the two children. Her niece and nephew, he surmised.

A table nearby held tubes of paint and an assortment of brushes. He opened a spiral sketch pad. Paper-clipped throughout were photos of dogs and cats. A colourful parrot of some sort. She'd sketched them and scribbled shorthand notes around the margins. The likenesses were remarkable.

"My human portrait work might be of more interest." Adeline said, startling him. "They're in the red sketchbook." She stood in the archway to the kitchen.

"I'm sorry. I didn't mean to be nosy."

Adeline shrugged. "It's okay. I'm just waiting on the toast, and then I'll head down. Okay?"

"Sure. I'll be close by."

He kept one eye on the kitchen as he opened the red sketchbook. The portrait sketches were more complex, and not all of them had photos. Adeline appeared, the breakfast tray in her hands. He flipped the red cover closed, and a photograph dislodged, fluttering to the floor.

He bent to pick it up. At first, the image didn't register. He was about to tuck it back inside the sketchbook when recognition hit. He froze, and then slipped it in his pocket.

What was Adeline doing with a photo of the warlock queen?

Fifteen

After breakfast, Joe took the kids, occupying them so Sarah's mother could examine her more carefully. She and her mom returned to their guest suite.

"Impressive," Sarah said, closing the door behind her. "The suite's already been cleaned." Everything about the ship was impressive. The staff were unerringly polite, their uniforms clean and pressed. She hadn't seen a single stain on the carpeting or a blemish on the furniture anywhere on the ship. And the food looked and tasted like they were in a Michelin-starred restaurant.

"Sit here and swivel toward the balcony," her mother said.

Sarah sat and turned in the chair. Her mother stood behind her and lifted her hands to either side of her head. "This reminds me of when I was a little girl," she said. "You would do this when I couldn't sleep."

"Even at a young age, you carried around enough worry to cripple a donkey. Not to mention guilt."

"Survivor's guilt. It's real. Being blessed with so much magic when Adeline got none? I still feel the weight of it. I wish I could talk to her about it, but she shuts me down if I try. She doesn't even know what I'm capable of."

"This crisis may have a silver lining," her mother said. "It's playing to Adeline's strength: fighting. It's how she copes. If she learns the warlocks are using her as a pawn, her anger will be the fuel she needs to fight her way out of their grip. And with the witches supporting her? Her resistance to magic might finally wane."

"That would be a relief. I'd have my big sister back. I would so love to tell her how far newborn bindings have come. The progress we've made. I'd tell her she was my inspiration."

"Hold still now." Her mother chanted softly as she worked. "I sense three folds. No wonder you're confused. Unfolding should ease the headache, but there's no guarantee the memories will come back."

"Just do it, Mom. The headache is draining me."

Her mother's magic flowed from her hands, guided by her whispers, warming her mind, easing some of the pressure.

"You might feel a tug," she said, shifting her hands.

The pain of the headache overshadowed any sense of a tug, and then her mother lowered her hands.

"That's one fold fixed. Your mind needs time to decompress before I unfold another. Lie down and rest."

She took to her bed. The soft click of the door closing as her mother left was the last thing she heard.

"Honey?" Joe said, shaking her shoulder. She roused.

"Where are the kids? What time is it?"

"Your mom's looking after them, and it's"—he checked his watch— "four o'clock. Morgan said she was able to release one of the folds. How are you feeling?"

Sarah gave herself a moment to assess. "The headache is better, I think."

"Do you remember anything more?"

"Hard to say yet." She sat up. "No. I do remember something. Beatrice has a warlock stone." She explained the stone's properties, and as she did so, she grew tense. There was more to the memory, but she couldn't recall it.

After another exquisite meal in the dining room, her mother followed them back to their suite. Olive and Jack hadn't yet acclimatized to the time shift. Sarah tucked in Olive, who had fallen asleep in her arms on the way back from supper. Jack fought his eyelids and settled in with a game on his tablet.

Sarah, her mother, and Joe pulled on sweaters and took in the fresh air on their small balcony. The ship was underway, heading south to Messina. Small waves marred the strait's deep blue water. They'd been told raptors were abundant in the area. Joe leaned his forearms on the balcony rail, a ship's pamphlet in his hand to help identify the birds.

Sarah's phone rang. "It's Adeline," she said, glancing at the display.

"Where are you?" she said, answering the call. "Mom and I haven't been able to reach you."

"At home. I'm just making Charlie's breakfast. Sorry about the phone. The signal is really weak where I'm staying."

"Where exactly are you staying?"

"An office tower in Coal Harbour. You know the one, with black windows near the Butcher and Bullock pub."

"Did you say office tower?"

"Yeah. Weird, eh? Have you remembered anything?"

"Mom was able to release some memories. Do you remember Beatrice?"

"Now that you mention it, yes. She was the older woman in the training centre with Silas. Carried a purse like it was a kettlebell."

"Probably weighed as much, too. That purse holds a warlock stone." Sarah again found herself explaining the finer points of warlock stones. "There's something else about her stone that I can't quite recall."

"She used her magic to force my hand to touch it," Adeline said. "In the GC meeting. You called her out for it. Blew the stone off the table."

"I knew there was more to it. Do you remember anything else?"

"No. My head still aches, though the Advil helps."

"How's it going with the warlock?"

"Better than I expected. He's here with me now. His name's Churchwell. He's a runecaster, and my shadow until they catch the warlock who attacked us."

"A runecaster? Damaras must have some pull with Lord Tanner."

"I suppose. Tell Mom she doesn't need to be concerned about my safety. Security at his place rivals a bank's vault. Guards on the door. Cameras in every corner. It's stifling."

"Sounds it. Why so much security?"

"Don't know. He's not sharing the why of it. Probably has something to do with the work he does for Lord Tanner. It's all very secretive. But on the plus side, Churchwell is teaching me how to use warlock magic. Yesterday we tackled compelling. It's the warlock version of conjuring."

"Maybe you should hold off on using the warlock's magic. Stirring it up might cause a reaction with your witch DNA. Has anyone checked your threads since you landed there?"

"No, but don't worry. Except for this headache, I feel okay. Has anyone heard from Marcus? Damaras told me he'd been attacked as well."

"No, and you're changing the subject. But I understand. Just be careful. I've got Marcus's number. I'll call him," Sarah said. "Do you know if anyone else was attacked?"

"No. That it was you, Marcus, and me makes sense, though," Adeline said. "You and I both saw him, and Marcus healed the damage to my arm. Damaras was operating with her usual efficiency, arranging refuge for the coven, so I don't think she's been hit. Silas and Beatrice would be targets, but Damaras didn't mention them."

"Is there any word about the warlock who attacked us?" Sarah said. "Do they know who he is? Was he working alone?"

"None of the above. That I know of, anyway. I haven't heard from Damaras."

"Neither have we. Mom left her a message, but she hasn't returned the call." Sarah's mother tapped Sarah's knee, beckoning for the phone. "Mom wants to talk to you. I'll pass you over to her. Ask her about her new diamond bracelet. I love you. Stay safe."

"Hello, angel. How are you?" her mother said, taking the phone.

Jack poked his head out the patio door and asked for a soda. She and Joe headed inside to give her mother some privacy.

With Jack once again occupied reading a book on his tablet, Joe turned to her. "Did I hear you say that the warlock protecting Adeline is a runecaster?"

She nodded. "And the level of security she described at his place makes me wonder how much danger she's really in."

·))) ● (((·

Adeline swivelled her head, checking to make sure Luke was out of sight. He'd insisted on accompanying her down the stairs.

"Charlie, your breakfast is here," Adeline called out. So much had happened since she'd last seen him that it felt like a week had passed.

"Welcome back," Charlie said, opening the door and pressing against the wall to let her pass.

Welcome back, she thought, confused. A clump of cheery grapes slipped by without remark.

"Did you have a nice long weekend?" he asked.

Long weekend? Had she missed something?

"Friday's breakfast delivery was a surprise," he said, closing the door. "Delicious, but not as good as yours."

Adeline faltered, pausing in the hallway. She had no recollection of doing that. Friday. Three days ago. Was she missing an entire day? The headache that hadn't left since her attack ramped up.

"You okay?" Charlie said, coming up behind her.

"Yeah, fine. Sorry," she said, and continued to the table with his tray.

"I hope it was okay to tip the driver. I never know if tips are included or not in services like that."

"I'm sure the driver was happy to get a tip. Remind me, which restaurant was it?"

"I have it right here," he said, and pulled the receipt from a stack of papers on the end of the kitchen counter. "Jam Café. Kitsilano. Never heard of it before."

Neither had Adeline.

Charlie didn't mind Adeline keeping the receipt, and he wouldn't accept reimbursement for the tip either. Luke rejoined her outside Charlie's door and escorted her back up the stairs. She tidied the kitchen, all the while poking at her memory, trying to loosen something up. Anything.

Churchwell leaned a shoulder against the archway to the solarium. "You're upset. Something happen with your tenant?"

She turned and rested her butt against the sink. "I'm missing a whole day. Last Friday." She pulled the receipt from her pocket. "Charlie had his breakfast delivered from this place. I don't know the restaurant, though maybe that memory's been taken from me, too. I feel so violated. Angry."

"I'm sorry. Is there anything I can do?"

"Can you release memories?"

"Sadly, no."

She turned to the sink and popped another pain pill. "How about headaches? You any good with those?"

"Perhaps," he said. "If you trust me to try."

She turned back. He hadn't moved from the archway. Did she trust him?

"I'm not the warlock who did that to you."

She hesitated, struggling against a lifetime of warnings, of prejudice.

"You don't have to suffer, but I understand. Are you ready to go?"

Was it possible she'd remember more if she wasn't battling the headache? This was day three, and it hadn't let up. She crossed her arms over her stomach. "I would like you to try."

He pushed off from the wall and came to stand in front of her. "Relax your arms. Close your eyes. Think of something pleasant."

His cedar scent came to mind. "What are you going to do?"

"Ease your headache. Now close your eyes."

She did, and soon after, with sunshine flooding the kitchen, the shadows of his fingers moved in an elegant dance near her face, around her head. The pain subsided. She sighed with relief.

"Better?" he asked.

"More than better. It's gone. Are you a healer?"

"No. But I'm glad it helped."

"Thank you." Perhaps Warrick wasn't the only exception to the *all warlocks are dogs* rule of thumb.

"I'm going to get my memories back. It's already started. This morning? When I spoke with my sister? I remembered more of my time in the training centre. The face of the warlock is blurry, but it'll come back. Friday will come back."

Alarm flashed ever so quickly across his features, then slipped away. "A word of caution? Be careful what you talk about in the tower. The cameras record everything."

Sixteen

Luke had to warn Adeline. If she was recovering her memories and spilled the details in the tower, Tanner would mine it for anything he could use against the witches . . . or a warlock. He wasn't particular, and Luke didn't want him to get any more ammunition.

Late that afternoon, back in the tower, Adeline took him up on his offer of another lesson. Until he could unlock her magic, Tanner would agree to him continuing to teach her. It wasn't like he was revealing anything she wouldn't have learned to do if she'd had witch powers. And he had to admit he enjoyed her company. At the very least, conversation with someone other than Tanner was an improvement over the past three years.

He didn't have to read her mind to sense that she craved the knowledge. Her eagerness shone through in the way she concentrated, in the delight in her eyes when she succeeded. His lessons would ensure her continued co-operation. They also had the benefit of keeping his magic unleashed for the lesson's duration.

With a sweep of his hand, he pushed the furniture out of the way. Adeline joined him, wearing long sleeves and yoga pants, her hair pulled back in a ponytail.

He called her closer. "What I'm going to show you is similar to compelling, but instead of creating an object from our magic, we're calling to us an object that already exists."

He offered her the silver tray with six new power cells. "Go ahead. You know how to put them on." Allowing Luke to reveal their power cells to witches reinforced the warlock lord's benevolence. On the surface, it would appear to the witches that Tanner had made a concession or slipped up. He hadn't.

He checked that she'd set the cells correctly, sidetracked momentarily by the coconut-and-honey scent of her, and then she pulled down her sleeve and they moved to the centre of the room.

"If you don't have a line of sight to the object you're calling, you can still call it if you know where it is and there're no solid barriers between you and it. You simply picture the object in its location." He began the demonstration with his phone, which he'd left on the kitchen counter. The next moment, it was in his hand.

Her eyes widened. "Did it vanish and reappear? Because I didn't see it move."

"It didn't vanish. It moves faster than the eye can track. As with compelling, the larger the object, the more power is required."

"So, if I had enough power, I could call my car to me?"

"If it was close enough you could, but it would take out a bank of windows on the way in and likely exceed the floor's load limit."

"Right," she said, mock admonishment in her features. "I meant hypothetically."

"How about we start with less tonnage?" Luke said, grinning. He had her call small objects he'd set around the room. A ring of keys, a wooden spoon, a box of tissues. None of the items landed in her hand. The keys flew past her shoulder, the wooden spoon rapped her knuckles, and the box of tissue landed on the floor by her feet.

"You'll get the hang of it." He recalled the items to reset them. "There's a weight-to-power balance that will come with practice." She repeated calling the items several more times, getting closer to landing them in her hands with each pass.

Given her curiosity about calling a car, he thought it would be prudent to demonstrate the danger of calling a larger object. He asked her to call one of the leather sofa cushions, which he knew were lighter than they looked.

She held out two hands, and the strong metallic scent of ozone told him she was pulling too much power. The cushion hit her in the chest and knocked her backwards, off her feet. She landed on her butt, gaping.

He helped her up. She wasn't hurt. She also wasn't deterred. It was as if her error in judgment spurred her on. She repeated the call until she had the cushion landing smoothly in her arms.

Tanner's phone rang, putting an end to their lesson.

"You get phone service here? I barely get one bar," she said.

"I've got to take this. Excuse me," he said, and headed to his office.

"What have you learned about Kai's lock on the witch?" Lord Tanner said.

"I believe he's put a rune on her. I haven't found it yet."

"She's been with you for three days. What's the holdup?"

"Her clothes. I'm trying to find it without compelling her to remove them. She's strong-willed. If the compulsion fails, we'll lose her co-operation."

"Are you telling me your runes aren't up to the task?"

"Adeline's mind has already been messed with, and her body's still recovering from the poisoning. A compulsion isn't necessary. Not yet. I've encouraged her to use the pool. If I can't find the locking rune when she's in a bathing suit, I'll develop a runecast." It was a last resort. A runecast to compel her could compromise her well-being. Tanner might force his hand, but Luke would avoid doing it if he could.

"Do not get attached to her. She's a witch, not a pet. Work faster. Meantime, I've asked Damaras to send over the binder witch, Beatrice. She'll check her over and bind any witch threads she finds. It'll keep her alive until you find the key to Kai's lock."

"Is Beatrice packing warlock powder?"

"You should assume so. We're not in a bargaining position. She's coming onto our territory to do our bidding. I've guaranteed her safety."

"Adeline can't take another dose of warlock power."

"Then you'd better make sure the binder doesn't feel the need to use it."

The intercom on his desk rang.

"That'll be for you," Tanner said, and he disconnected.

"Yes," Luke said, punching the intercom button.

"Boss? It's Connie." Of course it was Connie. Who else would it be? "Beatrice is here. Were you expecting her?"

Luke smoothed a hand down his face. "Yes. Hold her for five minutes then please send her up."

He had to prepare Adeline for the binder's arrival. He found her in her bedroom with the door closed. He knocked. "Adeline?"

She opened the door, shrugging into a thick terry robe. A bathing suit peeked out from underneath. A one-piece bathing suit. He tried not to let his disappointment show. He'd been hoping for a bikini that would reveal a rune in the middle of her back. Looked like he had a night of research ahead instead.

"Lord Tanner has arranged for your coven's binder to check in on your witch tells. She'll be here in a few minutes. Do you want me to send her in here?"

Adeline stiffened. "My sister is Stonewater coven's binder, and she's out of town. Who did the coven send?"

"A woman named Beatrice."

Adeline yanked on her robe's ties. "I don't want that woman anywhere near me."

He creased his brow. "Why not?"

She pressed her lips together. "I don't trust her." But Luke sensed there was a whole lot more to it.

"Is there someone else who can monitor the incompatible magics?"

She pulled out her phone. "Damn it. Still no bars. My sister might know someone, but I don't."

"Beatrice is already in the building. If I stay with you while she conducts the examination, would that ease your mind?"

Adeline pursed her lips. She tugged on the robe's ties.

"What is it?" Luke asked.

She gazed up at the camera in the hall behind Luke, did an about-face, and walked into her dressing room, leaving the door open in invitation. He stepped inside. Empty built-in racks and shelving covered the walls, and an island with drawers occupied the centre of the room. A full-length three-way mirror took up one corner. Adeline stood with her back to an empty rack at the back, the island between them.

"Close the door," she said.

He did. The room felt incredibly small.

"I remembered something. Earlier. When I was talking with my sister. Beatrice has a warlock stone."

He nodded, wary, but not for the reasons Adeline would assume. *What else has she remembered?* "Tanner has guaranteed her safety. I can't harm her. But I can protect you—if she tries to use it, that is."

"Trust me. She's not beyond using it."

"Oh?" If Adeline remembered being doused with it, she'd remember the events in the clearing.

"She used her magic to force my hand onto it."

Not the dousing. *Good.* But he understood why Adeline didn't trust her.

"I don't think she'd try to use warlock stone here, even if she has it with her. She's outnumbered. She might neutralize one or two of us, but not everyone."

Luke's phone dinged. "That'll be them. What do you want to do?"

Adeline's struggle reflected on her face.

"Don't tell her you remember," Luke said. "Co-operate. See how she plays it. That'll tell you more than refusing to see her."

Adeline tipped her head. "You're cunning."

He winked at her. "I'm a strategist. Shall we answer the door?"

·))) ● (((·

Adeline asked Churchwell to answer the door while she changed. She felt too exposed meeting Beatrice in a bathing suit.

"Hello, Adeline," Beatrice said, when she joined them in the living room. Adeline forced what she hoped was a genuine smile. There was no sign of her purse.

A woman Adeline didn't know stood off to the side. She had a generous, dimpled smile and an unimposing demeanour.

"This is Connie," Churchwell said, introducing the woman with no additional explanation.

Adeline approached her with an extended hand. "Adeline. Are you here with Beatrice?"

"No. I work for—"

"She's my . . . PA," Churchwell said. "She escorted Beatrice through security." He addressed Connie. "I'll call you when we're done here."

Connie didn't look happy about being dismissed, but she left without question.

"You're looking well," Beatrice said to Adeline. "How are you feeling?" Beatrice was doing a stellar impression of a nun, sweet and serene.

"Good, other than a persistent headache. Do you have any word on the warlock who attacked the coven?"

"Not yet, but it's all Damaras and Lord Tanner are working on. We'll find him." Beatrice turned to Churchwell, beaming with gratitude. "Thank you for taking such good care of her."

"It's been my pleasure," he said, his features softening. He glanced at Adeline, and she got the impression he was being sincere.

"Where would you like me?" Adeline said, anxious to get the reading over with so she could send Beatrice on her way.

"There is fine," Beatrice said, coming to stand in front of her.

Churchwell joined them. Beatrice gave him a curious glance.

"Her magic is unpredictable," he said, by way of explanation. "I'll intervene if she loses control." Adeline nearly laughed at the alarm on Beatrice's face.

"All right," Beatrice said. "Thank you." Her attention fell to Adeline. "Just relax, dear."

Dear? That was hardly the sentiment that came to Adeline's mind. Looked like Beatrice was putting stock in Adeline's memory having been wiped.

She raised her hands to Adeline's head and released her binder's magic. As the warmth of it slid over her, Adeline relaxed. She closed her eyes. A binder's magic was painless. It was something she'd endured repeatedly since her first failed unbinding. Just this past week, her sister had read her several times.

The soothing magic flowed around her head and down to her shoulders. Readings she'd had in the past had taken only thirty seconds or so, but Beatrice was taking her time. Adeline's first thought was that she was being ridiculously thorough, but then the pressure in her head ramped up. A painful tug, followed by a sharp stab, drew a gasp out of her. She winced and knocked Beatrice's hands away, leaning away from her. As she retreated a step, a whooshing sound fell around her. And then silence. Her headache roared to life.

She spun around, feeling the cool walls of an invisible dome around her. Her fingers flared red. She sought out Beatrice, and when her gaze landed on the woman, anger fuelled the fire pouring out of her hands. Adeline pointed in her direction. Beyond the barrier that enveloped her, protected from her fire, Beatrice dropped the serene nun facade, revealing her true colours: a snarling pit bull with hunched shoulders. Beatrice removed a small vial from her sweater pocket and aimed it at Adeline. She was pretty sure it wasn't bear spray.

Churchwell backed away from them, hands up and lips moving fast. His body language was aimed to calm Beatrice, to de-escalate the situation.

From the direction of the hallway, two guards came running into view, with Connie on their heels. Beatrice turned her back to Adeline and slid the threatening vial into her pocket. She glared at Adeline once more before allowing Connie to lead her away.

Five minutes passed before Churchwell returned. With a complicated swish of his hand, the dome disappeared.

"What happened?" Adeline said.

"You tell me."

Adeline seated herself. "At first, Beatrice was just reading me. The binder magic felt like it always does, until it intensified. I thought maybe she'd found a witch tell. And then she jabbed into my head with a sharp pain."

"What was she after?"

Adeline shook her head. "I don't know. But it's a safe bet she had malicious intentions."

"You would have burned her if I hadn't dropped that shield around you."

"You should have let me." Adeline looked at her fingertips. "What was that?"

"Warlock fire."

Adeline had seen it before. Where? She leaned forward, elbows on her knees, and rubbed her temples. "The headache's back."

"Do you want me to help?" He came to stand in front of her and squatted.

She nodded and closed her eyes. She sensed him fluttering his fingers again. The pain in her head dulled and then vanished.

"I wish I could do that for myself," Adeline said. "Thank you." His chain winked out at her from the hollow at the base of his neck. She stared at it. "I've never seen anything quite like the chain you wear. It's almost iridescent. What's it made of?"

He stood and straightened his shirt collar. "I don't know. It was . . . given to me." She looked at his back as he retreated to the kitchen. An odd way to react to a gift, she thought.

He brought her a glass of water, and she asked him if Beatrice had reported her findings. "Not to me. I can ask Lord Tanner."

"I'm not sure she'll tell the truth. No one witnessing our exchange would be able to see that it wasn't just binder magic she'd inflicted on me. It would look like I'd attacked her."

"You didn't strike first. I dropped the shield around you as soon as you pulled away from her."

He'd protected her. A warlock. "Thank you. Again."

He shrugged. "You didn't trust her, so I was prepared."

She couldn't guess Beatrice's game. Was she looking for something in her mind? Trying to hide something she'd remembered? "I need to call my sister. Can we get out of here?"

"Did you not say she was in Italy?" Adeline nodded. "They're—nine? —hours ahead of us."

"Right." She leaned back. "Do you know the symptoms of incompatible magic?"

"Fever, chills, nausea, muscle aches."

"Sounds like a flu."

"A deadly flu. Are you having chest pains? Difficulty breathing?"

"No. None of that." She pressed a hand to her chest. "How do you know the symptoms?"

"I looked them up after I was charged with giving you refuge. Can't have you dying on my watch."

"Headaches aren't on that list of symptoms, are they?"

"No. I wouldn't have risked easing them if they were."

Adeline's attention was once again on her fingertips. "The blast in the training centre—was that warlock fire?"

"Some form of it, I expect."

"Will you teach me how to use it?"

SEVENTEEN

"Thank the stars you picked up," Sarah said. It had been torture waiting until it was morning again in Vancouver. "I've got you on speaker with Mom. Where are you?"

"At home. Getting Charlie's breakfast ready. I was going to call you when I was done. Hi, Mom."

"Hello, angel. Where's the warlock?"

"Churchwell? I don't know. Not here. We're having a moment. It started last night."

"Does that comment need explanation?" their mother asked, exchanging a worrying glance with Sarah.

"Later. And that's a fine question coming from the woman who's been sketchy on details about her new diamond bracelet."

Sarah hid a smile at her mother's eye roll. "Fine. It's from a gentleman I've been spending some time with. His name is Anderson Schubert, and I've become quite fond of him."

"That's wonderful news, Mom. I'm happy for you," Adeline said.

"Me, too," Sarah said. "When do we get to meet him?"

"Enough about me." She fluttered her hand in a shooing motion. "Tell Adeline what we learned."

"I've remembered more," Sarah said. "Mom released the second fold. I can see his face again—the warlock who attacked you." Recovering the memory felt like a victory even if she didn't know her foe.

"Describe him."

"Fortyish, rusty-brown hair, thin face, freckles."

"And his eyes are a weird colour, right?"

"Yes. The same rusty shade as his hair. You remember too?" She squeezed her mother's hand.

"Just now."

"I thought this might happen," their mother said, nodding. "Your memories are triggering each other's."

"I also remember that Simon did a regression on you," Adeline said.

"He did? When?" Being told she'd done something she didn't recollect made her question her sanity.

"A day or two after the attack. You told me he got a clear likeness."

"Huh. I have no memory of that. If the warlock is local and they have his picture, shouldn't they have an ID on him by now?" Someone had to know who he was.

"Maybe he's not local. Or they can't find him."

The ship's whistle sounded, startling them.

"Stars, that was loud," Adeline said. "I should have asked, where are you?"

"Still in the Mediterranean basin," their mother said. "We're nearing Corfu."

A heavy sigh from Adeline. "Sounds lovely."

"Do you recall that before the warlock vanished, he told you to 'Tell Luke that Kai has served his sentence'?"

"Yes, I do. You and I talked about it. About what it meant. Did we figure it out?"

"Other than that Kai had committed some crime," she said, shrugging, "no. But you didn't want me to tell Damaras."

"Charlie told me something interesting. His breakfast on Friday was a delivery from a restaurant I've never heard of. I can't imagine I'd do that, but Friday is a total blank."

"I'm sorry," Sarah said, pinching her forehead between her thumb and forefinger. "Not remembering is frustrating. If it wasn't you, whoever did it knew your routine."

"Damaras and Silas knew I made Charlie his breakfast. Tanner and Churchwell, too, though Churchwell didn't react when I mentioned the mystery breakfast delivery to him. Oh, and Beatrice paid me a visit." Adeline told them about Beatrice's warlock stone and her visit to the tower. "You were right about her, Mom. She can't be trusted."

"Agreed," Sarah said. "There's more. At the GC meeting, one of the junior war mages suggested that your new warlock magic might give you access to their inner workings. It was Daniel. He wanted you to spy for us."

"Damaras must have been all over that," Adeline said. Their mother brought her fist to her lips, sharing Adeline's sentiments.

"She wasn't. She told them you wouldn't do it. I told them the same, that you wanted the magic out of you. That was before you blew up Silas's box and changed your mind."

"Churchwell told me about the explosion. I only remember flashes."

Sarah folded her arms over her stomach. "Do you have any recollection of your warlock magic draining us while Silas had you in that box?"

"No. I did that?"

"They're afraid of you, Adeline," Sarah said.

"Maybe they should be. Churchwell tells me the flames that erupt from my hands are called warlock fire. It's what we argued about. I wanted him to teach me how to use it. He wants to teach me flower arranging instead."

"Flower arranging?" their mother said, her eyes twinkling with curiosity.

"Might as well be. Moving things with magic. Rearranging them. I can shoot fire from my goddamn hands, and he wants me to concentrate on *foundational* magic. I nearly killed Beatrice. Not that Grandma Bea would be a great loss to witchkind, but surely learning to control warlock fire trumps moving spoons and boxes of tissue around."

"That does seem a rather bizarre order of priorities, given the circumstances," their mother said. "We're missing too many pieces to this puzzle. If this Kai character was sentenced to forfeit his power, why give it to a witch? No warlock court would sanction that."

"Warlocks don't want witches to learn their magic any more than we want them learning ours," Sarah said. "They know you have it. They could overpower you if they chose to. So why haven't they siphoned it out of you yet?"

"And they're teaching me how to use it."

"Yes, but only the flower arranging variety—nothing lethal," their mother said.

"They're biding their time," Adeline said. "What are they waiting for?"

Adeline's stony silence on the drive to her house convinced Luke that she needed time away from him. The wards would protect her in his absence. Perhaps after she talked to her family, she'd climb down from her horse. He accompanied her to the porch with a reminder to await his return before she delivered Charlie's breakfast.

After his warnings about the tower's cameras, she must have known that security would catch the two of them disappearing into her dressing room. The moment Tanner had found out, he'd torn into Luke like a dog with a pound of bacon. But he'd bought Luke's explanation that Adeline had warned him about Beatrice's warlock stone. That she hadn't wanted her betrayal of the witch's secret on video. Luke had managed to spin it into a positive: she was coming to trust him.

And now look where they were. Warlock fire was higher magic. Tanner wouldn't budge about teaching her. He didn't mind that she might kill someone.

Luke pulled away from the curb, powered down the windows, and trolled the neighbourhood for the scent of magic. Kai had to know they were hunting him. His old friend was wily. At full power, Kai would strike hard and fast, but that wasn't an option in his current condition. It didn't make him weaker; it simply forced him to resort to a different skill set: stealth and conniving, at which he excelled. Luke knew without doubt that Kai was also deftly replenishing his magical repertoire.

Luke returned to Adeline's house and trotted down the driveway. She was vulnerable to Kai outside her wards, and it was about time for her to deliver her tenant's breakfast.

He hadn't expected the grey-haired man to be sitting like a gnome in the back garden. "Hello," Luke said, caught off guard.

Charlie offered a cool smile. "Churchwell, is it?"

"Yes. I don't believe I caught your name last time we met."

"Charles," he said, not offering his hand.

"I'm meeting with Adeline," Luke said, feeling rebuffed. He stuffed his hands in his pockets.

"You must have missed her front door. It's back that way," he said, gesturing down the driveway.

He was feisty for someone who looked to be pushing seventy.

"Charlie?" Adeline said, exiting the upper door with the tray in her hands. "You want your breakfast outside? I can fetch you a blanket."

"No. Just enjoying the sunshine. Let me get the door for you."

"Churchwell," Adeline said, her tone flat.

She and Charlie—Charles to him—disappeared into his suite. Adeline must have been delighting in Luke's discomfort because she stayed inside far longer than it took to deliver a meal. When she finally emerged, she did so without a word to him and then climbed the stairs and disappeared into the kitchen.

Luke stalked to his car and stalled. He smelled ozone, and there wasn't a storm cloud in sight. Warlock magic. It was concentrated around his vehicle. He plucked a coin from his pocket and etched a rune on it. He then stepped away and tossed it in the air. The coin tumbled above the car and pinged as it hit the roof, pulled there like a magnet.

Adeline's front door opened. He spun and called to her. "Stay inside."

Surprise flitted across her face. She closed the door and gazed out through the door's diamond pane.

With her safe inside her ward, he closed in on the car and peeled off the coin. Underneath it was a tracking rune. Kai had been there.

They crossed the vestibule, and the guard retreated to his side of the door. Luke excused himself and turned into his office. He'd considered not telling Adeline about the tracking rune, but didn't want to erode her trust any further. And now that she knew, Tanner would have to be told. Luke wouldn't burden her with keeping it a secret. He prayed Kai was smart enough to stay away from him. Luke didn't want to lose another friend.

He crossed the carpet to his desk and stopped short. A silver cuff lay on it. Waiting for a wrist. Who this time? He picked it up and studied the runes etched inside.

Evan Minter. Luke exhaled. He didn't know him. The warlock's crime was being in arrears with his tithes. He owed Lord Tanner a hundred grand, had already received two warning shots across his bow, and now he'd been given two weeks to pay up or lose a hand.

He set the cuff down and carried on to the private bathroom. When he emerged, he stopped in his tracks.

"Put that down." His tone left no room for argument.

Adeline stood in front of his desk with the cuff in her hands, tracing her fingers around the runes inside. "I've seen one of these before," she said, squinting at it.

He reached across the desk and held out his hand.

"These are runes, aren't they?"

"No. Just . . . an old language," he said, blurting the words out as they came to him. "Please." He wiggled the fingers of his outstretched hand.

She placed the cuff in his palm, and he stuffed it in his pocket.

He thanked her, feeling more relief than she could know. "You were looking for me?"

Her attention had drifted to his *Book of Runes* that lay on his credenza. He cleared his throat.

Her gaze snapped back to him. "Oh . . . yes. I thought I'd make dinner. Would that be okay?"

"You don't need to cook."

"I'm going to fork my eyes out if I don't have something to do. It's one dinner. I won't poison you. Promise."

"Sure," he said, glancing at the flashing light on the intercom. "I'd like that."

She left, but he checked down the hall to ensure she was clear of it before he returned to the intercom and pressed the button.

"You're home. Good," Connie said. "Are you expecting Evan Minter?"

"Let me guess," Luke said. "He's here?"

"You know it," Connie said, playing a game he'd long tired of.

Two of Tanner's camo-wearing private militia brought in Evan Minter. One escorted him inside the conference room and remained standing behind his chair. The other stood guard in the hall outside. These weren't the king's nulls. Tanner wouldn't invest that kind of money to terrify a warlock Luke didn't know personally.

Luke nodded to the hall guard and entered the conference room. The door swung closed.

"You know why you're here?" Luke asked. The man he addressed had a wrestler's build and wore a T-shirt that showed off his physique.

"You're one of Tanner's henchmen?"

"You owe the lord a hundred thousand in tithes. He's done waiting." He tossed the cuff at Evan, who caught it readily. "Looks like that goes on your left wrist. You have fourteen days."

"He'll get his money, but I'm not wearing that."

"You're right. He will get his money. And you are wearing that. This isn't a discussion."

Evan shot to his feet, his hands already forming the runes that he released with a punch. Nothing came of it. Anger followed his surprise. He set his jaw.

Luke crossed his arms. "Left wrist. Put it on." The room's shields were calibrated to allow only the magic of whoever Tanner chose, and it was never the warlocks sent to Luke for cuffs.

Evan glanced at the guard, and then at Luke, gauging if he could make a break for it. And then he made the right decision and slipped the cuff over his left wrist. The metal snugged up.

Evan stormed around the end of the table, snarling. Luke stood his ground, ready to shield at the first sign of the man's fist. Evan took his frustration out on the door handle instead, hammering it and shoving the door open. Expletives spewed from his mouth, complete with matching hand gestures.

Luke straddled the conference room's threshold, watching Evan test the guards' fortitude. "The cuff will release when Tanner has his money. If I were you, I'd get it to him sooner rather than later. The guards will escort you out of the building."

When the front door closed behind them, he took a breath and hung his head. Doing Tanner's bidding tore a chunk out of him. It made him feel dirty, worthless, an accomplice in a regime he loathed. And he had as much hope of escaping his fate as did Evan, or Kai, or any of the other dozens of warlocks he'd fitted with cuffs.

He straightened his spine and crossed back to his office only to stop short. Adeline stood at the top of the hall, the expression on her face a mix of horror and revelation.

"That was a cuff. You're Lord Tanner's enforcer?"

He stepped into his office and closed the door.

EIGHTEEN

Adeline walked back to the kitchen, her head swimming, her chest aching. Churchwell had punched her in the gut and knocked the legs out from under her.

He'd lied about the silver bracelet. He'd lied when he'd agreed that cuffs were barbaric. He was quite comfortable with them, after all—his job was enforcing their use. Amputating limbs. It was the warlock practice she abhorred above all others. And she'd let him touch her mind. God, she was naive. This tower wasn't a refuge. It was a nightmare. She had to get away from it.

Last night, when she'd asked, Churchwell had told her they hadn't yet found the warlock who'd attacked her. He'd seemed genuinely surprised to learn that the attacker's likeness had been conveyed to Lord Tanner, but she no longer believed him. She'd fallen for his finesse with lying before. It wouldn't happen again.

Sarah had raised the question of why the warlocks hadn't tried to siphon the magic out of her. A barren witch with no magical defence? She'd been in their clutches for days now. *What are they waiting for?*

Did they imagine removing the warlock's magic would kill her and cause an accord-level ripple in the peace deal? Or maybe the warlocks had already tried to siphon it and couldn't. Was that the memory that had been hidden from her?

Regardless of her unanswered questions, one thing was certain; if the warlock who'd attacked her was tracking them, he was close by. He'd be caught soon. Her time in the tower was coming to an end, and she wasn't giving up her warlock magic without a fight.

She just had to keep that fight away from Charlie.

Charlie. She remembered the silver bracelet. Could picture it in her mind's eye on the laundry room window ledge. She'd thought it was

Charlie's, but that didn't make sense now that she knew what it was. Despite what Churchwell had said, the etchings inside the cuff were runes. She was certain of it. She'd been drawn to them just as she'd been drawn to the markings on his back and the leather-bound *Book of Runes* that sat on the credenza to the right of his desk.

She helped herself to a very expensive bottle of Churchwell's wine and poured herself a large glass. Churchwell wasn't the man she'd thought he was. He hadn't been kind or funny or genuine. He'd been following orders.

And she was being played. But that ended right now.

Years of mental conditioning kicked in. She calmed her mind. Clean slate. She was physically capable and highly trained. And she had added to her repertoire. She now had warlock fire. Anger triggered it, and, fortunately for her, she had a boatload of that at her disposal.

Churchwell hadn't wanted to teach her how to use the fire, and now she suspected he had ulterior motives for keeping her in the dark about it. He hadn't taught her nearly enough, but she could build on that without his help.

One day at a time, she reminded herself. Tomorrow, she'd brainstorm with her sister and mom. Tonight, she'd cook dinner, drink Churchwell's expensive wine, and pretend he hadn't gutted her.

Adeline found the remote to the music system and powered it on. The rhythmic thrum of a double bass plucking out a jazz melody drifted from the speakers. She pulled the lasagna from the oven and set it on the stove. The garlic bread would be ready by the time the lasagna had cooled enough to serve. The table was set, the Caesar salad prepared, and another bottle of pricy wine sat open.

Churchwell hadn't been out of his office since he'd crawled into it hours ago.

At the sound of the front door opening, Adeline walked down the hall to greet her dinner guest.

"I'm so pleased you invited me," Connie said, beaming her dimpled smile.

"Glad you could join us," Adeline said, and the two of them walked back to the kitchen. "Do you drink wine? I've got a bottle of red open, but Churchwell has a stocked bar if you'd prefer a spirit."

"I'd love a glass of red," she said.

She poured the wine. "Do you live here in the tower as well?"

"Downstairs. Luke arranged it right after he hired me. It's very convenient for the odd hours he keeps."

"Luke?"

"Churchwell. I call him boss, but his friends call him by his given name, Luke. Churchwell sounds so formal to me."

Another lie exposed. This was turning into a banner day for revelations. A few hours ago, she would have chalked up her not knowing Churchwell's given name to happenstance, but not now.

Tell Luke that Kai has served his sentence. It now made perfect sense. The cuff she'd found in the laundry must have been Kai's. It must have gotten tangled in her clothing the night of the attack. And it wasn't the quality of her paintings that had drawn Churchwell to her home. He hadn't been looking for a portrait. He'd been looking for Kai. He'd known the identity of her attacker all along.

Connie was interesting company. Adeline had sensed the tension between her and Churchwell during Beatrice's visit. That's why she'd ask the guard to contact Connie and invite her for dinner. She wanted Churchwell to feel as uncomfortable as he'd made her feel. She hoped Connie's quick, tinkling laughter would irritate the hell out of him.

"Speaking of our host," Connie said, looking around, "where is he?"

"In his office, I believe," Adeline said. "Would you mind tapping on his door while I set out dinner?"

Dinner was delightfully tense. When dessert was finished, and Adeline had run out of excuses to draw out the evening, she walked Connie to the door. By the time she returned to the kitchen, Churchwell, whom she'd called Luke all evening, had magicked the kitchen clean.

He stood near the windows, his gaze following Adeline's reflection in the wall of glass. "Do not. Ever. Invite that woman into my home again." He had a tumbler of something amber over ice in his hand.

"Oh? Why's that?" Adeline tilted her head. "Afraid she'll tell me something you don't want me to know?"

His expression turned glacial. "What you don't know would fill an ocean. And Connie will never tell you anything she has not calculated would benefit her."

Adeline replayed that back in her head. "Doesn't sound like there's a lot of trust between the two of you. Maybe you should find another assistant."

"My business in this tower is none of your concern. Stay out of it." He swirled the glass and brought it to his lips.

Adeline crossed her arms. "I've neglected to pass along a message. Didn't realize it was for you until tonight . . . when I learned your name was Luke."

Luke raised his eyes to meet hers in the window's reflection.

"Kai says to tell you he's served his sentence."

Luke spun from the window. "When?"

"The night he attacked me. He called you Luke, so I assume he's a friend of yours? Or was."

"You should be careful with your assumptions, Adeline."

Adeline pulled her blankets and pillows off the bed, dragged them into the dressing room, and rearranged them in a nest on the floor. She'd never been comfortable with the cameras in her bedroom and no longer cared if she violated her host's expectations or house rules, or whatever it was. She didn't plan to be there much longer. The one power cell remaining at her elbow had a little juice left in it. Would it be Churchwell she'd drain from when her last cell evaporated?

Her bedroom door was slightly ajar. The moment Churchwell's bedroom door clicked closed, she sat up. She'd seen Churchwell enter his office enough times to know he didn't keep it locked, just closed. She needed to open that door to create a calling path between his office and her dressing room. Closing her eyes, she visualized the door's handle. She pictured her hand pressing down on it. The sensation in her hand felt like the door had given way, but she couldn't be certain. There was only one way to find out. With her arm outstretched, she called his *Book of Runes*. The book flew past her shoulder, hit the wall, and landed in the nest of blankets. *Shit. It had worked!* She quickly stuffed the book under the covers.

Seconds later, Churchwell soft-stepped it down the hall. He entered her bedroom without a word, and slinked around until his gaze settled on her sitting cross-legged on the floor in the dressing room.

"I heard a thud," he said. "Everything okay?"

"Yeah. Called my phone. Used too much juice."

He gazed around the small space, checked behind the door. Didn't say a word about her new sleeping arrangements.

"Good night," he said, and crossed the bedroom floor, closing the door behind him.

She waited five minutes, expecting him to come charging back in to demand the book. When he didn't, she pulled the leather-bound volume out of the blankets and flipped it open.

L uke had blown Adeline's trust completely. Her hostility was a sheet of hardened ice under a fragile facade of politeness. At least she'd figured out the cameras. Luke wished he had the luxury of sleeping without Tanner's goons watching him. He couldn't scratch his balls without them knowing about it.

Her rant in the living room hadn't launched Tanner into orbit, which was a relief. Tanner must not have been bothered that she knew Kai's name. And he was probably delighted to know Adeline was now disgusted with Luke. At any rate, the guards didn't show up after her change of sleeping arrangements, so Tanner was probably still treating her as an asset. She wasn't in any danger. Not yet. But Luke sensed Adeline would make a run for it. He had to impress upon her how that was a bad decision.

When they arrived at her house the following morning, Adeline started up the steps. "You can meet me back here in an hour," she said.

"I need to speak with you. Inside."

"Something you can't say here?"

"I'd prefer not to, and inside the car wouldn't be wise."

She stopped her ascent and turned. "Tanner records you in the car? You ought to get another job."

"Another job is not an option. May we speak inside? Please."

She paused, keys in hand, as if considering his request. "I'll give you five minutes. Then you leave and wait for me outside. And, just so you know, I don't need magic to kick your ass out the door."

He nodded his agreement. She continued across the porch and opened the door. He followed but met resistance from the ward on the threshold. *Odd.* He'd been inside before. She dropped her keys on the hall table. "You may come in," she said over her shoulder, and the ward released him. She had to invite him in each time? Whoever had set the ward was a powerful witch. And smart. So why hadn't she enclosed the back stairs? Or, come to think of it, the porch?

In the kitchen, Adeline moved into her breakfast routine with the efficiency of a short-order cook.

"I'm sure you have questions," Luke said. "This is one of the few places I believe I can speak freely. Ask me anything you want."

"I don't have questions, Luke. Not any I'd trust you to answer honestly, in any case."

She pulled a cast-iron pan from the oven and set it on a burner.

He spoke to her back. "Kai is . . . was a friend of mine. We grew up together. He's from a wealthy family. Socializes with influential warlocks, royalty. Siphoning magic is something he does for entertainment. He was caught. Third offence. Might have gotten away with it, but he picked the wrong mark—someone who moved in the king's circles. Tanner came down hard on him, in part, to ingratiate himself with the king. Slapped a cuff on him."

"Don't you mean *you* slapped a cuff on him? Your friend. From childhood."

He ignored her jibes. "Tanner sentenced him to forfeit his magic."

"Ah, this is where I come in," Adeline said. She laid three strips of bacon in the pan.

"Normally, a cuff releases when the terms of the sentence are fulfilled. We were notified that Kai had served his sentence, but the cuff's conditions hadn't been met. Kai had somehow gotten around them. Tanner was furious. He charged me with finding him. A cuff's residual magic is detectable, but not for long. I was able to trace it here."

"You don't need to go on. I know the rest of the story. I'm living it." She cracked an egg on the lip of a bowl.

"I'm not sure you do. Kai will come back for the magic he left in you. He won't give up what he's spent a lifetime collecting. That's why he tried to track us."

"So what? I'm his piggy bank? He'll swagger up and withdraw what he deposited?"

"Yes. If he can."

"I don't suppose I have a say in this?" The egg took a more vigorous beating than required.

"No."

She dropped the fork and looked up at him. "So what's your job, Luke? Serving me up to your friend? Or are your loyalties with Tanner?"

"If Tanner gets his hands on your magic, he'll be even more dangerous."

"I'm unclear about why he hasn't just taken it already. It's not like I have an effective defence against warlocks."

"Kai locked his magic inside you. We don't know how, but I expect he's left a rune on you."

"Let me guess. Tanner wants you to remove the rune so he can drain me?"

"I doubt Kai will have made it that easy, but yes. That's Tanner's plan."

She narrowed her eyes. "Why are you telling me this?"

"Because you're upset with me. I don't want your anger to cause you to do something foolish—like ditching my protection. Kai is lurking."

"I'm confused. You don't want Tanner to get my magic, but you don't want Kai to get it either. Are you hoping to get it for yourself?"

"I'm a runecaster. I don't need Kai's magic. But if Tanner gets his hands on him, he'll use a runecast to compel Kai to produce the key. Once Tanner has the key to unlocking your magic, he will siphon every last drop of it, and then he'll kill Kai for defying him. And if he can't get his hands on your magic, he won't let you live. Tanner won't abide a witch possessing warlock magic. And if Kai prevails, Tanner will end me. He will see it as a betrayal. There are no winners here."

"Tanner is stronger than you."

"For the time being."

"How the hell did you get messed up with him?"

By underestimating him. Biggest mistake of his life. "I can keep you safe from Kai. He can't challenge me with his magic depleted. When he comes after you, and he will, I'll endeavour to convince him to leave you be and steer clear of Tanner."

"And if you can't?"

"Then none of us are safe."

Nineteen

"**M**om's here with me," Sarah said. "She was able to release the last fold in my memories. The headache is finally gone, thank the stars. Not everything has come back, but some of it has."

"How is your headache, angel?" their mother asked.

"Good for now. Churchwell was able to quell it. *Luke* Churchwell."

"Luke?" Sarah said. "As in '*Tell Luke that Kai has served his sentence*'?"

"Yup. Same one. And turns out I'm just a repository for Kai's magic. He's coming back for it. Unless Tanner can get it out of me before then."

Sarah and her mom listened while Adeline peeled off the layers of lies she'd been wrapped in. "I suppose the good news is Tanner won't kill me as long as he thinks he has a chance of getting his hands on the magic stuck inside me. And, for the time being, keeping me alive is in Luke's best interests."

Sarah's mother bristled. "The best chance of keeping you alive is to let one of them remove the magic from you," her mother said, her tone hardening. "Which one does it is of no consequence. It's the only way to guarantee the incompatible magic won't kill you."

Sarah sucked in a breath, waiting for the explosion on the other end of the line.

"How can you ask that of me? I finally have magic. Real magic. And you want me to toss it away?"

"It pains me to say it, but I must," her mother said, her tone softening again. "You're not thinking straight. I love you. I can't bear to lose you. You have to let the warlock's magic go."

There was a pause on Addie's end of the line. And then, "I hear you, and I love you, too. But I can't give this up. Not yet, anyway."

"Angel—"

"No. This is my decision. But if the magic makes me sick, you have my word that I'll let it go. Okay?"

"Hardly, but it seems you've made up your mind. I will hold you to your promise, though." Her mother's shoulders slouched.

"If you want to keep the magic, you have to find the rune that's protecting it before Luke does," Sarah said.

"I know. I've looked, believe me. But finding it won't be enough. I need to learn how to break it."

"No!" Her mother lurched toward the phone in Sarah's hand. "If the magic makes you sick and you've broken the lock, how will we get it out of you?"

"Maybe I was wrong about seeking out Warrick." Sarah offered her mother an apologetic smile.

"You weren't wrong," their mother said. "That man's nothing but trouble."

Sarah had to agree, though she'd always appreciated the handsome packaging. "True, but he's also a rebel. He might be the only warlock willing to shed light on that rune."

"Luke mentioned something that might be useful. He told me there were runes to prevent unwanted magic. I would bet unwanted magic includes siphoning. I've . . . borrowed . . . his *Book of Runes*. But finding the rune that prevents someone from siphoning my magic isn't going to be easy. The book is written in a language I can't read. It also depicts more than Odin's runes. There are symbols I've never seen before. Almost like hieroglyphs."

"Work quickly," her mother said. "You need to return that book before the runecaster notices it's missing. Warlocks are feral when it comes to protecting their precious runes."

"What about Carolyne? The archivist," Sarah said. "She'd have access to everything we know about runes."

"We can't trust anyone from the coven," their mother said. "Not until we know what happened."

"It's coming back to me," Sarah said. "More and more every day. Marcus said the same."

"Where is Marcus?" Adeline asked.

"At his dad's place in Halifax on the east coast. He's got access to a healer there."

"Interesting," their mother said, and Sarah realized she hadn't shared that with her yet. "I'd like to know if Damaras was behind his return to the coast."

"What are you thinking, Mom?" Adeline asked.

"Nothing, angel." She shot Sarah a knowing look. "Only that it's terribly inconvenient no one is close by to support you."

·)))●(((·

Adeline pushed open the kitchen door and started down the stairs with Charlie's tray in her hands. She paused and looked to the back garden. The grass and shrubs had what appeared to be a beautiful dusting of frost on them—which was impossible given the temperature was several degrees above freezing.

Luke lurked near the garage but stayed out of sight. She continued down the stairs. This morning's healthy addition to Charlie's breakfast was garlic-roasted cherry tomatoes. The scent of them wafting off the tray made her mouth water.

Charlie met her at the door. "Thank you," she said, as he opened it. He stuck his head out the door, glancing up and down the driveway.

"I don't see that Churchwell fella this morning."

"He'll be here. He's sitting for me again," she said, repeating the story she'd come up with to cover his presence. "Probably will be all week."

"He's an early riser, that one."

"He certainly is." Adeline set the tray down on the kitchen table.

"Will Jack and Olive be visiting this week?"

She swivelled her head up with a look of chagrin. "I forgot to mention. They're in Europe, visiting my mom."

"That's too bad. Well, great for them, of course. When will they be back?"

"I'm not sure. It was a last-minute trip. Mom was able to book them into a guest suite on the ship."

"That must be some cruise Morgan's on. I hope she's enjoying every minute of it."

"Can I get you anything else?"

"No. Thank you. This looks wonderful. Though I don't know about those shiny red things." He looked at her with a good-humoured raise of an eyebrow.

"They're full of lycopene. Fights cancer," she said, turning to leave. She heard the scrape of his chair as he settled in to eat.

She started up the steps, but halted and let out a squeak when a figure materialized one step up, facing her. Kai. She tripped and would have fallen, but he grabbed her wrist. He met her gaze, and there was a wild look in his rust-coloured eyes.

Her training kicked in. She stepped up and pushed her wrist into him, twisted her arm, and broke free. She turned to run down the staircase, but he once again materialized in front of her.

Right. Magical bastard. She punched her arm forward and splayed her fingers, reaching for warlock fire. But her mind was a blank. Nothing happened. He tilted his head, a quizzical look on his face. And then his body bent at the waist, and he was flying backwards through the air. He hit the driveway with a grunt, and Luke came into view.

She turned and raced for the safety of her wards.

Inside, she rushed to the kitchen window, but there was nothing to see. And when she opened it, she didn't hear sounds of a fight. She sniffed the air. The sweet, metallic scent of ozone came to her. Warlock magic. She'd never scented it before—barren witches couldn't—but Sarah had described it perfectly. One of the warlocks was containing the fight, hiding it from human ears.

She checked all the windows on that side of the house: the laundry room, the staircase landing, the closet. She moved to the front of the house and looked out the diamond pane of the door, then the front window. She saw nothing. Chirping birds and a lawnmower a few blocks over were the only sounds.

She examined her wrist where Kai had grabbed her. He'd gotten to her. Just like Luke had said. If Luke hadn't been there . . .

She shoved one of her living room armchairs against the outside wall, away from the windows, and sat in it, pulling her feet off the floor and wrapping her arms around her knees. The front door sat across the room diagonally to her right, the back door through the dining room to her left.

In a physical confrontation, muscle memory and years of training gave her the confidence to tackle anything. Anyone. But she had no magical muscle memory. Zero years of training with warlock magic. What had she been thinking? Compel a few pairs of dice, shoot fire once or twice, and she'd be able to take on a full-grown warlock?

She was an idiot.

It was a long time before a knock came at her front door. "Who is it?" she called, not moving from the chair.

"Luke. May I come in?"

It sounded like him, but she couldn't be sure. Warlocks could glamour as well as witches. "What's the password?"

"Penny."

"Luke may come in," she said to the ward. "No one else."

A moment later, Luke stood on the living room's threshold.

"What happened to Kai?" Adeline feared he'd killed him. The fall from the back stairs alone would have broken the back of anyone but a warlock.

"He's gone. For the moment."

"You weren't able to persuade him to stay away?" He shook his head. "So he's coming back?"

"I've no doubt."

"What's his plan?"

"It hasn't changed. He wants his magic back."

"Did you learn anything about what's locking it in place?"

"No. But Kai sensed that you care about Charlie. Your tenant is not safe here any longer. Kai will use him to get to you."

"Couldn't you stop him?" Her voice came out harsher than she'd intended.

"Not without killing him. And I'm not doing that."

"Can you shield Charlie? Make it so Kai can't see him? Can't get to him?"

He shook his head, almost mournful. "Not with the wards on the house in place."

"What about one of your guards? Could you station them here?"

"They work for Tanner. They wouldn't protect Charlie—they'd use him to lure Kai within reach."

"Do you not have anyone?" she said, letting out her frustration. "Not one person who's loyal to you?"

He gave the smallest shake of his head. "Not anymore."

Goddamn warlocks. She pulled out her phone and dialled her sister. She explained Kai's unwelcome visit and the situation with Charlie. "Do you trust Odette?" A principal spellcaster might be able to weave a protection spell for Charlie.

"Odette doesn't know you. Let me call her," Sarah said.

Five minutes later, Sarah called Adeline back. "She's in Cambridge, Massachusetts, with her family, recovering. I didn't know, but she's also been attacked."

Adeline hung up, wondering why the spellcaster had been targeted. She didn't have first-hand knowledge of Kai or his attack on Adeline.

"I can compel Charlie to stay in the house," Luke said. "He'll be safe from Kai inside the wards."

"He goes for a walk every morning at seven. Rain or shine."

"Then we'll be here at seven. I'll walk with him. We'll keep him safe until we can figure this out."

Adeline watched as Luke drew a rune on a coin. "I'll slide this under his door on the way out. It'll expire at 7:00 a.m. tomorrow. Are you ready to head back?"

"Tell me again why I shouldn't just stay here?"

"I won't stop you if you choose to stay. But if you leave the protection of your wards, you're vulnerable. Charlie's vulnerable. And if I return to the tower without you, Tanner will be on your doorstep."

Damn it. There was no escape. "I've got to make a phone call."

"I'll wait."

Adeline went up to her bedroom and closed the door. She sat cross-legged on her bed and dialled. "Hello, Warrick. It's Adeline."

TWENTY

L uke held the car door open for Adeline and remained vigilant. He didn't want to take any chances after the encounter with Kai.

Adeline asked Luke to stop by Jam Cafe in Kitsilano. It was a dead end. No one at the restaurant remembered who'd placed the order that had been delivered to Charlie on Friday. Whoever it was had paid in cash. That much was written on the receipt.

Luke had flitted in and out of Adeline's mind a few times since she'd first accompanied him to the tower. She still hadn't remembered the events in the clearing. It occurred to him that she and her sister might not even have had those memories. Both women had been held in some sort of witch spell by the other witches while their priestess negotiated with Tanner. And the confusion caused by the compressed memories made Adeline's mind harder to read. It wasn't the open book it had been before.

His thoughts turned to Kai. He'd been a busy little siphoner in the week and a half since he'd dumped his old magic into Adeline. But he was no match for Luke. During their encounter, other than pulling him away from Adeline and protecting himself, Luke hadn't deployed magic. It would have been unfair and cruel. Instead, their confrontation had been a war of words. Kai had spat venom at Luke, throwing out every horrible betrayal Luke had perpetrated since their failed coup. Luke tried to reason with him. If Kai could just get past his anger, he'd see that Luke wasn't the enemy. Tanner was. It had always been Tanner.

Luke would kill Tanner himself, but he couldn't with Tanner's chain around his neck. And he wouldn't risk anyone else doing it for him. The bastard had too many spies, too many people he'd coerced into loyalty. The chain kept Luke in line, and it wouldn't let him explain its purpose. So, to everyone on the outside, Luke was a traitor. Freely doing Tanner's bidding.

Luke couldn't hold Tanner off much longer. Tanner wanted the magic Adeline harboured, and Luke was running out of excuses. He'd spent the previous afternoon studying his *Book of Runes*, and had devised a runecast that would locate Adeline's rune. After he got a look at it, he'd be able to create another runecast to unlock it.

But until Tanner forced his hand, he wouldn't use it. Using it would spell the beginning of the end. Adeline would be alive, but she'd feel betrayed, and furious. Kai would also be alive, but he would never speak to Luke again. And Tanner would become impossible to kill.

Back in the tower, he and Adeline went their separate ways. He reported Kai's failed visit to Tanner, who scraped him for every detail. Eventually, he headed to the gym. Adeline was swimming laps in the pool. Front crawl one way, butterfly back. Her no-nonsense bathing suit was built for a workout, not posing. He admired her for not playing up that angle. She could, easily—she had the lean, toned body of an athlete. She glided smoothly through the water, her strokes graceful. She applied graceful strokes in her art as well, adding minute detail to the portraits that brought them to life. He found himself regretting that she would hate him when this was over.

In the suite, after he'd showered and changed, he helped himself to a juice and saw their lunches had been delivered. Adeline came out of her room dressed in workout gear.

"I'm out of power cells. May I have more?" She paused, her features pinched. "That came out a little more like Oliver Twist than I'd intended."

Luke laughed. "Of course you may." He pulled their plates from the fridge and left them on the counter, then headed back to his office. With the door locked behind him, he approached the gilded frame of a door-sized mirror mounted to the wall. He pressed a hidden button, and the framed mirror swung open. Luke stepped inside. Automatic lights came on. The vault pulsed with clear gelatinous globes the size of basketballs. Every shelf around the room and up the centre aisle held row after row of super-sized power cells. He selected one, pinched out six small discs, and applied them to his inner forearm. He then pinched out six more and set them on a tray.

Returning to the kitchen, he saw that Adeline had unwrapped their salads and set them on the table with cutlery. A serving of blackened salmon lay atop a bed of spinach dotted with candied walnuts and orange slices. He handed her the tray of power cells and took a seat.

"When I leave the tower, will I have access to these power packs?" she said, taking her seat. She lifted her fork.

He didn't dare meet her gaze. She well knew there was a good chance she'd not have her magic when she left. This conversation was for Tanner's benefit.

"I don't know," Luke said. "That'll be up to Lord Tanner."

"He's been generous, offering me this refuge, giving me so many of the power packs." She took a bite of salmon. "You said they were expensive."

"Very."

"Then me getting access to them after I leave is probably a moot point. I couldn't afford them. I've still got a mortgage."

"You're a witch. Why would you have a mortgage?"

"Not really a witch. Remember? And I have my pride. I've earned that house and everything in it. No magic involved."

Luke finished eating and excused himself at the sound of the intercom ringing in his office.

"It's Connie. Guards are on their way up. Another collection."

"Thank you." He took his finger off the button. Inhaled. Water running in the kitchen sink told him Adeline was occupied. He unlocked the vault and prepared the package. With it secured in a special carrier, he met the guards at the door and handed it over.

"Trouble?" Adeline asked, when he strolled back to the living room.

"No. Why do you ask?"

"I saw the guards. They don't usually come inside unless they're escorting someone."

"No trouble. Just collecting something for Lord Tanner. Are you up for another lesson?"

"If it's not too much bother, but I'd like to practise what I've learned first. Would you spot me?"

Luke agreed and rose to move the furniture, but she stopped him.

"Let me."

He nodded, giving her the room. He positioned himself with his back to the windows. He scented ozone like a coming storm as she drew the magic. She pushed out her hands, and the furniture moved, slowly at first. She was testing her strength. Smart not to use too much to start.

She checked her packs before continuing. With more experience, she'd learn to trust the feel of the pack in the crook of her elbow. And then he corrected himself. These sessions in the tower would likely be the only experiences with magic she'd ever have.

He watched as she compelled a plate and then, one by one, a dozen ping-pong balls, which she landed on the plate and balanced perfectly. And then she did something he didn't expect. One by one, the ping-pong balls disappeared, and so did the plate. She inhaled a self-satisfied breath.

"I didn't teach you that," he said.

"You didn't have to. Reverse engineering. I figured if I could visualize the objects appearing, I could also do the opposite."

"Impressive," he said, nodding his head. She was intuitive. She'd learn to use Kai's magic with or without him.

Adeline smiled, pleased with herself. She adjusted her feet, shoulder-width apart, and shook out her hands. After a long exhale, she closed her eyes. And then she disappeared.

Luke pushed off the window, alarmed. "Adeline?"

Her voice came from down the corridor to their bedrooms. "It worked."

He raced toward her room. She stood in her bedroom, giddy with excitement.

"What did you do?"

"Visualized myself somewhere else, and voilà. Here I am."

Luke pressed a hand to his forehead. Tanner would blow an artery. This was not foundational magic.

"Why do you look like I killed your puppy?" she said, and then alarm crossed her face. She yanked up her sleeve. "Whew. It's okay, there're two left. I didn't kill anything."

His phone rang. He exhaled. "I'll . . . have to get this," he said, and started for his office.

As he'd expected, it was Tanner.

"I'm on my way. Be in your office."

Whatever she'd done had stirred up a whirlwind in Luke. He'd disappeared out of her room at a trot. She guessed it was Tanner on the phone. He seemed to be the only one who ever called. She cringed. It was creepy how closely she was being monitored. What were they afraid of? It's not like she was using warlock fire. And even if she was, Luke was a runecaster. The most powerful of their kind. He could suppress any fire she might start, repair any damage.

She retreated to her dressing room to change.

The previous night, she'd returned Luke's book. Without interpretation, it was no use to her, and she didn't dare chance him discovering it missing. The rune designs were fascinating. They called to her creative side. She recognized Odin's twenty-four original runes—every witchling learned those. But there were dozens more besides. Individually, the runes were elegant in their simplicity, but they were designed to be combined, either overlapping or stacked atop one another. Each rune's addition and position complicated the design, made it more intricate, more complex. There were endless combinations.

Luke's shoulder markings came to mind as she stripped out of her clothes. With a flash of inspiration, she found a pen and drew a rune on her left forearm. She added another, mirroring it, and then another flipped upside down. She added flourishes until she ran out of forearm. Then she sat in her nest of bedding and doodled more runes on the tops of her feet, along the arch at the base of her toes. Satisfied with the design, she stretched her legs out and admired her work.

Churchwell would go apoplectic if he saw the designs. In her bathroom, she scrubbed the ink off her forearm. But she left the runes on her feet. No one would see those.

She walked to the kitchen and made herself a latte the hands-on way. No point in needlessly wasting her remaining power packs.

Raised voices, or rather one raised voice, floated down the hall from Luke's office. Her ears pricked up at the word *witch* slapped out like an insult. It wasn't Luke who'd said it. His softer voice filled in the spaces between what sounded like a solid dressing-down.

She took her mug to the sofa and pulled a cushion into her lap. Footsteps echoed in the hall. Whatever had gone down in Luke's office was headed her way. She tensed.

Luke emerged from the hall, and she noted that his demeanour had hardened. His jaw was set, his eyes narrowed. The stocky man walking ahead of Luke stopped in front of her. She set the pillow aside and stood.

"Hello, Adeline. I'm Lord Tanner."

"You look familiar. Have we met?" He wore a hand-stitched suit and a silk tie, as if he'd arrived on the heels of a power lunch.

"I understand your memories are impaired. I can help you recover them." He extended his arm. "Take my hand."

Adeline gazed at his hand then up to his face. "I have met you before." She had a flash of his hands on hers. It wasn't a pleasant memory.

"Yes, you have. Now, take my hand," he said again.

Memories of the man came in tiny flashes. Him kneeling beside her. Her lying on the grass. A red glow from his hands. Her instincts told her not to let him touch her. "I ..." She crossed her arms.

She glanced behind him. Luke's hands were moving, his fingers weaving magic. Her eyes widened. "No, don't do this," she said to him, pleading.

She tried to take a step back, but the sofa was in her way. And then Luke's magic hit. Her will left her. She cried out in her head, unable to utter a sound. A whispering breeze surrounded her, caressing her skin. It blew across the nape of her neck and into her scalp. The gentle wind touched every inch of her. And then it stopped.

"The rune is on her left foot," Luke said.

There was no rune on her left foot, other than her own handiwork. What was Luke up to?

Tanner put a hand on her shoulder and pushed her down to the sofa. She folded like a paper doll. He stood beside her and looked back to Luke. "Get her shoe off."

Luke approached with his emotions locked down tight. He crouched in front of her, undid her lace, then tipped her shoe off. He removed her ankle sock, and his hands stilled. He looked into her eyes, his own narrowed and questioning.

"What is that?" Tanner said, bending to see for himself. He rubbed his thumb over the mark and stared in disbelief at the smudge of ink. "She did that herself?"

"Must have," Luke said. "It's not my style. And it's too artistic to be Kai's work."

"Witches know some of our runes, but not those," Tanner said, straightening. "How did this happen?"

"I don't know."

"Find out. Read her mind."

Tanner strung the words together casually, as if requesting Luke scan through last week's news. A minor effort.

Inside her head, she shouted for him to get away from her.

Luke gazed to the floor and inhaled. He closed his eyes.

At the first sense of his probing, she shrieked again, though no sound came out. He flinched. The invasion of her mind was an assault, a violation. Anger raced through her veins like gasoline on fire. She fought the wave of panic that threatened. *Stop reacting. Centre yourself. Think.* Though unable to move, she could still visualize. She pictured herself in her living room, in the nearby bedroom. Nothing happened. She imagined a hailstorm, a tornado, to no effect. Luke's spell had snuffed out her magic.

Each of his probes felt like a defilement. She growled in her mind for him to get out of her head. He flipped his eyes open and met her gaze, surprise in his features. The probing stopped. *Had he heard her?*

"What is it?" Tanner said.

Luke stood. "She carries the will of someone else. Another witch. Adeline is unaware of it."

That couldn't be true. Surely she'd know if someone else was behind the wheel in her own head.

"What is this other witch's will?"

"Rune magic. The witch has compelled her to find the secret to our runes."

It had to be Damaras. She'd sent her into the wolves' den with a steak strapped to her head.

"And has she?"

"No. She has no access. You'd have seen it on the security cams if she did. But it does explain her unhealthy curiosity."

"Are you able to remove the witch's compulsion?"

"There's a risk. It's intertwined with her compressed memories. If I pull it out, the memories could come out with it."

"Do it. We can't let witches get their hands on rune magic."

Luke went down to his knees. Sorrow clouded his features. He rubbed his hands together then placed one on each side of her head.

Don't do this, Adeline said. A question lingered in his eyes. He had heard her?

I'm sorry, he said, and the words came to her mind, not her ears. And then darkness descended, consuming her.

TWENTY-ONE

"It's done," Luke said, adjusting Adeline's body so she lay more comfortably on the sofa.

"Get the rune off her foot," Tanner said, standing with his arms crossed. "I don't want it interfering with the removal of Kai's magic."

"She'll need to recover before you siphon her. You risk killing her otherwise."

"A dead witch is a good witch, as I like to say. Remove the rune."

Luke stood and pulled a photo from his pocket. He handed it to Tanner.

"What's this?"

"I found it at Adeline's. It was in her sketchbook. I think someone may have hired her to paint that portrait."

"Ophelia? The warlock queen? Impossible."

Luke shrugged, giving off the impression he didn't care one way or the other.

"Why are you just showing me this now?"

"You didn't let me finish my report before you left my office to find Adeline."

Tanner scrutinized Luke's face and then strode to the wall of windows and gazed out. The entire time, he flicked the photo against his palm. Tanner, Luke suspected, was considering if killing Adeline was worth the risk. She might be in the queen's favour. Perhaps even under her protection.

"How long until she recovers?" Tanner asked.

"Depends on how much damage I've done. I won't know until she wakes."

"I want a report as soon as you know."

Luke's violation of Adeline weighed heavily on his conscience. He didn't know for sure if she would remember what he'd done. He hoped not. The runecast he'd released on her had found dozens of runes. Her left forearm, both feet. As soon as Tanner had left, he'd moved his *Book of Runes* back to the safe. He'd only had it out to develop the new runecast. Had she somehow gotten her hands on the book without the cameras picking it up?

While she'd been unconscious, he'd placed fresh power cells on her arm. It was a small gesture, but one he hoped would prove he held no ill-will toward her.

Adeline didn't stir until after the sun set. She groaned and rubbed her temples. He'd been sitting in an armchair listening to an audiobook, and he removed his earbuds. "How are you feeling?"

Her eyes opened a crack. "My head's killing me. What did you do?"

"What do you remember?"

She turned her head. Her gaze landed on him like a punch. "What did you do?"

When he didn't answer, she pulled herself up and swung her legs to the floor. She cradled her head in her hands. "I'm going to be sick," she said, and clambered to her feet.

Luke rose to help her.

"Stay away from me," she said, holding up her hand.

She tripped her way down the hall to her room. Luke followed a step behind. She picked up her pace and ran across the bedroom, making it into her bathroom in time to retch into the toilet. Luke stood on the threshold. When Adeline finished retching, she lay across the toilet, not moving.

"Why are you still here?" she said.

"Can I get you something to settle your stomach?"

"You can get the hell out of my room. Shut the door behind you."

Luke compelled a sleeve of saltines and a bottle of ginger ale and left them in her dressing room.

That night, Luke lay in bed, his hands laced behind his head. In addition to the nonsensical runes Adeline had drawn, he'd found the rune Kai had left on her. But that wasn't foremost in his mind. The shock that Adeline could mind-talk hadn't left him since he'd heard her first scream. He and Kai had developed that very rare talent in childhood and had honed it over the years. But ever since Tanner had chained him, Luke hadn't been able to hear or speak with Kai that way.

But he'd heard Adeline. Had she heard him? Was there a weak link in Tanner's chain?

He closed his eyes and sent a thought to Adeline. *"I'm sorry. I had no choice."*

A minute passed, and then another. His hopes sank. He rolled over and punched his pillow.

"Stay out of my head."

He stilled. *"Adeline? Are you away from the cameras?"*

"I'm in the dressing room. How are you in my head?"

"You're not speaking out loud, are you?"

"No. What is this?"

"The best thing that's happened since I've been here." He tamped down his smile and inhaled several times to settle the elation that threatened to burst out of his chest. *"It's Kai's magic. You've accessed more of it. We called it mind-talking."*

"You and Kai?"

Luke had spent the earlier evening hours contemplating what he'd tell Adeline if he could. How much he could disclose without putting them in more danger. *"There is so much I need to tell you."*

Luke dressed and was in the kitchen nursing a coffee at 6:00 a.m. Without seeing Adeline's face when they'd mind-talked the night before, Luke couldn't truly gauge if she'd believed him. He'd been cautious about what he'd told her. She could turn on him, and he wouldn't blame her. But she also wanted to get back home, and the only way to do that was to convincingly pretend she hadn't remembered anything that would jeopardize Tanner's chances of getting his hands on Kai's magic.

She walked into the living room and spotted him. Then she pointedly ignored him and stormed into the kitchen. She made herself a latte and plopped down opposite him.

"How did you know a witch had planted something in my head?"

"I saw it when I probed your mind."

She became very still. Though he wasn't proud of it, he'd removed her memory of his mind-probing when he'd removed the witch's compulsion. He justified it as saving her the humiliation. But the truth was he didn't want her to hate him for invading her privacy.

Since then, everything had changed. She'd agreed to hear him out, to possibly help him. Telling her about the mind probing was a peace offering.

"You can get inside my mind?" She narrowed her eyes. "Good to know."

She looked away, shaking her head in disgust.

He deserved her ire. He'd earned it. Had he lost her?

A long few minutes later, she spoke again. "Did you see the witch who did it?"

Oxygen rushed into his lungs. She was still playing the game. "Sadly, no."

She cradled her cup, glaring at him. "Don't ever do that again. I don't care if it's for my own good or not. Stay out of my head."

That hadn't been part of their script. "I'm sorry. Please forgive me."

"I'll think about it." She blew across the top of her mug and tested the temperature with a small sip. "Lord Tanner wasn't upset, was he? About me having the witch's spell in my head?"

"No. He knows you were unaware of it."

She nodded, thoughtful now. "I'm glad. He's been good to me. He offered to help me remember, right?"

"Yes. Do you remember?"

She scrunched her face. "It's fuzzy. Did you draw a rune on my foot?"

He hesitated. "Yes. To help you remember. Did it work?"

"I don't think so. But my headache's back. Can you do your thing?"

"Sure." Standing, he walked around behind her, grateful for the opportunity to do something kind for her. "Close your eyes." He then formed the runes beside her head that would ease the pain.

"Thank you," she said, sighing as she reached for her phone. Alarm lit her face. "We have to go. We're going to be late." She jumped up and headed to the kitchen with her mug.

"We still have a half-hour," Luke said.

"No. It's eggs Benny day. That takes longer to make. Come on."

Luke glanced at the closest camera. A moment later, the shield fell. They'd done it.

Adeline assumed their performance had worked because the guard let them out. She didn't hear Luke in her head and didn't dare try mind-talking for fear she couldn't keep her body language out of the conversation.

Mind-talking. She'd never heard of such a thing. And, until a few minutes ago, she also hadn't known Luke could probe her mind. She'd have to find a rune to put an end to that as well as the siphoning.

She bounced a knee during the drive, unable to keep her nerves in check. She prayed Kai wasn't lurking outside Charlie's door. The minute Luke put the car in park, she was out of it. She strode past the front walk to glance down the driveway and pulled up short. Luke nearly walked into the back of her.

"What's that?"

Adeline smiled. "That is a '71 Harley-Davidson Super Glide." She sprinted down the driveway, glanced around the backyard, and found the side door to the garage ajar. She pulled it open.

Warrick turned when her shadow fell across the floor. "Hello, beautiful." His words came out in a purr that caressed her body. He'd removed the dust cover from her matching Harley and had a rag in his hand. His hair was a tousled mess, and he was covered in road dust and bug guts. She didn't care. She threw her arms around him and held tight.

"Whoa," he said, pulling her even closer. "You okay?"

"I am now," she said, her voice a whisper in his ear.

"As much as I'm enjoying this," Warrick said, "you should probably introduce me to your friend. He looks like he wants to eat me for breakfast."

She loosened her hold. "Thanks for coming." She turned to Luke, who blackened the doorway. "Luke Churchwell, meet Warrick Flynn. My ex-husband." She felt the tickle of Warrick's magic under his palm on the small of her back. She'd missed that.

"Ex-husband?" Luke said, sounding incredulous. "He's a warlock."

How did he know? Did warlocks have a sixth sense?

"You noticed," Warrick said, a mischievous grin on his face.

"You married . . . a warlock?" Luke said, looking from her to Warrick.

"Actually, I married a witch. She married a warlock," Warrick said, thoroughly enjoying himself.

"Best ten minutes of my life," Adeline said. She disentangled herself from Warrick and took his hand, dragging him toward the door. She shooed Luke out ahead of them.

They were nearly level with Charlie's door when it opened, and he stepped outside.

"Thought I heard a motorcycle," Charlie said, taking in the three of them. He addressed Warrick. "This yours?" His attention turned to the bike.

"Every inch of her," Warrick said, but he was looking at Adeline when he said it. He winked at her and dropped her hand. "The name's Warrick," he said, extending a hand to Charlie. Charlie admired the bike, and the two of them talked motorcycles like they were talking about pinup girls.

"Perhaps we can chat some more when I come back from my morning walk," Charlie said, patting Warrick's shoulder.

"How about I come with you? I could use some limbering up. Been on the bike for hours."

"I'll have breakfast ready for you both when you get back," Adeline said, and he and Warrick carried on down the driveway.

"Want to tell me what's going on?" Luke said, his voice bringing her around.

She walked toward the front of the house. "I invited him. He's here for Charlie."

"You sure about that?" Luke asked.

She turned back to him. "What's with the tone?"

He took a beat. "Sorry. You just . . . caught me by surprise."

They mounted the stairs, and Adeline unlocked the door and crossed the threshold. Luke hung back, knowing he couldn't cross, and that small hesitation made her feel like she'd regained a modicum of control in their very unbalanced relationship.

"You may come in," she said.

Luke stepped inside and started through the living room toward the solarium.

In the kitchen, she washed her hands and fell into her breakfast routine.

Luke was sizing up the backyard through the solarium's windows. He came to lean against the archway to the kitchen. "Tell me about Warrick. How'd you come to marry a warlock?"

"The short version? I was angry. We both were. Me about the not-really-a-witch thing. Him about his father's expectations. He was the dynamite. I was the detonator. It was a glorious explosion." She set a pot of water on the stove. "But after the satisfaction of blowing up our respective families' expectations, we realized that love wasn't going to be enough to overcome our differences."

"Is he the reason you know more about our runes than you should?"

"Why did you wait until this morning to tell me you could pry into my mind? You could have told me last night."

He glanced up, hesitating. A pained expression crossed his face. "Tanner needed to see some authenticity. Your reaction was convincing."

"Feeding me information like that makes me feel like your puppet. Don't do that. And stay out of my head. That's a hard line for me." It felt good to say it, not that she could stop him. She pulled the last of the cooked potatoes from the fridge. She'd have to boil a few more before she left for the tower.

"How long's he here for?" Luke said.

"As long as it takes."

"He just dropped everything and came running?"

She turned from the chopping board. "That's what friends do." She paused. That was cruel. "I'm sorry. I know friends are in short supply for you right now."

"How much does he know?"

"He knows that Kai attacked me and that he's trying to get his magic back. That you've been charged with protecting me. I'd tell him the rest if I could trust my memories."

"Have you remembered anything else after last night?"

"You mean after you ripped the witch's compulsion from me?"

"Would you rather Tanner have done it?"

She finished chopping the potatoes and set them aside. "I remembered that Damaras told me Lord Tanner could learn the identity of the warlock who'd attacked me. He just had to touch me. We were in the clearing. The last memory I have is waking on the ground. I looked up, and there was Tanner, his arm glowing red and vise-gripped to my hand. Just like when Kai burned me." She exhaled. "The rest is blank. Sarah may be able to fill it in. I'll talk to her before we leave."

Adeline finished the breakfast prep, making an extra serving for Warrick. Heavy paper ruffled from the solarium as Luke flipped through her sketchbook.

She was buttering the toast when footsteps sounded up the back staircase.

Warrick opened the door and stepped inside. "Charlie's home," he said, sniffing the air. "And that smells great."

"I made you a plate. Have a seat."

Luke appeared in the archway with a scowl on his face, his hands in his pockets.

She cut the toast and set it on a side plate. Toast was overkill when the egg came on an English muffin, but she knew Charlie kept a few jars of jam in his bar fridge and a toaster oven on the counter. If he didn't eat it now, he'd rewarm it later. She slid a fruit cup onto Charlie's tray and placed a plate in front of Warrick.

"I'll be back after I deliver Charlie's eggs."

"I'll watch your back," Luke said, holding the kitchen door open. Adeline picked up the tray and headed down the stairs.

When Luke had planted himself out of Charlie's line of sight, she tapped on Charlie's door.

"Warrick's an interesting fella," Charlie said, following her to his kitchen table. "How long ago was it you were married?"

"I was nineteen. Way too unstable to be getting married." She set his tray on the table. "But I'm glad we're still friends. You have anything exciting planned for today?"

"Nothing I'd call exciting, but I'll probably head to the Legion to chinwag with the lads at some point."

She wished him a good day, and Luke escorted her back up the stairs. "Any sign of Kai?" she asked.

"No. But if he's lurking, he'll have seen that Charlie won't be an easy target."

Adeline nodded, but she wouldn't relax about Charlie's safety until the threat of Kai was neutralized.

Warrick had finished his plate and turned sideways in his chair, his long legs stretched out in front of him. He toyed with his coffee cup on the table. "Thanks, babe. That hit the spot." He upended his coffee mug and stood. "I need a shower. See you in twenty." He loped down the hall and took the stairs two at a time to the top floor.

Luke was back in the archway. "Warrick crossed your wards without an invitation."

Adeline pulled three potatoes from the bin under the sink. "Is that why you were scowling earlier?" She scrubbed them and put them in a pot to boil.

"That wasn't a scowl. That was me not trusting your ex."

"You just met him. You don't know enough about him to mistrust him."

"You'd be surprised how much I've garnered. He's pretty transparent."

"He's a good man."

"I'll reserve judgment. How'd he cross your wards without an invite?"

"He has a standing invitation."

After Adeline explained that Warrick could come and go as he pleased, Luke skulked off to the solarium. As she tucked the Tupperware dish with the cooked potatoes into the fridge, she heard Warrick coming down the stairs. The three of them converged in the living room. Luke took a post by the front window. Warrick relaxed in a chair, and she sat on the edge of the sofa.

Adeline studied the two men. Luke: brooding, sleek, cunning. Warrick: relaxed, rugged, cagey. How their magics compared, she didn't know. A runecaster was powerful, but Warrick? He'd never played the power game, at least not around her. It had never been important to either of them. Back then.

"Tell me again," Warrick said, addressing Adeline. "I want to know every detail about the warlock's attack. From the beginning."

Adeline took a breath and dove in, adding names to the Stonewater coven players who were involved in the aftermath and the other witches whose memories had been compromised. And finally she told him about the witch's will that had been planted inside her.

"Damaras is Princess Dumbass?" Warrick said.

Adeline smiled, remembering how thoroughly she'd skewered the woman's very existence when they were married.

"And Moonmere's coven has a warlock stone. Interesting." Warrick turned to Luke. "How dangerous is Kai?"

Luke's arms were crossed, his expression unreadable. "He's clever, wealthy, has powerful connections. He's also the best siphon I've ever met. And now he's enraged and motivated. I'd say he's very dangerous."

Twenty-Two

Luke had chosen Kai to join his rebellion, to be his right hand, for those very reasons. Though back then, the anger and motivation they shared had been directed at Tanner.

Warrick looked to Adeline. "I know how you felt about magic before. What about now? You want to keep it or not?"

It was inconceivable to Luke that anyone would voluntarily give up their magic.

"Kai had no thought for my life when he contaminated me with his magic. He could have killed me. I'm keeping it."

"Despite the risks of incompatible magic?" Warrick said.

"I know the signs now," Adeline said, shooting a grateful smile at Luke. "I'll be vigilant. Sarah will be too when she gets back."

Warrick studied her, nodding. "Okay. Then we've got work to do." He addressed Luke. "You're the runecaster. How do we make this happen?"

"The situation is more complicated than that," Luke said. He explained the no-win predicament he faced that would leave either Kai, Adeline, or him dead.

After the telling, confusion clouded Warrick's face. "There's no dilemma here. The solution is clear. Tanner's got to go. Weave a protection rune for Adeline and explain carefully to Kai that he's forfeited his magic."

"Luke can't kill Tanner, and he can't talk about the revolt he started or the underlying reasons for it," Adeline said.

"Back up," Warrick said. "You staged a revolt. What the hell did Tanner ever do to you?"

Luke pushed his voice into Adeline's mind. She repeated what he said.

"Tanner inserted his loyalists into every warlock organization in his territory. Made deals that enriched him and his cronies. Tithed lower-ranking warlocks into poverty. Refused to approve magical training to off-spring of warlocks who held different views than him. The powerful were getting more powerful, the weak weaker. Need I go on? Need he go on, I mean," Adeline said.

Warrick glanced between Luke and Adeline. Held up a hand. "You tried to unseat him, and you failed," Warrick said. "Now Tanner's wiping his ass with you. Do I have that right?" A snarl formed on his lip.

Luke uncrossed his arms. His opinion of the swaggering prick dropped another notch.

"Why the hell not just kill you and be done with it?" Warrick asked.

"He finds me useful," Luke said. "He also enjoys tormenting me."

Adeline told Warrick about Luke's chain, which Tanner could use to dampen Luke's magic. "He can't talk about what the chain does," Adeline said, explaining that it also tracked his location.

Luke was grateful she didn't mention his role as Tanner's enforcer, or the cuffs.

"If Luke can't tell anyone about the failed coup or his chain, how do you know?"

"Kai could mind-talk with Luke. I've accessed that part of Kai's magic."

Alarm crossed Warrick's features as he shifted his attention to Luke. "Tanner knows this?"

Luke shook his head. "I don't think so. There was always more value in keeping it secret, so Kai and I kept it to ourselves. In the tower, Kai's magic is suppressed. We haven't used it since I've been there."

Warrick rubbed a tatted knuckle against his lips. "If Tanner is keeping you on a short leash, why does he allow you to come here?" he said. "What if he's using that chain to listen to everything you say?"

"I tested it. Right here. Told Adeline what Tanner was up to. If he'd heard that, I wouldn't be here."

Adeline shot him a worried look. "Could you not find a less lethal way to test it? I'd really prefer you don't die on me right now."

Luke quirked an eyebrow. *Right now?* "Thank you for clarifying."

"What I mean—"

"He knows what you mean," Warrick said, standing. "Mind if I have a look at that?" He indicated Luke's chain.

Luke lifted his chin, wary, then nodded his assent and opened his collar. He flicked his fingers, and a small ball of undulating red light appeared in his hand.

Warrick eyed the bright ball. "Afraid?"

The arrogant bastard smiled. Putting on a show for Adeline, without doubt. Luke kept his eyes narrowed. He'd take prepared and alive over proud and dead any day.

Warrick approached, and his eyes slid from Luke's to the chain. He pulled Luke's collar and studied the chain, moving in a full circle around him. Wisely, he didn't touch it.

"I know a jeweller who may be able to remove it."

"A jeweller?" Luke's opinion of Adeline's ex dropped another notch. He extinguished his energy ball.

"A special kind of jeweller," Warrick said, in a derisive tone. "But it'll cost you. She doesn't come cheap."

"Ballpark?" Luke asked.

"It won't be money." He headed back to his seat but sidetracked to the sofa to address Adeline. "I don't see the iridescence in the chain that you mentioned earlier."

"No?" Adeline said. "I can see it from here."

"Huh. You sure you're feeling okay? No symptoms?" Warrick said.

"No. Why?"

"That fern in the hallway. Have you looked at it lately?"

Adeline shot to her feet. "Oh no." With a pained expression on her face, she scooted out of the living room.

Luke poked his head down the hall.

"There's nothing wrong with the fern," she said, her voice loud enough for Warrick to hear. She poked a finger into the soil. "It's not even wilted."

"Is it glowing?"

Adeline's head came up. Her features tensed.

Luke shot a concerned glance at Warrick. Only witches saw the halo glow of living things. If her witch powers were developing, she was in trouble.

She drifted back to Luke, her eyes on his chain, and then she stepped around him and opened her front door, sweeping her head in a slow arc.

The door closed. Adeline returned to the living room.

"I take it that's a yes," Warrick said.

Adeline nodded.

"You're certain you aren't running a fever?" Luke said. "No muscle ache or nausea?"

She shook her head. "I feel perfectly healthy."

"Interesting," Warrick said. "Maybe it's a quirk of your unique physiology." He turned his attention to Luke. "You realize what this glow means? Your chain was made with witch magic. It appears Lord Tanner is keeping company with the enemy." Warrick glanced at Adeline with a smirk on his face. "Scandalous."

"Unless the witch high council's rules have changed, witches are forbidden from meddling in warlock affairs," Adeline said. "I wonder if your chain meets the bar."

Luke returned his gaze to the window. His chain had been made with witch magic? That intel could change the political dynamic substantially.

"You still have faith in your jeweller?" Luke asked.

"If she can't spring it, no one can."

Luke turned. "How soon can she get here?"

"I'll have to track her down," Warrick said. "If she can get it off, what's your plan?"

Luke had spent three years working on just that. But Adeline's involvement complicated things. He looked at Adeline and spoke to her mind. *I can't speak about what the chain does. Please tell Warrick that Tanner will be notified the moment the chain releases. When that happens, he'll ramp up his security. I won't be able to get near Tanner to take him out.*

Adeline nodded and repeated what Luke had said.

Warrick looked to Luke with disgust. "You want someone else to do your dirty work?"

Luke inhaled pointedly. "No, that is not what I'm suggesting. But Kai's co-operation is critical. He's the only one I know with the connections to bring Tanner, the jeweller, and me together without raising a red flag. A reception, perhaps, or an auction." And when the chain was removed, Luke wanted Kai by his side. Kai had been motivated once to take out Tanner. He could be motivated again.

"But he won't help you, because you're protecting me," Adeline said.

"Yes. And he's not going to stop going after you until I can convince him to stand down."

"You already tried to reason with him once," Adeline said.

"I know. But that was before I found the locking rune he left on you."

"What?" Adeline shifted in her seat. "When?"

"The runecast I used in the tower. It found the faded doodles you'd scrubbed off your arm, the ones on your feet, and his. In your right eye."

"And you waited until now to tell me?" Adeline said.

"Because I can't unlock it," Luke said. "I can only break it. And that would blind you. That's why Kai put it there."

"Bastard!" Warrick said.

Adeline dropped to the sofa, looking like someone had let all the air out of her.

"When Kai learns I've located his locking rune, he'll come around because he knows a runecaster can break it. If I were to do that, it would leave his magic vulnerable for anyone to siphon out of her."

"Kai knows Tanner wants her magic?" Warrick asked.

"Of course he knows. Vengeance is one of Tanner's core values, and Kai embarrassed him when he circumvented his cuff. I need to draw Kai out. Talk with him."

"What's to prevent Tanner from locking Adeline in the tower until the rune is found and disabled?" Warrick asked.

"Stonewater coven's witches. Tanner won't risk the penalty he'd incur if he hurt Adeline while she's under his protection, so he'll keep trying to find the rune and unlock it." He turned to Adeline. "I was able to hold him off until you're recovered from removing the witch's will. But he's going to attempt another siphon soon."

"It won't work though, right?" Adeline said. "Tanner doesn't know where the rune is, does he?"

"Not yet. I can buy us more time. But if I don't soon tell him where the locking rune is, Tanner will assume I'm stalling to give Kai time to reclaim it. He'll bring in his own runecaster to find it. And when Tanner learns it can't be unlocked, he won't hesitate to break it."

"And blind me," Adeline said, expressionless.

"Then it's a good thing Adeline is in the care of a runecaster," Warrick said. "A runeglyph would give her protection from siphoning, would it not?"

Luke pressed his lips together. He'd considered it. "It's dangerous," Luke said, speaking to Warrick. "If she develops incompatible witch magic, it could prevent a binder from getting in to fix it. And the mark could be fatal for a witch. It's never been done."

"What's a runeglyph?" Adeline said.

"A unique mark etched onto your skin to protect you from siphoning," Luke said. "Unlike a tattoo, it's permanent. There is no way to remove it."

"Is that the mark across your shoulders?" Adeline asked. Luke nodded. "And runecasters make these?"

"I can create a design, yes," Luke said. "But I've never marked a witch before. And if I do, Tanner will eventually find out. If Tanner can't siphon you, he'll kill you."

"And we're back where we started," Warrick said. "Tanner needs to stop breathing. Your chain won't let you kill him. Adeline can't challenge him magically, and the tower is impenetrable."

"We're not there yet," Luke said. "As long as Tanner thinks he can retrieve Kai's magic, Adeline is safe."

"Speaking for Adeline," said Adeline, "I'm not comfy waiting for Tanner to lose patience. Every minute in that tower, my life is in more danger. I've never had witch tells. Ever. I can't imagine that's going to change. I'm willing to risk it. How long will it take you to design a runeglyph?"

"If I have access to my research material? A few days. But I can't design it in the tower. Tanner will recognize it as a runeglyph."

"Putting aside the uncertainty of a timely runeglyph," Warrick said, shooting Luke a scowl, "you're right about being in danger. You have to learn how to use Kai's magic to defend yourself."

Adeline crossed her arms. "How about we start by calling it my magic?"

Luke resigned himself. It was entirely his fault that Adeline had ended up in this position. Kai would never have parked his magic in her if it wasn't for the cuff. And Kai wouldn't have been sentenced to a cuff if he'd committed the same crime in anyone else's jurisdiction. The harsh treatment was Tanner's attempt to curry favour with the king. It also ensured Luke was irrevocably tainted and stripped of allies and friends alike.

Kai didn't deserve that. Adeline didn't either. Luke was the one who deserved it. He'd started the revolt, recruited the soldiers. It had been his plan. And it had failed. He had failed. But he could make amends. He could help Adeline wield Kai's magic.

"Warrick makes a good point," Luke said. "I don't know the full extent of the magic you harbour, but you haven't learned nearly enough to protect yourself. We've got some time right now. What do you say?"

"Not here," Warrick said. "She'll drain Charlie."

"I'll let her tap me," Luke said. To Adeline, he communicated silently, *Lord Tanner wouldn't approve of Warrick learning about our power packs. He hasn't been vetted. Let's not add that complication.*

"I'm game. Show me how," Adeline said. Warrick parked his butt on the living room's front windowsill.

Luke walked her through how to intentionally link to him as a power source. When she felt the connection, her face lit up. With a mild sense of satisfaction, Luke noted Warrick crossing his arms. Served him right. He could have been the one to make the power offer, but Luke had beat him to it.

After he let Adeline get a good sense of how the process worked, he cut her off. *Use your power packs. Without looking, how many do you have left?* Luke asked.

All of them, Adeline said.

Tell me if you deplete the last one, and we'll stop.

She gave a small nod, and he began. He stalked her, a panther on the prowl. She kept her front to him as he circled her beyond striking distance. "What's the first thing you do when confronted by an enemy?" he asked.

"Assess intent," she said. "Avoid or deflect if possible. Engage only if there are no other options."

"If a warlock confronts you, they're already engaged," he said, still creeping around her at arm's length.

He circled for another rotation then stopped and took a step toward her. She backed up. He dematerialized and re-formed behind her. Before she sensed what he'd done, he had an arm around her throat. She reacted on instinct, driving an elbow backwards. But her elbow hit a solid force, sending a shockwave of pain up her arm. She spun around.

He retreated. "That's armour," he said. "It's a warlock's most important defence. The stronger the warlock, the stronger the armour. Shall we give it a go?"

He taught her how to use her hands to direct the power coming out of her core and down her arms. How to mould the power to cover her body in a flexible wrap that moved with her.

Adeline's smile broadened when Luke tested her armour with a punch. She'd staggered back a step but reported that he hadn't hurt her.

Luke grimaced as he shook out his hand. "That's good. It's also strong enough to prevent absorption of minor magic. Never warlock stone. But it'll allow you to step through a minor runecast. In time you'll be able to strengthen the armour to deflect knives and other projectiles. Not bullets."

"You'll also need to know how to throw up a shield," Warrick said. "A shield will protect you against an elemental attack—or allow you to protect someone or something else."

Luke resented the way Warrick was taking over the lesson, but he graciously stepped aside.

Warrick showed her how to form a net of magic, much like snapping sand out of a beach towel. But when she began stretching out the shield, the wards made their presence known.

"We'll have to go somewhere else to get you fully trained," Warrick said.

"That's enough for today," Luke said.

"But I haven't even broken a sweat," Adeline said. "Let's do some more. I know of a clearing out by the university."

Check your gel packs.

Adeline bent her elbow, and her eyes widened. *Shit, they're gone.*

"It'll have to wait until tomorrow," Luke said. "We're already late returning."

Adeline walked to the hall and shot a worried glance toward the kitchen.

It's okay, Luke said. *You didn't kill anything. I let you drain my gel packs. But we're done for today. Any more practice and you'll be tapping into Charlie.*

I'm sorry. I didn't realize.

You'll get the hang of it. We've got to go.

"I hate the thought of going back there," Adeline said, returning to the living room.

Warrick wrapped his arms around her, mumbling something in her ear. He was taking advantage of her vulnerability. Making himself at home. Luke needed her focused, not distracted by an ex whose moves suggested he wanted to get her into bed.

"Take care of Charlie," she said to him. "He's going to the Legion sometime today."

"I'll stick to him like a tattoo," Warrick said, and hugged her again.

Luke's phone vibrated. He cleared his throat. "Tanner just texted. We have to go."

TWENTY-THREE

Something about seeing Warrick stirred unrest in Adeline. It wasn't that she didn't want to see him naked and in her bed; she most certainly did. But she wanted her life back. Her uncomplicated life. The one where she sketched and painted portraits, didn't worry about Charlie's safety, and could have Jack and Olive over to visit. The one where Warrick stayed a few nights, not to protect Charlie but to spend quality time with her.

She didn't want the chaos that surrounded Luke Churchwell. As for the magic . . . well, she'd take the magic. It was a fun and oddly creative outlet she wanted to explore. She had absorbed Luke's lessons with a sense of awe. Linking her magic to a power source freed her. While he'd let her, she'd conducted his power like she was the baton and he the orchestra, drawing that first trickle out of him and building it to a steady stream. His power, like heat, rose and cooled inside her, guided by the graceful movement of his hands on hers. Without anger and pain driving it, her magic was free to flow in harmonious chords, a beautiful song. Power surged at her command, and she loved it.

She couldn't wait to do it again tomorrow.

On the short walk from her house to the car, Luke reminded her not to reveal her knowledge of the warlocks' power packs to Warrick. "We can't risk Tanner tracing a leak of that information back to us," Luke said.

"Do you have more power packs on you?" she said.

"I keep an emergency stash in the glovebox. Help yourself."

During the drive to the tower, she shored up her resilience. Until Luke came through with the protective runeglyph, she would have to play a pawn in Tanner's chess game. Her frustration eased somewhat when she imagined herself punching him in the windpipe and kicking his knee into an unnatural position.

She'd subdued her anger by the time they'd reached the elevator, but when the doors swished open at the top, her irritation surfaced again.

"Tanner's here," Luke said.

There were two guards at the door, not one. "Can't wait," Adeline said, the note of sarcasm echoing.

Luke inhaled sharply.

"...to show him what I've learned," she said, desperate to recover. It was easy to forget that every word out of her mouth was being recorded. One of the guards opened the door, and Adeline walked ahead.

After she'd cleared the vestibule, Luke's office door clicked open. Tanner appeared, a solemn smile in place.

Adeline stopped. "Hi," she said.

He tilted his head. "Adeline."

"I'm sorry," Adeline said. "About the compulsion spell. I didn't know. They shouldn't have done that."

"Indeed," Tanner said. "How are you feeling?"

"Tired. I fell asleep at the house today." It was perhaps a futile attempt, but Luke said Tanner would be reluctant to siphon her until she recovered from the removal of the witch's will. She had to try. "Don't know what's gotten into me. I'm usually stronger than this."

Tanner nodded a benevolent blessing on her weakened state. "Luke? May I have a word?" He stepped back into Luke's office. Luke didn't even glance in her direction as he followed Tanner inside.

Adeline stared at the closed door, and then at the guards, who didn't scurry away like they usually did. "Hey," she said, with an awkward wave. She turned and headed to her dressing room.

Making it through another night felt like an impossible task. She had no idea what Tanner and Luke were discussing. For all she knew, Tanner could be ordering him to throw another runecast at her. To find the locking rune, to unlock it or break it, to drain her, to kill her. How could she possibly protect herself?

Fire, unbidden, shot from her fingertips. She stifled a squeal. Setting Tanner's building on fire would not help her cause. Her thoughts turned to the ball of energy Luke had formed. Knowing how to do that would be useful.

But she couldn't count wholly on magic until she could wield it with more than a passing level of skill. Her advantage would have to come from her martial arts training, at least for now. Warlocks wouldn't expect a physical defence. She stretched and moved into a honed tai chi routine that settled her mind.

It was during that routine that another thought struck her. She straightened. Tanner didn't consider her a magical threat. She'd not hit any resistance using magic in the tower.

Could it be that simple? Maybe she already had everything she needed to defend herself. Closing her eyes, she compelled a collapsible bo staff. When it landed in her palm, she laughed out loud. Then she compelled a baton. And then a hunting knife. She considered compelling a gun, but she'd never fired a weapon. Inexperience with a deadly tool wasn't worth the risk. She nixed the gun idea and threw the other weapons into her tote. From now on, she'd leave her dressing and bedroom doors ajar, giving her a barrier-free path to compel the weapons at any time, with no need to magic a door open first.

With a renewed sense of independence, and the six new power packs on her arm from Luke's glovebox, she returned to the living room. Down the hall, Luke's office door remained closed.

Flopping on the sofa, she played with her magic. She opened a kitchen cupboard and called out a glass, levitating it beneath the water dispenser on the fridge door before activating the water. When she gauged the glass was full, she called it to her, marvelling that she'd managed it. Concentrating, she opened her hand and let her magic move the glass to the coffee table. A smile crossed her lips. This unexpected gift of magic made her feel whole, something she hadn't felt in a very long time.

She thought back to her childhood lessons, and the elemental magic she'd learned in her studies before . . . She cut off the thought. That was the past. She had to stop letting it have power over her future. The magic that had once been out of reach was hers now.

Witches and warlocks both could manipulate the elements. Was warlock magic similar to the lessons she'd learned?

She reached her hand out and called the water. The water came to her. Without the glass as its vessel. It flowed through the air and rested above her hand like a blob of mercury. Her magic held it there. Her eyes widened, and a sense of wonder came over her. She swirled her finger in a lazy circle and the water formed a funnel, twirling in mid-air. This was the sort of magic she'd seen elemental water witches do. She flicked her fingers outward. The water burst into a million droplets and hovered in the air like rain suspended.

With a downward push of her hand, the rain fell. It splashed on the table and soaked into the carpet. Droplets beaded on the leather sofa. Raising both hands, she called it back up, watching in awe as the water pulled itself out of the carpet and up from the coffee table, re-forming in raindrops. With a twist of her wrist, she sent the drops back to the glass. She reached down to touch the carpet. It was dry.

If she could control water, could she also control the other elements? She blew a breath into her hand and released it toward the water glass. The surface of the water rippled. Which meant she could also knock the glass over if she pushed enough will into it. Air element's box got a big check mark.

She compelled a small pot of soil and a bean seed, pushed the seed into the soil, and called water from the glass to moisten it. With her hand above the soil and her thumb and fingertips touching, she pulled upward, prodding the bean to sprout. The surface of the soil didn't move. She closed her eyes and concentrated, gently pulling with her hand. When she opened her eyes, she was rewarded with the sight of a crooked bean head tenting the soil. Further pulls grew the sprout an inch. At two inches, it straightened out.

She sent the pot to rest by the water glass and sat back. The earth box also got a big check mark. The fire box was already ticked. Earth, air, fire, water. The elements were at her disposal.

Awestruck, she sat back. Years of being denied elemental magic had been swept away in minutes. Her imagination swam with new possibilities.

It wasn't until she fully relaxed, letting her head fall back against the sofa, that she caught sight of a camera—and realized what she'd done. Damn. In the rush of excitement, she'd exposed her new magical potential to Tanner. She cursed her oversight and prayed Tanner would recognize the magic she'd displayed as juvenile, a danger only to carpets and furniture. It was no threat. She couldn't wield it like a weapon. Not yet.

As her thoughts turned to defending herself, an idea formed. A ridiculously simple idea. She visualized herself across the room, and then there she was. Unbelievable. She could visualize herself away from any threat, be it from Tanner or Kai. Why hadn't she realized that before now?

Luke had said the only way in or out of the suite was through the guarded door. Could she visualize herself on the other side of the door? On her front porch? Maybe she wasn't trapped after all.

She closed her eyes and visualized herself outside the suite, in the hall near the elevator. She felt forward movement moments before pain burst across her forehead. She'd hit the inside of the door hard, face first, and dropped in a heap, arms and legs akimbo. Her vision narrowed. The wind had been knocked out of her. She couldn't catch her breath.

A voice cut through the pain. Luke. Her vision swam. She sensed herself being lifted, moved. Another voice. "Set her here."

A damp cloth was pressed to her forehead. Luke's voice sounded in a murmur, and then warmth infused her. He was healing her.

When the nausea passed, she opened her eyes. Luke stood behind the sofa. Tanner sat opposite.

"What were you trying to do?" Luke said, his voice unexpectedly cold. "Knock yourself out?"

She didn't have the energy to give him a dirty look. "I was practising visualization. Thought I'd try transporting myself into the hall. It feels like I hit the door at full velocity."

"This suite is shielded," Tanner said. "No one gets in or out without going through that door."

"Luke mentioned that," Adeline said, gingerly sitting upright. She caught the damp rag as it fell from her forehead. It was covered in blood. "It's why I aimed for the door. I must have missed and hit the shield."

"The guard has to let you out," Tanner said. "It's for your own safety."

She felt woozy and steadied her swimming head with her arms planted on either side of her hips. "I get why a guard would have to let someone in, but out?"

"You only have to knock," Tanner said. "They'll open the door."

"What if they're away from their station and a fire breaks out? Or someone gets in through an outside window? How am I supposed to escape?"

"That's not going to happen," Tanner said. "As I said, the suite is shielded. You're perfectly safe here."

She inhaled a ragged breath. "I think it's time I went home. Thank you for being a gracious host."

"Kai is still out there," Tanner said. "You're safer here, and I did promise refuge to your priestess."

"You've fulfilled your promise. Thank you again. I'll explain my decision to Damaras. And if I see Kai again, I'll visualize myself away from him."

"It's safer for you here."

"I'm sure it is. And I appreciate all you've done for me. But I feel trapped. I can't stay." She stood and abruptly sat back down for fear she'd fall. Her head wasn't co-operating with her planned exit.

"You're not well enough to leave," Tanner said. "And that's my fault. I should have explained about the shield."

"By the time I've packed my belongings, I'll be well enough to go."

"I must insist you stay," Lord Tanner said.

Adeline pinched the bridge of her nose. "Then I must insist you alter your shield so I can visualize out of here if I need to. Otherwise, I'm going home."

Lord Tanner rose in a huff and turned his back to them. With his hands on his hips, he wagged his head back and forth. "That's a mistake, but if it's the only way to keep you here—to keep my word to priestess Damaras—then, against my better judgment, I'll do it."

"You will?" His response stunned her. "All right. Then I'll stay. If you'll excuse me, I think I'll go lie down." Luke escorted her to the bedroom, where she collapsed on the bed and drifted off.

It was dusk when she woke again. Her head pounded, and she still felt woozy. She sent a silent question to Luke. *Is Tanner still here?*

He left hours ago.

Did he alter the shield?

Said he did. I have no way of checking.

Are you able to make this dizziness go away?

Call my name. I'll come to you.

"Luke? You out there?" she called.

A moment later, he appeared in her doorway.

She hadn't arisen for fear the vertical wouldn't last. "Can you do that thing that makes my head stop aching?"

He approached the bed and sat close to her. "Close your eyes."

The warmth of Luke's magic chased the pain away. As the warmth moved down her throat, she opened her eyes. His fingers flittered in a complicated dance as he worked down her chest and over her stomach. The queasiness faded.

"Are runecasters healers as well?"

"Runes are the foundation for all higher warlock magic."

"And you can't teach me about them?"

"Before a runecaster ever begins training, we must swear a blood oath to never share the secrets of the runes."

"Blood oath?"

"It's an acknowledgement that we forfeit our life if we break the oath."

"Harsh," Adeline said. Her arm lay across her stomach. Luke brushed his fingers from her elbow to her fingertips.

Warrick still has feelings for you.

Our relationship is...complicated.

Do you love him?

I love the idea of him. I always have. But the reality is more difficult.

You trust him?

With my life. Why are you asking?

If his jeweller makes a mistake, you will need to count on him to keep you safe.

Adeline's eyes widened. *Why? What will happen?*

Luke straightened. A smile settled in place. "Are you feeling better?"

A chill went through her. Luke's chain was a cuff.

Twenty-Four

Sarah thanked the Uber driver and dragged her suitcase and her tired butt out of his car. She stood at the foot of the driveway and stared up at the darkened windows of Adeline's house. She was probably still asleep in Luke's suite at the tower.

She squinted up toward the garage. Was that Warrick's bike? It looked like Adeline had followed through with calling him. It also explained why she'd gotten only a text from Adeline yesterday. She hadn't *run out of time* to call Sarah, she'd gotten busy with her ex. Sarah smiled, a tiny bit envious.

She let herself in. The house was quiet. She tiptoed to the sofa and lay down. If she was very lucky, she'd get another hour or so of sleep before anyone stirred. She conjured a soft blanket and fell asleep.

Footsteps coming down the stairs roused her. The descent paused before continuing. She sat up just as Warrick came in.

"Sarah? I wondered whose suitcase that was."

He hadn't changed one wink. Still looked like trouble. Cocky smile, a twinkle in his eye.

"Warrick." She stood and folded into his open arms, accepting his welcoming hug.

He held her at arm's length. "Look at you. You're all grown up."

"It happens to everyone except you, apparently. You haven't aged a day." She stepped away with a yawn and straightened her clothes. "I'm glad you came."

"I'll always have your sister's back," he said. "She didn't tell me you were coming. Thought you were in Europe. When did you arrive?"

"A few hours ago. Adeline doesn't know I'm here. Didn't want to wake her."

"She'll be here soon," he said, checking his watch. "I'll put a pot of coffee on."

She conjured a steaming cup of it and handed it to him.

"Thanks, but Adeline likes to make it the human way."

She followed him to the kitchen, admiring the blue jeans that fit him to perfection. "Did she catch you up? About the attack?"

"If I get my hands on the bastard who did this to her, I'll kill him myself."

"You met Luke Churchwell?"

"Yesterday. Where does she keep the coffee?"

She pointed him to the cupboard above the microwave.

"What do you think of him?"

He blew out a breath. "I don't trust him. He's under Tanner's influence and loyal to the lowlife who attacked Adeline."

"That wasn't the answer I was hoping for."

While the coffee brewed, he told her what he knew of Luke's situation. "Adeline needs to learn how to use the magic, and quick. We're heading out to a clearing she knows when she's done here. I'll teach her what she needs."

He finished the coffee Sarah had conjured and pushed off from the sink. "Charlie's stirring downstairs. I'd better get outside."

Adeline had been right to ask for Warrick's help. But as her gaze followed him through the kitchen door, she hoped he wouldn't break Adeline's heart. Again.

Moments later, the front door opened, and Adeline walked in. Sarah hurried down the hall to greet her. She gave her sister a hug and pulled back. "What happened here?"

Adeline touched the nearly healed cut on her forehead. "Would you believe I walked into a door? Well, more like flew into it."

"Seriously?"

"It's a long story."

"Warrick put coffee on. We need to talk." She tugged her sister by the hand.

"Ahem," came a voice from behind them.

"Sorry. Come in," Adeline said.

"You must be Luke." Sarah offered her hand to the tall man with hair and eyes the colour of coal. He wore a finely knit sweater and dress slacks. She'd seen him before but couldn't place where.

"This is my sister, Sarah," Adeline said. "Let's talk in the kitchen."

"Wait." Sarah stopped her and sent her binder's magic in search of Adeline's threads.

"What do you see?" Adeline asked.

"Nothing witchy."

"You're sure?"

"Yes. Why?"

"Because I can now see the glow I've been told only witches can see. The one that surrounds living matter. And yesterday I learned I can control the elements."

"You didn't tell me about the elements," Luke said.

"Sorry. It was before I smacked into the door. Sarah checking my threads just now reminded me."

"Are you feeling okay? Mom said to watch for flu-like symptoms."

"So far, I feel fine."

They continued to the kitchen. Luke and Sarah took seats at the table while Adeline prepared Charlie's breakfast.

Luke raked his fingers through his hair, and Sarah suddenly remembered where she'd seen him before. The knowledge chilled her. She addressed him. "I remember the night at the clearing. Unless I'm mistaken, you were there. Were you not?"

"I was. Along with one of Tanner's lieutenants."

At least he wasn't trying to hide it.

Adeline turned from the stove. "You never told me you were there."

"I did. I told you the priestess showed us a vision of you using warlock fire. I thought you knew that took place in the clearing."

"I guess I didn't put those pieces together," Adeline said. "So tell us: what did you see that night?"

"Nothing that will shed new light. I was across the clearing. Damaras approached with her war mages. She and Tanner negotiated a deal. Tanner agreed to a financial penalty and punishment for the warlock responsible. He also agreed to siphon the magic out of you to save your life."

"That is not what the council agreed to," Sarah said. "Tanner's touch was only to learn the identity of the warlock behind the attack."

"Damaras lied to us," Adeline said. "I know my memory is spotty, but I can't imagine I'd agree to let anyone root around in my head, let alone siphon magic from me."

"You didn't," Sarah said. "You were quite clear about that. As soon as Tanner rendered you unconscious, I raised the alarm. But Daniel reassured me that Tanner's touch was going as planned. It was you who figured out something wasn't right. I don't think Tanner was expecting you to come to. When you did, you kneed him in the head."

"And broke his nose," Luke added, sounding proud of her.

"Next thing we saw were fireworks shooting from your hands," Sarah said. "Beatrice doused you with warlock powder to snuff it out, and you collapsed. I called the wind and blew as much of the poison off you as I could."

"It's a good thing you did. Warlock stone can be lethal in large doses," Luke said.

"The rest of the council contained us. You and me," Sarah said. "They thought we were acting against Damaras. Against the witches."

"Me, I understand. But you? Acting against the coven? They believed that?" Adeline said.

"I don't know. At that point, I was focused on you, not the others. My last clear memory is Silas approaching the witches who were holding us immobile. Then I was phoning Joe, and we were whisked onto a plane. It was at least thirty-six hours until I spoke with you again."

"The missing day," Adeline said.

"Warlock poison can take several hours to clear your system," Luke said. "If Sarah was blowing excess powder off you, it must have been a substantial dose. I wouldn't be surprised if it took a day."

Luke pushed his chair back and stood. He walked to the kitchen door and checked through the window. Looking for Warrick? He turned and crossed his arms. "There's something else you don't know."

Adeline stopped flipping bacon, the tongs mid-air.

"Your priestess knew Tanner wanted your magic. She used you as a pawn to get damaging the grid elevated to an accord-level infraction."

"And you're drip-feeding me this now?" Adeline said. Her face flushed a dangerous shade of red. "Anything else you care to share?"

"Me telling you doesn't change a thing. It's just one more detail you shouldn't know that could trip you up with Tanner. But it just occurred to me that any change to the accord would have to be approved by the warlock king and your high priestess. Those details would have to be documented. There may be information in those records that would prove your priestess colluded with Lord Tanner against your best interests."

His explanation didn't soften Adeline's scowl.

"Surely, they wouldn't be stupid enough to put something like that in writing," Sarah said. "Then again . . . I think it's time I returned to the sanctuary and paid a visit to the archives."

"No," Adeline said. "It's not safe for you there."

"True, but Damaras doesn't yet know I'm back in the country. If she hasn't revoked my access, I can slip in and out when the place is deserted."

"If you do that, she'll suspect you're on to her," Adeline said.

"Good. I hope it keeps her up at night. Because I don't think it was a warlock who folded our memories," Sarah said. "I think it was a witch."

The line between Adeline's brows deepened. "Luke learned that a witch's will had been planted inside me. That I'd been compelled to learn what I could about rune magic and disclose it."

"Daniel!" Sarah said. "He'd made a play for that scenario. Proposed it at the GC. We told him no."

"We?" Adeline asked.

"Damaras and I."

"Lip service," Adeline said. "Damaras has to be working with Silas. Daniel and Kylie don't make a move without his blessing."

"The elementals weren't at the clearing, so I don't imagine they're involved. Marcus and Odette were present, but their memories were also wiped," Sarah said.

"What about Simon?" Adeline said. "You trust him?"

"I do, but he has a mile-high crush on Kylie. He would have done anything she suggested."

"I think it's safe to say that anyone whose memories were wiped was opposed to what Damaras and Silas were up to. The rest were either unaware—or in on it."

"What are we going to do?" Sarah said.

"What we should have done after Dad died," Adeline said. "Find the proof we need to expose them."

When Warrick returned after seeing Charlie safely home from his walk, Luke asked about his jeweller.

"She's intrigued. She'll be here tomorrow," Warrick said.

"Jeweller?" Sarah whispered to Adeline.

"We'll talk later," Adeline said, under her breath. She pushed open the door with her hip, Charlie's tray in hand.

Sarah followed her down the stairs, swinging Adeline's car keys by the fob. "Tell Charlie I said hi." She split off from Adeline at the bottom of the stairs. Luke kept watch as Adeline greeted Charlie at his door. As soon as they were inside, Sarah threw up a veil to hide her activity. If Kai was lurking, she didn't want him following them.

Sarah disappeared inside the garage and backed out Adeline's Jeep. Moments later, Adeline and Warrick exited the house and joined her. Luke would stay behind and watch over Charlie. They had one hour.

The clearing was a ten-minute drive away. Warrick's instruction started from the back seat. "Sarah, ward yourself, or Adeline will draw power from you. Adeline, you're going to shield the clearing."

Sarah parked by the footpath along the side of the road. The university's forested area had gotten smaller over the years as the student body had grown and more buildings were required, but it was plenty big enough for their purposes.

"This is perfect," Warrick said, gazing around at a thick ring of mature trees. "Trees are second only to people when it comes to power sources." He taught Adeline how to tap into the power. Sarah watched as the luminescence rising from the forest was redirected to her sister. First it came through her fingertips, but eventually her whole body seemed to absorb it, as if she'd become a sponge.

Sarah sat on the sidelines in awe. She'd never been a fighter like Adeline. More the dancer type. Hence her years of ballet training.

Adeline mastered everything Warrick threw at her with an athlete's concentration and stamina. Adeline's fireballs and crackling lightning sounded as fierce as they looked. And the more Adeline used her magic, the smoother her red threads became. Adeline and Warrick flashed in and out, criss-crossing the clearing with increasing speed. Warrick taunted Adeline, tracked her. She met his challenge every time. Warrick's hour of training flew by far too fast.

Back in the Jeep, Warrick continued. "You'll get stronger and require less power with practice. Remember: it takes as much power to create one baseball-sized weapon as it does to create four that are golf-ball sized, or a hundred the size of ball bearings. Warlock fire seems to be your go-to, so if your opponents know you, they'll be expecting it. Surprise them. Show me the runes I taught you. From behind the driver's wheel, Sarah could see only snippets of the runes Adeline formed for wind, earth, water, and fire, but she felt their effect despite Warrick's dampening efforts.

Luke met them in the front hallway, standing with his hands jammed into his pockets, the picture of impatience. "We've got to go," he said the moment they breached the threshold.

"Did something happen?" Adeline asked.

"Not yet, and I'd like to keep it that way. Come on," Luke said, starting for the door.

"You make any progress on Adeline's runeglyph?" Warrick asked Luke.

"Some. I'll do more research back at the tower."

"Let's aim for completion tomorrow," Warrick said. A scowl escaped from behind Luke's polished manners.

"What's a runeglyph?" Sarah asked.

"It's a mark that will protect her from having her magic siphoned," Luke said. "Let's go."

"Thanks, Warrick," Adeline said, hugging him. "Sarah, I'll see you tomorrow."

Sarah watched Luke pull away from the curb with Adeline in the passenger seat. "Did he seem a little anxious to get her out of here?" A sense of foreboding settled in her chest.

"She's a prize to him. I just can't decide if he favours awarding her to Tanner or to Kai."

Twenty-Five

As intrigued as Adeline was with this new magic inside her, she had difficulty shaking the unease she'd felt since learning that Luke had been at the accord meeting in the clearing.

She mind-talked to him on the drive back to the tower. *Why did Tanner involve you in the accord meeting? It's not like you're besties.*

Tanner suspected Kai was the one who'd attacked you. He knew that Kai and I were close once. That I knew his magical capabilities better than anyone.

You've known all along who attacked me?

Yes. Keeping you in the dark kept you under Tanner's roof.

You could have told me any time we were at the house. And you didn't. You also let me tell you about Beatrice's warlock stone when you were already aware of it. You knew she'd poisoned me with it in the clearing.

You're right. I could have told you about all of it. And I was tempted, but it would have been a mistake. Every time I reveal information to you, I'm throwing the dice. If you slip up when Tanner's people are listening? A pause. Adeline swung her head in his direction. He met her gaze briefly and looked forward again. *As soon as Tanner suspects you know he's after your magic, your time's up. I know you don't want to hear this, but the less you know, the better. Trust me.*

Trust you? She was feeling less and less inclined to do that. She stared out the side window, unable to even look at him. There was only one person she could count on in the tower. Herself.

The moment the guard opened the door to the suite, Luke disappeared into his office.

An hour later, the door to the hallway opened. She set her sketchbook aside as footsteps approached and Tanner appeared. He glanced up at a camera and ran a finger across his throat.

Why would he cut off the camera feeds?

"Hello, Adeline. Where's Luke?"

"His office."

Tanner made a casual gesture with his hand toward Luke's office. Alarm raced through her. Had he locked Luke into his office?

"You and I have things to discuss." His smile seemed off. He usually hid his disdain better.

He sat beside her. Too close. She adjusted her seating to create more distance. He leaned in. She stood, collected her sketchbook, and moved to an armchair. "What would you like to discuss?"

He straightened, inhaling. "I'm afraid I can't let you keep the magic."

Adeline stiffened. "That hardly sounds like a discussion."

"You're right. It's not." Tanner stood. "Your co-operation isn't necessary, but it would be preferable."

Had Luke lied to her again? Betrayed her? She flashed herself to the kitchen, putting the island between them. "You want to steal my magic?"

He approached casually, confident of his power over her. "It's not your magic."

"This is not what the priestess agreed to," Adeline said. She needed a moment to think. Dare she call to Luke and hope he wasn't a part of this? If he was, she'd have to fight them both. Magically, she couldn't beat either of them. And Tanner had no doubt already altered the shield to remove her ability to visualize out of there.

Tanner threw his arm out, his fingers splayed. She visualized herself behind him, surprising herself to find she'd succeeded. Whatever magic he'd let loose hadn't hit her. She would have to knock him out cold before he could immobilize her with magic.

He turned. She didn't hesitate. She threw her weight behind her arm and knuckled him in the side of the neck, a pressure-point strike. He hit the coffee table on his way to the floor. In a blink, she visualized herself at the front door. With her fist raised to knock, Luke stepped out of his office.

"What's going on?" Luke said.

She pulled on her magic. A ball of fire appeared in her hand.

Luke raised his arms and backed away. He turned his head toward the crashing noises coming from the living room. "Who's in there?" Luke asked, already turning to run into the fray.

Adeline rapped her knuckles on the door. There was no answer. Not surprising.

Adeline visualized herself on the other side of the door just as it opened. The guard jumped back, surprised. Adeline lost her balance and stumbled. The fireball dropped and landed on the carpet, where the guard made quick work of stamping it out. The heavy door swung closed. "Are you all right, Ms. Thorne?"

"Yeah. Thanks," Adeline said, bewildered. She'd visualized herself out of the suite.

"Do you need an escort?" the guard said.

Adeline frowned. Something wasn't sitting right. Surely the guard knew what Tanner had been up to. Why hadn't Tanner revoked her ability to visualize out of the suite? *Wait.* Where was the second guard that travelled with Tanner? Something didn't line up.

Adeline visualized herself back inside the suite, where Luke and Tanner were squared off against one another. Luke had a gash on his forehead. Tanner's lip was split.

"You're asking me to lay down my life for you," Luke said.

The pair of them circled one another, keeping an arm's length apart.

"Sounds like a fair trade to me," Tanner said.

"Use your head," Luke said. "You didn't think he was going to let me walk away, did you? This is the price I paid."

Adeline stood out of view, feeling like she'd entered an altered reality.

Tanner jerked his head back. "Pretty comfy jail cell you managed here, buddy. Or should I say traitor? Doesn't look like much of a sacrifice to me."

Buddy? Traitor? Their conversation didn't track.

"He has ruined me. Taken everything. But we can fix this."

"Last time you tried to fix this, your revolt nearly got us all killed," Tanner said.

Except it wasn't Tanner.

"If you siphon Adeline, Tanner kills me. And then he'll kill you. But if you walk away, you can rebuild your magic. We both live to fight another day."

Oh, goddamnit. It was Kai. He was in body glamour.

"It took me years—years—to build that magic. It would take me a decade to rebuild it."

"I know. But you'd be alive," Luke said. "Please. Don't do this. I can't lose another friend."

Kai, who still looked like Tanner, noticed Adeline. He swivelled his head in her direction.

She held out her hand, called her bo staff, and quickly extended it. She gripped it close to one end, ready to strike.

"I thought you said we couldn't use magic in here? Looks like she doesn't have any trouble with it."

"She's no threat to Tanner."

"Kai, I presume," Adeline said. "You can drop the glamour. I know who you are."

"He can't, actually," Luke said. "That would require the use of his magic, which he can't access in here."

"Then how'd he get in here?" Adeline asked.

"My guess? He glamoured before he got to the building and waited long enough for the scent of the magic to dissipate. The guard missed it."

"And it's a very good glamour," Kai said, looking entirely too smug.

"You could have killed me," Adeline said to Kai, swinging the staff.

"You look pretty healthy to me," he said.

Adeline's temper flared. She positioned her feet and punched the staff, knocking him backwards.

He recovered. "You think I'd risk killing you and losing my magic? You're a barren witch. The perfect vessel."

"Your presumption was a guess at best. You don't know anything about me. You took a chance with my life. As far as I'm concerned, you forfeited your magic the instant you pumped it into me."

"That magic is mine," Kai said.

Adeline twirled the staff, feeling the instrument's perfect balance. "You want it? Come and get it." If he reached out, she'd strike, breaking his hand. If he approached, she'd grip the end of the staff and punch him back.

Kai's lip curled. He took a step forward.

"Kai," Luke said. "That would be a very big mistake. Back away."

Kai raised his arm in a futile attempt to use magic to disarm her. She swung her staff out and connected with bone. He howled and pulled in his injured wrist, holding it tight to his body. It occurred to Adeline that magicals were useless without their magic. Worse than teenagers with big mouths and nothing to back it up. She had no inherent magic, but she could sure as hell back up her threats.

"Bitch!" Kai said.

"That's witch to you." She visualized him outside in the hall.

Kai disappeared.

Luke blinked. He let out a breath. "How did you . . .? Never mind. Thank you. You probably just saved his life."

"I'm not sure he deserved it."

"Nonetheless, thank you."

Adeline felt a pinch of sorrow for Luke. He looked genuinely relieved. Though she was still angry with him for spoon-feeding her information like a toddler, it couldn't be easy for him, betraying his friends on Tanner's orders. Not being able to explain himself.

Luke's phone rang. "I've got to take this," he said.

"If that's Tanner, put him on speaker," Adeline said. She collapsed her bo staff and sent it back to her room.

Luke ignored her and headed toward his office. Adeline flashed away and reappeared in front of him. "Put him on speaker."

Luke stopped. "He won't take kindly to an ambush."

She crossed her arms.

Luke's mind-voice came through in a low growl. *The cameras are back on. If you want to take a piece out of someone, take it out of me. Away from the cameras. Let me deal with Tanner. I know where the landmines are. You don't.*

"Excuse me," Luke said. He disappeared into his office and closed the door.

Adeline marched to her dressing room and changed into workout gear. Being drip-fed critical information when it was her life—her magic—on the line infuriated her.

When she knocked on the door to get out, two guards accompanied her down to the gym. Security had been beefed up, she was told. She hit her workout with a vengeance, and didn't return until she'd expended every ounce of the anger she couldn't hold inside.

After her shower, back in her dressing room, as she towelled off, she put her thoughts in order. She knew exactly what she had to do, and it started with Luke's runeglyph. More than just her magic needed protecting. She was amending her requirements.

With that settled, she grabbed hold of the duvet she'd been using as a mattress and shook it out to re-fluff it. After she laid it out on the floor again, she stood. A down feather, light as air, gently floated downward. *Light as air.* The thought was in her mind for just a moment before her feet lifted from the floor.

Twenty-Six

In his conversation with Tanner, Luke kept the details sparse. Kai had glamoured to gain entry to the suite. He'd threatened Adeline then provoked a fight with Luke. As soon as Adeline figured out that Kai was posing as Tanner, she visualized Kai into the hall outside the suite. He made it sound like Tanner was her hero for having the foresight to adjust the shield, which allowed her to expel the threat.

Satisfied that Luke's explanation matched the guard's version of events, Tanner let slip that Kai had escaped. Not sensing the body glamour and then letting Kai get away? It was going to be a very bad day for the guard.

Luke was still talking with Tanner when he heard Adeline leave the suite. To the gym, hopefully, to blow off steam.

"No more delays," Tanner said. "The witch has recovered well enough. Tomorrow you will find Kai's locking rune. I want this done and Adeline out of there before our runes are exposed."

"As soon as I find the rune, I will begin working on a runecast to unlock it. I'll do some preliminary research this afternoon."

At least Tanner wouldn't question why he was poring over his *Book of Runes*. The additions Adeline had asked him to integrate into her runeglyph would make it as complicated as his own. It might take him all night, but he would finish it.

And tomorrow, he'd set wheels in motion that couldn't be stopped. A witch with a warlock runeglyph was unprecedented. He couldn't decide if he was breaking all the rules or making up new ones.

Luke wouldn't survive Tanner's wrath when he learned about the runeglyph, but Adeline might. She would have Kai's considerable magic at her disposal and Warrick, undoubtedly, at her side.

He'd already incorporated two more compound runes into the design in his head for Adeline when the hall door opened and closed. Light foot-steps that he now recognized as Adeline's carried on down the hall.

She opened their mind-talking link. *We have a problem. Tomorrow is Saturday.*

Why is that a problem?

I don't make Charlie breakfast on the weekends. Tanner might know that.

That's not our only problem. He explained about Tanner demanding he find the locking rune. *If he knows you don't cook on the weekends, he'll be here first thing.*

Tell him my sister has arrived from Europe. That I'll be spending the morning with her.

That might work. We can give it a try. Come to my office and have that conversation with me. If Tanner doesn't hear it himself, it'll be reported to him.

Luke had his doubts that Tanner would give any consideration to Adeline's sister being in town, but when Luke called him, Tanner leaned into it. A few extra hours was an acceptable price to pay to keep Adeline from suspecting anything was amiss.

In the car the next morning, Luke opened the mind-link. *I've been working on a plan to recruit some help. Would you be willing to play interpreter?*

Absolutely. Where? When?

I don't know yet.

Sarah was on a video chat with Joe and her kids when Adeline and Luke arrived. She waved from her seat on the sofa.

Warrick had made himself at home in Adeline's kitchen, surrounded by a mound of dirty bowls and pans. "Morning, babe. French toast and maple bacon coming right up," he said, patting himself on the back. "Be ready in five minutes." Adeline approached the stove, resting a hand on Warrick's shoulder. He took advantage of her proximity and pecked her on the cheek. Did Adeline sense that Warrick was staking out his territory?

She crossed back to the coffee pot. "You want a cup?" she asked Luke.

He accepted. Better to have something to do with his hands other than wrap them around Warrick's neck.

"Liza Patel will be here within the hour. She's the jeweller," Warrick said. "Is Adeline's runeglyph ready?"

"It's in here," Luke said, pointing to his head. "Just need to sketch it out."

Sarah joined them as they took seats around the kitchen table and Warrick set a stack of food in front of them.

"How are Joe and the kids?" Adeline asked.

"The kids are fine. They're durable. Joe less so." She laid a napkin in her lap. "He's been fielding calls from friends in the coven who've heard rumours that a warlock attacked the GC. He's worried they're going to get out their pitchforks and worsen the divide."

"Damaras, Silas, and whoever else was involved are probably feeding those rumours," Adeline said. She forked a half slice of French toast onto her plate.

It made sense. Chaos had a way of stoking the fires of rage, keeping the witches from examining the facts too closely.

"Did you learn anything at the archives?"

"Nothing useful. Carolyne recorded the attack on you, but there's no record of Simon's regression on me. There's no ID on the warlock and no record of reparations. There's also nothing about the second attack and no suggestion of a change to the terms of the accord." She reached for the syrup. "Maybe because the outcome is still undetermined? Still, it's unusual. Events involving warlocks or the accord are usually recorded promptly. The warlock attack on the grid was recorded the very next day."

"What attack on the grid?" Luke asked.

"It was just before Kai assaulted Adeline," Sarah said. "In the southwest. It was the worst one yet. Resulted in a tear."

Luke tilted his head. Worst one yet? He'd read about grid attacks, but only in a historical context, long before the peace accord.

"If the coven learns it was witches who attacked the GC and butchered our memories, those responsible will be hauled up before Lady Brighton," Adeline said.

"After you left yesterday, I called Marcus and Odette," Sarah said. "They're on their way home. Neither of them can put a face to whoever messed with their memories."

"Who are Marcus and Odette?" Luke asked.

"Marcus is the coven's principal healer," Sarah said. "Odette is our principal spellcaster."

"Lady Brighton could order a regression on someone else who was present and may have seen it happen," Adeline said.

"I doubt she'd insult Damaras or Silas by opening an investigation without a stitch of proof," Sarah said.

Adeline bunched her forehead and pressed her lips together. "It feels like we're missing something."

Their heads came up at a knock at the front door.

"That'll be Liza," Warrick said, scooting back his chair.

Adeline went with him to answer the door. Luke hoped it was because she was the only one who could invite anyone past her wards. Sarah walked ahead of Luke into the living room.

Liza, a pint-sized warlock with skin the colour of warm copper and a striking blonde buzzcut, was immediately intrigued by Luke's chain.

Luke mind-talked with Adeline to instruct Liza on the finer points of it, especially its explosive capability. Sweat prickled his forehead as Liza circled him, using a metal rod to lift the chain in places.

"Whoever created this was diabolical," she said. "There are three possible releasing clasps. A little game of Russian roulette for anyone who tries to open it."

"Can you remove it?" Adeline asked.

Not here, Luke said, reminding her. *Tanner will be alerted. He'll descend on your house like the plague.*

Liza stepped away from him. "Not today. I'll have to tap my friends in the business. See if anyone has dealt with something like this before."

Luke exhaled, the tension leaving him. But disappointment soon rushed in, catching him off guard. He hadn't realized he'd placed that much hope on a positive outcome.

"Thank you, Liza," he said. "I'm happy to compensate you for your time today."

"Not necessary. But we'll talk again when I find a solution."

Though he appreciated she'd said *when,* he had no expectation a solution would be coming in time to save his ass. "If you'll excuse me," Luke said, "I've got work to attend to."

Luke left Warrick and Liza talking with Sarah and Adeline. In the solarium, he cast a shield to prevent unwelcome eyes from observing the runeglyph he'd designed. He compelled a board and parchment and propped them on Adeline's easel. A crystal bowl came next and hovered in the air beneath his wrist. He opened a vein to collect enough blood to sketch the design. The fountain pen would need to be filled with blood many times to complete the runeglyph.

He began as he always did, drawing in the critical foundation runes and then building them out to incorporate the core directives. The complex rune to prevent siphoning sat beside the equally complex rune that would prevent access to her memories. A third intricate rune prevented mind-reading probes. When he was satisfied the structure was sound, he began applying the cover design that would hide the rune work he'd done. An hour passed before he stepped back to look at his creation. It was beautiful and fierce. Fitting for Adeline. The design would sit between her shoulder blades and trail down her spine.

Luke felt spent when he rejoined the others in the living room. He'd crammed into a few short hours a design that would normally have taken days to complete. Liza had left. Sarah and Adeline were bookends curled on opposite ends of the sofa, Adeline with a pillow in her lap. Warrick's legs were a tripping hazard, stretched out from one of the armchairs.

Luke addressed Adeline. "It's done."

Twenty-Seven

"May I see it?" Adeline asked, eyeing the small square of paper Luke held. If she was going to bear the mark for the rest of her days, she wanted a preview.

"No. The rune's been cast." He slipped the paper in his pocket. "Have you changed your mind?"

Sarah sat forward, interjecting. "Adeline tells me the runeglyph could prevent a binding should her witch threads develop. Is there a way to test that before it's a part of her?"

"I'm afraid not. But we don't have to go through with it." Luke walked to the only empty armchair and perched on the seat's edge. He tented his hands, elbows on his knees.

Sarah turned to Adeline. "We have options. There's a big old world outside of this house. A lot of interesting places where no one would find us."

"You and the kids? Joe? Mom and Charlie?" She'd never upend their lives to take them on the run with her. And that's what she'd have to do. "You'd all become targets. Kai's already threatened Charlie. Tanner would do the same with Jack or Olive."

"The runeglyph's fallout could kill you," Sarah said. "Mom would never recover from that. Neither would I, or the kids."

"The only other way out of this predicament is to let Kai reclaim his magic. Which will get Luke killed. And if Tanner gets the magic, I'll be blinded. And I know blind is better than dead, but that's a shit choice." Adeline tossed the pillow aside and stood. The injustice of the situation infuriated her.

"Adeline." Sarah's voice was a warning, and her eyes were trained on Adeline's hands.

Adeline glanced down. Fire curled around her fists. "Sorry," she said as she shook them out.

"The way I see it," Adeline said, "I can make a choice with a terrible outcome, or I can make a choice with an unknown outcome. Given that I've never had a witch tell, it's unlikely I'd develop one. And even if I do, Luke doesn't know for sure the runeglyph will prevent a binding."

"What if you're wrong?" Sarah said. "You're seeing the life force that feeds the grid. That's new. Only witches see that. It might be a sign that your witch magic is waking up."

A derisive laugh escaped her throat. "I've been waiting my whole life for my witch magic to wake the hell up. I'm done waiting. Everyone in this room has magic except for me. Until now. So maybe you can't understand how I feel. You've never experienced being left behind while everyone you know claims their magical inheritance. But now, because of a messed-up chain of unfortunate events, I finally have magic. I can't give it up."

"If you go through with this, Tanner or Kai might kill you for denying them the magic they're so desperate to get their hands on."

She rubbed her forehead. "I am so sick of people assuming they have some kind of right to take my magic, to take my life, to take my sight. If they want a part of me, they're going to have to fight for it. Bring it on. I'm ready. I know you're worried. I'm worried too. But I'm willing to take the chance that I can keep this magic. I want the runeglyph."

"Then you can't go back to the tower," Sarah said. "Luke's already told us that Tanner would sooner kill you than allow you to keep the warlock magic."

"Will he know I have a runeglyph?"

"Not unless he sees it or tries siphoning," Luke said. "That won't happen today."

"You sure about that?" Warrick said.

"Tanner has gone to some lengths to maintain Adeline's cooperation. Killing her will create a mess he'd have to clean up with the witches. He's insisted I find the locking rune today, but I've already told him I need extra time to create a runecast to open it. That gives us another day."

"Unless he decides to break the lock instead of waiting for you to unlock it," Sarah said.

"That's a possibility, but Adeline is under his protection. If he hurts her, he'll have extensive reparations to make. He'll only resort to breaking the rune when he learns the unlocking rune doesn't work. And it won't."

"An extra day is fine and well, but how does that help?" Warrick asked.

"I put wheels in motion earlier today. They'll either pay off, or they won't. And if they don't, Adeline will stay behind, here, when I return to the tower tomorrow."

"But . . . he'll kill you." Adeline would have gladly traded the fatalistic trend in Luke's thinking for the annoying aloofness he'd shown when they'd first met.

"He's going to kill me anyway," Luke said, pointing to his chain.

"But there's still a chance Liza can get that off you," Adeline said.

"The jeweller was always a long shot. And we're almost out of time. I wish there was another way. At least with the runeglyph, your odds are better of keeping the magic."

"And your eyesight," Sarah said. "I can hide the runeglyph with glamour, if that helps."

"You don't have to return to the tower today if you don't want to," Luke said. "But if you don't, you can't stay here."

"I won't just leave you—"

"Tell us about these wheels you've put in motion," Warrick said, straightening and pulling in his legs.

"Tanner has a lot of enemies. I know most of them, but I haven't been able to speak with them. I can now. Earlier, I sent coded runes to locations where they'll be found by the right people. When they show up, Adeline can speak freely for me. I'll broker a deal."

"Where are these enemies of Tanner's showing up? And how many?" Warrick asked.

"I won't know the details until they contact me."

Warrick stared at Luke with narrowed eyes. He swung his attention to her. "How do you feel about that, babe?"

She looked from him to Luke. "I think it's worth a shot. One more day?" She glanced back at Warrick. "I'll be safe enough if I can use magic and have the protection of the runeglyph."

Warrick nodded, but he looked unconvinced. "You're sure?"

"I am. Let's get on with it. Luke? Are you ready?"

"If your wards will allow it."

"Sarah?" Adeline said.

Sarah stood and approached Adeline. "Are you absolutely certain about this? It can't be undone."

"Yes," Adeline said, and she pulled her sister into an embrace. "I've hated not having magic. This is a new beginning for me. Please try to see this from my perspective."

When Adeline pulled back, Sarah had tears in her eyes. "Okay," she said wiping them away. "I'll adjust the ward."

"Thanks, sis." Adeline turned to Luke. "Where's the best place to do this?"

"You should probably be lying face down, comfortable. Your bed?"

Sarah remained on the main floor to adjust the wards while Luke, Warrick, and Adeline made their way up to her bedroom.

"Your back will need to be bare," Luke said.

Having Luke and Warrick in her bedroom shrank the room to half its size and felt terribly awkward. More so when she thought of baring herself. She closed her bathroom door and stripped from the waist up. Her robe hung on the back of the door. She snagged it and put it on backwards, like a hospital johnny.

When she returned to the bedroom, Luke stood back while Warrick helped position her and adjusted the pillow. When she was comfortable, Warrick exposed her back and shoulders.

"Is this going to hurt?" she asked.

"Yes. I'll warn you before I start. But first I need to sterilize the area."

He compelled a bottle of isopropyl alcohol and a sterile pad.

"I'll do that," Warrick said.

"Oh? Do you know what area needs to be sterilized?" Luke said.

The protectiveness in Warrick's voice was a comfort, given how vulnerable she felt. But Luke wouldn't hurt her. She knew that. He'd already defended her against Kai and was actively holding Tanner at bay.

By the time Sarah arrived, Adeline's skin was prepared.

"Warrick, Sarah," Luke said. "You'll need to leave."

"Oh, I'm not going anywhere," Warrick said.

"Your instinct will be to interfere, and that can't happen," Luke said. "If she is moved, even slightly—say, by the shifting of your weight on the bed—the runeglyph won't function the way it's intended. And I won't be able to fix it."

Warrick leaned down to her ear. "You okay with this?"

"Go. Please. Let's get this over with."

"I'll be right outside."

"Me, too," Sarah said.

The closing of her bedroom door sent a chill through her. She was standing on a precipice. Behind her was the barren witch. Over the cliff, on the other side, was the warlock witch.

"Are you ready?"

The moment she uttered yes, the room sealed shut. Absolute silence fell. She knew then that no one would be getting in or out until they were done.

"Last chance to say no," Luke said.

"Do it."

"Close your eyes, and I'll begin," Luke said.

The moment she did so, the first tendrils of his magic hit her. It rendered her unable to move, unable to speak. Even the panic that would normally cause her heart rate to escalate didn't materialize.

Luke's voice flitted around her, a chant that increased the air pressure in the room. A brilliant light flashed, and then a wave of heat hit her. A low drone began to build until it was a deafening roar. And then her back was on fire with the stings of a thousand angry hornets.

Her screams were silent.

An agonizing eternity passed before her shrieks gave way to groans. A tear fell and dripped across her nose. Someone wiped it away. Luke, she assumed, but couldn't know.

Slowly, she became aware that he'd released his freeze on her muscles. She opened her eyes.

Luke leaned against the wall by her window. "It's done. The magic is yours to keep. If you can stay alive."

"Thank you," she said. She shifted, and the stinging started up again.

"Stay still. It'll settle down in an hour or so."

He made a complicated gesture with his hands, and the pressure in the room dissipated. Sounds from outside returned, including a persistent banging on the bedroom door.

"It's open," Luke said.

Warrick and Sarah spilled into the room. Sarah stopped at the foot of the bed, her gaze glued to Adeline's back. Warrick's face was a storm cloud. He almost made it to Luke before he, too, was drawn to whatever it was Luke had put on her back.

"It's beautiful," Sarah said. "Have you seen it?"

"No. It still hurts to move."

Sarah pulled out her phone and took a photo. She held it so Adeline could see.

The runeglyph was nothing like what she'd expected. The piercing blue eyes of a snow leopard stared out at her, its long tail trailing down her spine. Black spots dotted the leopard's silver fur. Its face exuded powerful majesty. The image was so realistic she thought, if she reached behind, that she would feel its thick fur.

Sarah magnified the details. The leopard's black spots weren't what they appeared to be from a distance. Up close, they were symbols. A pentagram on its shoulder, the moon's phases down its tail. Adeline imagined runes hidden in the others. A series of small spots on its forehead looked remarkably like the outline of an eye.

Sarah glanced at Luke. "A third eye?"

He crossed his arms. "Well, she is a witch."

"It's beautiful," Adeline said. "I've never seen anything like it. I guess I imagined my runeglyph would look like yours."

"No. Someone else created mine. That one is uniquely yours."

"What made you choose a snow leopard?" Adeline asked.

"Because it's you. Rare, lethal, and beautiful."

An awkward silence hung in the air. Warrick sat on the bed near the pillows. He stroked her hair.

"I'll go fix the wards," Sarah said, heading for the door.

"Speaking of the wards," Luke said, holding his hand out to stop her. "Why didn't you include the back stairs?"

"Wards are stronger if they don't have to stretch out over open air." She addressed Adeline. "Can I get—"

"Why not the porch?" Luke said.

Adeline smiled at Sarah's expression, which suggested he was daft. "How would anyone be able to knock on her door? Ring the doorbell?"

Sarah returned her attention to Adeline. "Can I get you anything when I come back? A cold compress?"

"No," Luke said. "When the pain subsides, you can glamour it and she can redress, but don't put anything on the runeglyph itself for twenty-four hours. It should be settled properly by then."

"Is it safe to read her threads?" Sarah asked.

"That, I don't know. Does a binder's magic flow into her body?"

"No. It touches her aura."

"Wait a few hours before you try," Luke said.

"How soon until we can test it against invasive magic?" Warrick asked, shifting his weight. Adeline inhaled sharply at the bed's movement "Sorry, babe."

"Ideally?" Luke said. "Not until it's healed."

"What happens if it's tested before I'm healed?" Adeline asked.

"The runeglyph will be fine, but you'll feel it. It won't be as painful as it was just now, but it won't be pleasant. After it heals, all you'll feel is a tugging sensation. A warning of an imminent threat."

"How long until it's healed?" Warrick asked.

"A month. But she doesn't have a month."

Twenty-Eight

Luke retreated to the kitchen while Sarah glamoured Adeline's runeglyph. He kept a safe distance from Warrick, whose anger simmered like bubbling lava, a molten minefield.

Warrick crossed his arms and rested his butt against the sink. Luke stood on the line between the hall and the kitchen, fingers rustling the coins in his slacks pockets.

"If you get back to the tower and Tanner learns you've runeglyphed Adeline, what's your plan?"

"Get her out of there. She doesn't have enough control of her power to beat Tanner magically."

Warrick jutted his jaw. "You and your buddy, Kai, put Adeline in this position. I could kill you for doing this to her."

"You'd be joining a very long queue."

Warrick pinned his gaze to the floor. "I asked around about Lord Tanner. Didn't find many warlocks willing to offer an opinion."

"Opinions aren't encouraged in this territory."

A nod. A pause. "It seems the king favours Tanner."

"I'm not surprised. Tanner kisses his ass."

Warrick looked up. "Do you know the name Judith La Croix?"

"Tanner's sister."

"She's also the king's secretary. Screens his calls. Prioritizes his visitors."

Luke stilled his fingers. He hadn't known that. Just how much ass had Tanner kissed to make that happen?

"This war you started with him is not going to end well for you."

Warrick didn't live in the territory. He hadn't gotten the email. The war was over. Past tense. The *not going to end well* part had already happened.

"You have to give Tanner points for rooting out the hostiles after the coup failed. Rumour has it you had a hand in that. Someone even suggested you were his new enforcer."

"Are you done?" Luke said. "Because this conversation is growing tiresome."

Warrick sprang away from the counter and stopped inches from Luke, who didn't flinch.

"I won't be done until Adeline is safely out of your orbit," Warrick said.

"Then you won't have long to wait."

At the sound of footsteps coming down the stairs, they staked out separate corners. Adeline appeared first. She looked from Warrick to Luke. "What's going on?"

"We should go," Luke said. "Unless you've changed your mind?"

"I haven't."

He addressed Sarah. "You've re-established the wards?"

"Yes."

"Good. I hope you don't need them. If Adeline returns tonight, take Charlie on a surprise holiday until the storm blows itself out."

"Love you, sis," Adeline said, hugging Sarah. She kissed a brooding Warrick on the cheek and turned to Luke. "Let's do this."

Luke opened a mind-link the moment they cleared the porch. *If I spot any of the people I tried to summon, I'll exit the car. Play along and accompany me.*

Luke had his head on a swivel, praying he'd spot one of his old friends along their route. He drove slowly, catching red lights and lingering at stop signs. The closer they inched to the downtown, the lower his optimism dipped. With the tower in sight, Luke smacked the steering wheel. His Hail Mary runes hadn't worked.

"What's this?" Adeline asked, holding up a coin she'd retrieved from the cupholder.

Luke glanced over, his eyes widening. He shook his head vigorously. "The lug nut key. Must have fallen out of the glovebox yesterday." She dropped the coin into his outstretched hand. He blew on it, and writing appeared on his palm. An address.

Tell me you want to stop at the Sinclair Centre to . . . shop or something, Luke said. . The Sinclair Centre was a busy hive of upscale shops.

"Ah . . . do you mind if we stop at the Sinclair Centre? Sarah's had her eye on a sweater in one of the shops. I'd like to surprise her with it."

"Sure," Luke said, "but be quick about it." At the next intersection, he detoured from their regular route and pulled into an underground parking lot. He got out of the car and signalled for her to come with him. After he checked his palm, he spun in a circle, searching for the correct stairwell, and then he took off at a jog.

Armour yourself, he said, *and stay close.* He pulled open the stairwell door and started down. At the lowest level, he exited and searched again, then started for the northwest corner. He stopped short of the last row of parked cars. A shield fell around them. Slowly, he turned.

Sutter materialized within the shield. He still dressed like the aristocrat he was, though his family had lost their fortune.

"So it really is you." Sutter's fingers twitched at his sides. "Didn't think you'd be foolish enough to actually show up."

A car length away, a second figure materialized.

"Rowan," Luke said, acknowledging another of his failed coup crew. In grey fatigues, Rowan looked like the enforcer he'd been. A very effective enforcer.

"Thank you for bringing the witch," Kai said, appearing to their right, seemingly peeling himself off a concrete pillar.

You invited Kai to the party? Adeline said. *What's wrong with you? He's baiting you. Don't react to him.*

Three times is not the charm, Churchwell.

"Thank you for coming," Luke said. "This is Adeline Thorne. She's agreed to speak for me." He nodded toward Adeline and then began.

"Until now," Adeline said, "I . . . Luke hasn't been able to talk about the revolt. But when Kai dropped his magic into . . . me, Luke learned that he and I could mind-talk."

Kai took an aggressive step toward Adeline. "Mind-talking is my magic, not yours."

"Back off, Kai," Luke said.

Adeline continued. "Luke's actions these past three years have not been his own. When Tanner captured Luke, he installed that chain around his neck and moved him into the tower. The chain is a cuff, and the tower is wired for round-the-clock surveillance."

"Yeah, I've seen the deplorable conditions Luke suffers under," Kai said. "Must be tough being forced to live in a plush penthouse, made to wear fancy threads, obliged to eat gourmet meals and guzzle fine wine."

"Luke must follow Tanner's orders," Adeline continued, "or the chain will activate. Through the chain, Tanner controls how much power Luke can access and when. It also prevents him from harming Tanner or telling anyone about the chain."

"Doesn't that bring new meaning to *yanking your chain*," Rowan said, smiling despite Luke's icy glare.

"He's been waiting for an opportunity," Adeline said, repeating Luke's words. "A way to escape. To finish what he started."

"We missed our opportunity," Sutter said. "Tanner's stronger than he's ever been."

"He's made new alliances and eliminated most of his opposition," Rowan added. "There's nothing to finish."

"Luke has a new plan," Adeline said.

Kai tossed his hands into the air. "Give it up, Luke. We lost. Accept it and move on."

"There's no moving on for me—for Luke, I mean. Tanner sentenced him to twenty-five-years wearing the chain, doing his bidding."

Adeline turned to Luke. "Jesus. Twenty-five years?"

"After what you've done to us, to your friends and soldiers, you've earned Tanner's sentence," Kai said.

"Luke doesn't deserve that," Adeline said, snapping her head in Kai's direction. "Tanner's a corrupt thug. His only goal is getting richer and more powerful at the expense of those he's supposed to protect. I thought you two were friends. Can you not see that Tanner is responsible for Luke's actions?"

Kai took a step closer. "This is warlock business, witch. Stay out of it."

"I would love to do that, but, thanks to you, I don't have that luxury. It's bad enough that you could have killed me with your magic, but worse? You put a target on my back. Tanner wants the magic you dumped into me. So Tanner is very much my problem."

"Not anymore." Kai flashed behind Adeline and wrapped an arm around her throat. He grunted as she rammed an elbow into his gut and spun out of his grip.

Luke shot his hand out, sending a blast toward Kai, but Sutter blocked it as he and Rowan moved in on Luke.

"That's Kai's magic," Sutter said. "We won't let you stop him from reclaiming it." They stood in Luke's path, armoured, fingers twitching with magic. Luke moved to lower a bell shield over them, but they saw it coming and countered it.

Visualize out of here, Adeline. Get back to the tower.

Another smack. Another grunt. Beyond Sutter and Rowan, Luke caught a glimpse of Adeline, whose face was a fierce knot of anger. Rain droplets hung in the air before her. He watched the drops turn into ice pellets, and, with a swift thrust of her hand, the hard balls pummelled into Kai. With his arm shielding his face, Adeline rushed him, knocking him to the ground.

Rowan took his eyes off Luke, spotted Adeline standing over Kai, and shot a blast of energy at her back. She dropped to her knees and wobbled.

Anger spiked in Luke, the likes of which he rarely allowed. Hitting her in the back was a low blow. He threw lightning at the shield, shattering it. Luke's next runecast was already in motion, shooting from his hand, but Sutter saw it coming and blasted a ball of energy at it, fracturing it.

Kai, having gotten to his feet, pushed a boot to Adeline's shoulder. She crumpled over.

"This is going to happen," Rowan said, stepping closer to Luke and blocking his view of Kai, who was now kneeling beside Adeline. Sutter threw his hands in the air, re-establishing the shield that hid them from public view. "A witch bearing warlock magic is unnatural."

Her scream rent the air.

Luke curled his fists. Another scream. A groan. Rowan and Sutter spun runes in the air, prepared to cause serious bodily damage should he move against them. He'd have to kill them, and he wouldn't do that. He closed his eyes against the pain Kai was inflicting, knowing the hell he was putting Adeline through.

Kai's breaths came in desperate huffs. Someone's feet scuffled for purchase on the concrete. "Let go of me," Adeline hissed. Luke glanced up. A moment lapsed. Fabric rustled.

"What have you done?" Kai said, his voice a menacing growl.

It was over. Luke shuddered with relief.

Rowan and Sutter turned from Luke. Kai was on his knees, his hands on his thighs, one still glowing red. He glared at Luke.

"What's wrong?" Sutter said.

Kai rose to his feet and stalked toward Luke. "Answer me. What have you done with my magic?"

"It belongs to Adeline now," Luke said, meeting his glare head-on.

Kai shook his head in disgust. "I'd kill you right now, but I don't need to bother, do I? Tanner will do that for me when he learns you've rune-glyphed a witch."

"What?" Rowan and Sutter said in chorus.

"Not only a traitor to the cause, but now a traitor to your kind," Kai said.

"Shut up, Kai." Adeline was now on her feet and dusting herself off. Her face was a reddened mask of fury as she marched up to Kai. "You're the traitor. You gave your magic to a witch. What kind of warlock does that?" And before he could come up with a retort, she punched him in the face.

He staggered backwards, blood dripping from his nose. Sutter stepped between them.

"Luke saved your sorry ass," Adeline shouted over Sutter's shoulder. "If you'd gotten my magic, Tanner would have hunted you down and executed you."

Kai curled his lip at Adeline and turned to Luke. "Tanner's going to kill you."

"Yes," Luke said. "But you'll be alive. And she'll be alive. And Tanner won't get his hands on more magic. I can die in peace."

"Luke is the one who will pay for your mistake," Adeline said, her voice another swat at Kai. "The least you can do is listen to his plan."

Kai pushed Sutter away and took a step toward Adeline, but she showed no fear. She squared off, her posture begging him to try again. Sutter re-established a presence between them.

"That's enough, Kai," Rowan said, turning to Luke. "Okay. We'll listen. No promises."

Luke mind-talked to Adeline, who repeated his words. "Tanner has set up a massive siphoning ring," Adeline said. "If the king finds out about it, he'll take care of Tanner for us."

"How do you know the king's not in on it?" Rowan said.

"That's the flaw in my plan. I don't," Luke said.

"Where's your proof?" Sutter said.

Luke rolled up his sleeve and showed them his power packs. "This is just a small sample of his inventory."

"Shit, I've heard of these," Rowan said. "Thought it was a rumour."

"Where's his operation?" Kai said, finally showing some interest.

"Before I answer that, how did you circumvent Tanner's cuff?"

Kai stared at him with narrowed eyes for an uncomfortable moment. Luke thought he wouldn't answer, and then he shrugged. "Child's play. Forfeiture was always a threat, so I was prepared. I've known about barren witches for years. Just had to find one. I'd read the cuff's runes. All I needed was a higher authority. A lord I know owed me a favour. He attended, created the illusion, and got us out of there when it was done."

"The unconscious driver," Adeline said.

"He was resting," Kai said. "Now, where's Tanner's power pack operation?"

"The tower," Luke said. "Thousands of people spend their days there, Monday to Friday. He's siphoning a captive audience."

"Hypocritical bastard," Kai said.

"Tanner was currying the king's favour imposing your stiff sentence for siphoning. And all the while he's been doing it on a mass scale. I doubt the king would approve. Especially when the witches find out about it."

"You think the king will take action against him?" Sutter said. "Set an example?"

"I'd put money on it," Luke said.

Kai rolled his shoulders and pulled down his cuffs. "What's your plan?"

TWENTY-NINE

"I'm fine," Adeline said, after the three warlocks had left. Her back still stung, but it was nothing she couldn't cope with. As they headed for the car, she brushed off the remaining dust, straightened her clothes, and fixed her hair.

What she wasn't fine with was Luke's revelation that everyone who worked in the tower was being siphoned to make the power packs she'd come to rely on. She felt sick about it.

Luke brooded, swimming in the guilt that he hadn't been able to stop Kai attempting to siphon her.

"Don't forget your sister's package," he said, as they drove into the tower's underground.

Adeline had forgotten. She compelled a peach-coloured sweater with pearl buttons, wrapped in tissue and nestled in a proper shopping bag. She shone with pride as she exited the car. It was the most complicated compel she'd accomplished to date.

Two guards were in position outside the suite. Adeline's heart rate kicked up. Tanner's guard looked them over as the other guard opened the door. They crossed the threshold and passed Luke's office. The door was open. Both of them glanced inside, but Tanner wasn't there.

"I think I'll go for a swim," she said, trying for nonchalance as they entered the kitchen. "Oh, hello." She'd spotted Tanner sitting in the living room, his arms stretched along the back of the sofa, an ankle resting on one knee. His gaze followed them into the room.

"Hello." He stood. "Luke, may I have a word?"

Luke dipped his head. "Of course." Tanner crossed in front of them, and Luke followed him to his office without a backward glance. Adeline understood better now how Luke played to the cameras. Unwavering obedience. It's how he stayed alive. Adeline didn't think she'd have the stomach for the constant humiliation he endured.

She carried on to her room, slipped into her bathing suit, and pulled on a robe. It seemed like a very good idea to keep out of Tanner's sight until he'd finished his business with Luke.

But after a lengthy workout, Tanner's guard was still lurking around the suite's entrance. She walked into the living room and stalled. Tanner stood with a second man Adeline didn't recognize. Her fight-or-flight instinct kicked in. She dripped power down her arms and armoured herself.

"Where's Luke?" she asked.

"Resting," Tanner said.

He wasn't resting of his own accord, of that Adeline was certain. Luke would never leave her to these two without so much as a mind message.

"This is my runecaster, Liam Nunez," Tanner said. "He'd like to examine you, if that's all right."

"Isn't Luke your runecaster?" Adeline said.

"I have several. Liam specializes in healing. We made a commitment to your priestess to monitor the magic inside you. It's been several days now since Beatrice checked. We'd like to ensure the magic is not compromising your health."

"I'm sure I'd know if it was. Flu symptoms, I'm told. I feel fine. My sister checked my threads just this morning. She's the coven's binder," she explained. "Nothing witchy in here."

"Still. Never hurts to be sure." He offered a benevolent smile to Adeline and turned to his runecaster. "If you wouldn't mind." He swept his hand toward her.

"Actually," Adeline said. "I would mind. No offence, but I don't know Liam." And more to the point, she didn't know what Tanner had tasked Liam to do. Find the locking rune, or break it? She wasn't going to wait to find out.

"I have to change," Adeline said. Her hasty plan was to get into the dressing room, from where she could visualize herself out of the suite.

Her mistake was turning her back.

She woke on her side in a haze, her head fuzzy. She blinked, and felt sand in her right eye. When she rolled onto her back, the skin between her shoulder blades burned. Unable to get comfortable, she sat up. Why was she in the bedroom? She was in her bathing suit. She gazed around the room, catching sight of the camera in the corner.

Memories flooded back. Tanner, Liam, the rune in her eye. With difficulty, she kept her escalating panic in check. It was six in the morning. She'd been out of it for twelve hours. She rose and walked to the bathroom mirror. Her right eye looked normal, but her eyelid told her otherwise. Years ago, she'd scratched a cornea, and this felt similar.

She turned her back to the mirror and glanced over her shoulder. Sarah's glamour was still in place. She pulled on her magic and felt it waiting, intact. At least he hadn't been able to take that. Two power packs remained on her arm.

Back in the dressing room, she noticed that the shopping bag she'd compelled yesterday had been moved. She peered inside. The tissue paper was wrinkled. Someone had inspected her handiwork. It could only have been Tanner or Liam. Could they tell she'd compelled it?

She changed and went in search of Luke. His bedroom door was closed. She continued to the living room and found him reclined on the sofa, an arm draped over his eyes.

"Luke?"

He jerked, glanced over, and sat up. "Hey."

"You don't look so good. Can I get you something?"

"No, but thank you. It's just a headache. I've taken something for it." *Tanner cut off my magic. He knocked me out. I'm sorry I couldn't protect you.*

Why would he do that? "If you don't mind, I'll make myself a latte."

"Go ahead." *He heard we'd detoured on our way back here. Sent Connie to check on us.*

Shit. She started for the kitchen. *How much did she see?* "Funny that I don't remember going to bed. I guess Tanner and Liam let themselves out."

"Liam? I didn't know he came by. It must have been after I'd gone to lie down. When you were at the pool." *She saw Sutter in the parkade's stairwell. Knew I was close by from the chain's tracker. Made assumptions. She's got no proof, but Tanner wasn't taking any chances.*

What do you know about Liam?

We've met. He's one of Tanner's puppets. He's a runecaster. A good one. I think he found Kai's locking rune. My right eye is scratchy, but he didn't get my magic. "I hope they didn't take offence that I turned down their offer to check on my health. Maybe if I knew Liam . . ." She shrugged.

Making Tanner believe she hadn't clued in to what he had done was critical. Otherwise, she could kiss goodbye any possibility of getting out of the tower again. "Do you have a first aid kit in here?" Adeline said. "I think I've scratched my eye."

"No, but you can compel one." *Is the glamour still in place?*

Yes, but my runeglyph is burning. "Right, of course. I keep forgetting. Old habits." She extended her arm and compelled a familiar brand of eye drops. The small squirt bottle appeared in her open hand.

Your sister's glamour prevented Liam from seeing your runeglyph. He must have tried to find the locking rune, and, failing that, attempted to force it. Though it didn't work, as long as Tanner thinks he has a shot at getting your magic, he'll keep you alive.

When her latte finished brewing, she took an armchair opposite Luke. She set the cup down, leaned her head back, and squeezed two drops of the soothing antibiotic drops into her eye. *I should never have turned my back on Tanner. My armour was useless against whatever he hit me with.* "I'll get in touch with Marcus. He can probably fix whatever I've done to my eye," she said. "I'll call him from Sarah's this morning."

"I think you mean tomorrow. You've got your days mixed up." *Tanner is suspicious enough. I don't want to push him. We need to stay here, set our trap, and pray he doesn't catch on.*

"Right. It's Sunday. I forgot," Adeline said. "Any word yet on Kai's whereabouts?"

"Not yet."

She checked the time. They had hours to endure before Luke's plan was set in motion. She pulled out her sketch pad. The scratch in her eye, though annoying, wouldn't prevent her from sketching. Her nerves were fried. Having a pencil in her hand always soothed her, made the world go away.

"That'll be Connie," Luke said, excusing himself a few minutes before seven that evening. As planned, he disappeared into his office to supposedly answer the intercom. When dinner arrived promptly at seven, as it always did, Adeline went down the hall to collect it. She thanked the guard, and, before the door closed, two new guards approached.

She left Luke to greet the new guards and carried on back to the kitchen. That Tanner had sent dinner was a positive sign. Then again, he could have poisoned their meal. She wouldn't dwell on that.

Adeline went about the usual evening routine of setting out plates and cutlery. Dinner was steak and roasted vegetables. Perfect with a bottle of wine, she thought, uncorking a Cabernet Sauvignon from Luke's bar.

How'd it go? Adeline asked.

We'll know soon enough. He poured them each a glass. "Cheers."

She'd never tried so hard to act casual. Across the table, Luke seemed to be doing the same. They were both overly complimentary about the food, laughing too hard, struggling to find topics for discussion.

Minutes dragged by. Then an hour. Adeline found distraction tidying the kitchen. She sat down again with her sketchbook but had difficulty concentrating on anything more than doodles. Luke remained quiet.

The moment she could justify it, she escaped to her dressing room for the night. She didn't change for bed. Better to be ready if the door burst open and Tanner stormed in.

Restless, she woke every hour during the endless night. When sunlight finally crept across the floor beyond the crack in her door, she breathed a sigh of relief. They'd made it through the night. Another hour and they'd be out of there.

After she used the bathroom, she slipped down the hall. Luke's door was still closed. Silently, she made her way to the living room. Everything was as they'd left it the night before, not tossed like a bomb had gone off as she'd half expected. She made herself a latte and pulled her sketchbook into her lap. The city had an ethereal glow in the early morning light, and she set about trying to capture it.

Luke arrived a short time later, looking as he always did: smartly dressed, clean shaven, black hair slicked back and still wet from the shower. A now-familiar waft of cedar trailed him.

"You're up early," he said.

"Good light this morning," she said. *Everything okay?*

So far. No word from Tanner. He made himself an espresso. *I suggest we carry on as usual.*

I want out of here so bad I could chew my way through the door.

Patience, Luke said, sipping his brew.

She put another two drops in her scratched eye and managed to waste another half an hour before she stood. "Let's go. Sarah will be waiting."

Luke looked up from his phone, a small smile curving his lips. He rose and stashed his phone in his pocket. "After you," he said.

She noticed him glance at the camera. His brow furrowed.

What's up?

The shield hasn't come down.

He could feel that? Why couldn't she? *Your magic?*

Still locked.

Keeping with their routine, she knocked on the door. When the guard opened it, Tanner and his guard were arriving at a clip.

"Going somewhere?" Tanner said, effectively blocking their exit.

Adeline swallowed. She smiled, hoping her unease didn't leak through. "It's Monday. I have to make Charlie's breakfast. And we'll probably be late. I've invited my sister over."

He glanced at her hands. "Aren't you forgetting something?"

"Shoot. Thanks for reminding me," Adeline said. She flung out her arm and called the bag with the sweater in it. The handles landed neatly in her grip.

"May I have a moment with you before you go?" Tanner said. He surged ahead, forcing them back into the suite. She and Luke pressed against the wall on the same side to allow Tanner room to pass. His guard blocked the doorway.

Luke handed her the car keys. "Wait in the car. I'll be down in a minute."

"Actually, I'd prefer she join us," Tanner said.

Armour yourself, Luke said.

Already there, Adeline replied. Not that her armour had helped in the last go-round with Tanner. At least she knew not to turn her back on him this time.

They followed Tanner into the living room.

"I had an interesting discussion with Connie this morning," Tanner began. "Seems she can't remember talking with you last night."

Luke furrowed his brow. "That's curious."

"Two packages left here at 7:00 p.m. Who did Connie say was collecting them?"

"I'm never given that information. Just told to have the packages ready."

"Did you recognize the guards who took them?"

"No. Why? What's happened?"

"It appears we've had a security breach. Who knows the procedure for releasing the packages?"

"You, Connie, me. If the guards are privy, I wouldn't know."

"The guards are not privy. I didn't authorize the release of those packages. Connie doesn't recall directing you to release them. Which leaves you. Unless Adeline here organized it."

Adeline's mouth dropped open. "Me? I don't even know what you're talking about," Adeline said. She realized she was seeing the real Tanner now, not the fake benefactor. Alarm shot through her. If this conversation didn't turn around, there would be no going back.

"No?" Tanner said, swivelling his head in her direction. "You've never wondered where Luke gets those power packs you so enjoy?"

She adopted a puzzled expression. "Actually, no. He already told me he makes them."

"Did he?" Tanner turned back to Luke. "Did you also tell her how you make them?"

Tanner could squish her like a bug. She needed to get away from him. "Whatever this is about, sounds like it's between you two," Adeline said. "I'll be in my room." She backed away from them with her hands in the air.

"You know what I think?" Tanner said, still addressing Luke. "I think you met with Sutter yesterday. And I think you organized for those packages to be released to his people."

"How?" Luke spread his arms. "Your guards hear every word I speak. See every move I make. I couldn't have organized such a thing without you knowing about it."

Adeline felt a crackling in the air. She froze.

Tanner's voice boomed. "Do you take me for a fool?" A bolt of lightning hit Luke in the chest. He dropped to his knees, and his face contorted in pain. Tanner backhanded him. Hard. Luke toppled over.

As much as it killed Adeline, she couldn't defend herself against Tanner's magic. She visualized herself beyond the door in the hall outside, but Tanner had closed her escape hatch. Pain spiked as she smashed into the door. Her cheek bounced off the hard surface. She'd been more cautious than last time, used less velocity, but it still knocked her senseless.

She found herself being pulled toward the kitchen, as if someone had a grip on the front of her shirt. Tanner stood, his fist outstretched, a gleeful smile on his face. "The only place where this traitorous liar was left unmonitored was inside your house wards. Care to enlighten me about what you two have been up to?"

"I don't know what—"

"Do not lie to me," he snarled. "He's recruited you, or you wouldn't have tried to escape."

She glanced at Luke, who hadn't moved except for an involuntary twitch of his hand. "After what you did to him? Escaping is the only sane choice."

"Luke Churchwell has crossed me for the last time. Tell me what you know, or I'll pry the information out of you with an ice pick. After which you can join Luke in the afterlife."

Tanner's invisible grip lifted her feet from the floor. "I don't think the priestess would consider either of those options any kind of refuge."

He threw a shock into her that bent her spine. "Last chance, witch."

Her voice strained through the pain. "Nothing is going on." She sucked in a ragged breath. "I don't know who Sutter is." Another laboured breath. "Luke didn't meet anyone inside my wards." Two more breaths. "He couldn't get anyone inside without me inviting them in." Another breath. "And I'm not in the habit of inviting warlocks into my home."

Luke had come to and staggered to his feet, his nose bleeding.

"The plates on that motorcycle parked in your driveway belong to Warrick Flynn. A rebel warlock of some renown. So it appears you are in the habit of inviting warlocks into your home." He adjusted the tilt of his head. "And you wonder why I wouldn't believe you. What else are you lying about?"

"Warrick is my ex-husband. He's there to protect Charlie because Kai threatened him."

Tanner's eyes widened ever so slightly. She'd surprised him. He loosened his hold, and she dropped to the floor, staggering like she'd had one drink too many.

Luke steadied himself. Tanner noticed, and nailed him with another body-blow of energy. Luke flew backwards, his arms akimbo, and hit the kitchen island. He grunted and once again fell to the floor.

"I heard the chime of the intercom last night," Adeline said. "If it wasn't Connie on the other end, then someone hacked your system."

"I'll give you credit for imagination, but your story doesn't pan out. The intercom is monitored. There was no call to this suite last night."

"Then messing with your monitoring system was part of the hack."

Tanner shook his head. "Such lengths you're willing to go to. For this piece of shit. Maybe you fancy him?"

Adeline called her bo staff. It landed in her hand with a satisfying smack. She unfurled it on instinct and assumed a fighting stance.

Tanner laughed. With a swipe of his hand, her bo staff dropped to the floor and melted into a molten puddle.

He reached out, crushing her windpipe from across the room. Her sight narrowed. Bright dots appeared at the edges of her vision. And then his breath was upon her face.

"You will not keep this magic, witch. It belongs to the warlocks." Though she couldn't see it, his hand wrapped around her wrist. Burning heat rose up her arm. His face appeared in her field of vision. Fingers pried open her right eye. She cried out at the first piercing of his magic. Many more followed. An agony unlike anything she'd experienced before shattered her.

She didn't see what force ended her suffering. She was simply grateful for it. Sharp pops of crackling magic exploded around her, followed by what sounded like water being sprayed on a hot pan. Wood splintered. Glass shattered. Dark shapes moved through the air, followed by loud thumps. And then quiet descended.

She came to, blinking. Her eyes hurt. Her vision didn't clear. The threat of Tanner had her gulping air, but the immediate area around her was quiet, as if isolated from its surroundings. She righted herself and took inventory. She was on the floor in the kitchen. Her left arm burned. The skin between her shoulder blades stung, as if revisited by the hornets. Breathing hurt. Blinking hurt. She struggled to her feet, steadying herself against the counter. The silence that surrounded her was absolute, as if she were the lone survivor of a nuclear attack. She squinted toward the kitchen cupboards. Blurry shapes that could be cabinet doors hung askew, as if their hinges had been broken. A large painting in the living room appeared to be cockeyed.

Tears flooded her injured eyes, worsening what little sight she had.

With her hands in front of her, she managed to find her way to an armchair but discovered it was overturned. She approached another that had been shoved against a wall. Glass crunched under her feet. Probably remnants of the coffee table.

She crawled into the armchair and cradled her head. She'd been injured and compromised in a way that left her disassociated from her body, but she knew she had to get away from there. Thoughts flitted in and out of her mind, taunting her to catch them.

She rose and stumbled down the hall. There was no sign of Luke or Tanner. With concerted effort and a hand on the wall, she made her way to the front door. She knocked, but the door didn't open. Tentatively, she reached for the handle and pushed down. It opened. She stepped out. No shield, no resistance. No guard presence. She followed the wall to the elevator, found the call button, and pushed.

When the ding sounded, she felt along the wall for the opening and stepped inside. She pushed all the lower buttons. One of them would be the lobby. She stayed put when the robotic female voice called out *first floor*.

Her burned arm chafed against her clothing. She held it away from her body and smoothed her hair with her other hand. She'd been wearing jeans and what was now probably a very dirty T-shirt, and she prayed she looked normal enough to pass through the lobby and get outside without drawing attention.

Exiting the elevator on the ground floor, she kept her good arm out in front of her. She shielded her eyes with her burned arm and headed toward the light and, she hoped, the street.

"Do you need assistance?" asked a stern voice. The screech of a walkie-talkie came from the voice's general direction. A security guard? She probably looked like a stumbling junkie. Dangerous. Unpredictable. Someone who needed to be removed from the premises.

That worked for her. "Would you help me outside?"

The guard took her uninjured elbow and guided her to a concrete bench outside. She sat and thanked the air where the guard had stood seconds earlier. He'd already abandoned her. Her phone was in her pocket. She caught her breath, then squinted at the screen and pressed on a blue blob she hoped was the voice command button. Warrick answered. Her voice cracked. She told him where she was. The phone was still in her hand when he materialized.

"Babe? Jesus." He took the phone from her. "Take my hand."

She did, and a moment later the warm touch of Warrick's magic, of her home, embraced her. Tears formed, real ones this time.

When she awoke next, quiet once again surrounded her. "Hello," she called. She couldn't open her eyes. Terror flashed through her.

"I'm right here," Warrick said.

"I can't see." Adeline's voice was a desperate cry.

"Marcus is here. I'll call him."

"Adeline," Marcus said, his voice a soothing balm. "I'm going to remove the bandages from your eyes. Don't fight me."

She felt the pull of tape, but when the bandages were lifted, she could see no more than vague shapes before her eyes.

"What's he done to me?"

"Quiet. Let me work."

THIRTY

After Tanner's initial lightning bolt, Luke's first thought was for Adeline. She had to get out of there to save herself, because he wasn't going to survive Tanner's fury. Tanner's second bolt landed him on the floor near the kitchen island. He came to as Tanner had Adeline in his grip, his hand glowing red. Luke tried to get to her, but his heart was skipping beats. His muscles wouldn't obey his commands.

He lay there, helpless. And then, inexplicably, guards rushed the room. Not Tanner's guards. Nulls. More than he'd ever seen in one place before.

They forcibly separated Tanner from Adeline, who was tossed aside like trash. Tanner put up a good fight, but the nulls had him trussed up in magical bonds within minutes. They hauled Luke to his feet and bound him the same way. Unable to use their magic, he and Tanner were transported from the tower's underground in a passenger van with blacked-out windows.

The bolts had left Luke with loose muscles and the taste of copper in his mouth. His right thumb sported a new ring. The black metal fit snugly, but not tight. Even so, he couldn't twist it or budge it. The ring must have been how the nulls had bound his magic. Tanner also wore a ring, adding weight to Luke's suspicions. Tanner's glare was a toxic cloud. Luke knew without a doubt that Tanner would have detonated his chain if he'd been able to wield his magic.

During the dark drive, Luke had too much time to contemplate what came next. After what he'd done under Tanner's orders, he had no illusion that any of his old friends were loyal to him. He and Tanner would both be painted with the same brush. Not that it mattered. Dead was dead, no matter at whose hands.

The stop and start of city traffic gave way to a long stretch of steady movement, and then they slowed again. One speed bump and then another. The transport van idled, and heavy boots made a slow circumference of the vehicle. Bomb inspection? And then a final lurch, a short drive, and the engine cut out.

As they were ushered out of the van, Luke squinted against bright sunlight, surprised they were at Tanner's mansion. Then again, it wasn't really Tanner's. It was the home of whichever lord the king chose for the territory.

He and Tanner were escorted through a side entrance and down a set of stairs and a long hallway, to a windowless holding cell of sorts. Their escorts cast runes to prevent them from talking and tethered them to separate stations.

Luke stretched out on the bench and rested. Had Adeline made it out of the tower? He hoped she had. She'd done well, improvising, playing her part. Her loyalty was the only loyalty he'd experienced in the past three years. He admired her spark and determination. If he ever fell for a witch, Adeline would be the one.

An hour passed, maybe two, before the nulls came back. They took Tanner away. Another hour or more passed before they returned for Luke. They brought him to a formal sitting room he'd never seen before. Dark colours predominated: slate grey, blood red, mahogany. Heavy floor-to-ceiling drapes covered the windows. Two warlords, a man and a woman, lounged beside a stone fireplace that dominated one wall.

King Lochlan sat in a wing chair behind an antique table, a null behind him on either side. A gelatinous power globe sat in the middle of the small round table.

Luke had been in the king's company before, but never under his scrutiny. His court wasn't as formal as some, but there were rules. The king was to be addressed as *Your Majesty* or *King Lochlan*, and *sir* thereafter. Men didn't have to bow at the waist and women didn't have to curtsy, but a bow of the head was expected. And one had to be very careful about asking questions.

"I'd like to hear your version of events," Lochlan said, sitting forward.

Luke's voice binding disappeared. "Where would you like me to begin, Your Majesty?"

"At the beginning, of course."

Luke nodded. "Eight years ago, when Baroness Erin was killed, you appointed a new ruler to our territory, Lord Tanner. He spent the first two years of his lordship laying the groundwork for a . . . transformation . . . of the territory." Luke's chain heated. "He installed . . . loyalists—" the burn began. He stretched his neck but couldn't escape it. "—in key positions—" Luke's words came in a hiss. He couldn't go much farther. "Bankrupted. Refused—" He grimaced.

The king rose to his feet and walked around the table, a null never more than a step away from him. He approached Luke cautiously, gazing at his chain. "What is this?"

Luke froze as the null stepped forward and pulled Luke's shirt open. He knew the skin around the chain would be red, possibly blistered.

"Fascinating," Lochlan said. "This chain has sentient magic. Tanner's doing, I take it?"

Luke couldn't say.

The king returned to his chair. "So. You're prohibited from talking about Tanner's business. Forbidden from talking about the chain you wear. Are you able to shed light on this power globe?" he asked, gesturing to it.

"The power is . . . collected . . . from the people who inhabit the tower. It's a slow drip. Most don't notice it."

The king leaned forward. "How is the power . . . *collected*?" He repeated *collected* as if the word offended him.

"A runecast."

"Your creation?"

"Yes, but not this version. I'd tapped into the forest on my estate. Tanner learned of it when I was captured and bent it to his own purposes."

"Tanner bent it?"

"No." Luke hung his head. He hadn't meant to mislead the king. "Only another runecaster could. Tanner ordered it, but I don't know for certain who carried it out."

"But you have an idea?"

Luke shifted his stance, uncomfortable with pointing a finger. "Lord Tanner's runecaster is Liam Nunez, but that doesn't mean he did it."

The king nodded, drummed his thumb on the desk. "What do you know of the witch who was attacked by one of our warlocks?"

"Her name's Adeline Thorne." King Lochlan's drumming thumb

stopped, as if he recognized her name. "Tanner tasked me with protecting her. He insisted she stay at the tower until the warlock who attacked her was no longer a danger."

The king steepled his fingers. "No longer a danger to whom?"

"The witch. Her coven." He would have added Tanner's name to that list, but that might lead to the fact that Adeline now bore Luke's rune-glyph. He would suffer the consequences of his actions, but he wouldn't risk endangering her.

"The warlock who attacked the witch is Kai Oxen? A friend of yours. A well-connected siphon who outwitted runecaster Liam's cuff."

"Yes. Kai and I grew up together."

"I understand she's a barren witch. That she now wields warlock magic. What does she know of our runes?"

"Nothing more than what witches have always known. She recognizes some basic forms but doesn't know how to use them."

"If I'd known the witch was in residence at the tower, I would have instructed the nulls to bring her here for questioning. Was she aware of the mass siphoning happening in the tower?"

"Yes."

He slapped his hand on the arm of the chair and cursed. He stood, turning away from Luke. "Take him back to his cell."

·))) ● (((·

Sarah lurked outside Adeline's bedroom door. She trusted Marcus and Warrick, but the magic Lord Tanner had used on Adeline had been raw. Brutal. The tears she'd shed were bloody. When Warrick had brought her home, Adeline had insisted on walking under her own power up the stairs to her room. She'd collapsed on the third step.

Marcus had healed her burned arm, but fixing the damage had exhausted him. He called in an apprentice healer to mend her broken ribs. Marcus and Adeline had slept for hours, resting, healing.

Sarah had insisted on reading Adeline's threads. The magic hadn't hurt her, but Sarah's binder magic couldn't penetrate the cloud of smoke that swirled around her head. She didn't know what it meant.

Now Marcus was back in Adeline's room, working on her eyes. What-ever Tanner had done had terrified Addie. Sarah's heart ached for her sister. Painting had been Addie's love and livelihood for years—the one thing that consistently brought her joy. To lose it would be devastating.

Marcus had been at it for an hour when the door opened. He motioned for Sarah to follow him. Down in the kitchen, she poured him a glass of water.

"Her corneas are abraded. It's bad. Looks to me like Tanner released an unlocking rune several times in her right eye. My guess is when that didn't work, he thought he had the wrong eye and hit the other eye, too. I've repaired what I could for today, but her body will have to absorb the magic before I can do any more. I've put healing ointment in her eyes, and patched them so the light doesn't hurt as much."

"Will she recover her eyesight?"

Marcus scrubbed a hand down his face. "I don't know."

"Hello, Marcus." Odette stood in the archway from the solarium to the kitchen. They embraced. "Sarah invited me."

"I thought we should talk about what's happened," Sarah said. "Figure out how to move forward."

They settled in the living room, each recounting their recollection of events in the clearing. None of them could recall the person responsible for folding their memories.

"All our memories end at the clearing," Sarah said. "For one warlock to fold the memories of four witches in a short time, in that setting . . . The mechanics of it don't work. A specialized fold like that takes time. He would have had to hold three of us in suspended animation while he worked on the other. He couldn't have done that in the clearing in the presence of the coven. So how'd he do it?"

"After the attack, Damaras approached me at the sanctuary," Odette said. "She suggested I visit my family in Cambridge until the crisis was resolved."

"I was in the lab," Marcus said. "Going to the east coast was her suggestion as well."

"Adeline was here when Damaras told her about the attack," Sarah said. "Joe tells me I was wandering on the grounds of the sanctuary when Damaras called him to get me to safety."

Odette sat forward, her features tense. "We were in the sanctuary when our memories were folded. It had to have been a witch."

"Yes. A warlock couldn't have broken through the sanctuary's wards," Sarah said.

"Damaras?" Odette said, testing the impossible idea.

"Silas, too," Sarah said. "Luke found a compulsion spell buried in Adeline's memories. One that compelled her to learn about warlock runes."

"Before the blast in the training centre, at the GC meeting, Daniel suggested Adeline spy for us," Marcus said. "A compulsion spell would fill that order."

"Daniel wouldn't have the clout to do that on his own," Sarah said. "I agree with you. Silas must have been involved."

Odette shifted uncomfortably in her seat. "Then Kylie's in on it too. They always stand together. But why would they do this? I don't understand."

"I think I do," Sarah said. "Damaras and Silas are working together to bury something that would unseat her."

She stood, collecting her thoughts as she wandered to stand behind the sofa. This wasn't a story she could tell sitting down. "It began seven years ago when Damaras and my mother were in the running for priestess to succeed Jonas. Mom was powerful and popular. Ahead of Damaras in the race. Damaras knew the election was the last chance she'd have at becoming priestess. She and Mom are the same age, and it's a lifetime appointment.

"So Damaras dug up Adeline's failed unbindings. She suggested those failures were because Mom's magic was weak. Adeline's spectacular rebellion added weight to her argument. Damaras blamed her behaviour on Mom's poor parenting. She declared it a character flaw that would lead to bad leadership for the coven. But no matter how low Damaras sank in her efforts, Mom remained ahead of her in the race."

Sarah self-soothed by running her hands over the fabric on the top edge of the sofa. "Until my father died. Unexpectedly. Damaras refused to investigate, and Mom gave up her quest to become priestess. We may never be able to prove that Dad was murdered, but Adeline made her suspicions clear to Damaras. She also continued to be a stone in her shoe.

"Adeline, however, was never a real threat to Damaras—until Silas witnessed the untethered power Adeline displayed in the training centre. He was unnerved by her."

Odette and Marcus remained quiet, still absorbing her words when she retook her seat.

Odette finally spoke. "Murder? Memory manipulation?" She shook her head. "I'm not saying I don't believe you, Sarah, but it's hard to imagine Damaras harming us. She's our priestess, sworn to protect us. We chose her."

"Damaras has set her sights higher than priestess of the Stonewater coven," Sarah said. "She's aiming for high priestess. Lady Brighton is getting on in years. Her retirement—or, stars forbid, her death—will be Damaras's last chance at the role."

"How do you know that?" Odette said.

"I've worked with Damaras for years. She doesn't hide her ambitions."

"What about Silas?" Odette said. "He's proven his loyalty to the coven time and again."

"Yes," Sarah said. "And Lady Brighton's successor can bring along their war mage."

"That might explain how Silas got two additional war mages on our GC," Marcus said. "The three of them carry more weight than any of us. And don't forget it was Daniel who raised the alarm about Adeline siphoning from us."

"Damaras and Silas already lied to us," Sarah said. "At the clearing, they told us they'd negotiated for Tanner to touch Adeline with the intent of learning the identity of her attacker. But Luke told us what they'd actually arranged was for Lord Tanner to siphon her magic. No one knew the warlock who'd attacked her had locked the magic inside her. By the time Tanner tried and failed, it was too late to hide from the coven the truth of what they'd agreed to."

"They fabricated the second attack," Marcus said, thinking out loud, "to whitewash their mess."

"That's the conclusion I came to as well," Sarah said.

"But why would the warlocks go along with that?" Odette said.

"To get their hands on Adeline," Sarah said. "Tanner wanted the magic for himself. He hoped to find the unlocking rune. And now that their cover-up is unravelling, Damaras or Silas will kill Adeline if they have the opportunity. They're afraid of her."

"Do we have proof of any of this?" Odette said. She sat on the edge of her seat, her elbows on her knees.

"I can testify to Adeline's physical condition," Marcus said. "What about the warlock? Luke. Will he testify?"

"I don't think Tanner would allow it," Sarah said. "And other than the initial attack on Adeline, there's no archive record of what happened in the clearing. I checked."

"That leaves us with hearsay and circumstantial evidence," Odette said. "It's not enough."

"Four of us against the coven? We're screwed," Marcus said.

A loud knock at the front door startled them.

Sarah rose to answer it. Warrick materialized on the stairs.

"It's Damaras," Sarah said, under her breath. Odette and Marcus retreated to the back of the house. Sarah forced a smile and answered the door.

"Is Adeline here?"

"Yes. Upstairs recovering."

"That's a relief. When I learned Lord Tanner had gone missing, I feared the worst. May I see her?"

"She's resting," Warrick said, coming to stand beside Sarah.

Damaras flinched. Warrick grinned.

"Kindly invite me inside," Damaras said, with a sweet smile on her lips.

Sarah knew better than to deny her. "Please come in." Damaras crossed the threshold and flicked her hand behind her, closing the door. She stalked into the living room. Sarah and Warrick followed.

"You must be Warrick Flynn," Damaras said.

"And you must be Damaras Deschene."

"I must say, I'm surprised to find you here," Damaras said.

"You shouldn't be. I'll always have Adeline's back. As she has always had mine."

"That's very gallant of you. But this is witch business, as I'm sure you're aware. I need to see her."

"And she needs her rest. I'll ask her to call you when she wakes."

Damaras pressed her lips together. "Do not make the mistake of interfering in witch business."

"I wouldn't think of it. If you'll excuse me." Warrick dipped his head and vanished. Upstairs, Adeline's bedroom door opened and closed.

"Hello, Damaras," Odette said, walking with Marcus into the living room.

Surprise flitted across Damaras's face. Her features quickly morphed into a pleasant facade. "I heard you'd returned. You're both well?"

"Yes, thank you. Glad to be home," Odette said. Marcus nodded in agreement.

"And your memories? Have they returned?" Damaras asked.

Odette shook her head. "No."

"Mine neither," Marcus said.

"The warlock who attacked us hasn't been found," Damaras said. "You should return to your families. Lie low until he's apprehended."

"I can't speak for Odette," Marcus said, "but I'm staying. Adeline hasn't recovered yet. I want to help her."

"I appreciate that. But you also have a duty to the coven. I don't want you needlessly risking your life." She turned to Odette. "You also have a duty to the coven."

"I asked her to come," Sarah said. "She's safe here within the wards, and I could use her support."

"Of course," Damaras said. "I'll leave you, then, and await Adeline's call."

Odette stared at the closed door after she left. "She never asked what happened to Adeline."

"And she clearly didn't want you and me here," Marcus said.

Sarah looked from Odette to Marcus as a troubling thought demanded her attention. "Damaras is one of the few people capable of breaking the wards on this house."

Thirty-One

Adeline dozed, saturated with the healing magic of Marcus and his apprentice. The bandages over her eyes pressed her into perpetual darkness. Sleep was a welcome reprieve from the ache in her ribs and the disconnect she still felt after suffering the force of Tanner's magic. Each time she stirred, Warrick's warming presence soothed her. Sarah was there too, quiet, but when she took Adeline's hand, she felt Sarah's strength and love.

She lost track of time. When she finally woke fully, she remembered Charlie with a start.

"He's fine," Warrick told her, offering a reassuring stroke of her shoulder. "We've taken care of him."

"Thank you," Adeline said. "Is Marcus still here?"

"He's close by. Do you need him?"

"I'd like him to check my eyes." She reached her feet to the floor and sat up, pushing her throw aside. The plush texture of the blanket was unfamiliar; Sarah must have conjured it. Warrick's chair let out a squeak as he shifted.

"It's only been an hour since he was here. He doesn't want to remove the bandages yet."

"The not knowing is killing me."

"I know. We're all anxious. Would you like me to read you today's headlines?" Warrick asked.

"Maybe later. Guide me downstairs? I need to get my muscles moving." She reached out, and Warrick took her hand. She stood, found her balance, then turned to the left, keeping a guiding hand on the edge of her bed.

"There's something you should know," he said.

"What?" When her hand failed to find the footboard, she stalled. "This isn't my bed."

"That's what I was about to tell you," Warrick said.

Out of nowhere, a deafening screech hit her like a body blow. She dropped to the bed, pulled away from Warrick, and pressed her hands to her ears.

He knelt in front of her, his hands on her forearms. "What is it?"

"The wards. They've been broken. We have to leave. Quick." She staggered to her feet again. "Sarah!" She lurched forward.

Warrick stood in her path, his hands on her shoulders. "Sarah's okay. You're okay," he said. "We're not at your house."

Footsteps rushed toward her. She covered her head and cowered.

"It's just me," Sarah said. "I came as soon as I felt it."

Adeline began to shake. Her blindness left her feeling so vulnerable she wanted to scream.

"Sit," Warrick said, guiding her back to the bed. "We moved everyone out of the house. Even Charlie. We're safe. Everyone's safe."

Adeline sucked in a ragged breath. "Why? What happened?"

"Damaras stopped by your place. Marcus and Odette were there. Sarah and me as well. She wanted to see you. I put her off. She didn't press the issue, but before she departed, she strongly suggested Marcus and Odette leave. None of us felt comfortable staying there after that, knowing she could break the wards if she chose to."

"And Charlie?"

"He's at a B&B. We told him you had norovirus and the house was being disinfected. He was relieved to get away from it."

"Where are we?"

"The Sylvia Hotel in the West End. Odette and Marcus are one floor down. Sarah, you, and I are in a suite."

Adeline let out a breath. "I hate this. Kai, Tanner, Damaras. I'm sick of them using me, trying to control me. They need to be stopped."

"They will be," Sarah said.

"Breaking your wards is the beginning of the end," Warrick said. "We just need to be patient."

Patience. The same thing Luke had cautioned. A wave of guilt that she hadn't considered his welfare before now washed over her. "What's happened to Luke?"

"We don't know. Someone in the tower suite put up a fight," Warrick said. "After you were home, I went back. The front door was unlocked.

There were no guards, no one inside. The centre of the suite had been trashed. The magic that had held the shields in place was in tatters. I brought back your things."

Sometime later, Marcus and Odette joined them. Despite Marcus's protests, Adeline insisted he remove the bandages.

"Close the drapes," Marcus said. "Her eyes will be sensitive to the light."

He proceeded to remove the gauze, and, even with her eyelids closed, the light was too bright. When he'd finished swiping something warm against her eyelids, she peeled her eyes open, squinting. All she could make out were murky shadows.

"It's the ointment," Marcus said, a little too quickly. "Give it another day."

Reluctantly, she let him reapply the bandages, relieved when the painful light snuffed out.

Sarah read her again but reported that she still couldn't get a take on her.

The following day, Adeline sat in the hotel suite's living room, nursing a cup of aromatic coffee while anxiously awaiting Marcus's arrival. He'd insisted she wait until noon to remove the bandages and, knowing her impatience, wisely kept away until then.

Sarah and Warrick had been taking turns distracting her. Mostly with food. The sweet pop of grapes, a creamy mug of seafood chowder, the crunch of a toasted bagel.

When Marcus's knock came, Adeline jumped. Coffee dribbled off her fingers.

"I'll get the door," Sarah said, pressing a napkin into Adeline's hand.

The door opened and closed. Footsteps approached. Marcus spoke. "You ready for this?"

After he had someone close the drapes, he removed the adhesive and slowly peeled away the gauze, giving her eyes time to adjust to the light. "Don't open your eyes yet. How are you doing?"

"It's bright." She felt hopeful.

His touch was gentle as he wiped a warm, wet cloth around her eyes. "This stuff's like Vaseline. It'll take a while to clear. Don't rub your eyes, but you can blink if that helps. Ready?"

At her nod, he instructed her to open her eyes. She did. Her vision was no better. Blinking worked some of the ointment away, but as it thinned, the scratching of her eyelids returned.

"Well?" Warrick said.

She shook her head, afraid her voice would crack if she spoke.

"Tip your head back," Marcus said. The ambient light felt like a dose of soap in her eyes. "I see improvement. Most of the smaller abrasions are healed already."

He worked his magic again and then reapplied ointment and taped fresh gauze into place. She was plunged back into darkness.

Warrick took her hand, sensing her fear. "It's only been forty-eight hours."

"Your abrasions were extensive," Marcus said. "The magic is speeding the healing. You should see some improvement in the morning."

Someone's phone rang.

"It's Damaras," Sarah said.

"Can she track your phone?" Warrick said.

"No. I've spelled all our phones to prevent tracking."

"Answer it," Adeline said. "See what she wants."

"I'll put her on speaker," Sarah said. "Hello, Damaras."

"Sarah. Where is Adeline?"

"Somewhere safe."

"I want an address. And I want it now."

"Why did you break the wards on her house?"

"Adeline was told to call me. She didn't. I don't beg for audiences with witches under my rule."

"She's still recovering," Sarah said.

"You, your sister, Marcus, and Odette will report to the sanctuary immediately. That's an order. Refusal will have life-altering consequences for all of you."

"We know what you did, Damaras," Sarah said.

The line went dead.

Tanner was removed from their cell for questioning once again, and he didn't return. Luke spent an uncomfortable night on the narrow bench. In the morning, he was given breakfast, and then the nulls brought him to stand before the king, this time in a room he was familiar with. Tanner's office. The king sat behind the desk, twirling a silver letter opener between his fingers. The nulls were present, but the warlords were taking a break.

"Do you know how few warlock lords make it to old age?" he said, raising a questioning eyebrow. When Luke didn't offer an answer, the king's attention drifted to the letter opener. "About sixty percent. I'm endlessly surprised the aristocracy is still interested in filling the roles when they become vacant. Lordships are fraught with danger. If the lord is too lenient, rogue warlocks set up shop, crime runs rampant, and tithes dry up. The territory goes to hell. If a lord is too harsh, rogues still move in and tithes still dry up, but the rogues' goals are different. They aim to usurp." He stilled the letter opener and glanced directly at Luke. "Which of those two rogues do you imagine is more dangerous?"

The question made it clear that he'd heard Tanner's version of events, and he'd put Luke squarely in the second camp.

"To the king? Neither. You have the power to quash rebellions, remove lords. But you didn't mention the fallout from a crooked lord. A crooked lord *is* the rogue, pocketing tithes and quietly growing his power until it rivals the king's."

The king nodded, thoughtful as he again began twirling the letter opener. "If you had succeeded in the coup you undertook—and yes, I'm aware of your actions—which of your soldiers did you imagine would replace him? Yourself, perhaps?"

"None of us. That's your purview."

He placed the letter opener on the desk in front of him. "Sutter's father was an acquaintance of mine, though I hadn't seen him of late. I know now why. Earlier, I spoke to him and a number of his associates."

Luke allowed himself to feel a ray of hope that Sutter's father had shone a light on Tanner's unquenchable greed.

"I assume you bear a runeglyph?"

"Of course."

"Then I have to trust you're telling me the truth." He leaned forward. "Unless I learn otherwise, which wouldn't be good for your health. What's your professional opinion of runecaster Liam Nunez?"

"He's competent. Loyal to Tanner. Created an impressive runeglyph for him."

"Competent? And yet a warlock of questionable repute outwitted his cuff?"

"Kai is smart and adept. I'm not entirely surprised he found a way around the cuff."

"And he locked his magic inside a witch. Are you able to unlock the rune holding his magic?"

"No. Kai tied it to his biometrics. It needs a fingerprint, or blood. I'm not sure which."

The king sat back again, thinking. "You might want to reassess your professional opinion of runecaster Liam. He was unaware of that fact. It does, however, explain why Tanner didn't succeed in siphoning her magic."

Lochlan stared at the desktop, thinking out loud. "Regardless, the witches will interpret Tanner's attempt as an assault, compounded by the fact that she was under his protection at the time. And I shudder to think of the fallout when the witches learn of the mass siphoning in the tower, if they don't already know. There'll be no mitigating that damage. The political embarrassment will cost us dearly."

Lochlan glanced up at him. "Tell me what you know about an attack on the witches' grid."

"Not a thing. I was unaware of it until a few days ago."

"The high priestess, Lady Brighton, has requested an accord-level meeting. Her sentinels have found something regarding the grid attack."

Luke was escorted back to his cell. Tanner still hadn't returned, but he didn't think the king had released him. If that were the case, Luke wouldn't be wondering anything. He'd be dead.

The hours crawled by. He paced until he was sick of it, then sat on the hard bench. When that became unbearable, he lay on the floor.

When the nulls came for him again, he brushed himself off. Darkness had fallen outside the mansion's sitting room. The king stood at the window, holding back the drapes. He dropped the fabric and turned when Luke was brought before him.

"Care to explain that?" Lochlan glanced pointedly at a photo that lay on the antique table. The image looked an awful lot like Luke, lit up in a spray of sparks.

Luke bent over the photo. "If that's me, I don't recognize it. What's it supposed to be?"

"You, attacking the witches' grid. The high priestess's sentinels were able to sharpen the image caught on CCTV footage from a warehouse nearby."

Luke picked up the photo and looked at it more closely. "Is this the right date?" The date stamp was a little over two weeks prior.

"Yes."

"Then that's not me. Whoever that is, they're not wearing a chain."

Lochlan paused. The nulls pushed Luke back and retrieved the photo, which they handed to the king. He looked at it carefully before glancing up at Luke. "Body glamour?"

"Likely."

"Witch or warlock?"

A witch? That would change the politics of the situation considerably. He'd have to give that some thought.

"May I ask a question?" Luke said.

"Go ahead."

"Why did you ask who bent my runecast to Tanner's purposes?"

"Why do you think?"

Luke took a moment. "Because if it was bent once, perhaps it could be bent again? To drain the grid."

Thirty-Two

"I won't think any less of you if you report to the sanctuary," Adeline said, knowing the heavy price Odette and Marcus would pay for disobeying Damaras.

Regardless, no one reported to the sanctuary. Marcus and Odette were now seeing Damaras in a different light. Until they knew who'd folded their memories, they didn't feel safe being confined with the priestess or the war mages, who had the power to hold them against their will.

They had proof that Damaras had broken Adeline's wards. It wasn't enough. The high priestess could order a regression to prove it was a witch who folded their memories, to prove Damaras had sold out Adeline and tried to cover it up. But the high priestess wouldn't entertain their request without significant proof. Suspicions were penny stock.

"Damaras can only guess what we suspect her of doing, and I'd bet she has a long list of offences to choose from," Adeline said.

"I hope it's driving her mad," Sarah said. "Desperation might cause her to screw up. Expose herself."

None of them voiced the unnerving possibility they wouldn't get the proof they needed.

"What's the plan?" Odette said. "We can't just sit here and wait for Damaras to screw up."

"If we could get inside her office, we might find something incriminating," Marcus said.

"She's good at covering her tracks," Adeline said. "There won't be anything left to connect her to what happened in the clearing."

"Maybe Silas isn't as good at the cover-up. He knows the truth," Odette said. "And he has an office in the sanctuary."

"We'd never get in. The wards will have been changed by now," Marcus said.

"Maybe, but it's worth a try," Sarah said.

"You're skilled with wards," Warrick said to Sarah. "Do you think you could break the one at the sanctuary?"

"I don't know, but out of all of us, I've got the best shot at doing it. But the wards are alarmed. Damaras and Silas would be notified immediately."

"Everyone is looking for us," Marcus said. "We'd never even get close."

"*We'd* never get close, but I know someone who could." Sarah didn't explain herself before she whispered a spell. The room's energy shifted, and then there was silence.

"Impressive," Warrick said, breaking the quiet.

"How did you learn to glamour like that?" Marcus said, his tone one of awe.

"Glamour?" Adeline said.

"Full body! Your sister looks the spitting image of Simon," Odette said. "Where did you find the spell? I've been looking for it for ages."

"In the old grimoires in the archives," said a voice that sounded like Simon's. "The dangerous grimoires are spelled to keep them hidden. I overheard Carolyne talking with someone on the phone about it. Mom confirmed it, though I'm sure she never expected me to go looking for them."

"My baby sister. The radical," Adeline said, smiling.

Simon laughed. "Baby? Well, I did hear she was younger than you."

The voice changed back, and Sarah countered each of their *it's too dangerous* arguments. "Body glamour won't fool the wards, but I only have to touch the door to know if I'm persona non grata. If that's all we learn, it's more than we know now, and then we can move on, maybe try to recruit someone."

When it became clear that Sarah was determined to test the wards, they devised a plan. If she could get inside, she would. If not, she'd get off the property before anyone from the coven knew she'd tried. They covered every angle, every misstep and outcome they could conceive. The exercise might not get them any proof, but doing something felt an awful lot better than doing nothing.

When they'd exhausted their list of potential disasters, Warrick kissed Adeline goodbye. The other three hugged her fiercely, and then they left.

Odette had wanted to stay, but Adeline bristled at the notion of a babysitter. She would not be the weak link that caused their plan to fail. They needed everyone in the field to support Sarah.

She sat with the phone in her hand and prayed they all made it back without incident.

A tense hour into the wait, her phone rang. She fumbled to answer it.

"Is this Adeline Thorne?" a man asked in a deep bass.

She didn't recognize the voice. "May I ask who's calling?"

"My name's Anderson Schubert. I'm a friend of your mother's."

Her mom's new beau. Or someone trying to fool her? "I don't mean to sound paranoid, Anderson, but I need proof you are who you say you are."

"All right. What proof may I offer?"

"You bought something for my mother recently."

"Ah, yes. You must be referring to a diamond tennis bracelet. It looks lovely on her wrist, if I do say."

He was the real deal. "Thank you for indulging my paranoia. My apologies."

"No need to apologize. You don't know me. But I hope to change that. I find myself here in Vancouver on business with a rare afternoon off. I'd like to invite you and your sister for a drink, if that's agreeable. I'm staying at the Fairmont downtown."

Her mother would be hurt if she offended him, but she couldn't. Not in her condition. "I'm sorry, Anderson, but this isn't a good time."

"Your mother told me as much. But I did promise her I'd check in on you both."

"That's very kind of you. I'll call her and let her know you've been in touch."

She heard his soft laughter. "You must not know the same Morgan Thorne I do. If you'd prefer, I can come to you. I haven't been to the Sylvia in years."

She jerked her head back. He knew where she was staying? Her surprise faded as she realized that Sarah had probably told Joe, who'd told her mom.

"I'd hate to disappoint Morgan. Please. A quick drink."

"Sarah is out. I don't know when she'll return. And, like I said, this really is not a good time."

"I know. So does your mother. Hence her insistence. I fear if you don't agree, she'll be on the next flight to Vancouver."

As much as she didn't want to, Adeline agreed to let him send a car. Him coming to the Sylvia was out of the question. He may have known she and Sarah were staying there, but the others wouldn't appreciate her exposing them.

They also wouldn't appreciate Adeline not being in her room when they returned. Not daring to blow Sarah's cover with a phone call, she used her voice assistant to text Warrick instead. Her phone read his response. If she didn't call him in an hour, he was coming looking for her. He had her back, and that was reassuring, but he couldn't afford to be distracted. She set an alarm to ensure she didn't miss her call-in.

The concierge sent a porter up to her room to guide her to the hotel's side entrance, where the car Anderson had ordered was waiting.

The driver advised her that Anderson would meet their car at the Fairmont. When they arrived, the car's door opened, and the scent of a man's cologne wafted in. She sensed a hesitation.

"Take my hand," a deep voice said, tapping her shoulder. The voice belonged to Anderson. He helped her from the car and tucked her hand in the crook of his arm. "Well, now. I see why you didn't want to meet with me." He guided her inside.

They walked a short distance with only the sound of their footsteps on the marble flooring. Soon after they hit carpet, he seated her in a plush chair. Music blended with quiet voices nearby.

"What would you like to drink?"

"A Cab Sauv would be nice."

He spoke to a server, and minutes later they had their drinks.

"It's a tall, stemmed glass," he said, pushing it across the table so it touched her hand. As soon as she had it successfully cupped, a hush came over them.

"You're a witch?" she said.

"No one will disturb us. Tell me what happened."

"I'm sure you can appreciate that I don't want to upset my mother. Our coven's healer is treating me. He has great faith that he can repair the damage. So please don't tell her. At least not until I can see well enough to reassure her."

"Is the damage to your eyes because of the locking rune?"

"Indirectly, I suppose. My mother told you?"

"About the warlock's attack? Yes. Tell me how this injury occurred."

"Lord Tanner tried to unlock the rune. He wanted my magic. He didn't get it."

"One of the king's lords tried to siphon you? How do we not know about this?"

"We?"

"What did your mother tell you about me?" he asked.

"Just that you used to work together."

"I was her contact on the high council. The high priestess, Lady Brighton, is my superior."

"Is?"

"Yes. She's here for an accord meeting with the warlock king. I'm here to support her. There are a number of items on the agenda, and this should have been one of them. She should have been forewarned about the assault on you."

Adeline's temper flared. "Why?" She spat the word, not intending to sound as harsh as she did. But if he said it was so the witches could demand more money or better concessions, she was going to combust.

"Why?" he said, sounding genuinely confused. "Suitable punishment must be arranged. We can't have warlocks—especially lords—assaulting witches. You were thinking something else?"

A pang of guilt hit her. "Sorry. For the temper. Damaras was more interested in money and concessions. I'm just so tired of being used."

"Your mother shares your sentiments. I imagine the injury doesn't help. Did you report the assault to Damaras?"

"No."

"Why ever not? This needs to be addressed."

"It will be. But Damaras and I are on the outs right now."

"I understand that's the status quo between you two," he said with a chuckle. "I suppose it means I won't see you at tonight's cocktail party."

"What party?"

"Damaras has invited the high priestess and her entourage to a reception this evening."

Adeline's thoughts raced to Sarah. "At the sanctuary?"

"No. Here. Upstairs in the Pacific Ballroom. Your entire coven will be here."

Adeline froze. "When?"

"A few hours. I'm told some have rented rooms and are already trickling in."

Fear crept up her spine, stiffening every muscle in her body. "They're looking for me. I can't be here."

·))) ● (((·

Sarah pointed to the right of the stairs in the distance. "Is that Daniel's bike?" She'd materialized, along with Marcus, Warrick, and Odette, on the grounds of the sanctuary. They stood near a stand of trees just outside security camera range. Warrick could already sense the wards on the building and wouldn't be able to get much closer than the parking lot.

"I think so," Marcus said. "And that's Silas's car." He pointed out a black Porsche Cayenne. "It looks like Damaras and Kylie have already left." Sarah could hold her own against everyone but Damaras and the war mages. With them out of the building, she had her best shot.

"I won't glamour until we see the last of them leave," Sarah said. "Can't hold it for more than ten minutes or so."

Odette disappeared to set up spells at two locations on the other side of the building. Distractions Sarah hoped wouldn't be necessary.

Warrick was taking the biggest risk. Warlocks and witches were prohibited from meddling in each other's affairs, so his *official* role, if, stars forbid, they were caught, was strictly transportation should any of them become incapacitated.

Sarah hadn't discussed any of this with Joe. He would have tried to stop her. Failing that, he'd only worry. She would call him when it was done.

After Odette returned, they settled in to wait. A steady stream of witches left the building, and the parking lot was clearing out.

"There's Silas," Marcus said.

The black car purred past their hiding place. A few minutes later, Daniel jogged down the stairs, securing the strap of his helmet. When his bike roared out of the parking lot, Sarah stood.

"Here we go." Sarah glamoured, and Odette spelled her with a finding spell should she be discovered and taken. Then Sarah dialled Odette, put her phone on speaker so the others could hear what was happening in Sarah's vicinity, and slipped the phone in her shirt pocket.

"Wish me luck," Sarah said in Simon's voice.

Sarah's Simon jogged down the driveway. She slowed to a walk through the parking lot and approached the stairs with one hand in her pocket, humming a tune. The picture of carefree *nothing-going-on-here-that-shouldn't-be* ease.

As she reached the stairs, the door at the top opened unexpectedly. Glancing up, her breath caught in her throat, and she tripped on the first step.

"Walk much?" Daniel said, letting the arched door close behind him. He started down the steps.

Simon's laugh came out strained. She continued up the steps on autopilot, hurrying past him. Her mind frantically searched for an excuse to turn around and leave without looking suspicious. They'd been wrong about the man who'd left on the motorcycle.

Daniel's footsteps stalled. "Shouldn't you be there by now?"

Where? she wondered. "Yeah, I'll be there shortly." Sarah's Simon turned and continued toward the entrance. When her hand touched the handle, she knew she was in trouble. The sanctuary's ward recognized her and wasn't letting her in. Rattled, she did her best to cover, smacking herself in the forehead as if she'd just remembered something.

She turned. Daniel was right behind her.

He tilted his head, his eyes narrowed. "Where's your car, Simon?"

A loud blast exploded on the other side of the building. Sarah's Simon squeaked in surprise at the concussive impact. Odette wasn't messing around. Sarah's Simon darted a glance in the direction of the explosion. She raced down the stairs, toward the chaos, praying she'd lose Daniel in the blast's fallout.

A second blast rattled the windows. Daniel appeared in front of her, casting a spell that dropped her to her knees. "Who are you?" He held his arm steady, pouring magic into her. Holding on to the body glamour though the pain of Daniel's spell took her breath away.

Kylie materialized near them. She looked from Daniel to Sarah's Simon.

"This one couldn't get through the wards," Daniel said. "Must be one of the rebels in glamour."

"Then the others aren't far away," Kylie said. "I'm on it."

Daniel didn't let up. Sarah couldn't hold the glamour any longer. She morphed back to herself. Daniel let go, shoving her so she fell to the ground.

"Look who it is. Miss goody two-shoes. Never thought you'd be reduced to this, Sarah."

Her hands were already in motion, but he was ahead of her. His second spell suspended her will. Her hands stilled. She lay there, unable to move.

Daniel dematerialized. She prayed the others wouldn't fall into his trap, but the healer in Marcus couldn't help himself. He appeared beside her and bent to her with reassuring words. She couldn't even shout at him to get away. As soon as he touched her, he dropped on top of her, immobilized by the same spell. After that, the others must have figured it out, because neither Odette nor Warrick came near.

Sirens wailed in the distance. Neighbours had sounded the alarm, but humans weren't welcome here. Any witches who remained in the building would be busy repairing the damage with haste, clearing away all evidence of the explosions. The blasts would be a mystery, and then a false alarm, and then the humans would forget they'd heard anything.

Silas materialized before the emergency vehicles arrived. "I've reset the wards to prevent them from leaving the sanctuary. Take them inside and rejoin me." He was addressing Daniel, who levitated Marcus, and Kylie, who did the same with Sarah. They passed over the threshold unhindered.

Daniel dropped Marcus in the vestibule. "Dump her here," he said to Kylie. "We need to get back out there and help repair the damage."

"Not here. If the emergency personnel insist on coming inside, they'll see them. Cloak room," she said, already on her way with Sarah. Kylie let her fall in a heap, and Marcus was similarly deposited. The door slammed closed.

Downward light leaked in through aerating slats in the door. Sirens in the distance grew louder. She and Marcus stared at one another, unable to do more than blink. She thought of her children. If she got out of this alive, Joe was going to kill her. Their mother would never forgive her. Sarah was supposed to be the level-headed one. The logical one not prone to reckless decisions. She'd really stepped in it this time.

She considered why Daniel and Kylie were needed to help with the repair. There should have been a dozen witches in the facility. It was never empty. Yet the war mages had dumped her and Marcus practically inside the front door rather than taking the time to get them to the secure rooms in the basement.

And, come to think of it, the parking lot had almost cleared out.

The emergency vehicles arrived, their sirens' volume levelling out. The vehicles must have stopped near the entrance. Vehicle doors slammed. Minutes passed. The vehicles with the sirens moved, but not far. Probably around to the side of the building. Silas would be stalling the humans, giving the witches time to fix the damage.

Marcus blinked hard, then hollowed his cheeks. He moved his head. For him, the will-dampening spell was beginning to lift, probably because he had more body mass than she did and the spell had been weaker by the time he'd been hit with it.

The sirens moved again, this time to the back, and, a short time later, the loud shrilling quieted. The damage must have been cleaned up.

A door near the rear of the sanctuary opened, and an alarm inside the building sounded. An emergency exit. Heavy footsteps approached. Sarah's heart thumped. The footsteps carried on. A radio squawked. The people inside must have been human officials. A lot of them. Voices seemed to come from every corner of the building. More doors opened and closed. The alarm fell silent.

Sarah swallowed. That tiny movement encouraged her. She followed Marcus's example and worked her facial muscles. Finally, she could turn her head.

Marcus had regained his voice. "Can you dematerialize?"

She shook her head. Not yet.

"You said the wards are weakest in the sanctuary's sunroom." She nodded. "Okay. That's where we'll go. And if we can't get out, we can play one hell of a game of hide-and-seek."

Sarah returned Marcus's smile. His defiance helped tamp down the disciplinary voice that was on a ranting loop in her head.

"Go," she said, her voice now a quiet rasp.

Marcus got an arm under himself and rose to his elbow. He reached for her hand. Warmth spilled down her arm before Marcus collapsed again, his elbow having given out. He'd helped her shake off the spell at his own expense.

"Not worth it," she said. But, thanks to him, the spell was loosening its hold. She sat up. Moved her head from side to side, stretched her shoulders.

Marcus got back up to his elbow. "Damn spell packs a punch." He sat and pushed himself to lean against the wall.

"Yeah, and body glamouring is frowned upon? That spell's worse." Sarah wiggled her toes, thrilled that they obeyed her.

Footsteps approached once again. Lighter footfalls this time. Sarah had been watching the door handle, so she was ready when it moved. She froze it. A small spell that even witchlings could accomplish. It taxed her.

"That won't hold them. Are you ready?" Marcus said.

Sarah nodded. As soon as Marcus faded, she released the spell. The door opened, and Kylie appeared, with Daniel right behind her. Kylie didn't get her spell cast before Sarah dematerialized.

THIRTY-THREE

Later that night, the nulls once again came for Luke. The thumb ring remained firmly in place. They silenced his voice and loaded him into the vehicle with the blacked-out windows. He didn't hide his surprise at the sight of Tanner, already inside and likewise trussed and silent.

Thirty minutes later, the vehicle stopped, and Luke and Tanner were escorted to a service elevator. The control panel identified the Fairmont Hotel. One of the guards punched the button for the conference floor. They exited, and the nulls ensured no one noticed them going into a room with a brass plaque that read *Boardroom*.

Inside, a crystal chandelier hung from a high ceiling. Grey and gold striped curtains framed tall windows on two sides of the room. The carpet, in rich shades of red, gold, and turquoise, had been custom made for the elegant space.

An oblong table with one chair at either end sat in the centre. Behind each end of the table, a semicircle of chairs had been placed. This is where the high priestess and the king were meeting. The arrangement mirrored their positions. They were equals, matched in power.

He and Tanner were seated, one at each end of the semicircle of chairs. As far from one another as possible. One null stayed behind to guard them.

A long stretch of time passed before another warlock entered. Liam. He wasn't wearing a thumb ring and smiled slyly as he was seated beside Tanner. Tanner's expression was one of relief, which sent a chill through Luke.

Next in were Kai, Sutter, and Rowan. Luke raised an eyebrow in question. Kai wore the thumb ring, but not Sutter or Rowan. Those two maintained neutral expressions. Kai was livid. Luke could almost see his anger writhing beneath his skin.

The king's warlords and runecaster took seats directly behind the empty chair at the table.

A war mage and a white-robed witch arrived next and took up two seats in the semicircle on the other side of the room. Another man entered, large and wearing a long silk tunic. Damaras, in her royal-blue cape, and her ammo-clad senior war mage took their seats.

Finally, the king, the silver-robed high priestess, and their respective guards arrived.

"Your Majesty," the high priestess said, addressing Lochlan. "I see you've brought the warlocks we identified. Shall we continue?"

"Our investigation on the matter concerning the grid is incomplete, Lady Brighton. May I suggest we continue and come back to it?" the king said.

"As you wish." The high priestess asked Damaras to proceed. Damaras outlined her charge against Kai Oxen for tampering with the memories of four witches in their coven.

Kai straightened in his seat, confusion mixing with his simmering anger.

"With their memories wiped, they can offer no proof, of course," Damaras said. "Lord Tanner agreed, and ceded, which is why he offered refuge. For which we thank him." Damaras dipped her head in appreciation. She retook her seat.

"Lord Tanner? Is this what happened?" the king asked.

A null stepped behind Tanner, releasing the hold on his voice. "I took the priestess at her word, Your Majesty," Tanner said. "Offering refuge was the only honourable thing to do." Tanner smiled like he knew the definition of honourable.

"Ceded with no proof?" the king said. "That's unusual, is it not?" It was a rhetorical question. "Kai Oxen, what do you have to say for yourself?"

After he regained his voice, Kai stood. His posture suggested he wanted to throttle someone, though he kept his voice under control. "I didn't erase anyone's memories, Your Majesty. Test me. You'll see."

"Fair enough. He's at your disposal," the king said.

At the high priestess's nod, the witch in white stood.

Damaras jumped to her feet. "The warlock has already proven he's untrustworthy."

"We will see what he has to show us," the high priestess said. "Proceed."

Damaras hardened her gaze as she retook her seat.

The white witch met Kai and his null guard at the midpoint beside the oblong table. She was given the date and a six-hour window to check.

"I will only read what I need to. You have my word," the white witch said. With a hand on each side of his head, she closed her eyes. A long minute later, she released him and returned to stand with the high priestess. "On the date and time in question, the warlock was not engaged in memory tampering."

"I'm not surprised," Damaras said, standing once again. "Who knows what magic he's used to hide his crime?"

"My apologies, sir," the high priestess said. "The coven's priestess is rightfully aggrieved about the attack on her witches. But we will stand by the results of our regression and strike this item from the agenda."

"Thank you, ma'am," the king said. "We will need more time to investigate the final issue. If you would be so kind, may we have the room?"

"Of course. I'll see you shortly." She rose, and the witches at her end of the table did the same. They each inclined their heads to the king as they filed out.

When the door closed, Lochlan dismissed everyone except Liam, Luke, and a contingent of nulls. The *final issue* was the attack on the grid. Had Liam and Tanner twisted the truth to put the blame on Luke? He steeled himself.

The king stood and turned to face them, casually resting his backside against the table. Liam and Luke stood. Lochlan tipped his head to the null behind Luke, who released his voice.

"My advisors tell me you are both highly skilled runecasters. As such, tell me: if a warlock could tap into the grid, how would they do it? Liam?"

Liam bowed his head. "I appreciate the compliment, Your Majesty, but I'm no expert in draining power." He offered a shy smile, lapping up the king's attention. "That would be Luke." Liam extended his hand in Luke's direction, palm up.

The king turned an expectant gaze Luke's way.

Luke dragged a hard stare from Liam and composed himself. "The runecast I created to support my household did not drain anything. Sustainability was the entire point of it."

"And how might this runecast of yours be adapted to tap into the grid?" the king asked, crossing his arms.

"It can't be adapted," Luke said, shaking his head. "The runecast operates like a trickle charge. It collects miniscule sparks and stores them. The grid is lightning. Connecting to it would fry the runecast."

The king lifted his chin in Liam's direction. "What are your thoughts, Liam?"

"My thoughts? Luke thinks too small. Extrapolating from Luke's trickle charge idea, I believe it's entirely possible to amp up the runecast and tap into the grid. It might take some trial and error, but yeah." Liam rocked back on his heels, boastful confidence in his expression.

"You have the skill?" the king asked.

Liam stared at the king. "Are you asking me to do it?"

Liam wasn't as astute as Luke had imagined. Even if the king wanted to act against the accord, which Luke doubted, he would never set up such an act in front of witnesses.

"I'm asking you if you have the skill to do it."

"I believe I do, yes," Liam said.

"You sound confident." The king tapped his forefinger against his biceps. A thinking gesture. "Do you have any experience?"

"No. Not with the grid, of course. That's forbidden—at least, without your blessing. But I've worked with a similar runecast."

"The runecast in the tower?" the king asked.

Liam nodded and clasped his hands behind his back. "At the lord's request. Yes. It's proven successful. I can do the same for you, if you wish."

Lochlan unfolded his arms. "You do know that siphoning is a violation of the accord?"

"Siphoning from witches and warlocks, yes. These are humans."

"You're certain no witch or warlock works in that tower? Visits that tower?"

"Perhaps there's a slim chance. But it's hard to argue the benefits don't outweigh the risks."

"That's one way of justifying it, I suppose." Lochlan drew circles with his fingertip on the table. "Just one more question." He glanced up at Liam. "If you were tasked with doing something that violated the accord, something like trying to siphon from the grid, how would you go about covering your tracks?"

Liam's face paled.

Sarah took form in the sunroom. Marcus stood with his back to the wall just inside the glass ceiling. He darted a glance up and then scanned the trio of glass walls that jutted into the garden in front of him.

"I've texted Odette," he said. "They know we're here. I don't see them. How do we break the ward?"

"Not yet," Sarah said. "We made it this far. Let's find the proof we need. Meet me in Damaras's office."

"Her office will have added protection. We won't get in."

"We have to try. Otherwise, what's all this been for?"

"They'll expect us to go there."

"Not if they think we're somewhere else, and I know all the somewhere elses in this building." Sarah sent a spell to the dining room. A loud crash followed. "That should do it. Let's go."

Sarah made it as far as the assistant's desk outside Damaras's office. Marcus came stumbling in beside her.

"Another ward?" he said.

"Looks like." Sarah searched the ward for a weak spot but didn't find one. They descended on the assistant's desk like vultures, each taking a side, rifling through the drawers.

"Nothing," Sarah said, standing. "Silas's office?"

"They won't fall for another distraction."

"They can't afford not to check it out." Sarah sent out a spell to the meditation room in the attic and smashed the floor-to-ceiling mirror. Marcus disappeared ahead of her.

They both re-formed inside the war mage's office and stood silent. No wards, no traps.

"Quickly," Sarah said, nodding toward the shelving. She rushed to the desk. Marcus took her cue, moving swiftly to the bookcase.

With each drawer she yanked open, her despair grew. Pens, pencils, paperclips. Rubber bands, protein bars, and a stapler. Why all the tools for paper and not a scrap of it anywhere?

"Found something," Marcus said.

Footsteps sounded outside. She and Marcus exchanged a worried glance. The door flung open, and she disappeared as Silas's stormy face appeared.

"Oh, thank the heavens," Sarah said, as Marcus materialized beside her in the sunroom. Stupidly, they hadn't made that arrangement ahead of time.

"Get us out of here," he said.

"Smash the glass when I tell you. All of it. That'll weaken the ward enough for me to break it."

The shattering glass would also attract the war mages, but she couldn't think about that.

She moved her hands and spoke quietly, weaving her spell. Silas may have cast the ward on the front doors, but it was Damaras who'd cast the ones around the building. She recognized her work. The wards were strong. But so was she. She concentrated, pouring all her power into the spell.

She took a deep breath. "Now."

Marcus threw his arms into the air, and glass rained down in a deadly, sparkling waterfall.

Sarah blasted her spell directly in front of them. The ward groaned. She cast a second spell, pummelling the spot with wind. Marcus joined in, pushing the wind's needle to gale force. They had to lean into the wash of rebound to keep themselves upright.

Another groan from the ward, and then finally it tore apart. They staggered backwards as the wind escaped through the tear. Kylie came racing in, buffeted by the dying wind. Sarah and Marcus spun in her direction. Marcus hit her first with a concussive blast that disoriented her. Sarah followed up with a firehose of water that had her staggering. They didn't wait to see her fall.

Back in the protection of the stand of trees, Sarah bent over, catching her breath. Marcus leaned against a trunk, gulping air. Odette and Warrick rushed to their sides.

"Let's get out of here," Warrick said. He grabbed Sarah's hand. Odette took Marcus's, and they dematerialized.

They took form inside their suite at the Sylvia.

"Are you back? Is everyone okay?" Adeline asked, rising from an arm-chair.

"We're good," Sarah said, still breathing heavily. "We're all okay."

"Speak for yourself," Odette said. "You scared the living crap out of me back there."

Sarah greeted her sister with a reassuring hug and then collapsed on the sofa. Marcus folded beside her. Warrick guided Adeline to a chair and stood behind her, a hand on her shoulder.

As they pieced the story together, Adeline's grip on the armchair tightened.

"You know what was really strange?" Marcus said. "The sanctuary was deserted."

"We noticed that too," Odette said. "The parking lot was empty. Where'd everyone go?"

"I can tell you," Adeline said. She rehashed her visit with Anderson and the impending cocktail reception with Stonewater coven, the high priestess in attendance. "Damaras is laying it on thick for Lady Brighton. It's too bad you didn't find something we could use against Damaras. I think Anderson would help us if he could."

"We did find something," Marcus said.

All heads turned in his direction. He fished three red books from inside his jacket. "Silas keeps a diary."

"No," Sarah said, her tone incredulous. "Way to embrace technology, Silas."

"I didn't have time to be more selective." Marcus handed one to Sarah. "That one covers the timeline your father was killed. These two are current." Marcus handed the second one to Warrick.

Odette leaned over Sarah's shoulder.

"Read to me," Adeline said.

"Hang on," Sarah said. "Wait until we find something worth reading."

Sarah flipped pages, stopped to decipher the writing, sighed, and read some more. Each page held such promise and then such disappointment. Marcus and Warrick were doing the same with their volumes.

It took a full hour to determine that Silas had written nothing incriminating. Unless tedious detail about every training session he'd ever conducted was a crime. Sarah could have thrown the diary across the room.

"Now what?" Odette said.

"I've had time to think about that," Adeline said. "It should be me who goes to Damaras. I dragged you all into this mess. But it's me she wants. She may not know it yet, but she can't hurt me. Banishment means nothing to me. And she can't take my magic. I'll plug my nose and apologize. Make a deal for the rest of you."

"She can lock you inside the sanctuary," Sarah said.

"No. She can't contain my magic. Not warlock fire."

"You're forgetting warlock stone," Warrick said. "That can kill you."

"And I don't think it's just you she wants," Odette said. "I've never seen Damaras this incensed. She'll make examples of us. Even if she doesn't, there's no deal you could make with her that I would trust her to uphold."

"I'm with Odette," Marcus said. "I don't trust her."

"She has to be exposed," Sarah said. "It's the only way."

"I agree," Warrick said. "And I think tonight's formal reception will be your best opportunity to confront her. Her reaction will be tempered in front of the high priestess."

"Confront her with what?" Odette said. "We still can't back up our accusations. We have nothing."

Adeline swung her head in the direction of Odette's voice. "She doesn't know we have nothing."

"What are you getting at?" Warrick asked.

"Do you think Silas lets Damaras read his journals?" Adeline said.

"Go on," Sarah said.

"What if I were to suggest to Damaras that Silas documented what happened in the clearing? That he'd named names," Adeline said. "We could make her think Silas created an out for himself. A parachute."

"Oh, I do like the way you're thinking," Warrick said.

THIRTY-FOUR

Adeline wished she was able to see the formal attire everyone had conjured to blend in. The men wore tailored tuxedos, the woman full-length gowns. Sarah had created a backless halter dress for her that fell to the floor. Adeline wanted her runeglyph on display tonight. Odette wove a spell that pulled her hair into an elaborate braided updo.

Warrick let out a low whistle when she presented herself. "Your gown matches your eyes."

Not that anyone would see her eyes. She wore sunglasses, but they didn't quite cover the bandages.

Sarah tried once again to read her for witch tells. "Sorry, Addie. I can't through the smoky cloud that's hiding your aura."

Adeline shook it off, reassuring herself that she wasn't feeling any flu symptoms.

Warrick and Adeline armoured themselves. Odette cast a protection spell for the others. Finally, Marcus conjured each of them an earpiece so they could communicate to coordinate their efforts and guide Adeline. Their efforts seemed scant protection in the face of a ballroom filled with powerful witches, where they'd be outnumbered and vastly out-magicked.

Earlier, they had pored over the online floor plans for the Fairmont Hotel and its Pacific Ballroom, which was located on the hotel's conference floor. They knew exactly where they were going and the ballroom's configuration, but they didn't know how the room would be set up.

Warrick dematerialized with Adeline, landing them on the roof of the Fairmont. Everyone else followed. Then Warrick handed Adeline off to Sarah. A heavy door opened.

"Handy trick," Sarah said, explaining that Warrick had placed his hand on the rooftop door to unlock it. They stepped inside and descended a handful of concrete steps. Marcus was the last in, and he snicked the door closed. Warrick went ahead, ensuring their path was clear. He waited for them on a lower landing. Another door lock clicked.

"Elevators are through here," Warrick said.

Sarah gripped Adeline's elbow. "Don't trip on the carpeting."

"We look like cocktail party refugees," Odette said with a rushed laugh.

They waited for the soft ding that announced their ride. The elevator doors swished open, and they piled in.

"Conference floor," Warrick said, and the doors closed.

Nervous tension in the elevator was palpable. The doors trundled open. When they left the elevator, they stalled.

"Pacific Ballroom," Odette said, sounding as if she'd just spotted a sign. "This way."

They were on the move again, crossing miles of carpeting. The din of voices in the distance grew louder.

"This is it," Sarah said. She pulled Adeline around to a stop.

Vivaldi's *Four Seasons* spilled out of the room. *Summer*, Adeline thought. It offered a soft counterpoint to the pitch and cadence of dozens of conversations.

Sarah continued. "Our backs are to the wall at the east end of the ballroom, where the stage is. There are three sets of double doors that lead into the room, spaced about ten metres apart. We'll be going in through the first set of doors to our left. Odette?"

"I'm ready. Going in through the same doors as you. Hugging the wall to the right and making my way to the back end of the room. Marcus, you're taking the left side?"

"That's the plan. Up to the stage if I can get there. Otherwise, straight across the room to the windows on the other side," Marcus said.

"Adeline, I'll stay a few paces behind you," Sarah said. "Warrick will go inside only if he needs to draw attention away from you." Warrick would be a warlock beacon drawing every witch's attention the moment he entered. "Everyone know what to do?"

"We've got this," Odette said. "After I'm in there, count to ten. Slowly."

She reported in. "Tall tables are set up around the perimeter of the room a good metre from the walls. No tables near the doors. Clear sailing through the centre of the room."

"Going in now," Marcus said. "Wow. The room's huge. At least half a football field long. String quartet to the left of the stage. Making my way around them."

"Finn just waved at me," Odette said. Finn was the coven's senior wind elemental. "Interesting. He doesn't seem surprised to see me."

"The high priestess is in a huddle on the far side of the room, down near the end, third set of doors," Marcus said. "Damaras is with her."

"Perfect," Sarah replied. "That's our cue."

Adeline groaned. "Says the one who's not blind and doesn't have to walk the length of half a football field."

"The more witches who see you, the less likely it is Damaras will make a scene," Sarah said.

"All right, then. Let's go." Adeline walked forward two paces.

"One more step, and then turn to your left," Sarah said. "That's it. You're in front of the door. Now straight ahead."

Adeline's instinct was to scissor her hands out in front of her or to shuffle her feet, anticipating a collision. She didn't do that. When she met Damaras, she wanted to project confidence, not weakness. She lifted her chin and walked forward, trusting Sarah to guide her.

She made it five paces into the room before the ambient noise changed. Whispers rose around her.

"I'm behind you," Sarah said. "Angle to your right. That's it."

"I could be mistaken," Marcus said, "but I think the warlock king is here. Two men dressed like nulls are tucked in by the curtains on either side of the stage. I'm skirting the stage now."

"It's him, all right," Odette said. "He's standing with the high priest-ess and Damaras."

"Well, then," Warrick said. "This is about to get interesting."

"I've spotted Silas," Marcus said. "He's a few arm's lengths from Damaras, behind the king, opposite the third set of doors."

"Looks like I'm needed after all," Warrick said. "My presence should keep Silas occupied. I'm going in. Third door."

"You're turning heads, Adeline, but no one's moving to stop you," Sarah said.

Of course she was turning heads. The sunglasses alone were as good as a flashing neon sign.

"Do you see this?" Odette said. "Witches are parting like Warrick is

Moses and they're the Red Sea. Oh, shit. He's approaching the goddamn king. What is he doing? The nulls will annihilate him."

"No," Marcus said, with a note of confusion. "The king's waving his guards away."

"Your Majesty," Warrick said.

"This is a pleasant surprise. I thought you were in California."

"Portland of late. How's the queen?"

"Splendid. You should drop by for a visit."

"I've been trying. Judith La Croix is proving very difficult to get around."

"I'm sorry to hear that. What brings you to town?"

"The usual. Trouble," Warrick said.

"Oh? Is she here?"

"I'll introduce you later," Warrick said.

"Lady Brighton, may I introduce you to my nephew, Warrick Flynn?"

"Nephew?" They all said at once. Adeline paused. Warrick had never told her. She'd have given her front teeth to see Damaras's reaction.

"Keep going," Sarah said. "Damaras has her back to you, standing between you and Lady Brighton."

Adeline recovered from her stall, shaking off Warrick's revelation.

"Damaras is five metres ahead of you," Sarah said. "Call her name."

Adeline stopped. "Damaras," she said, projecting her voice. "May I have a word?"

Sarah laughed. "Damaras is putting on a pretty good fake smile. She's excusing herself. The high priestess sees you."

Adeline dipped her head. "Lady Brighton."

"Shoot. Daniel has spotted you," Odette said. "He's coming from your left, Adeline."

"I've got him," Marcus said, and then Marcus called Daniel's name.

"Hello, Adeline," Damaras said. "Come with me." The words were tipped with ice. Her footsteps didn't slow as she approached. She grabbed for Adeline's arm, but her fingers couldn't find purchase on Adeline's armour. They simply slipped off. Adeline spun away from her, hoping it looked like she was just getting out of Damaras's path. She didn't want to trigger Lady Brighton's guards.

"She would like a word with you here," Sarah said, her voice to Adeline's right.

Adeline sensed the failed snatch-and-spin had effectively switched her and Damaras's positions. She now faced the stage end of the room, and Damaras, in front of her, faced the king and the Lady Brighton.

"You dare approach me in the company of the high priestess?" Her words were delivered with a hiss.

"Seemed like a good precaution," Adeline said.

"Kylie is making a beeline for you," Odette said. "I'll cut her off."

"You don't belong among us," Damaras hissed. "You were never a witch, and you are mistaken if you think Lady Brighton will take kindly to your intrusion." Adeline pictured Damaras gritting her teeth behind a wide smile.

"Are you aware that Silas keeps a journal?" Adeline said.

"I would suggest you leave before the high priestess proves my point."

"A very detailed journal."

"This is hardly the place or time—"

"I'm told they're a cheery red colour. You must have seen them."

"Get to your point, if you have one, or get out. You are embarrassing the entire coven."

"Silas's journals are full of interesting information. Enlightening events. The one that caught my attention happened in a clearing. You'll be happy to know he spells your name correctly. And that of Lord Tanner," Adeline said. Silence stretched on for a satisfying moment. She'd surprised her.

"I don't believe you," Damaras said.

"And yet," Sarah said, "your reaction tells me you aren't as sure as you'd like to be."

"Get out."

"Before you cast that spell, Damaras," Sarah said, "you might want to take a closer look at what the king's nephew holds in his hands."

"Those journals you're still wondering about?" Adeline said. "The high priestess will be very interested to read what's inside them."

"Hello, Sarah, Adeline," Silas said, materializing in front of them. "It's time for you to leave."

"Are you missing some journals, Silas?" Adeline said.

"Odette and Marcus are waiting for you in the hall," Silas said.

"If you force us to leave, those journals will be delivered to the high priestess," Sarah said.

"Adeline tells me the journals in the warlock's hand are yours, Silas. Is that true?" Damaras asked.

"Those are training records. Nothing more. Sarah, Adeline, let's go. And don't make a scene."

"Well, if you insist. Goodbye, Damaras. And good luck," Adeline said.

"Do not fall for their lies," Silas said quietly, she assumed to Damaras. "I'll deal with that warlock when these two are contained."

Sarah took Adeline's arm, and they turned for the third set of doors.

Silas's gasp was audible. He was versed in warlock magic. He'd know what the marking was on her back. She paused to turn her head, letting him know she'd heard him, and then resumed walking toward the door.

"Let's not be hasty," Damaras said. "Silence them. Hold them inside the room, near the wall over there."

Adeline strengthened her armour, extending it over her sister. They kept walking. When Silas's silencing spell hit, she felt the force of it. "Sarah?" Adeline said.

"It missed," Sarah said.

Bounced off her armour, Adeline suspected. A test. She felt her sister turn to look behind them. "Silas's face is almost as red as his journals."

"Well, hello, Adeline." The voice belonged to Anderson. She stopped abruptly, and Sarah stumbled. "I didn't think you'd be joining us this evening. You must be Sarah."

"Anderson Schubert, this is Sarah Booth," Adeline said.

"It's so good to—"

"Excuse my interruption," Silas said. "Unfortunately, these two were just leaving. It's a security issue. Damaras's orders."

"Don't take them too far," Anderson said. "I'll be having a word with Damaras momentarily."

Despite Damaras's instructions to hold them inside the room, Silas walked them out into the hall, his hand on Adeline's shoulder armour, pushing her. Adeline imagined he was doing the same with Sarah. She noticed he didn't touch her runeglyph, but he would have felt the slick armour that coated her body.

"Damaras is not going to be happy with you," Sarah said. "You disobeyed her."

"Shut the fuck up," Silas said.

When the noise spilling into the hallway faded behind a closing door, he lassoed them with some kind of magical dampening spell and towed them down the hall.

"Where's he taking us?" Adeline said, grasping her sister's hand. The senior war mage was second only to Damaras in power. She and Sarah couldn't defeat him with brute-force magic. They'd have to ride this out.

"Don't know yet. We're walking down the hall outside the ballroom. Just passed the stage end of the room. Turned right. Must be another room down here."

"I said shut up."

A lock clicked. A door opened. They were pulled forward again.

Sarah lurched, tugging Adeline's hand. "What have you done?" She pressed forward against the magical restraint.

"What is it?" Adeline asked.

"Odette and Marcus are here," Sarah said. "They're on the floor, unconscious."

"They're not unconscious," Silas said. "They're not breathing. And you two are next."

Sarah stiffened.

"You were warned of the consequences of ignoring Damaras's order," Silas said.

Adeline's thoughts streamlined instantly. They weren't riding this out. And, though she wasn't stronger than Silas magically, she wouldn't go down without a fight.

"Hang on to me," she said, tightening her grip on Sarah's hand. She visualized herself and Sarah outside of the magical lasso. Silas's footsteps faltered. It had worked. They'd escaped the lasso, but she was left disoriented. She had no sense of where she and Sara stood in relation to the room, in relation to Silas.

"Adeline, duck!" Sarah said. The moment she did, what sounded like a missile passed over her crouched form and hit the wall with a thud.

"Where is he?" Adeline said, bringing her hands around. Anger, swift as wildfire, raced down her arms.

"Directly ahead, reloading his spell," Sarah said.

Adeline shot her arms forward and blasted warlock fire out in front of them, sweeping her hands in a semicircle.

But she heard no reaction from Silas. She'd been too slow. "Where is he?"

"Ceiling, behind us," Sarah said. "Move!" Sarah shoved her aside as another blast of power hit the floor. Sarah yelped in pain.

Adeline shot her arms into the air, the heat of her fire flowing freely. "Guide me," she called to her sister. Instead, her sister tackled her at the waist. Adeline felt herself being pulled along in a swirl of Sarah's molecules. They landed in a painful twist of limbs.

Sarah's breath came in ragged pulls.

"What happened?" Adeline said, rolling to knees. She reached out for her sister and found her lying on her side. "You're hurt."

"He got my shoulder. Stars, that smarts."

"Any blood?"

A pause. "No." Adeline helped her sit upright. Sarah began to tremble. "Marcus and Odette," she said, her voice breaking. "How could he do that to them?" A fire alarm blared, but it was cut short. There'd be no emergency personnel coming to distract anyone.

"He'll pay for that," Adeline said, her own chest tightening. "Where are we?"

"At the elevators."

"Has anyone seen us?"

"I don't think so," Sarah said, sniffling.

"Let's get up before someone does." Adeline helped Sarah to her feet. Sarah straightened her dress and then helped Adeline do the same. She'd lost her sunglasses. The hall was eerily quiet. "Where is everyone?"

"The ballroom, I expect," Sarah said.

"They would have heard Silas's blasts, the fire alarm. They should be swarming these halls right now making it all go away."

"I don't know what's going on, and I don't care." Sarah left her side. Adeline heard her repeatedly hitting the elevator's call button. "I'll get us to the Sylvia. Just need a minute." Sarah's voice cracked.

"We have to get back into the ballroom," Adeline said.

"They killed Marcus and Odette! I'm not going back in there."

"Sarah," Adeline said, patting about for her sister. She found her and cupped her face. "If we leave now, they'll cover this up. Just like they did with Dad. Marcus and Odette need us to expose their murders."

"I can't. I can't leave my kids," Sarah said, sobbing now.

"You're not leaving your kids. You're showing them what a badass you are. Now get me back in there," Adeline said.

Sarah's breath hitched. "I can't lose you, either. Please."

Adeline realized that Sarah had hit her limit. It was unfair to push her further. "I love you," Adeline said, pulling her sister into an embrace. "Get somewhere safe."

Using the position of the elevators to get her bearings, Adeline retraced what she prayed were the steps she'd taken to get to the ballroom the first time. She made it several steps before she stumbled, having veered off the carpeting.

"Damn it, Adeline," Sarah said. Her sister's hand slid under her elbow. "If they don't kill you, I'm going to." Sarah sniffled back her tears. "I can't believe I'm taking you back in there. A room bursting at the seams with ill intent. Let's have a nice visit with our powerful enemies. Maybe we can help them wash the fresh blood off their hands. Sounds like fun."

Sarah's rant had the effect of focusing Adeline. Never again would she back down from these people. They would pay for their sins. She would make certain of that.

"Second set of doors," Adeline said. "I want to be in the middle of the room."

Sarah stopped when they got to the ballroom. "We're here, but something's not right. It's too quiet. All three double doors into the ballroom are closed."

"Sealed?" Adeline asked.

Sarah left her side and returned. "No."

"Send out your binder's magic, tell me what you see."

A moment of silence followed. "A dozen people, possibly more. Witches and warlocks."

Adeline inhaled, steeling herself.

"It might be a trap," Sarah said. "We don't know who's in there."

"Warrick wouldn't leave us, and if he's inside, I'll be okay." She squeezed her sister's hand. "I can do this on my own. Go."

"Leave my blind sister? I'm not doing that."

"Think of Jack and Olive," Adeline said.

"I am," Sarah said. "Let's go. The doors are two paces dead ahead."

Adeline squeezed her hand one more time, then strode forward and pushed open the doors.

"This can't be good," Sarah said.

Thirty-Five

Luke watched with professional interest as the nulls initiated Liam into the thumb-ring crew. Liam had fallen face first into the king's trap. A trap Liam had helped create when he'd climbed on top of a shaky pedestal. He must have thought everyone in power was as crooked as Lord Tanner.

"Put them with the others," the king said to the nulls. "We'll reconvene after the festivities."

The nulls led Liam and Luke across a wide hall, through another door, and up a few steps onto a darkened stage. A curious place to hold prisoners, Luke thought. Was it a convenience or something more foreboding? He scanned the ceiling for a noose, the floor for a trap door, but found nothing. Kai and Tanner were already there, sitting obedient and quiet but for Tanner's piercing glare. Luke ignored him and took his designated seat. Frustration with his bindings gnawed at him until he was distracted by the spicy aroma of cloves. Witch magic. Curiosity replaced his frustration.

Gold-coloured floor-to-ceiling curtains covered one end of the stage. Partial curtains hung in the wings. Beyond the curtains, tittering laughter, low conversation, and the tinkling of glasses painted the picture of a party. The festivities the king had referred to. Witches and warlocks intermingling? Interesting.

A half-hour into the party, the mood changed. The tittering died down, and whispers replaced it. Loud voices called out above the din. He thought Adeline's voice was among them and strained to hear, his spirits lifting, but he couldn't be certain. The noise level decreased dramatically, and then slowly built back to its earlier twittering. He added unquenched curiosity to his frustrations.

The cheerful exuberance beyond the curtains hung in stark contrast to his grim thoughts. Tanner would have been within his rights to kill Luke outright for his role in the uprising. Would the king follow through on that? Or would he now become the king's prisoner?

The party atmosphere changed abruptly with the deep screech of a wrecking ball hitting something close by. The vibration of it travelled up through the floor, setting Luke on edge. The four nulls scrambled positions, and one of them exited in a rush. Another loud crash rent the air. The disturbance was coming from the room they'd vacated.

Panicked voices broke out in the party room. A fire alarm blared and then abruptly cut out. In short order, a woman's voice rose above the noise, asking everyone to leave the building and get to safety. Within moments, the room quieted, as if the crowd had simply disappeared. Which they probably had. Three heavy doors slammed closed in quick succession.

Minutes ticked by. He and Kai traded *what's-going-on* glances. Tanner and Liam did the same.

Closing his eyes, Luke concentrated to hear beyond the curtains, but he couldn't make out the words, just the tone. A woman's voice. Apologetic. A man's low bass, steady and strong. The woman again, irritated. And then quiet.

The null who'd exited briefly returned, and, after a brief discussion with the other nulls, they escorted Luke and his fellow prisoners off the side of the stage and into the party room.

He took in a grand room in sumptuous red and gold colours as his eyes adjusted from the darkened stage. In the centre of the room, the king and the high priestess sat on a dais. Three chandeliers graced what had to be a twenty-foot ceiling. Richly coloured carpet ringed a hardwood floor. The scent of clove in the air was strong.

What was Warrick doing here? He clutched a few slim red volumes and stood on the floor close to the king, alongside the king's warlords and runecaster. The high priestess's party from the earlier meeting, including Damaras and her war mages, stood on Lady Brighton's side of the room.

There was no sign that a raucous party had just cleared out. Not a dirty glass, not a discarded napkin. Witch magic.

All those gathered stood facing three double doors, apparently waiting for something. What?

Minutes ticked by. And then the middle door opened.

Luke went rigid.

Adeline. Her eyes. *Tanner*. The bastard. He'd kill him slowly for this.

The heavy man in a long tunic walked to meet Adeline. Sarah was with her. "We've been expecting you," he said. This was the man with the low voice he'd heard earlier. "I was explaining to—"

"Silas murdered two witches tonight," Adeline said, sparking chaos among the witches. She stood defiant and stunning, despite her rumpled gown and the gauze covering her eyes.

"This is outrageous," Damaras said, and she turned to the high priestess. "You see what I've been contending with? Her entire family is a disgrace."

"I can take you to where we found them," Sarah said.

"And you are?" the high priestess asked.

Sarah nodded toward Adeline. "Her sister."

"Silas, you and your war mages will stay here," the high priestess said. She nodded to the witch in white. "Go with her."

The white witch followed Sarah from the room. In the ensuing silence, the man with the deep voice quietly described the room's occupants and layout to Adeline. He didn't mention Luke's name, and he didn't think Sarah had seen him; she'd been too laser-focused on Damaras's circle of witches. He desperately wanted Adeline to know that he was there, that he'd avenge her, that he'd eviscerate Tanner for what he'd done.

Minutes dragged on.

The white witch returned. Sarah stopped beside Adeline. The white witch continued to the edge of the raised dais. "The witches are alive, but they need a healer. I've made arrangements."

"Thank you," the high priestess said to the white witch. She addressed Damaras. "It appears this is an internal matter. We will deal with it in private."

She turned to the king. "My apologies. Shall we move on?" At the king's agreement, she called Anderson, the large man, to speak.

"Lady Brighton, King Lochlan. This is Adeline Thorne," he said, introducing her. The king's gaze swivelled to Warrick, who nodded. It was almost as if the king and Warrick knew one another. "She was attacked by the warlock Kai Oxen, who forcibly forfeited his magic to her, and secured it from siphoning with a locking rune that he placed in her right eye."

"Pleased to make your acquaintance, Ms. Thorne," the king said. "I wish it were under different circumstances. I am aware of the transgression and offer you my personal apology." The king addressed Anderson. "I am also aware that this matter has already been dealt with."

"Indeed," Anderson said. "But it's come to our attention that while Ms. Thorne was under Lord Tanner's protection, she suffered egregiously at his hand. His failed attempt to unlock the rune for the purpose of siphoning Kai Oxen's magic has blinded her."

The king's eyes widened ever so slightly. He'd known about Tanner's siphoning her; the nulls had caught him red-handed. But he hadn't known that Tanner had blinded her in the process. "I am truly sorry, Ms. Thorne. If this is true, the lord responsible will be punished." He addressed the high priestess. "May we examine her eyes?"

"Is this acceptable to you, Adeline?"

She agreed and was seated. The king's healer arrived. He removed the bandages and proceeded with a lengthy examination.

"She's not blind, but the corneal abrasions are a result of rune magic and have compromised her vision," he declared.

"No murders, not blind," Damaras said. "See how she twists the truth?"

"Quiet," the white witch said, moving closer to Damaras.

The king's healer spoke to the king. "Would you like me to repair the damage?"

"If she consents, yes."

"Stonewater's healer is already treating me," Adeline said.

"I'm sure your healer is trying, but he or she is just a witch."

"Just?" she said, indignant.

"What I mean to say is that the damage to your eyes was done with warlock magic. Only warlock magic will heal it."

The warlock's pronouncement stunned Adeline.

"Do you wish me to proceed?" the king's healer asked.

"Gods, yes," she said.

"The healing will be uncomfortable, but it won't take long."

Adeline didn't care how uncomfortable or how long. She'd endure anything to have her sight returned. With her head tipped back, the shadow of his fingers flickered, and then a bright light bore down on her. She was unable to blink or close her eyelids as the light burned. Left eye, then right. Tears flooded her eyes and dripped down her temples.

Pain made time move at a glacial pace. When the light receded, she was finally able to close her eyes. She straightened and took the tissue he offered. The scratching sensation was gone.

"You'll be sensitive to light for a few weeks," he said, and she heard him step in front of her. "Go ahead. You can open your eyes now."

Barely breathing and praying to all the gods, she did just that. The next batch of tears were real. Her composure crumpled with the relief of it. She greedily absorbed every detail, every nuance. The healer's dark complexion, the thick curl of his lashes.

"Thank you," she said, through her tears. The healer bowed his head and retreated.

The colours and textures and lights were overwhelming.

"Well?" Sarah said, coming around her chair.

"I can see. Perfectly." She cupped her sister's cheek, inhaled the scent of her, revelled in the blue of her eyes, the delicate arch of her brow. "You are so beautiful." Adeline stood and pulled her into a hug. "I thought I'd never see you again. This is incredible." She held her sister at arm's length. "Gorgeous." Sarah wore an emerald-green, off-the-shoulder dress like a goddess.

Over Sarah's shoulder, she spotted Warrick, grinning at her, the red journals still in his hands. The king and high priestess sat in high-backed chairs on a raised dais.

"Thank you, Your Majesty, Lady Brighton," she said, bowing deeply, her gratitude overflowing.

She glanced around, drinking in the richly appointed room, the people spread out before her. The sight of Luke drew a smile out of her. He appeared unharmed. They exchanged a silent greeting, but he didn't respond to her mind-talk, so she knew his magic was quelled. Tanner and Liam glared at her. She didn't give them the satisfaction of a reaction, but prayed their magic was also contained because Luke still wore the chain.

On the other side of the dais, the only witches she recognized were Damaras and the war mages. None of them appeared happy to see her.

"This is wonderful news, and we will celebrate later, but we must move on with our discussions," Anderson said, resuming his official role. His physical size fit his voice, Adeline thought, seeing him for the first time.

The king's warlord cleared his throat. He spoke to Adeline. "Was there a witness to the assault?"

It took her a moment to regain the thread of their earlier discussion. "Luke Churchwell was there, but Lord Tanner had incapacitated him. I don't know if he saw it," Adeline said.

"Allow him to speak," the king said. The null behind Luke made a motion with his hand.

Luke shook his head in apology. "I heard her screaming but couldn't get to her. Couldn't see her or Tanner, and he was the only other one there." Luke addressed the king. "But your nulls saw it. They interrupted it. He'd already blinded her by then." And then Luke turned to Tanner, venom in his voice. "What was that? Your third attempt to siphon her? Fourth? This corrupt, immoral miscreant deserves no mercy."

Tanner struggled against his bindings, his face reddening with hatred. He lurched toward Luke, his eyes on Luke's chain, which caught the light as both men struggled against their invisible bindings. A snarl curled Luke's lips.

Adeline swung her head to the dais. Surely someone would intervene. Lady Brighton watched the melee, her eyes focused on Luke. Adeline's attention flipped to the king, who slashed his hand. Luke straightened. Tanner stopped moving. Tanner had been willing to risk losing his hand to detonate Luke's chain. She exhaled in relief.

"What do you have to say for yourself?" the king asked Tanner.

Tanner spewed the moment he had his voice back. "Luke Churchwell is a practised liar. Any of his acquaintances will tell you the same thing. Of course he'd take the side of a witch against me. He'd do anything to discredit me after his failed coup."

"Are you claiming it wasn't you who compromised this witch's sight?" the king asked.

"No. That was not my intent. At her priestess's request, I agreed to try to extract the incompatible warlock magic, which is a death sentence for a witch," he said. "I agreed to save her life!"

The king's gaze hardened as he glared at Tanner.

The high priestess froze. She turned to Damaras. "You requested this?"

"To save her life," she said. "I couldn't just let her die, no matter how disagreeable she is."

"Was Ms. Thorne made aware of the risks of this . . . procedure?" the high priestess asked.

"No one knew what the risks were," Damaras said. "A witch wielding warlock magic? It's never happened before."

"Ms. Thorne? I'd like to hear your thoughts on the matter."

The moment the high priestess's attention was off her, Damaras's gaze slid to Warrick, and the red books under his arm.

Adeline stood, shoulders back. "Damaras told me and the other witches that she'd agreed to let Lord Tanner touch me for the purpose of identifying the warlock responsible for leaving his magic in me. She lied to us. His touch was meant to siphon the magic out of me. It didn't work because he didn't know about the locking rune."

The high priestess inhaled an exasperated breath. She turned to Damaras. "Who was present at this negotiation?"

"My war mages, Silas and Daniel."

Lady Brighton nodded knowingly. "That's unfortunate. Unless you're willing to set aside your war mages' inviolable status and allow a regression?"

"The secrets they guard protect all of us. I won't compromise them to disprove the lies of this witch."

"Of course. I understand," Lady Brighton said.

"Excuse me," Silas said, bowing his head to Lady Brighton. "May I have a word with Damaras?"

Lady Brighton nodded once, a silent agreement. Silas and Damaras put their heads together and spoke in quiet voices.

"I was present," Sarah said, drawing the room's attention. "The two injured witches were as well. Each one of us would agree to a regression, but our memories have been erased, just like Adeline's."

"That is curious," Anderson said. "Almost sounds like someone is trying to cover up something."

Damaras stepped forward. "In order to clear my good name, I will allow a regression of Daniel, only if he agrees. Daniel?"

"As you wish," Daniel said.

Adeline mumbled under her breath. "That was too easy."

The high priestess raised her hand. "Sarah, would you agree to a regression?"

"Of course, Lady Brighton, but as I said, my memory has been compromised."

Damaras cleared her throat. "Daniel has already agreed," she said, louder this time.

"Yes, and thank you, Damaras, for the offer. I may take you up on it, but not just yet." The high priestess tipped her chin toward the witch with the white cape. "Attend Sarah and confirm that what she says is true."

Though proud of her sister's bravery, Adeline sent a prayer to the heavens that the regression didn't backfire on them. She was pretty sure body glamouring to break into the sanctuary and pilfering Silas's journals would be frowned upon.

The white witch approached Sarah. "Would you like to sit?" Adeline's chair drifted into place behind Sarah. She took the hint and sat. The white witch asked her for the date in question. Placing her hands alongside Sarah's head, she began the regression. She closed her eyes and tilted her head, left then right, repeating the motion.

When she finished, Sarah sagged in the seat. "The witch does not lie," she said, addressing Lady Brighton. "Her memory has been folded multiple times. It's been partially repaired, but there are substantial gaps."

Lady Brighton nodded, thoughtful. "Are you able to restore the memories?"

"What?" Sarah said, finding the energy to straighten. "That's possible?"

"Yes," the white witch said. "I believe so. Ma'am?" Lady Brighton held the white witch's gaze, and a knowing look passed between them.

Adeline thought back to moments earlier, to what the warlock healer had said to her. It took a warlock to repair damage caused by warlock magic.

As a wash of understanding hit her, Adeline darted a glance at Damaras. The witch's sycophantic facade melted, replaced by a seething anger which was aimed at Sarah. Years of martial arts training drew Adeline's notice to the dip of Damaras's shoulder. That dip, Adeline knew, telegraphed Damaras's intent, and it wasn't a baseball in her hand.

Adeline acted on pure instinct and dove in front of Sarah, intercepting the underhanded lob of Damaras's spell. But the spell was stronger than Adeline's armour. Her protection shattered, and she was sent hurtling into the air, her back bowed.

Strangely, she experienced no pain, just euphoric relief. Her body had no weight to it, her mind no burdens. A sense of calm overcame her. She floated above the chaos that had broken out below, disconnected from the sounds, unable to feel or control her body. Sarah's scream sounded like it was coming from very far away.

Her shoulder bumped a chandelier, causing it to tinkle. The sparkle amused her. Below her, Sarah was bent over a figure on the floor. Such a shame to ruin her beautiful emerald dress. Lady Brighton was there too, kneeling by the figure. The dress that pooled on the floor was the same colour as Adeline's. A lovely shade of blue, she thought, as she drifted toward an open window.

The stars outside shone brightly in the night sky. They called to her, and she knew she belonged to them. She glanced down one last time.

Warrick was helping Sarah to her feet. He'd always been such a gentleman. The king joined the small gathering. Lady Brighton got to her feet, revealing the prone figure on the floor. Adeline caught a glimpse of a snow leopard on the figure's back, its sapphire-blue eyes staring right at her.

Thirty-Six

Such alluring eyes, Adeline thought, drifting toward the call of the stars. A cool night breeze met her at the window. That sensation was followed by another, an odd tingling between her shoulder blades. Confused, she glanced at the people below.

Lady Brighton looked up, scanning the ceiling. She found Adeline and locked gazes with her. The lady's hand shot up, and magic spilled out, grabbing for Adeline.

No! Adeline shrieked, annoyed at the intrusion. But her protest went unheeded. The lady's magic snared her and hurtled her downward. With a crack of lightning, Adeline hit the body on the floor.

The rude reawakening drew a groan from her throat.

The white witch insisted she lie still until her examination was complete. "No broken bones," she declared, and then hands were helping her up. Warrick and Sarah. They got her to her feet and promptly sat her in a chair.

"Glad to have you back," Warrick said, holding her hand.

Sarah crouched beside her. "How are you feeling?"

"Like an elephant stomped on me. Are you okay?"

"I'm fine. It was you who took the full force of Damaras's spell."

"What the hell was that?" Adeline said.

"She separated your soul from your body," Lady Brighton said, materializing in front of them. "It's a dreadful spell. You would have lingered in that state until your body died of old age if I hadn't been able to call your soul back."

"I owe you my life. Thank you," Adeline said.

"No. It was my fault. I exposed Damaras without first securing her. She responded before I was able to stop her."

"I don't understand," Sarah said.

"I think I do," Adeline said. "When the white witch confirmed she could repair your memories, she was telling Lady Brighton that a witch had been responsible for the folding. If it had been a warlock, she wouldn't have been able to repair it."

"That's right," Lady Brighton said. "And the white witch has a name. Shea." She spoke to Sarah. "She'll repair your memories after we take care of some other business. Adeline, are you well enough to join us in the other room? Sarah, Warrick, you as well."

Warrick and Sarah helped her to her feet. Her hair had fallen loose. They walked onto the stage and out through the stage's back door, across a wide hall, and returned to the room where Silas had tried to kill them.

"Odette and Marcus?" Adeline asked, remembering her injured friends.

"Recovering in the infirmary," Sarah said.

"At the sanctuary? Is it safe there for them? We don't know who else Damaras may have poisoned against us."

"My guards are with them," Lady Brighton said. "They're perfectly safe."

The null stationed at the door opened it for them.

"Take a seat behind me, and don't speak unless I ask you to. Warrick, you'll be seated behind your uncle." She walked ahead, with that reminder lingering in her wake.

Uncle, Adeline thought. Oh yes, she'd be having a chat with Warrick when this was done.

Inside the room, the king stood at one end of an oblong table. Lady Brighton took her seat opposite. After they sat, their respective parties took their seats behind them. Luke, Tanner, and Damaras were lined up against a wall. Luke didn't belong with them. Luke and Tanner had their own null guard. One of Lady Brighton's guards stood behind Damaras. Adeline offered Luke a warm smile. It was all she could do.

The king greeted the high priestess and then thanked her for the photographic evidence she had provided concerning the attack on the grid.

"I'm sorry to say that I can't agree with your assessment that Luke Churchwell is the warlock in the photo," the king said. "Luke wears a permanent chain and has for three years. The person in that photo does not." He floated the photo through the air, and it landed gently in front of the high priestess.

She looked up from the photo. "May I see this chain to which you're referring?"

"Luke Churchwell, please step forward," the king said. Adeline's heart lurched in her chest. Did they know the chain was a cuff that could detonate? She tried to meet Luke's gaze, but his attention was on Lady Brighton.

She stood and approached him. "Show me your chain."

Though Luke looked confused, he loosened his collar. He stiffened visibly when she slid her fingers under the chain.

She dropped her hands. "You cannot remove this?"

"He cannot," the king replied.

"It's a cuff, then?" she asked. Adeline let out a breath of relief. They knew.

"Warlock justice may be harsh in your eyes, but it effective," the king said.

Harsh in anyone's eyes, Adeline thought.

"Thank you," Lady Brighton said to Luke, and she retook her seat.

The king nodded at Luke. "You may step back."

Adeline shivered, thanking the stars that was over. She sought out Luke's gaze, and this time he met it, though only briefly.

Lady Brighton addressed the king. "What is your conclusion, given that photo?"

"It's someone in body glamour. As to whether it's a witch or a warlock, I don't know."

"Whoever it is knows what Luke Churchwell looks like, so it's not likely a witch."

"Regardless, we can't know for certain."

"No. I don't suppose we can." She drummed her fingers on the table, thoughtful. "Whose chain is it that Churchwell wears?"

"Lord Tanner's."

"May I speak with him?"

The king beckoned Tanner forward. He took a half-hearted step. His null nudged him to take another.

"Lord Tanner," the high priestess began. "Luke's chain is your creation?"

"Yes, Priestess," he said, in a gravelly voice.

But he'd had help, hadn't he? Adeline glanced at Damaras, who had her gaze glued to her feet.

Tanner cleared his throat and straightened. "He earned it when he tried and failed to overthrow me." Indignation dripped from his words.

"Are you aware," Lady Brighton said, "that when a new priest or priestess is elected, I gift him or her with a special kind of magic? It ensures their magical superiority over their coven."

Lord Tanner shifted his feet, perhaps sensing he was the frog in a pot of water.

"No?" Lady Brighton said. "But surely you know that witches can see the life force that contributes to the grid. We can see magic. That chain you created was made with the same magic I gifted to Priestess Damaras. So either you siphoned that magic from her to create it, or you colluded with her. Which is it?"

Adeline didn't see that coming. Siphoning or collusion? Rock and a hard place.

Thirty seconds passed. Tanner pressed his lips together.

"Given your silence, I would suggest you colluded," Lady Brighton said. "Damaras would have known if you'd siphoned the magic from her. She wouldn't have taken kindly to that. She would have sought a remedy."

Tanner looked over his shoulder to Luke. "I should have taken your head off long ago."

"Silence. Step back, Lord Tanner," the king said.

"Damaras, are you able to remove this chain without harming the warlock?" Lady Brighton said.

"I can. For a price. What do I get in exchange?" Damaras said.

Lady Brighton stood. "Leniency. But if the warlock is harmed in any way, I will show no mercy."

At the king's request, Luke stepped forward once again. "Do you wish to have Priestess Damaras remove your chain?"

Luke sought out Adeline's gaze. She nodded, encouraging him. Damaras had been promised leniency. Adeline didn't know the sentence for collusion, but if leniency was on the table, it was bad. Damaras wouldn't risk losing the promised lenience.

Luke inhaled. He looked to the ceiling and blew the breath out. "Yes, Sir. I would like the chain removed."

Adeline wrapped her arms around her torso, praying the godforsaken cuff didn't detonate.

Lady Brighton approached Damaras and hurled a spell at her that caused Damaras to stumble. "That's to keep you from dematerializing when I release your magic. Do not make the mistake of thinking you can escape me."

The surprise on Damaras's face told her that was exactly what she'd planned.

The king approached Luke.

Shea stood and spun a ward around the witches. A warlock on the other side was doing the same with a shield. They were protecting everyone from Damaras—and any blowback if Lady Brighton or King Lochlan had to get involved. A smart precaution.

Lady Brighton wove her spell, releasing Damaras's magic. Damaras inhaled like she'd been starved for air.

Adeline felt the tension in Luke like it was her own. One mistake, intentional or not, and he'd be dead. The only thing worse than trusting his life to Damaras was trusting his life to Tanner. But if he wanted out of the chain, those were his only options.

Damaras approached Luke with a sneer. He sucked in a breath when she slid her finger under his chain. She smiled. She liked that. Adeline would have loved to wipe that smile from her face.

"Stay very still," Damaras said. "An unexpected move would be . . . Well, we'd create a mess, wouldn't we, if we activated this by accident?"

Adeline stood, her jaw clenched. She'd taken a few steps in their direction before Shea lifted her hand in warning.

Damaras fingered her way around Luke's chain twice and then reversed course. It seemed to Adeline that she was using the three clasps the jeweller had found like a spinning combination lock. When it released, the chain dropped into her hand.

Luke immediately stepped back from Damaras, and his hand shot to his neck. He sucked in a ragged breath. Adeline sagged with relief.

"I'll take that," Lady Brighton said, holding her palm out to Damaras.

Damaras tilted her head, giving off the distinct impression she was considering if she had any options. She didn't. The chain disappeared from Damaras's hand and reappeared in Lady Brighton's. Within the span of a breath, Damaras's magic was once again contained. The protection ward around the witches fell.

The king approached Luke. "Your assistance with these matters has been noted. Consider your sentence served." He drew a pattern with his fingers. Luke inhaled deeply. "You may leave, but do not leave the territory. I'll have further questions for you."

Luke bowed his head. "Thank you, Sir."

Adeline took a step forward. *Are you back online?* she said, a hopeful tone in her voice.

She stood between him and the exit, and he was approaching fast. *You look stunning. I've been wanting to tell you that since I laid eyes on you.* He reached her, stopped, and without a hint of warning, he dropped his lips to hers and wrapped her in an embrace. His kiss was hard and hurried, but much more than a thank-you. He broke the kiss and took in her features with unabashed yearning. It was the stress, she thought, a release. It had to be. He smoothed her hair back from her forehead. *And I don't mean tonight.*

"Goodbye, Adeline." He left her and turned for the exit. *I have fences to mend, but I'll be back.*

Adeline watched him leave but didn't know what to do with the emotions that crashed over her. She was stunned. Happy. Confused. Giddy.

"What is it with you and warlocks?" Sarah said, coming up beside her.

"I believe this concludes our accord discussions," the king said to Lady Brighton.

"It does. Thank you for your time, Wyn."

"Likewise, Lochlan. It was lovely to see you again."

It was the only time Adeline had heard the king and the high priestess address each other without their titles. They bowed their heads to each other, and then Lady Brighton and her entourage took their leave.

Adeline wanted to hang back and wait for Warrick, but the nulls closed the doors.

Sarah met her in the hall. "We've been ordered to the sanctuary."

Thirty-Seven

S arah took great comfort in the sight of one of Lady Brighton's guards standing at the sanctuary's entrance. But she and Adeline had changed into their fighting clothes, just in case. It was after midnight when they landed at the foot of the stairs.

"Shea is expecting you in the infirmary," the guard said, opening the door. They sailed through the wards.

"Impressive," Sarah said. "Shea's work, I think." That witch was powerful. Shea had to be Lady Brighton's second-in-command.

They reunited with Odette and Marcus in the infirmary, interrupting a lively conversation.

"Look at you two, lounging around, yakking it up," Sarah said, and she hugged them both. They were dressed and sitting in adjacent beds.

"We'll be lounging for a while after that number Silas pulled on us," Marcus said. "He was prepared to kill us to protect Damaras from being exposed."

"He was protecting his own ass," Adeline said. "If Damaras was found out, he'd never sail in on her coattails to become the most powerful war mage at the high council."

"Shea tells us that if the healers hadn't gotten to us when they did, Silas would have succeeded. We wouldn't be here," Odette said. "Guess we owe you."

"No. It's me who owes you," Adeline said. "It was my mess you were helping clean up."

"You'll be revisiting that opinion when Shea is done with you," Marcus said.

"You have your memories back?" Sarah asked.

The door opened behind them, and Shea walked in. "Good. You're here. I'd like to get started. Are you ready, Sarah?"

"Now?" She felt like she needed time to brace herself.

"If you wouldn't mind. I have a very full schedule."

"Of course," Sarah said, though she wished she had more time to talk with Marcus and Odette about what to expect.

Shea had her lie down. Her hands hovered near Sarah's head as she whispered her spell, drenching her in magic. When she finished, Sarah could only blink at what she'd learned. She turned her head in Adeline's direction. "We were right."

"Would you like me to attempt a recovery of your memories, Adeline?"

"I don't think the runeglyph will allow it."

"Shall we test it?" Shea asked.

"Not today. My body's had enough punishment."

Shea nodded. "Then we should go. We're convening in the gathering hall."

The sanctuary's gathering hall wasn't as large or grand as the ballroom at the hotel, but it was adequate. It was where they held celebrations and unbindings, weddings and funerals. Witches milled about, not many yet seated in the chairs that had been arranged in rows of semicircles.

She and Adeline received a mixed reaction as they walked through the room behind Shea. Sarah saw surprise, anger, and confusion, but also the occasional warm smile. In front of her, Adeline was on high alert, her gaze darting around, her hands loose at her sides. This despite the guards in the room. Shea guided them to the first row.

When Lady Brighton arrived, the crowd parted. She spoke to no one as she made her way to the front of the room. Anderson and Lady Brighton's war mage followed.

Shea asked for everyone to be seated.

When the room quieted, guards brought in Damaras and the war mages. By the pained expressions on Daniel and Kylie's faces, they knew nothing good would come from today's events. Damaras and Silas remained defiant, all hard stares and pinched faces.

This gathering wouldn't resemble any notion of a trial in the human sense. It was a summoning for judgment. The high priestess's word was the law, and after being duly chosen by the priests and priestesses to rule, she was granted the power to enforce it.

The high priestess ruled for life, unless she chose to step down. The same was true of priests and priestesses like Damaras. It was rare for one of them to fall from grace. And what Damaras had done was worse than that; she'd punched grace in the gut and kicked her to the curb.

"Damaras Deschene," Lady Brighton began. "You must answer for colluding with the warlock lord. For interfering in warlock affairs. For malicious intent and injury to the witch Adeline Thorne. For unlawfully altering the memories of four witches in your coven. For directing your war mages and governing council members to engage in unlawful activity."

Lady Brighton turned to the audience. "From what I and my advisors witnessed in the accord meetings, and what we have learned from the regressions of the witches whose memories have been restored, there is no question of Damaras Deschene's guilt. She is responsible for a grave injustice to me, the Stonewater coven, and the territory's warlocks.

"Damaras Deschene, it is with a heavy heart that I sentence you to expulsion from the Stonewater coven and banishment from all other covens. Further, you must leave this territory and never return. Finally, I sentence you to permanent magical binding."

A collective gasp rose amongst the witches, but no one spoke out in Damaras's defence.

Lady Brighton turned to Silas Vance and read off some of the same charges, adding malicious injury to Odette and Marcus. He was similarly sentenced.

Kylie and Daniel got off a little lighter. But following orders didn't excuse their poor judgment. They were to be magically bound for five years and forbidden from ever holding a formal role in any coven. They'd be relegated to private citizens, so to speak.

When Lady Brighton was finished, she and Shea followed the heavily guarded guilty parties from the room. Lady Brighton would perform the bindings herself in a warded cell in the basement.

Anderson took the floor and outlined the procedure for the election of a new priest or priestess. Lady Brighton would oversee the process. Candidates could put their names forward in the coming week.

"You've all had a long night," Anderson said in his soothing bass voice. "Go home. A new chapter for your coven begins tomorrow."

The witches dispersed. Sarah and Adeline spoke briefly to Anderson, agreeing to a longer visit before he left Vancouver.

"Come back to the house," Adeline said to Sarah as they stood outside the sanctuary. "Stay the night. We'll call Mom, have a sleepover. Drink too much wine."

Sarah checked the time. It was 2:30 a.m. Close to noon for their mother. "I'll go back to your place to call mom—reassure her we're still alive—but I can't stay over. Joe and the kids are on their way home from Europe. I've got to be at the airport at six o'clock to pick them up."

"We'll make it an all-nighter," Adeline said. "Haven't done that in a while."

Back at Adeline's they dialled their mother.

"Your father's murder is still unsolved," their mother said, after the retelling. "His blood is on Damaras's hands. She got off light."

"Not having magic?" Adeline said. "I can't imagine a worse fate."

Sarah nearly choked on her wine. A playful smile bloomed on her sister's lips. Sarah mirrored it. Her sister was coming back to her.

"I'm delighted to hear you say that, angel. Speaking of which, when was the last time Sarah checked you for witch tells?"

Sarah set down her wineglass. She sent out her binder's magic, but what she saw confounded her.

Adeline raised a questioning eyebrow. "What is it?"

"I—I don't know. You have no threads, witch or warlock. And the smoky fog from your runeglyph has thinned somewhat, revealing a glimpse of your aura. But it's . . . changed." She searched her memory for an explanation, but nothing came to mind.

"Focus, Sarah," Adeline said. "What do you see?"

She sat back, boneless. "Your aura. It's purple."

Adeline's frown deepened. "What does that mean?"

"I have no idea," Sarah said.

"Do you feel sick?" their mother said.

"No. I feel fine. Perfectly normal."

Sarah considered Adeline's unique situation. She had witch's DNA and warlock magic. Not one or the other, both. A combination. "When warlocks use magic, their aura is red. A witch's aura is blue. Red and blue."

"Purple," Adeline said. "A hybrid."

When Adeline finally disconnected the call, they both felt drained.

And though neither of them wanted to rehash the day's events, they couldn't help themselves.

After a few moments of silence, Adeline asked, "How is it done? A permanent binding."

Sarah toyed with her wineglass. "The witch's elemental threads are teased out and severed. Their aura is shattered. It's horrible. Fortunately, it's a rare occurrence."

"I've never thanked you," Adeline said. "For your binder's magic. For sticking by me even when I was a pain in the ass. I'm lucky to have you. Thank you."

Sarah took her sister's offered hand. "We're both lucky." They shed some tears but they were happy tears, grateful tears, and in their state of exhaustion, the tears soon turned to giggles, and then irrepressible laughter.

It had been an eventful day and a long night. So when the doorbell rang at nearly four in the morning, they looked at one another and groaned.

Thirty-Eight

Adeline trudged to the door. Warrick grinned at her through the diamond pane, and suddenly, she didn't feel so tired. He followed her into the living room, greeted Sarah, and they both collapsed on the sofa.

"Tanner's dead," Warrick said. "The king ordered his execution after learning he and Damaras were selling those chains to the highest bidders. The buyers were essentially enslaving warlocks. No crime required. Maybe the only decent thing Tanner did was hand over the buyers' names."

"I'm happy to hear that brutal practice has come to an end," Adeline said, and then she filled him in on Damaras's fate.

"I hope Damaras socked away some of her ill-gotten cash. She's going to need it now that she can't rely on magic to pave her way."

"Who's going to replace Tanner?" Sarah asked.

"Don't know yet. Tanner's death will create a power vacuum if the king doesn't plug it with a new lord, and soon."

"Speaking of your *uncle*, what the actual hell?" Adeline said. "You said your father was a lawyer. That you didn't want to join the family business."

"He is a lawyer. The king's lawyer. Or, I should say, one of my uncle's many lawyers. And the king's court is the family business. You know me, Adeline. I'm not one for rules and order. Nine-to-five would kill me, and official functions bore me to distraction."

"But your last name is Flynn," Sarah said. "The king's surname is Kinnaird."

"Flynn is my dad's name. My mom is the Kinnaird—King Lochlan's sister."

"And you never thought to tell me?" Adeline said. "You could have pleaded our case to your uncle after I first called you. None of this shit had to happen."

"I tried. Believe me. But Tanner managed to get his sister into the king's court. As his secretary, no less. She's a bloody bulldog. Wouldn't let me get anywhere near him. And as for others in his court? Well, you know my reputation. No one wanted to risk the king's ire by taking my case forward." He took Adeline's hand. "I'm sorry. I would have done anything to prevent what happened to you."

"Oh my stars," Sarah said, gasping. "You're a prince."

"In name only. And I wish you'd never learned of my heritage. I didn't want to be a part of that world. Still don't. Like you, Adeline, a witch in name only. We had that in common, you and I."

Sarah's phone alarm pinged. "I've got to go. Joe's flight is landing. He's been on single-dad duty for a week. The man deserves a rest."

"He deserves more than that," Warrick said with a wink. He gave her a hug goodbye.

Adeline walked her into the hall. "I'm so proud of you," she said, squeezing her sister in an embrace. "Thank you for everything."

Sarah had no sooner dematerialized than Adeline felt Warrick at her back. He pulled her close.

"Do you realize this is the first time we've been alone since I arrived?"

She relaxed into the cradle of his arms. "I've got my life back."

He rested his chin on the crown of her head. "Do you have feelings for Luke?"

"Are you referring to his kiss?"

"It looked like a declaration. I didn't see you slap him."

"He took me by surprise."

"So? Do you? Have feelings for him?"

"I don't know. I don't want to see him hurt. Why do you ask?"

"Because I want to take you to your bed and ravage you until you're a puddle in my arms, and I'd prefer if he wasn't in the room with us."

Surprise had her turning in his arms. "There's nothing between Luke and me. I've only known him for ten minutes. You, I've known all my adult life."

"Is that a yes?"

"That is most definitely a yes."

They climbed the stairs one delicious step at a time and landed on her bed in a tangle of arms and legs and very little clothing. She'd forgotten how beautiful his body was, how perfectly it fit with hers. He'd always been a generous lover, and mind-blowingly creative. None of that had changed. They made love until the sun came up, and she fell asleep wrapped in his arms. Happy. Sated.

When they roused in the early afternoon, they made love again. There was no awkward morning after. Just laughter and the warmth of a deep connection. After they showered, he watched her cook him breakfast.

"Remind me why we got divorced," he said.

When they were happy like this, it was easy to forget what had driven them apart. "We wanted different things. Have you forgotten our epic fights, after which you'd disappear for weeks? It just wasn't meant to be." She wanted the picket fence; he wanted the wind at his back.

"Last night didn't feel like *wasn't meant to be*."

She laughed. "Our problems were never between the sheets. Grab the plates?" she said, taking the pan to the sink. She poured two glasses of juice and joined him at the table. "I'll call Charlie today. Let him know it's safe to come home."

"Ouch! That's a quick change of subject."

His pout was endearing. "I loved every minute of last night. I love our friendship. This ease between us. I want to hold on to this for however long it lasts. But no expectations."

Over breakfast, he filled her in on more of what had happened in the king's court.

"We know who attacked the grid. It was Tanner's runecaster, Liam Nunez. His loyalty to Tanner vanished in a heartbeat when the king laid out his suspicions."

"Suspicions?"

"There wasn't just one tower set up to mass-siphon. Tanner has a chain of them. Liam is working with the nulls to dismantle them. We're not enlightening the witches, which is why I didn't mention it when Sarah was here."

Warrick's phone dinged. "Looks like the political manoeuvring has begun. My uncle's throwing a party tonight to ruffle some feathers and assess his options for the new lord. The queen has asked if you'd attend. She'd like to meet you."

"Why?"

"Who knows? My uncle probably told her he'd met you. She's always been curious about the witch I married, and she just happens to be in town."

Adeline agreed to go. It was the least she could do for Warrick, who had done so much for her. It was another formal affair.

"Runeglyph showing or not?" she wondered aloud.

"In a room full of back-stabbing warlocks?" Warrick grinned. "Showing. Definitely."

Adeline created a floor-length gown in black velvet, with a plunging back, and put her hair up. Warrick donned a tuxedo with a matching velvet cummerbund. He was irresistible in jeans, sexy in a suit, but smouldering in a tux, especially when he looked at her like she was the whipped cream he planned to lick off the Adeline sundae at the first possible opportunity.

Taking her hand, he transported them to the handsome mansion. "This is the warlock seat for this territory. When my uncle appoints the new lord or baroness, they'll live here."

"Suitably stately." She hated to admit it, but she was intimidated by the imposing stone facade, the perfectly manicured grounds, the number of guards. She was a witch once again entering a den of warlocks. But this wasn't the tower, she reminded herself, calming her nerves.

Inside, a riot of colour awaited. Her artist's eye caught every hue, every shadow and play of light. It was a painter's paradise, a smorgasbord for the eyes. Gratitude for her vision once again overwhelmed her. She'd never take it for granted again.

As they strolled through the guests, Warrick kept a hand on her. If it wasn't on the small of her back, he'd pull her hand into the crook of his arm. They encountered curious glances, brow-arching surprise, and suspicious glares. She was an outsider here. That was how she'd felt in the sanctuary, too. She didn't wholly belong in either camp.

The warlocks to whom Warrick introduced her were careful to fawn and offer their warmest smiles, as if he might have some influence with his uncle in the selection of the new lord.

But one face in the crowd caused her to slow. "What is Kai Oxen doing here?"

"Don't worry about Kai. He's toothless tonight."

"The king invited him?"

"Kai has friends in high places. He also has an innate ability to sniff out magical traits—a skill the king values. They've come to an agreement, but the king will be keeping him on a short leash."

"Was Luke invited?"

"He had other commitments," Warrick said, a little too quickly. He placed her hand on his forearm. "My uncle awaits."

Ahead, whoever had been speaking with the king bowed and stepped away. The king turned his attention to Warrick.

"Uncle, allow me to introduce Adeline Thorne," Warrick said.

"Pleased to meet you under better circumstances, Ms. Thorne. It's about time my nephew introduced you."

"Your Majesty. Thank you again for allowing your healer to repair the damage to my eyes. I'm most grateful."

"You're welcome. I owe you my thanks as well."

Adeline tilted her head. What had she done for the king?

"You knew Lord Tanner was creating power globes by siphoning the tower's occupants. Yet you didn't disclose that knowledge to the witches. Why?"

"To protect Luke Churchwell, Sir. I feared Tanner would have killed him if the witches learned about it."

"Given your history," he said, shooting a sideways glance at Warrick, "I suppose I shouldn't be surprised that you would protect one of us."

"Luke did the same for me. He's the one who gave me the runeglyph."

"Yes, that's quite a statement." Something drew the king's attention behind her. His face lit up.

"Darling. Warrick." A woman's voice. She walked around Adeline to stand beside the king.

Adeline failed to hide her surprise. She gaped. It was Mrs. Doppler. She was a warlock.

"Queen Ophelia, may I introduce Adeline Thorne?" Warrick said.

"I believe Adeline already knows me. Do you not?" the queen said.

Indeed, she knew every nuance of her face. The eyes she'd spent days perfecting didn't do her justice. "I do, Your Majesty. But the gallery told me your name was Mrs. Doppler."

She laughed. "A precaution. We're a secretive lot. Sadly necessary."

"You painted my aunt's portrait?" Warrick said.

"I did. It was an anniversary gift." She turned back to the queen. "You knew who I was." It wasn't a question.

"Yes," the king said. "Imagine my surprise when your name came to the top of the list of portrait painters for my consideration."

"And I love it," the queen said. "You are very talented, Adeline."

"But . . . I'm a witch."

"Not just any witch," the queen said. "The witch who stole my nephew's heart. I'm glad I finally got to meet you."

EPILOGUE

Adeline strolled through the gardens of the sanctuary, enjoying the last of the pink-tinged, milky-white blooms of the Japanese dogwoods and the rainbow colours of primula underneath. Roses perfumed the air. It was summer solstice. The longest day of the year.

"We should make our way inside," her mother said, walking quietly beside her. "Anderson is holding seats for us."

Her mom and Anderson had arrived the night before for Jack's unbinding. They would return to the cruise in three days' time. Claiming they didn't want to be a bother, they'd booked into a hotel. Adeline and Sarah had a quiet giggle at their mother's attempt at a smokescreen.

They headed inside to find Anderson on his feet, scanning the gathering crowd for them. They joined him and took their seats.

"Where's Joe?" Adeline asked. She knew Olive would be with the under-twelves, sequestered with a magician to distract them.

"There," Anderson said, pointing near the front. Sarah wasn't seated with him. She was sitting in a semicircle of chairs on the dais at the front of the room. Being the coven's principal binder, she was also the one who performed the unbindings. But not on Jack. Binders weren't allowed to bind or unbind their own children. The rule protected the family bond should anything go wrong. But she refused to dwell on that today, allowing herself only positive thoughts for Jack.

Adeline imagined Joe and Sarah were a bundle of nerves, along with all the other parents of children who were present for their unbindings: earth for thirteen-year-olds, air for fifteen-year-olds, water for seventeen-year-olds, and fire for nineteen-year-olds.

When the binding for their element was removed, it was customary for witchlings to wield the element for the first time in the presence of the coven. In Jack's case, the element was earth, and he would be wielding something small: a sprouting seed, a blooming flower. Jack had been studying the hand motions for months.

At the toll of a bell, the gathering room grew quiet. Carolyne stood. She's been the principal archivist under Damaras and was now the new priestess. She was a good choice. Kind, level-headed. She'd run on a platform of using history to guide her. Their mother approved. She considered Carolyne a strategist who knew where all the bodies were buried.

After Carolyne's introductions and the formalities were finished, the unbindings began. First up was the youngest group, the thirteen-year-olds here for their first unbindings. One by one, they approached Sarah. Adeline swallowed her unease. She'd never witnessed her baby sister in this role. Sarah looked impressive in her finely embroidered binder's robe. It depicted every element's colour in a scene that represented their power.

Sarah spoke quietly to each child, putting them at ease. It seemed to Adeline that she didn't begin the ritual until the child appeared calm. She took her time with the more timid children. And when they were ready, she would begin. Sparkling white light flowed downward from her hands, which she held aloft to create a dome over the child. The children's faces lit up with wonder. And then Sarah unbound a single thread, teasing it out with a gentle pull of her fingers. Adeline's heart was in her throat each time. But Sarah's technique was flawless, and when the thread was free, she lowered her hands. Sparkles settled on the child's head, their shoulders, the floor around them, and slowly winked out. After they swore a solemn oath to practise the element responsibly and uphold the laws of magic, she invited them to wield the element.

The pride on the children's faces, when they succeeded in manipulating the element that first time, was second only to the joy of their parents.

Jack was the last to approach Sarah. A witch Adeline had never seen before rose from his chair. He bowed his head to Sarah, and they spoke a few words. Even from a distance, Adeline could see Sarah's reluctance as she left Jack and took her seat beside Joe. But Jack was in good hands. Sarah was an exceptional binder, and she'd hand-picked the binder for Jack.

After Jack's unbinding, he turned to the audience. He beamed at his parents and then sought out Adeline. When he found her, his smile lit up Adeline's heart. He worked his magic with a flourish that was pure Jack, and produced the white bell flower of a lily of the valley. Sarah's favourite.

The remaining unbindings rolled out in textbook-perfect fashion, even with a jinx in the room.

During the proceedings, Adeline's mind wandered to Luke. She hadn't heard from him since his kiss. It had probably been a heat-of-the-moment gesture on his part. She understood—but still thought of him often. Still wished he'd call her and let her know how he was doing. But she was careful not to visualize him calling.

A reception followed the formalities. Adeline caught up with Odette and Marcus. There were still witches who gave Adeline a wide berth, but she didn't let it bother her. She didn't expect she'd ever be fully accepted. In her first address to the coven following her election, Carolyne had specifically acknowledged Adeline, removing any question that she was a member of Stonewater coven. Though Adeline appreciated the gesture, she steered clear of the sanctuary.

Giving herself permission to use her new powers had been a struggle. Old habits did indeed die hard. She still preferred to cook Charlie's breakfast the old-fashioned way. Ditto for making coffee. It felt like living her life rather than floating through it. She made an exception for scrubbing pots.

A few days after the king's party, he'd sent her a gift. His runecaster had arrived with a pumpkin-sized power globe. He'd set it up in her bedroom closet and created a runecast to keep it fed, drawing on the biggest trees in the neighbourhood.

Her powers got stronger with use, and new ones popped up regularly, which sometimes created awkward moments. She could now unlock doors with her mind. That little gem she'd learned when she'd arrived at Leung's grocers, unaware they hadn't yet opened. She'd been in a hurry, had simply grabbed the door's handle, and it had opened. It was only after the owners rushed in from the back wearing looks of alarm that Adeline realized what had happened. She felt guilty about the clerk who'd closed out the previous night and was sure to get an earful.

Her knowledge of warlock magic was growing, and using it often tired her, but that was the nature of magic: it demanded a price.

Later that evening, Jack repeated his flower-blooming magic at his party until everyone present had a lily of the valley to take home with them. "Magikin!" Olive said, squealing with delight when it was her turn. Olive was sitting on Adeline's lap when Jack bowed and produced a daisy for her. He shot a sideways glance at Adeline, who smiled proudly. He was showing off, having studied secretly to learn not just one flower, but two. Adeline high-fived him and told him what a wonderful job he'd done today.

Olive was still too young to understand that magic was real, but she'd spent the afternoon with a magician, his magic hat, bunnies, and a pony. It would be many years yet before she was exposed to the truth. In those years, she'd enjoy her childhood safe from the dangers of unbound magic.

The thought stopped her. It was something Adeline never imagined she'd be grateful for.

As the evening wore on, Olive was carted off to bed, and Jack started to sag. Adeline said her goodbyes and joined the stragglers who were headed home.

Safely inside her wards, she poured a glass of wine, sent her new jazz playlist to the speakers, and wandered into the solarium. Light spilled out from Charlie's suite below. Tomorrow's breakfast was a poached egg. A few slices of the ripe cantaloupe in the bowl on the kitchen counter would make their way onto his tray.

Not all of her father's orchids had survived her inadvertent draining of them, but the few that had were doing well. Sarah had contributed a replacement for one of the empty discs, and she'd purchased another. Eventually, she'd repopulate the collection.

Her new commission was taking shape on the easel. Business had picked up significantly after word got out about the warlock queen's portrait.

Warrick's likeness stared out at her from the painting of him she'd done years ago. She'd moved his portrait to the front of the stack on the floor for inspiration. She'd painted it when they were madly in love. The sass of his posture as he leaned against his bike, the way he looked up from under his dark brow, the come-hither in his eyes . . . The man dripped sex.

She missed him. The wind had called to him again. But his leaving didn't hurt this time. She had her home, her family, Charlie. She and Warrick still had each other's backs and would always be friends, but the road and the picket fence were mutually exclusive endgames. So they'd gently let each other go. He'd be back when she called, or when he needed the comfort of a home for however long it lasted. She could live with that.

She turned out the lights and headed up the stairs with the last of her wine. Her sketchbook lay open on her bed. Filling the page were charcoal likeness of another man who'd disappeared from her life. Luke. He never had sent her the photographs she'd asked for, back when she though he wanted her to paint him. She'd drawn him from memory. As always with her, it was the eyes that were most captivating. His were intelligent, secretive, and as black as onyx.

She flipped the page. The runes she'd sketched from the photos she'd taken of his *Book of Runes* still puzzled her. She hadn't yet found the language that might unlock their secrets, but maybe one day.

Her doorbell chimed. She closed the sketchbook. It was after eleven. Was Warrick back already? She set down her glass and descended the stairs, turning on the porch light when she reached the bottom.

She glanced out the diamond pane. Not Warrick.

"Your bad penny's come back."

THE END

Thank You

Thank you for reading *The Never Witch*. If you enjoyed it, please tell a friend or consider posting a short review where you purchased it. Reviews help other readers discover the book and are much appreciated.

—JP McLean

Read on for a sneak peek of *Hexborn*

Excerpt from Hexborn

Book 2 of The Thorne Witch Novels

Witch by birth, warlock by trade.

Adeline Thorne is a witch. The magic inside her is not.

The warlock magic coursing through her veins is volatile, incompatible with her witch blood, and growing more unstable by the day. When Luke Churchwell, a powerful runecaster, returns and sees how far her magic has spiralled, he steps in to train her—but every lesson is a gamble, and his desire for her may take them both down.

Far across the country, the hexborn are tracking a killer whose trail leads straight to Adeline.

The hunter is closing in. And the secret that created him is deadlier than the man himself.

One

Adeline Thorne stood at the foot of her bed, flipping through her sketchbook. The runes she'd drawn were intriguing—promising even—but they were useless without knowing how to cast magic into them.

At the chime of her doorbell, she glanced up. Half past eleven. Late for a visitor. She closed the sketchbook and set her empty wineglass on the dresser. Thankfully, she hadn't yet changed out of her party dress. She pulled her bedroom door closed and descended the stairs, turning on the porch light when she reached the bottom. Through the door's diamond-shaped panes, in a pool of light, stood Luke Churchwell. Her pulse quickened. She opened the door, and the faint scent of cedar drifted in.

"Your bad penny's come back," he said, one hand in his slacks pocket, the other hanging loose at his side. The corner of his mouth quirked into a tentative smile, as if he weren't sure of his welcome.

Adeline hugged her torso and leaned her shoulder against the doorframe. "It's been a while." Three months, and until a moment ago, she hadn't realized how much she'd missed him—not romantically. She'd missed his company. He'd risked his life for her, and vice versa. And yet she'd never known the real Luke Churchwell, just the edited version his jailer allowed. He looked good in a bespoke jacket with a black dress shirt unbuttoned at the collar, but the shadow of a beard suggested he'd had a very long day.

"It has. Sorry for the late hour. I've just returned. Came straight here." He swept his dark hair back, leaned in, and lowered his voice. "I've learned something you should know. May I come in?"

She frowned, searching his tired features, his midnight eyes, and then straightened. "All right. Please, come in." She led him across her warded threshold and into the living room. "Have a seat. Would you like a drink?"

"No, thanks." He folded onto one end of the sofa. "You look like you're dressed for a party."

"I am. Was. Today was my nephew's first unbinding ceremony. There was a party afterward."

"Ah, yes. Summer Solstice. How'd it go?"

She quirked an eyebrow at him. "You don't have to pretend with me." Warlocks felt the same way about witches binding magic as witches felt about warlock jewellery that amputated limbs.

"I'm evolving," he said, smirking.

"I see." She sat in an armchair opposite him. "In that case, it went well. Better than well. He wielded earth elemental magic like a pro."

"Happy to hear. How about you? May I assume your magic is behaving?"

She stifled a laugh. "I've not seen any sign of incompatibility, but I can't say it's behaving."

"Oh?"

"You know Kai better than most. The eclectic array of magic he pilfered over the years has spawned more than one awkward moment. Some days I feel like a five-year-old with a loaded wand." Kai Oxen was the warlock who thought he could evade his sentence of magical forfeiture by dumping it into her—a magically barren witch, a vessel from which the arrogant bastard presumed he could retrieve his magic when it suited him.

"I expect that's quite a challenge. If I can help in any way, call on me. Please."

She dipped her head in acknowledgement. "What is it you've learned that I need to know?"

His attention slipped to his hand as he dipped into thought, absently caressing the arm of the sofa. He wore a heavy ring she'd not seen before.

"News of a witch possessing warlock magic has gone viral in the warlock community."

It wasn't a shock. Kai's assault of Adeline had threatened a decades-old peace accord between witches and warlocks. Word of the attack had also rippled through the network of covens.

Luke continued. "But knowing there's a witch who wields warlock power, and tolerating it, are two very different things. You need to be careful."

"You sound like Sarah." Adeline's sister had said the same thing. "She tells me there are witches who think I'm an abomination, that I'm a threat to them."

He glanced up. "You *are* a threat to them."

"That's not true," she said, scowling. "I would never siphon their magic. And I wouldn't siphon their power. Not intentionally. I don't even know how."

"Maybe not today. But Kai could siphon magic from the shadow of a witch or warlock half a kilometre away, so you can too, should you choose to do so."

"And what do the warlocks fear?"

"That your loyalty is to witches and that you'll expose our rune magic."

"Which I can't do, because none of you will teach me."

"Is that so? Because rumour has it you've been behind closed doors with Queen Ophelia on more than one occasion."

"And you think she's teaching me your sacred rune magic?" she said, her expression doubtful. "Do warlocks not trust their own queen?"

A dark chuckle escaped his throat. "Unseating royals has been a favourite pastime among warlocks for centuries. King Lochlan and his queen are very good at the power games, but they're not bulletproof. Queen Ophelia's secret meetings with you are stirring unease."

"Secret?" she said, taken aback. "Where are you getting your information?"

"Are you forgetting I led a coup against Lord Tanner? It may have been unsuccessful, but I didn't go down that path without well-positioned informants."

"Evidently, you need better informants. My meetings with Ophelia are not secret. Her secretary pens an invite that's delivered by her courier, and a null escorts me to and from her home. None of that is concealed. Everyone knows." Just as everyone knew that Adeline had been commissioned to paint her portrait, though that was before she'd known her subject was the warlock queen.

"Ah, but she meets with you in private."

Adeline frowned in confusion.

"When anyone else meets with the royals, nulls are present. But not when she meets with you." Nulls were royal guards who served for life and were immune to all but the king's magic.

"I'm under her protection. She considers me family."

"That—right there—is the heart of the problem. When you and Warrick married, he brought a witch into the royal family. That's never been done before. It doesn't matter that you're divorced now. The prejudice against witches runs deep. Probably as deep as witches' prejudice against warlocks."

Adeline exhaled. "I can't fix that. None of it. It's exhausting." She dragged herself upright. "But I will mention it to Ophelia." She stood. "I'm having a glass of wine. Can I change your mind on a drink?"

She poured him a Lagavulin and joined him on the sofa. "How did your fence-mending go?" The last time she'd seen him, moments after the king had released him from his imprisonment, he'd kissed her and then rushed away to seek forgiveness from those he'd been forced to harm while trapped by Lord Tanner. She was still uncertain if the kiss was genuine interest or a spontaneous burst of relief that he was finally free. Given his long, quiet absence, she leaned toward the latter.

He shook his head. "As good as could be expected."

"I'm sorry."

"Time may heal the wounds." He filled his lungs, shaking off the disappointment. He met her gaze. "Warrick's bike is gone."

She paused. He must have checked the garage for her ex's Harley before he'd rung her doorbell. Luke and Warrick were not buddies. The only things they had in common were her and believing they were the better man. "He's on the road again. California, I think." Warrick was allergic to anything that tethered him to one place for any length of time.

The hint of a smile crossed Luke's face as he swirled the amber liquid in his glass. Their conversation flowed easily despite the months that had passed. There was a trust between them, forged in battle. She imagined it was the same trust shared by soldiers who'd fought shoulder to shoulder and survived.

He asked about Charlie, her first and last bed-and-breakfast guest. The elderly gentleman had booked a one-night stay in her renovated basement suite and never left. He was a tenant now, though she still brought him breakfast on weekdays.

She asked about Luke's sister and her family. He'd hidden them from Lord Tanner before his attempted coup.

"Lord Mandal has agreed to find wards to train her sons, my nephews. Lieutenants, no less." He said it with pride, a sentiment she'd not heard in his voice before.

"Mandal? His territory is in the northeast. Peace River?"

He tilted his head, a question in his expression.

"Ophelia is schooling me in royal politics, which includes knowing the warlock lords, ladies, and their territories. And in exchange, I'm explaining coven governance and witch hierarchy."

"Ah," he said, nodding. "Then not runes?"

"Not yet," Adeline said with a playful smile, then she grew serious. "This wall of prejudice between witches and warlocks is toxic. I like to think, if we knew more about one another, if we invited each other in, that—just maybe—we could loosen the mortar on old misunderstandings. Poke a hole in the wall."

He nodded, thoughtful. "It's possible, I suppose. In theory. But how do you peel away generational layers of prejudice? A history lesson and a tea party aren't going to do it. It's inbred, in both our kind."

"I know. Like I said, it's exhausting."

"You also said you couldn't fix it."

"Doesn't mean I shouldn't try. *We* shouldn't try." She set down her empty wineglass and stifled a yawn.

Luke upended his glass. "I'd best get home and make sure it's still standing."

Adeline grew still in concentration. "Can you hear that?"

He tilted his head to listen. "No. What do you hear?"

"Not in my ears—in my head. Like when you and I mind-talk." They'd discovered that Kai's magic had also passed along to Adeline his ability to mind-talk with Luke, and so far, only Luke. "It sounds like a child's voice. It's faint. She's tired and wants to go to her bed."

"You've heard her before?" he said, closing his eyes. A line formed between his brows.

"A few times. I chalked it up to more of Kai's magic developing."

"I'm not hearing it. Have you tried talking back?"

"Only once. But my *hello* frightened her away," she said, rubbing her temples. "Do you know over what kind of distances you and Kai could mind-talk?"

"A few city blocks, not much more."

"Then whoever this is, is close."

Mind-talking, Luke knew, was a very rare ability. He and Kai had discovered it when they were children, and though they'd never met anyone else with the ability, they'd heard rumours about others like them. Now he wondered if Kai had been completely honest about only being able to mind-talk with Luke.

But it was also dangerous, an advantage best left hidden. He and Kai had never disclosed their secret, which had saved both their hides many times during the coup—at least up to the point Luke was captured and Tanner installed a magic-dampening chain around his neck that also tied his tongue. He'd still be chained, still doing Tanner's bidding, if Adeline hadn't been dropped into his orbit. He owed her his life.

"The voice may sound childlike, but it could be a trap. A warlock hunting for someone with mind-talking ability to sell off for siphoning."

"Wow. That's where your mind goes? You need a vacation."

He chuckled. "That was rather dark. It appears I've spent too much time with the dregs of warlock society."

"You're also forgetting the snow leopard you drew on my back. Your runeglyph?" Absently, she pulled her impossibly long braid over her shoulder. "If it's all you promised, I don't need to worry about siphoning."

He took in Adeline's teasing smile, the hollow at the base of her throat, the perfection of her collarbones. The grace of her every movement. He'd thought the time he'd spent away would have diminished his feelings for her, but from the moment she'd opened her door, he'd known he was in trouble.

"I'm keeping you up," he said, setting his empty glass aside. He stood and offered her his hand. She let him tug her off the sofa, and he held her there, wanting to pull her close, to know what she felt like in his arms, but instead he kissed the back of her hand.

At the front door, he turned. "I meant what I said earlier. Call me if I can help you sort out your magic. Any time. Name the place, and I'll be there."

She looked up at him, dark lashes framing sapphire-blue eyes. "I'd like that."

Emboldened, he leaned down, his cheek nearly touching hers as he breathed in the sweet coconut scent of her hair and whispered, "Make it soon."

The next day, while the coffee brewed, Luke stood barefoot in his rustic kitchen and gazed out at a forest of ancient trees he knew as well as his reflection. They'd been powering his magic since he'd bought the place years ago. It had been dark the night before when he'd returned from Adeline's, and he hadn't yet had the chance to lay eyes on them and say a proper hello.

He swung open the leaded-glass double doors, inhaling the sweet scent of the climbing roses that tumbled over arbours at the edge of the dew-dampened patio stones. He stepped outside, the slate cool underfoot. Dew lay thick on the grass beyond the patio—more moss than grass, he noted—relishing the soft touch of the earth that grounded him. He made his way into the forest and to the massive trunk of a Douglas fir. The giant tree wasn't old growth, but at almost six feet in circumference, she was at least a hundred years old.

He walked in a circle around her trunk, weaving his hands in a familiar pattern, runecasting his magic along the forest floor, letting it encompass the nearby arbutus and red cedars. Then he swirled his hands in upward circles, pulling up the magic until it had fully scanned the precious trees for their enemies: the Douglas-fir beetle, the cedar-tree borer, and others of their ilk. Satisfying zaps signalled the harmful insects' demise in the web of his magic.

Confident he'd banished any tiny threats, he laid a hand on the Douglas fir's rough bark, absorbing the pulse of energy she emitted. "Any time, old girl," he said, patting her bark before heading back to the stone cottage.

In his study, with a coffee in hand, he flipped through the mail left there by his cleaning service. Warlocks were largely traditionalists, eschewing digital correspondence in favour of embossed linen stationery for invitations and announcements of weddings, engagements, births, and mentorships. There were no such crisp linen envelopes in Luke's stack of mail—just form letters from local politicians, charities seeking donations, and colourful flyers from neighbourhood businesses.

It would be a long time before he'd be invited into inner warlock circles again, if ever, and he couldn't blame them. After the failed coup, Lord Tanner had ensured they witnessed Luke carrying out the lord's dirty work firsthand. He'd humiliated Luke at every turn, branding him a traitor. Reputation was one of the few things magic couldn't buy.

The apologies had gone better than he'd deserved, the forgiveness more generous than he'd hoped. He'd also helped King Lochlan rout out Tanner's cohorts—those in power who'd abused their positions and enriched themselves in the process. The king was holding them accountable, and the new lord he'd appointed to the territory, Clive Redd, was repairing the damage he'd inherited, reinstating titles and returning money and property Tanner had extorted.

Even if his friends never trusted him again, Luke took solace in seeing them whole and happy again. And he was deeply grateful to King Lochlan for believing him and releasing him from Tanner's chain. He might be ostracized by his peers, but he was also blessed: to be alive, to be in the king's favour, and to have Adeline in his corner.

Adeline. She hovered in the background of his thoughts most days, but with increasing regularity as the vitriol about a witch having warlock powers refused to fade. The simmering anger had spread to outlying territories, where unaffiliated warlocks threatened vigilante retribution. And because she bore his runeglyph on her back, the reckoning wouldn't be as easy as siphoning the magic out of her. They'd have to kill her.

Acknowledgements

The Never Witch has been an absolute joy to write. The story tumbled out of my imagination faster than I could capture it with the keyboard. That has never happened before. I took it as a sign and ran with it, chasing the wonder of magic and the mystery of witches and warlocks. The possibilities are dizzying.

Like all books, The Never Witch had a lot of help getting to the point of publication.

Thank you to the readers who reach out and ask for more. Readers who help me choose book titles and character names. Readers who oohed and aahed at the early snippets I shared. Your support and encouragement warm this writer's heart.

To my critique partners, Elinor Florence and Donna Tunney, thank you for pushing me when I dig in my heels, for cheering my wins, for being handy with a ladder when I fall into a hole. For making me smile when I want to scream or cry or give up. You're the best!

Not only is Donna Tunney a generous critique partner, but she's also a stellar structural editor. She's proven that once again with The Never Witch. Thanks for smoothing out the rough patches. I am equally grateful for the talents of Amanda Bidnall, whose editing touched on and improved every detail of The Never Witch. And finally, for her fine eye for detail and stalwart support, thank you Jasna Tosic.

One of the things I enjoy most about being a writer is being part of the larger author community. I'm endlessly grateful to the authors who lift each other up, share craft and marketing tips, and understand the tremendous ups and downs of writing and publishing. Authors like Wendy Hawkin, Joanna Vander Vlugt, Andy Patten, Annie Siegel, Kristin Butcher, Diana Stevan, Marie Powell, Debra Purdy Kong, and Susan Toy . . . There are many others.

Thanks to my mom and dad, who are always in my corner, and my big sister, who can make me laugh so hard my stomach aches and my eyes leak.

And finally, thanks to my husband, who often asks, "Where are you?" when I'm sitting right beside him, staring off into space. Thanks for tugging me back to Earth and encouraging me to "just breathe."

Cast of Characters

Beatrice is a witch and the principal binder from Seattle's Moonmere coven.

Lady Wyn Brighton is a witch and the high priestess.

Suzanna Bolt is the owner of Bolt Gallery and carries Adeline Thorne's paintings.

Joe Booth is a witch, Sarah Booth's husband, and an architect.

Jack Booth is a witch and Adeline's nephew.

Olive Booth is a witch and Adeline's niece.

Sarah Booth (née Thorne) is a witch and Adeline Thorne's younger sister. She's married to Joe Booth and has two children, Jack and Olive. Sarah is a principal binder and member of Stonewater coven's governing council.

Buck is a witch, Stonewater coven's principal earth elemental, and a member of the governing council.

Cameron is a witch and Stonewater's coven's principal potioner.

Casey is a witch, Stonewater coven's principal fire elemental, and a member of the governing council.

Luke Churchwell is a warlock runecaster who started a failed rebellion against Lord Tanner.

Connie is a warlock and Luke Churchwell's personal assistant.

Daniel is a warlock and one of two junior war mages.

Damaras Deschene is a witch, Stonewater coven's priestess, and a principal spellcaster.

Odette Dion is a witch, Stonewater coven's principal spellcaster, and a member of the governing council.

Mrs. Doppler is the subject of Adeline Thorne's current portrait.

Lady Erin was a warlock, and Lord Tanner's deceased predecessor in the territory.

Finn is a witch, Stonewater coven's principal wind elemental, and a member of the governing council.

Warrick Flynn is a warlock and Adeline Thorne's ex-husband.

Jonas is a witch and the former priest of Stonewater coven.

Marcus Janson is a witch and the coven's principal healer.

Sutter Keats is a warlock aristocrat and a former comrade in Luke Churchwell's rebellion.

Lochlan Kinnaird is the warlock king.

Ophelia Kinnaird is the warlock queen.

Kylie is a warlock and one of two junior war mages.

Judith La Croix is a warlock, Lord Tanner's sister, and the person who screens the king's visitors.

Evan Minter is a warlock in arrears with his tithes.

Natalie is Sarah Booth's hair stylist.

Nulls are warlocks who serve as the king's guards and are immune to all but the king's magic.

Liam Nunez is a warlock and runecaster loyal to Lord Tanner.

Carolyne Okada is a witch, Stonewater coven's principal archivist, and a member of the governing council.

Kai Oxen is a warlock, a childhood friend of Luke Churchwell, and a comrade in Luke's rebellion.

Liza Patel is a warlock known as a jeweller who specializes in picking locks.

Anderson Schubert is a witch, Morgan Thorne's love interest, and a member of the high priestess's high council.

Shea (aka the white witch) is the high priestess's healer and a member of the high council.

Simon is a witch with the ability to search a witch's memories.

Stonewater Coven is the local coven.

Nicholas Tanner is a warlock and the territory's lord.

Rowan Thibeaud is a warlock and a former comrade in Luke Churchwell's rebellion.

Adeline Thorne is a witch who is barren of magic. She's a fourth-degree martial arts black belt, a graphic designer, and a portrait painter.

Morgan Thorne is a witch, a widow, a retired principal archivist, and the mother of Adeline Thorne and Sarah Booth.

Charlie Tucker is Adeline's basement tenant. He's a senior, a veteran, and a grandfather figure to Adeline's niece and nephew.

Silas Vance is a witch, Stonewater coven's principal war mage, and a member of the governing council.

Willow is a witch, Stonewater coven's principal water elemental, and a member of the governing council.

About the Author

JP (Jo-Anne) McLean is a bestselling author of urban fantasy and supernatural thrillers. She is an Eric Hoffer award winner, a two-time silver medalist in the Wishing Shelf Book Awards, a finalist in the Chanticleer International Book Awards and the Independent Author Network Awards. She is a B.R.A.G. medallion honoree and four-time Literary Titan Gold Award winner. Reviewers call her books *addictive*, *smart*, and *fun*.

JP holds a Bachelor of Commerce degree from the University of British Columbia's Sauder School of Business, is a certified scuba diver, an exploratory chef, and an avid gardener.

Raised in Toronto, Ontario, JP now lives with her husband on Denman Island, which is nestled between the coast of British Columbia and Vancouver Island. When she's not writing, you'll find her cooking dishes that look nothing like the recipe photos or arguing with weeds in the garden. She enjoys hearing from readers. Contact her via her website, jpmcleanauthor.com, or through social media.

Sign up for JP's monthly newsletter for FREE short stories and insider scoop at jpmcleanauthor.com.

Find her on Goodreads ~ goodreads.com/jpmclean
Like her on Facebook ~ facebook.com/JPMcLeanBooks
Follow her on Instagram ~ @jpmcleanauthor